Strung Along

A CHERRY PEAK NOVEL

HANNAH COWAN

Copyright © 2024, By Hannah Cowan

ISBN: 978-1-990804-33-5

Cover designed by: Andra @andra.mdesigns

Edited and proofed by: @oneloveediting

Interior Illustrations by: Jordan Burns @joburns.designs

Playlist

Daylight — Taylor Swift	4:53
On My Way To You — Cody Johnson	3:33
Take It From Me — Jordan Davis	2:54
The Tree — Marren Morris	3:26
Shoutout To my Ex — Little Mix	4:06
Strip It Down — Luke Bryan	4:02
Does Heaven Even Know You're Missing — Nickelback	3:44
Sleep Without You— Brett Young	3:08
Better Than Revenge (Taylor's Version) — Taylor Swift	3:40
Cool Anymore — Jordan Davis, Julia Michaels	3:20
Potential Breakup Song — Aly & AJ	3:38
Cowboy Hat — Jon Pardi	3:18
Made That Way — Jordan Davis	2:54
Why Should We — CHASE WRIGHT	2:51
Trouble — Josh Ross	3:35
Match For My Memory — Robyn Ottolini	3:00
When She Comes Home Tonight — Riley Green	4:10
180 (Lifestyle) — Morgan Wallen	3:09
Before He Cheats — Carrie Underwood	3:20
Night Crawling — Miley Cyrus, Billy Idol	3:09
Still Gonna Be You — Jade Eagleson	3:22

Authors Note

Before diving into this book, please know that there will be mention of a parental death. It does not take place on page, but is described in small detail.

Thank you,

Hannah xx

Dedicated to every single one of us who has ever dreamed of being the heroine in a small-town cowboy romance. May Brody Steele and Cherry Peak help fill that void.

1

Annalise

THERE ARE FEW THINGS I HATE IN THIS WORLD AS MUCH AS A
thong.

Between the string trying to crawl inside of me with every
shift of my thighs and the perpetual feeling of having a wedgie,
I'm usually stuffing any I've been peer pressured into buying
into the back of my drawer. Panty lines? I embrace them. They're
better than having my butt cheeks flossed.

If it weren't for the birthday surprise I suspect Stewart is
planning for me tonight, I would have slipped on my favourite
pair of 100 percent cotton briefs instead of the red thong with the
tag still attached. His favourite dress of mine is a tight, silky
thing from one of my favourite boutiques that doesn't allow for
underwear. Not the visible kind. It will be worth the pain,
though. I know it will be.

I smooth my hands down my generous hips and dart my
eyes to where my phone lies on the bed. For the third time in the
past couple of minutes, the screen is dark, no new messages
waiting for me. Like every time before, I brush it off. Stewart
didn't have to tell me that he's planning anything for me to
know he is.

We've been dating for three years, engaged and living

together for just over two of them. He's always done something grand for my birthday. His giving soul is one of the things I love most about him. The incredibly successful, classically handsome man I met after one of my sister's animal shelter fundraisers turned a girl against marriage into one who didn't hesitate to say yes when he dropped to one knee at our special spot—the Oak Bay Marina in Vancouver—and asked me to be his wife.

Every year since, we've celebrated my birthday with a big party on his company's yacht despite the slight chill of October in Vancouver. Last year, he hired a string quartet to play me a collection of my favourite songs. I've tried not to let my expectations for this year fly too high, but I'm only human.

With a final brush of my fingers through my pin-straight hair, I nod and spin to grab my phone. A swipe across the screen tells me there still aren't any new messages. But after a quick look at our shared location, I know he's at the marina, most likely so busy finalizing everything that he forgot to tell me when I should be there. I figured six o'clock was a safe bet since that's when the party was last year. My sister's lack of response to my text asking when she was told to arrive only confirms that she must already be on her way.

It takes half an hour to get to the marina from our high-rise condo, but the drive is easy. The long walk from the parking lot to the docks is the more tedious part, especially in these wedges. My deep red nail-polished toes wink at me when I step out of the car and into the setting sun's light.

A spark of confusion appears in my mind at the lack of familiar vehicles in the parking lot. My mom's new Jeep—a gift from her new husband—is hard to miss with its new orange paint job, but it's nowhere to be seen. Maybe I'm just early.

"Oh my gosh, you shouldn't have," I gasp, beginning to practise what I'll say when I arrive. "This is the sweetest thing ever! An ice sculpture of my perfect figure? You've outdone yourself this year."

My following snort is loud and gross. An ice sculpture would be beyond my expectations, but I'm definitely not opposed to it.

The Band-Aids I stuck to my heels in preparation for the walk to the docks work like a charm when the marina finally comes into view and not a hint of a blister has appeared. The cool ocean breeze sweeps through my hair and over my warm skin, reminding me of why I love it here so much. Seagulls soar through the air above the dock, leading the way to where the yacht waits.

It's quiet when I approach the back end and step on board, the water softly lapping at the sides, rocking it side to side. Climbing the stairs that lead to the sliding glass door, my stomach rolls, a prickle of doubt nestling into my mind at the continued silence.

The door slides open, unlocked. "Stewart?" I call softly, step-ping inside.

Worry pierces my chest. There's no sign of a party. No sign of anything or anyone besides the open back door.

Each one of my steps clicks on the wood floors as I walk through the open layout of the kitchen and sitting room. I focus on the open door that leads to the first deck. "Stewart?"

Nobody replies. It's too silent . . . until a high-pitched cry punctures that quiet calm. My pace kicks up into a jog as I rush toward the door, snagging the fire extinguisher from where it sits in the corner of the sitting room on my way. I don't even know *how* to use a fire extinguisher—which is a *total* safety hazard—but I won't be using it to put out a fire. I'll smash it into some-one's face if I have to instead.

The sound of flesh slapping against flesh turns my blood cold. A deafening whoosh fills my ears. Each step out the door feels sluggish.

"Stewart?" I call, the name sounding pitifully weak.

It takes all I have not to collapse on the deck as my knees wobble. The scene unfolding in front of me is nothing more than a cruel, cruel joke. I'm having a nightmare, my real body tucked nice and safe and happy in our bed. *Our.* Bed.

My shaky gasp hits the air like a gunshot. It's the woman who notices me first, her pale green eyes going wide as her cheeks pale. The red flush that was there a blink ago is gone. But the sweat on her forehead is still there.

She doesn't look away, and neither do I. Not even when she drops her legs from where they were just wrapped tight around Stewart's waist, and certainly not when she raises a shaking hand to her swollen lips and then has the decency to at least cover her bare chest with her forearm.

"You said she was gone!" she shrieks at my fiancé.

My stomach threatens to fall to the floor when he whips his head to finally stare at me.

Stewart's shoulders are bare to match the rest of his body. The scratch marks zigzagging across the expanse of them are new. Lord knows I've never felt enough pleasure from sex with him to mark his skin that way. His always perfectly swooped chestnut hair is messy, sticking up every which way. From her fingers, no doubt. Not mine.

Not my fingers. Not my scratches. Not my legs that were just wrapped around him. *Not. My. Anything.*

The rock on my finger suddenly weighs a million pounds. The silver ring burns my skin like acid.

"Anna—"

"It's my birthday," I blurt out, as if that means anything now.

He rubs his eyes, blinking repeatedly, as if he can't believe this is actually happening. That I'm here. That I spoiled his plans.

"It's my birthday, and this is what you're doing." I will my voice to remain steady, hard. The cold weight in my hands is a reminder that I don't have an open one to smack him across the face. "Three years wasted on you."

"Anna, baby. I don't know what happened—I just—*fuck.* Time got away from me, and I just forg—"

I release a tight, painful exhale. Each breath feels like I'm swallowing fire. "Time got away from you?" With a shake of my head, I push forward. "How long?"

The strong cheekbones I loved to trace while we watched movies or drank wine on the terrace are suddenly too deeply etched. Plump lips I used to kiss at any given chance revolt me. His every feature turns and twists into something I hate the longer I stare at him.

"It was an accident."

The woman he's still *inside* gapes at his words. She's beautiful, I realize. Even with her mouth twisted in disgust, she's beautiful. All long limbs, perfectly placed muscles, and flawless skin. My stomach sinks further.

"Only now it was an accident? What about the first fifty times?" she asks him.

Betrayal morphs into rage. My body overheats with it. "How long has this been going on?" I ask through clenched teeth.

"Months!" the woman screeches. Finally, she shoves him away from her, and I glance at the sky when they separate. "For months, he's been taking me here!"

"She's lying," Stewart blubbers.

With a careful sweep of my eyes, I take him in as he shoves his dick into his pants and frantically zips them up. He leaves them unbuttoned. Those perfectly ironed suit pants he loves so much, now crinkled and dirty.

My palms are slick around the fire extinguisher, but I don't let it slip from my grasp. When I adjust my hold on it, Stewart glances down.

"Why do you have that? Put it down," he orders. "Don't do anything crazy."

I follow his eyes, focusing on the silver handle that's tucked beneath my fingers and the pin that remains in place. The woman shuffles where she's sitting, most likely trying to put her clothes on.

"Crazy?" The laugh I let rip through the space between us is anything but sane.

"Yes, crazy! You're freaking me out. Relax before you do something stupid."

"Do something stupid," I echo, stroking the side of the fire extinguisher. "Like fucking someone who isn't your fiancée? Who isn't the woman you're about to marry in a year? The one who has already bought her dress and told everyone she's marrying a good man? You don't get to call me crazy. You don't get to tell me to *relax*."

The nameless woman slinks off the dining table and stands beside him. She doesn't try to leave despite the way he spoke about her. My chest cracks wide open as I finally register the way she admitted they've been together for a while. Often.

My hold on my emotions is faltering. I've always been bad at remaining calm when I'm upset, but this . . . this isn't some small fight or misunderstanding. This is so much more than that.

There's no going back from this.

It's that thought that has me pulling the pin on the fire extinguisher and squeezing the lever, dousing the couple in white foam.

2

Annalise

I CAN STILL FEEL THE EXTINGUISHER FOAM ON MY FINGERS THE NEXT morning despite how many times I scrubbed my hands. My sister is practically burning the carpet with her frantic pacing, rage lighting her usual soft eyes. They're a bright blue, so unlike my brown.

She apologizes for what feels like the millionth time, and I tell her to cut it out for the millionth and one.

When I showed up at her rental house last night after nearly tossing my ring into the marina and sobbing in my car for an hour, she took me in without a word needing to have been spoken between us. One look at me and she knew. The apologies came once I told her what happened. Every gut-wrenching detail of it. It took everything in me to convince her to hold off until today to enact our revenge.

We took one step into the condo Stewart and I share—*shared*, I guess—before she was stalking off to the bedroom to find my luggage. An hour later, all of my clothes and important belongings are tucked away, ready for a new home. I wish I felt the same.

There's nothing about this condo that expresses who I am, yet it was home. The place I thought I would be coming back to after my wedding. Where we would start our newlywed life together and create a lifetime more memories. Good ones and bad ones, but not like this.

"I should have checked my phone sooner," she huffs, eyeing the suit jacket on Stewart's side of the closet. My half is empty. Absolutely empty amongst the expensive suit jackets and golf shirts.

"Knock it off, Braxton. I would much rather you have been taking care of my sick nephew than dealing with my problems," I chastise her. "Not to mention you were out all day with your in-laws."

She curls her fingers into fists. "Either way, I want to string that guy up a flagpole by his tiny balls!"

Her husband, Maddox, winces from where he watches us from his position in the doorway. Sympathy is heavy in his stance, and I continue to ignore it. Sure, my heart might ache like a mofo right now, but this is not the end of my world. Stewart doesn't deserve to have that power over me.

Maybe if I repeat that over and over and over again, it might help take the pain away as well as the bottle of wine did last night.

"Oh, don't give us that look, Anna. You've never turned down the idea of dishing out a healthy dose of revenge." Braxton tightens her stare on me. "There are ideas in that beautiful head of yours, I know it."

"Of course there are. I'm just trying to work out what I want to start with."

Maddox winces. "That's never a good sign."

"You know what else wasn't a good sign?" I pause, waiting for them to guess the answer to my rhetorical question. Anger flushes my cheeks. "That he refused to let me snoop on his phone! Work, work, work, he always said, but I should have known better! Nobody needs to take their phone to the shower in case of a work call! God, I'm naive. A naive idiot who sat back in la-la land while their fiancé was hooking up with a gorgeous woman who was *not* me," I rant, a sharp sting attacking the back of my eyes.

Braxton stomps toward me before dropping to a squat, hands on my knees. I hate the way tears drip down my cheeks. Hate that my wounds are still so fresh, my sense of self-worth cracking further and deeper with each reminder of them. Being in this bedroom, a place that was once a happy, safe space . . .

I want to shatter the walls and ruin everything he's ever loved. But more than that, I want to curl up on the bed, breathe in his cologne, and cry for the foreseeable future. Three years of my life I've spent with Stewart. I'll never get that time back.

"What am I supposed to do now?" I ask her, my voice little more than a whimper.

"I think you need to get all your shit out of here and then start embracing the rage prowling beneath your skin. Once you've let it have its moment, you work on healing yourself. You repair the damage he caused while moving on with your life. You're too strong to allow this man to stop you from accomplishing everything you've ever wanted in life. He was never worthy of you."

Thick black curls fall into my sister's eyes, and I fight back a weak smile when she lifts a hand to flick them away. I used to always want hair like hers, and she wanted hair like mine. We used to waste our shooting star wishes on somehow swapping styles when we were younger. My sister is my best friend. Nobody has ever been able to compete with her, even when we used to spend too many days picking on one another growing up.

"If he was never worthy of me, then why did you approve of him?" I ask her.

"I never did," Maddox puts in. The cheeky grin he gives us has my sister flipping him off.

"You're a no-good suck-up, Maddox. Go do something useful and keep watch for Ewie Stewie."

I shake my head, the small flicker of humour that had

sparked inside of me quickly snuffed out. "He won't be home for a few hours."

He came home last night begging and pleading for me to speak to him. *To just listen to what I have to say,* he said. But after ten minutes of me screaming at him to go loud enough to wake the neighbours, he took off with his tail between his legs and a promise to try and speak with me again after work today. *Once I've calmed down enough to listen.*

"You know what, Anna? Get up," Braxton orders with a slap to both my knees. After rising to her feet, she goes right back to the closet, beginning to yank hangers off the rod. "Get up and wipe your tears. I'm not allowing you to wallow. Not when you're still so angry. *Rightfully so.*"

"What do you want me to do? Throw a tantrum?"

Maddox lingers still, watching his wife toss hangers of expensive clothes on the bed behind me. "Are you sure I have to watch the door? I think it's about to become incredibly entertaining to watch."

"The last thing we need is that piece of shit interrupting us. Can you please watch the door? If he shows up, you have full permission to get him out by any means necessary."

Like magic, Maddox darts out of the room. Braxton looks at me again before dragging her eyes to the pile of clothes. I swallow the lump in my throat—from emotion or the aftermath of my tears, I don't know—and focus on the navy blue button-up on the top of the mountain of clothes. I don't think he's ever worn that shirt, but I remember gifting it to him last year for his birthday. Another pang in my chest, this one threatening to steal my breath.

Braxton doesn't wait for me to speak before she's storming out of the room. I don't have it in me to follow her. Tentatively, I pinch the bottom button on that blue shirt and exhale. The longer I hold the smooth, cold button, the tighter my grip becomes. When I finally tear it from the string attaching it to the shirt, I feel a rush of relief. Some of the pressure in my chest releases. When the second button tears free, another tiny bit of relief has me moving button by button until none remain.

"Catch," Braxton says.

I barely manage to catch the bottle of ketchup in my hands before she's throwing one full of mayo. Then mustard and barbeque sauce. She doesn't dare throw the heavy jug of bleach that's swinging in her left hand, though.

"What's that for?"

"What? This?" She swings the bottle slowly.

"I don't know about that look in your eyes . . ."

Maddox shouts from the living room, "She's vicious! Make sure all of your things are tucked away, Anna!"

"Don't listen to him. He's just jealous he isn't about to take part in this destruction. Take the jug," Braxton orders, extending the bleach to me.

My fingers itch with the urge to take it, and I no longer have it in me to resist the rage warming my blood. "Fine."

The sudden weight of it threatens to tip me off balance as I loop my fingers through the handle. I steel my spine and take the cap off. The smell is immediate, and I scrunch my nose before turning to the bed.

"Let it out. He deserves to feel your wrath," Braxton coos.

"My wrath?" I want to laugh, but it dies in my throat.

"That's right. The wrath of a scorned lover. A bad bitch's revenge."

I've never considered myself a bad bitch, but maybe that's part of my problem. This is my initiation, it would seem, and I refuse to not make the club.

With one swing of my arm, the clear liquid is splashing over the bed and settling over the pile of expensive clothes. The scent of it fills the room, burning my nose, but I don't stop dumping it. Not until only a few drops linger, splattering onto the ruined dress shirt, and then . . . nothing.

Dropping the bottle onto the ground, I prowl to the ensuite bathroom and dig through the cabinet beneath the sink until I find the small bottle of blue toilet bowl cleaner. Unscrewing the top, I step in front of the closet and squirt the thick substance over the clothes still hanging on the rod. Suit jackets, folded pants, a long wool coat that he claimed was too luxurious for the streets of Vancouver.

When that's empty too, I move on to the dresser drawers. One after the other, I alternate between the condiments Braxton brought from the fridge, soaking the clothes with ketchup, mayonnaise, and vinegar. The stench is almost stomach churning, but I can't stop. Tears burn my eyes, pain heavy in my chest. A pain that only dulls when I'm destroying an item that I know means something to him. It's evil beyond belief, but I don't allow myself to focus on that guilt too much.

The moment Braxton silently hands me a bag of flour, I'm spinning to deposit it on the bed. Clouds of white fill the air as I hit the clothes. Over and over, my palms make contact, the slick of bleach mixing with powder beneath them, sticking to my fingers. A cry climbs my throat and pierces the silence before I use all of my strength to shove the clothes off the bed. They fly across the room and land on the floor with a wet plop.

My hands are shaking. I wipe them on my thighs and then realize I've smeared the white goop all over them. Tears burn my cheeks. They don't stop coming, regardless of how furiously I blink. My breaths are shallow and tight. Each one is more painful than the last. My sticky fingers curl into the chest of my shirt, tugging and tugging.

Arms wrap around me, and I bury my face in my sister's shoulder. Her hold is warm and familiar and comforting, but the sobs don't stop. Only once I've cried so long my throat is raw and my eyes are so swollen that they're hard to keep open do I peel myself away and wipe at my face.

Maddox lingers in the bedroom now, a pained expression on his face. I focus on my sister and the shine in her blue eyes. Her smile is as wobbly as mine.

"Sorry," I mumble.

"Don't apologize. You needed that," she replies. Her hands cup my shoulders and then squeeze. "Ready to go?"

I take in the room and swallow my gasp. It's a disaster. One I'm almost a little proud of. He's going to lose his mind when he sees what I've done, but isn't that karma? At least now he has an idea of the destruction in my chest.

There's no future for us anymore. If he ever wanted one with me in the first place, the events of the past twenty-four hours would have been nothing but a nightmare. This isn't my home. It never was.

I stare at the ring on my finger and fight another wave of tears, these ones angry and bitter. The thin silver band slips off easily.

When I toss it on the bed, it hits the dirty comforter with a thump so loud it echoes in my mind long after we wheel my luggage out of the condo and I shut the door for the final time.

3

Annalise

I NEVER PICTURED MYSELF LIVING IN A SMALL TOWN. GROWING UP IN Vancouver, British Columbia, I'm used to city living. The traffic jams during rush hour and busy streets with street performers on every corner.

Cherry Peak is the opposite of Vancouver. Not only is it in an entirely different province, but it's a town small enough to have only one family-run grocery store, a library that splits a building with the town hall, and one school that houses all grades, kindergarten to twelve.

My life in Cherry Peak, Alberta, is a far shot from how it was back home, and that's exactly what I need right now.

The November breeze runs through my hair as I walk down Main Street, taking in the smells from the singular coffee shop and the farmers' market on the corner. Flowers, coffee, and fresh air. The number of looming trees that surround the town was overwhelming at first glance, but I've grown a bit more used to them now. If you know where to look, you can spot the Rocky Mountains peeking through the shorter, white-tipped trees. I still haven't gotten used to the beauty of the snow-peaked mountains. They're a punch to the gut every morning. A good punch.

I've been a resident of this *blink-and-you'll-pass-it* town for two weeks now, but this is the first time I've had the confidence to walk this street. Before today, I found more than a few excuses to keep myself locked away in my new rental home, only slinking into the real world to work at the hair salon that took me in like a lost puppy the day I came begging for a job. Unpacking, cleaning, internet stalking my ex—I've come up with just about every reason not to have to converse with the people living here more than necessary. But I can't be a hermit forever.

I can't hide from real life, even if the thought of starting a new one here makes my chest ache and my head throb.

Like every time I walk around this town, heads turn, and curious eyes watch me. When I'm working, it's easier to ignore the attention. I can concentrate on my job and not the questions they're dying to ask me. *Where did I come from? Why did I move here? How long am I staying?*

Only a handful of clients have asked me those questions, and it's easy to distract them when I have scissors in my hands and their hair poised between the blades. Now, though? I fear it may not be so easy.

I keep my head high and my mouth set in a soft, natural smile. There was a reason for today's venture other than making my presence known to every single person in this town. My destination is the bridal boutique that has undoubtedly seen better days. I've driven it past it a handful of times in the past few days, and while it looks like it's inside of a shoebox-size space, it will have to do.

Today is the first day I've had the nerve to even contemplate stepping foot inside of it. Sweat beads on the back of my neck at the mention of being surrounded with white tulle and fake bouquets again.

While Braxton was selling my wedding dress at a consignment shop in Vancouver before I moved out here, I was busy trying to forget the man responsible for that dress and my shattered heart. I want nothing to do with anything related to a wedding, but for my sister, I'd do just about anything, even torture myself with the reminder of everything I've lost. That's my reasoning behind agreeing when she all but begged me to still come with her to Maddox's teammate's wedding in two months. I couldn't go back on my agreement from months ago. Not after everything she did for me post-Stewart. Just the fact that I can even think his name now without sobbing is half due to her help during the start of my grieving process.

The street ahead of me fills with voices, some soft and some hard. Shoes crunching over snow-covered pavement and jingling bells from above shop doors have my pace slowing. Every person in town has to be at the farmers' market. It's most likely the last one of the season, with the snow starting to fall heavier and heavier each day. I should have known today would be a terrible day to come . . .

"A new face!"

I freeze, knees locking at the loud voice.

"Don't be so aggressive, Bryce."

"I'm not being aggressive! I'm being welcoming."

"If you're so welcoming, then why does she look like she's going to hack all over the street?"

I blink, taking in the two women moving toward me. The shorter of the two, Bryce, from what I've gathered, is intimidating as all hell, even from the healthy distance between us. With night-black hair and sharp blue eyes, she reminds me of Braxton. A much scarier version of her.

She's incredibly fit. Muscles flex beneath her long sleeves, even as she stands still, observing me. Her black vest is snug over her chest, and the puff on the top of her toque bobs with every step she takes. Two rows of gleaming white teeth flash as she grins at me, and suddenly, she's the opposite of intimidating.

The woman beside Bryce appears far more harmless, even without smiling, with soft brown eyes and hair to match. Her skin is warmer than Bryce's, like she's used to spending long hours in the sun despite the cold, while Bryce maybe tends to do the opposite. She's built similar to me, with thighs filling the tight material of her jeans, hips that flare wide, and a generous chest that, from experience, is why we have to go up a size in tops despite our slimmer waists.

"Sorry, I have a habit of being a bit too loud sometimes," Bryce apologizes, wincing slightly.

I return her smile and extend my hand. She takes it easily. "Don't be sorry. It's nice to have someone else make the first move. I'm Annalise. Anna for short."

"You're the new hairdresser," the second woman notes, piecing something together in her mind. Recognition sparks in her eyes, and she ignores my outstretched hand. "I'm Poppy! I own Beautifully Bold. We're neighbours."

In a surprising move, she swats down my hand and wraps me in a tight hug. I stand frozen for a beat before awkwardly wrapping my arms around her and then pulling back. She doesn't seem to care about my awkwardness.

Bryce picks up on it, though, offering me another apologetic grimace. "And you were giving me a hard time for being aggressive."

I laugh at that. "Beautifully Bold . . . that's the pole studio, right?"

"That's the one, but don't get her started on it. She'll end up forcing you into coming for a lesson," Bryce says.

Poppy rolls her eyes and shoves her friend's shoulder. "I don't force anyone. It's more just gentle marketing, I promise."

"I'm all ears. Give me your best-selling speech." I nod in encouragement when she hesitates.

I've never done pole before. I'm not much for exercise, if I'm completely honest. Walking up and down the basement stairs to do my laundry is enough to have me huffing and puffing, but I can't say that I'm completely against the idea of pole. I've seen the women who do pole work, and they're incredibly strong.

Poppy tucks some loose hairs from her bun out of her face as the wind picks up but straightens and smiles brightly. "Beautifully Bold is a space for those who may not feel comfortable to go to a public gym but still want to get a bit of activity into their day in a different, fun way. It's mostly women who join the classes, but it's open to anyone interested. We have classes every Wednesday, Friday, and Saturday at four thirty for an hour, and they're usually full of both those who have never tried before and those who have been doing it for years. Really, it's just a safe place for people to have fun while working out in a safe environment."

"Don't forget your selling point, Poppy," Bryce reminds her.

I roll my lips to fight a laugh while Poppy huffs. "I was getting there, Bryce." Focusing solely on me, she adds, "The side window faces the front of the fire department. The yard, specifically. Where the volunteers work out in the summer. The view is always a great motivator."

"I have to peel her tongue from the window more often than not," Bryce teases.

Poppy glares at her. "You're not much better."

"Never said I was," Bryce sings.

My eyes bounce between the two of them, a bite of jealousy growing in my gut. It's not like I've never had a friendship like this . . . well, I guess I haven't, really. Unless you count my sister. Which, really, is just sad if I do.

I've never *not* wanted a close friendship with other women before. I have and do work with more than several women, but I can be a lot, and I try to hold back so as to not overwhelm other people. A few years ago, I wouldn't have cared how extra I was, but something I've realized over the past month is that all of those subtle digs Stewart made about my loud laugh and tendency to speak without being spoken to first did indeed dig into my subconscious. I hate that I allowed myself to take his hateful words and find truth in them. Let them poison my opinion of myself.

Watching Bryce and Poppy be so open and free with one another in such an obviously close friendship makes me undeniably jealous. I want that. Badly.

"I think I'd like to come to one of the classes," I blurt out.

Both women pause, gazes shooting to me. Poppy is the first to break free of her surprise and clap excitedly. Bryce's eyes tighten as she takes me in, almost as if she's searching for the thoughts I was just thinking. The softening of her stare a beat later makes me swallow, hating that I wear my emotions so obviously for everyone to see.

"That would be amazing!" Poppy cheers.

My cheeks warm as her excitement snags the attention of a few of the people walking by. The jealousy ebbs away, replaced with a blooming sensation of excitement.

"I doubt I'll do well, but I'm down to give it a chance."

"It took me three weeks to get the grasp of a simple back bend, so I wouldn't worry about your skill. You'd be surprised how long it can take to nail a move," Bryce says.

My smile is a silent thank you. She tips her chin in reply.

Poppy takes a step toward me while slipping her hand into the pocket on the thigh of her leggings. "Why don't we exchange numbers, and I'll send you all of the sign-up info? You can let me know what day you want to come, and we can go from there. Are you living in town?"

I shrug my purse from my shoulder and pull my phone free, exchanging it for hers. "I'm by the school. It's just a rental for now, but I figured in town would have been better. This province is still new to me."

"You're not from Alberta?" Bryce asks.

Once I finish adding my number to Poppy's phone, I hand it back and take Bryce's. Poppy hands my phone to her friend a beat later.

"I'm from BC. Vancouver, specifically."

"And you moved from there to *here*? *Why?*" Poppy scrunches her nose, darting her eyes to the snow piles lining the street.

"Would you believe me if I said I preferred the prairies?"

Bryce snorts a laugh. "Not at all."

"There's a story behind this move, isn't there?" Poppy asks.

With a tired smile, I swap phones with Bryce. "One for another day."

I'm grateful when they both accept that and let it go. I don't want to ruin a good meeting with the mention of Stewart. He took too many things from me to allow him to take this too.

"Well, just shoot me a text whenever you want, okay? We can figure out your pole class and maybe a drink out or something?" Hope glimmers in Poppy's eyes, and it makes my smile grow.

"I'd like that."

The two friends say goodbye a moment later, and I watch them disappear into the crowd before continuing toward the bridal shop. A spark of excitement has my steps moving a half beat quicker than before.

4

Annalise

As if I've had my mouth shoved full of all this tulle and lace, my tongue grows dry, sticking to the roof of my mouth. The bridal shop is far more stocked than I was anticipating, and one look at the rows and rows of dresses has me fighting to keep from spinning back around.

I can hear the quick tapping of heels on the floor as the camera facing the door announces my arrival. And five minutes later, I blow out a long, strained breath when I'm left alone to try on the five dresses the associate deemed appropriate for my body and style.

The older, dainty woman who owns the shop is sweet and kind, but the longer I stand here, basking in the reminder of everything I've lost in the past few weeks, the harder it's going to be to not lose the effort to do what I'm here to do.

A heavy, pastel pink curtain acts as a barrier for the dressing room, and it brushes my back when I spin to face the dresses hung on a rod. According to Braxton, the bride of this wedding is a real stickler when it comes to her black-tie theme, so every dress hung before me is what I think is the most appropriate. The longest of the five dresses has a slit that travels to nearly mid-thigh, and the shortest will hardly brush my knees at my five-six height. I'm not awfully tall, so I don't even want to know how short you'd have to be to not flash a bit of panty in that dress.

I shrug out of my clothes and start with the safest option—a shiny black dress with a sweetheart neckline and a laced bottom hem that should sit around my mid-shin. A ball sticks in my throat when I tug it over my chest and let it swoosh along my legs. The mirror is directly across from me, and I grow stiff as I take myself in.

I've never been ashamed of my body. With a sister who evokes such confidence about hers, it's hard not to follow in her footsteps. We both have our mother's body type, with more meat on our bones than we know what to do with sometimes. I was always a bigger girl growing up, but I slimmed out quite a bit once puberty hit. I've never been able to get much smaller than I am now, though. I love my curves, even if Stewart liked to hint at hitting the gym with him regardless of how many times I turned him down.

Yet another thing the asshole did that I didn't pay attention to. A red flag that should have had me running for the hills long before he decided to cheat.

Lifting my chin, I shove those thoughts away and focus on the mirror. The dress is cute, but it isn't me. It's dainty and soft-spoken, and I am neither of those things.

The next option is another too similar to the one I'm wearing. I skip it, choosing to try the one with the slit in the leg instead. *Go big or go home, Anna.*

The small space grows hot with the effort of stripping and dressing again, but I push past it. The moment the silk glides over my warm skin, I exhale, forcing myself not to look away from my reflection. The neckline is lined with gems that sparkle beneath the small light above me and is swooped enough to show a good bit of cleavage. It's a sexy dress, one that says I'm single and ready to mingle. Or at least that I look ready to mingle. It's still to be said if I will be or not.

A twist of my hips and I gawk at the length of exposed leg poking through the slit in the silk. Warmth blooms on my cheeks at the thought of others seeing this much bare skin.

I grab my phone from the small bench littered with my discarded clothes and snap a couple of photos of myself in the mirror before sending them all to my sister.

> Me: Be honest. Maybe not brutally so . . . but still honest.

Her reply comes instantly. She's most likely been waiting for it since the moment I told her I was heading to look.

> Big Sis: H. O. T. *heart eye emoji*

> Me: It's not too much?

> Big Sis: There's no such thing as too much when it comes to you, Banana.

> Me: What if I flash someone with the slit?

I would never get over that trauma.

> Big Sis: They're welcome.

> Me: I'd scar the children.

> Big Sis: Good thing children aren't allowed at the wedding then. Buy the dress. You look stunning.

I hesitate with a reply, tapping the back of my phone instead of the screen. Another text comes through a beat later.

> Big Sis: Don't ignore me. BUY THE DAMN DRESS. IT WAS MADE FOR YOU!

> **Me:** I need to send it to the planner first.

> **Big Sis:** I almost forgot about that. Fine. But buy it regardless of what she says.

Nerves clamp down on me as I copy the phone number from our conversation into the New Message tab.

> **Me:** Hi! Is this dress approved for the Morales wedding?

I attach the most modest of the pictures I took, only allowing a bit of my leg to show, and then send the message.

God, that's such an awkward text. In my defense, who makes their wedding guests send their outfits for approval? I get wanting your wedding to be perfect, but holy. That's a bit much, if you ask me.

I didn't plan on having a theme for my wedding . . . but I guess that doesn't matter anymore, does it? I'm done with weddings for the rest of my goddamn life. No more.

I've only begun to take another look at my reflection when my phone buzzes. One look at the screen has my cheeks on fire, the dressing room suddenly too stuffy.

> **17805559540:** Yes.

> **17805559540:** What do I have to do to get plus one approval?

STEELE RANCH

Brody

MY BACK ACHES. Fuck, all of me does.

The bar smells like frying oil and sweat. Something sticky tugs at the bottom of my boots beneath the table, like a drink was spilled earlier but never mopped up. It's too damn loud in here for a Saturday afternoon.

I keep my face hidden beneath the brim of my hat and tap my fingers on the side of my whiskey glass. It's grown warm in the time we've been sitting here, slick with dew.

"You're one surly son of a bitch today," Caleb notes, not hesitating to gulp down his cold beer.

Wearing his Cherry Peak Fire shirt and an easy grin despite the long day of volunteering at the station, he rolls his neck and finishes his drink.

Peakside is usually our location of choice to get dumb drunk after a long day, but ever since Caleb and his wife had their daughter nearly a decade ago, these evenings have grown few and far between. It's why I took him up on his invite after lunch.

A few of the men who volunteer alongside him joined us after ignoring the withering glare I shot Caleb when they appeared. *Just us*, he promised. Bullshit.

"Yet you still invited me," I reply smugly.

"Wouldn't kill you to smile once, though. You're scaring the waitress."

I ignore him, raising my glass to my mouth and finishing the whiskey off. It burns the entire way down, hot in my stomach.

One of the new volunteers decides to chime in. "Told you not to invite him, Caleb."

"Caleb doesn't go anywhere without his ball and chain," another puts in.

"You talk a lot of smack for a virgin," Caleb tosses back.

I should know the names of these guys by now, but I don't give enough of a shit to try. Reclining back in the booth, I peer behind the head of the man beside me and flag over the waitress. She doesn't look scared of me. Maybe intimidated, but that's not unusual. I'm not exactly the friendliest person, especially not to strangers.

"Another?" she asks me, voice too timid for a rowdy place like this.

Caleb responds for me. "Might as well bring him the whole bottle, Jewel. He's in a mood today."

I attempt to soften my scowl, but when Caleb barks a laugh at me, I know I look like a fucking idiot instead. "A water, please."

She scurries off with little more than a tip of her chin. I ignore the brief slash of guilt that follows her quick disappearance and tighten my stare on the deep gauges in the table instead.

Peakside has been around since before I was born, and it hasn't changed at all in the twenty-eight years since. The twin gouges on this table are from a teenage Brody and Caleb, though, our mark on the place courtesy of my pocket knife the first night we ever came here.

"Water?" It's Caleb's turn to frown.

I nod. "Gotta be up at the ass crack of dawn tomorrow."

My grandpa has been planning our trip to the auction a few hours north of here for weeks now. He'd swat me across the back of the head with the newspaper hard enough I'd see stars if I cancelled on him because I drank too much whiskey the night before.

"The auction," Caleb says before I can tell him. "Why does he need you to go with him again?"

"Wants me there to look at whatever he decides to buy before pullin' the trigger on it."

"Haven't forgotten how to work beneath the hood of a tractor yet, Popstar?" Darren asks, another of the volunteers, but one I can stomach having a conversation with.

His subtle dig annoys me, but not enough to have me picking a fight with him.

"Couldn't forget if I tried," I grumble.

Caleb smirks. "Brody has spent more time beneath hoods than he has women."

"Not includin' your mother, right?" I ask, reaching up to flex the brim of my hat.

Caleb's not even all that wrong. I've been beneath more hoods than I could ever think to count or remember. Before life took me down a different path, I thought I'd still be working on heavy equipment when my bones turned brittle.

The table breaks out in loud, howling laughter, and the waitress stumbles a step while approaching with my water. With a flash of a smile, she sets it on the table, and one of the volunteers pushes it toward me before starting a new conversation about how he found a stray cat beneath the wheel of the fire truck last week.

I zone out, drinking nearly the whole glass of water in one gulp. The whiskey scorched away the lingering ache in my throat from singing after avoiding that strain for a couple of weeks, but it's already coming back. The water coats the rawness with another flash of relief that I know won't last. The pain will disappear by the morning, so long as I don't let Caleb convince me to get drunk and sing karaoke all damn night.

But the odds of that happening are so low they're nearly nonexistent.

"You gonna tell me what's got you in such a terrible mood before you leave?" Caleb asks, the question quiet enough across the table that I know it's meant just for me.

"Rita was here this morning. Wanted to hear how the vocal rest was coming along."

His eyebrow twitches but doesn't lift. "And?"

"I'm still here."

"You pushed yourself too hard on that damn tour. I'm glad you're home. I think the whole town is, honestly. So, you won't find me disappointed that your voice hasn't even healed yet for you to take off again."

The stark honesty in his words rattles my chest. "It's nice

being back at the ranch. My grandparents need the help anyway."

"I'm going to assume Rita didn't share our opinion?"

A gigantic understatement. "She wants me to finish Killian's tour. I agreed to open for the entire thing, and then I just left. It makes my entire team look bad. Pissed off the fans too."

The angry messages and emails are now being filtered through people Rita hired over the past couple of weeks. I don't have the passwords to anything anymore.

"It's for your own well-being," she said.

I didn't disagree. Still don't.

"If you had finished the tour, you could have damaged your voice bad enough that a small break wouldn't have been able to fix shit," Caleb hisses.

"I know. That's why I'm still here."

Some of the anger leaches from his expression but still gleams in his eyes. We're like brothers. One willing to fall on a dagger for the other. His protectiveness doesn't surprise me. I would be the same if he were in my position.

"Next time Rita slithers into town, send her to the station. We'll have her running back to Nashville faster than she can say Carrie Underwood."

"Who are we sending back to Nashville?" Darren asks, shoving himself into the conversation.

I finish off my water as Caleb says, "None of your business, Nosey Nelly."

My phone vibrates on the table, screen facing up, and Caleb zeroes in on it. That brow arches now, amusement curling his mouth.

Snapping out his hand, he sets it over my phone. "Is there another reason you've stayed in town that you haven't told me?"

"What?"

"Don't try and play coy."

My mouth hardens as he grabs my phone and guesses my

passcode on what seems like the first try. "Don't go lookin' through my shit, Caleb."

He doesn't reply. His lips part in silent surprise instead. The other guys seem to clue in to what's happening, and we become centre of their attention. One by one, they lean toward Caleb, trying to sneak a look at whatever he's found on my phone.

"Does he have Shania Twain's number in that thing?" one of the volunteers asks.

I rub my temple and lean back in the booth.

"Well, this is a first for me," Caleb finally utters. When Darren tries to look at the screen from over his shoulder, he angles the phone away and stares at me. "Looks like we've got an accidental text on our hands, guys."

Interest skims beneath my skin. I lean forward again, resting my forearms on the table. "What?"

He flips the screen, and alarm replaces that initial interest. The photo of the woman on my screen is a Rita-classified nightmare. I swipe my arm out to take the phone when Caleb tugs it back to his chest, shaking his head.

"No fucking way. I'm rolling with this," he decides.

"You're not. Delete the message and the picture. Nobody should have my number."

Especially not the woman who sent me a photo of herself—or I assume it's her—in a dress with a long pale leg peeking through a high slit and her cleavage on display. It doesn't matter that both of those things were blaringly attractive even after only a millisecond of view. The photo didn't even show above her shoulders, which raises more than a few alarms.

Caleb's fingers fly across the screen far faster than if he were doing what I told him to. I push myself over the table as far as I can go without climbing onto the fucking thing and try to take the phone from him. His laugh is rough and loud and a massive fuck you that I don't plan on forgetting anytime soon.

By the time he finally tosses the phone toward me, I look

desperately at the screen and feel my stomach turn hollow. He's replied to her not once but twice.

> **Me:** Yes.

> **Me:** What do I have to do to get plus one approval?

5

Brody

THE AUCTION GROUNDS ARE PACKED. HARSH WINTER WIND BITES AT my face and neck as we stand beside a group of wrinkled ranchers Grandpa hasn't told to get lost yet. The old man knows just about everyone who owns so much as a lick of farmland in this province. *"They're connections,"* he says. I think he's just a goddamn hoarder of acquaintances.

The thick wool socks I forced myself to wear inside my boots are paying off with the quickly dipping November temperature. It's a damn shame my Stetson doesn't come with ear warmers.

"Brody, come here," Grandpa huffs.

Snow crunches beneath my feet as I join the group, trying not to focus on the bitter judgment that flicks in the eyes of the old men. I knew my choice to leave Cherry Peak would rub a few members of the community the wrong way, but while the majority of people understood . . . these men did no such thing.

I don't say anything as I sidle up beside my grandfather, taking note of the familiar hat resting over the top of his shoulder-length silver hair. He refuses to cut it, even when Grandma chases after him with her scissors. I can't tell him to cut it either, considering I refuse to do the same thing to mine.

Blue eyes so similar to mine land on my face and stay there, watching as I tip my chin at the men. "Hey."

"Brody," George grumbles. He's the toughest of Grandpa's friends, a millionth-generation cattle rancher similar to the Steeles. "You didn't tell us you were bringing your grandson, Wade."

My grandpa blows a foggy breath into the cool air. "'Course I was. He's helping me pick a good buy today."

George's eyes sharpen. "You haven't forgotten how to lift a hood in the time you've been gone?"

And so it begins. My shoulders tense as I slip my hands into the pockets of my jacket. "Some things aren't easily forgotten."

"So you say," George grinds out. "We'll see inside, won't we?"

Cool tension ripples from my grandfather as he takes a single step toward his friend and slaps a hand between his shoulders. "Brody doesn't need an old ass pissin' all over his foot. Let me him be and head inside."

George glances at the other two men, who don't have the nerve to stick their noses in whatever problem he has with me, and they wait for him to lift his glare from my face before following him toward the auction gates.

Grandpa lingers beside me, a heavy silence swirling between us until he slices through it with two words. "Ignore him."

"Been ignorin' him since I got back to town. He doesn't make it easy."

"They're stuck in their old ways."

It's more than that. They're protective of the old man, and that's a good thing. But also a pain in my ass. "I'm not their enemy. I'm not here to cause trouble with your little cadre."

"Cadre," he echoes, barking a rough laugh. "Is it such a bad thing for an old man to surround himself with friends?"

"No, it isn't. Even if they've got nearly a century of sticks up their asses."

Another laugh, this one hoarse, highlighting the damage caused by a lifetime of smoking cigarettes. "I recommend you don't say that to their faces unless you're prepared to taste leather, boy."

I shrug. "They'd never catch me."

The crow's feet beside his eyes tighten when his mouth twists. He shakes his head, silver hair flying in the wind. I laugh softly, not risking strengthening the pain in my throat.

"Suppose you got a point there. If we linger out here any longer, they'll take all the good shit on purpose," he says a beat later.

I sniff and let him lead the way inside.

A DISGUSTING AMOUNT of money later, my grandfather is off making delivery plans for his new purchases while I linger by his truck, breathing into my hands to bring some warmth back to them. It was a stupid decision not to bring gloves, but fuck if my grandfather won't just let me sit inside the cab while I wait.

Most people leaving don't pay me a lick of attention—either from being used to seeing me around for my entire life or just not giving enough of a shit to bother gawking at me—so it's easy to tell who the out-of-towners are. The muttered words spoken between friends as they stroll by, wide-eyed at my presence, are enough of a giveaway.

Citizens of Cherry Peak don't bother whispering when they're speaking about anyone, even when it comes to their "hometown celebrity." They're loud and unafraid of the damage their words could cause.

Maybe it's the out-of-towners' effort to hide their curiosity that has me acknowledging the two teenage boys with a half-smile when they pass by, their eyes bright with surprise and misplaced awe. I slip into the mask I wear when meeting fans and watch as they grin and shuffle past, not making any move to come speak to me. I'm grateful for that.

A familiar buzzing rhythm moves along my thigh before I use frozen fingers to pull my phone free. One look at the text and my guard shoots up, invisible snakes hissing in my mind.

> 16045557841: That picture wasn't meant for you.

A cool reply from the stranger Caleb couldn't resist replying to yesterday. When she didn't respond back to him—or me, I guess—I figured she tucked tail and blocked my number after he sent that ridiculous flirty fucking answer. Maybe I should have been the one to block the number just to be safe. To avoid this exact situation.

Not even a heartbeat later, another message comes through.

> 16045557841: You didn't like . . . keep the photo, right? I would appreciate if you removed it from your spank bank if you did.

I scoff, smoke puffing out of my mouth. As if.

> Me: I'm not that desperate.

I read the words again and wince, but I've already sent the message. That didn't exactly come out how I meant it to, and when she replies, I know I've fucked up.

> 16045557841: Desperate? DESPERATE? Alright. Leave it up to me to even accidentally text a world class asshole. How typical.

I tap my thumbs on the screen, tonguing my cheek. My grandpa's voice rings through the parking lot, marking his return. I don't miss the anger-bitten words he hollers to George before stomping toward the truck. With my fingers moving with a slow numbness, I type out four quick words and hit Send before slipping my phone away.

Me: That came out wrong.

Grandpa reaches me two breaths later, and we slide into the truck, heading back to the ranch. He's normally a quiet man, but this isn't a normal silence. For the majority of the drive, he *broods*, as Grandma would describe.

I let him sit in his silence for the hour-long drive back but halt him when we pull up outside of the house and he goes to get out of the truck.

"What happened?"

He stiffens, freezing with one hand on the door handle. "Nothin' you need to worry about."

"Tell me anyway."

"You were perfectly fine not carin' about our problems for a long while, boy. You don't gotta start up again now." He grinds the words out, avoiding eye contact.

I swallow, my chest tightening, but focus on keeping my voice level. "I've been wonderin' how long it would take you to finally admit how you felt about me being back here. Took longer than I thought."

"I didn't admit anythin', smartass. Get inside. Your grandmother is waitin'."

"I'm not a young kid you can boss around anymore," I point out, the words steely.

Something happened in that goddamn auction to bring this out. I've been walking on eggshells since I got back, just waiting for him to finally let me know how pissed he was when I left the ranch to pursue music. Of course, the bullheaded man refused to be honest about his feelings until now. When someone said something to him to spark this reaction.

"By all means, spend the night with the pigs, then," he growls before carefully shutting the truck door and stalking up the porch steps.

I straighten my spine, following after him. His head whips back when I shut the truck door harder than I should. "What happened to ignoring them? That golden nugget of advice only carries weight when it comes to me bitin' *my* tongue?"

The porch door swings open, and soft footsteps on the freshly stained wood can only belong to one woman. I fight to keep from looking at my grandmother. Her husband does the same, his narrowed eyes focused solely on me. The hurt I find lying there is gone in a blink, leaving me to wonder if it was ever there at all.

"Careful, Brody. You might be too old for me to boss around, but this is still my house. You'll speak to me with respect while you're here," he snaps.

I bite down hard on my tongue to keep my retort from spilling out. The words he left unspoken are crystal clear. *I'll treat him with respect while I'm here, however long that will be this time.*

A fleeting look at my grandmother has my stomach sinking like a rock in a pond. Her soft green eyes are torn, the mouth that's always lifted in a smile turned down. The wind whips her short black-and-silver hair against her cheeks, and she doesn't bother to brush it away.

I flash her a weak smile before spinning on my heel and striding toward the shop, not ready to coexist in the house with them for a good while. Neither of them tries to stop me.

The weather has only gotten worse, the temperature dropping alongside the sun. But it'll be warm in the shop, so I don't hide from the chill or the sting on my frozen cheeks. I've spent more time in the shop these past few weeks than I have the guest house I've moved back into. God knows I love my grandparents, but the guilt that followed my return—hell, followed my leave two years ago—keeps me from settling back into how things used to be.

Grandma treats me the same. I think she's just happy to have me back. But Grandpa tries to play it off, especially in front of the community and his closest friends, but those who know him well see right through it. The hurt and nagging feeling of abandonment. The fear. It's right below that calm exterior, and moments like just now show me how deep those feelings run.

Shouldering the shop door open, I step inside and take a heady lungful of fuel and oil. Something settles deep in my chest. A sense of rightness, maybe.

I fall into a familiar sense of mind as I pick up my metal box of tools from the shining silver workbench and carry it to the same tractor that's been pissing hydraulic fluid for a solid two days.

An hour later, I've changed out the line and reattached the connectors. I wipe my greasy palms along my thighs and stretch out my neck, noting the lack of tension there. Only a nip of it lingers, and it's guilt more than anger with my grandfather.

There's black beneath my nails when I pull free my phone and scroll through the notifications, finding three text messages from the stranger. Each one makes my guilt grow.

> 16045557841: You know what? Fuck you. As if I'd let myself be insulted by someone who could very well be a disgusting human being.

> 16045557841: I'm HOT. Very hot. You'd be struck stupid if you ever saw me in person. Which you will N O T.

> 16045557841: Lose this number.

She doesn't lack confidence, that's for sure. Or spunk.

I contemplate my reply, knowing damn well I shouldn't even bother. It's more effort than it's worth. I don't owe her an apology. But that's not how I was raised—to insult women, even accidentally.

> Me: I didn't mean it that way. Your body is great.

I delete the words with a grimace.

> Me: I meant that I'm not desperate enough to use a stranger's photos in that way.

Fuck. I erase that message too.

> Me: I didn't mean it that way. I'm sorry.

I send the message before I can talk myself out of it and wait for a reply. Five minutes go by before the message changes from Delivered to Read. Another two minutes pass. Then another.

A low laugh crawls up my throat when she leaves me on Read, not responding.

Touché, stranger. Touché.

6

Annalise

MAYBE I SHOULD GET A CAT.

Sleeping alone after three years of having a warm body wrapped around mine is jarring. It seems silly, but I've been sleeping terribly, waking every couple of hours with my hand reaching toward an empty, cold spot beside me.

I'm not a dog fan, with their barking and dripping tongues, but a cat? I think I could handle one of those. My fur allergy was always tedious when I was growing up, but with medication, I think it'd be fine. I'd go as far as to bribe the cat to sleep on the bed with buckets of catnip just so I didn't feel so alone. Gosh, that's sad.

My new winter boots sink into the fresh snow courtesy of a night-long, relentless dumping. I make a mental note to shovel the sidewalk when I get home. It's been years since I've had to shovel a sidewalk, back when I was a teenager being punished for something I did without thinking of the consequences.

Beautifully Bold is nestled between the town's flower shop and hair salon. The sign is a muted pink with white cursive writing and hangs above the entrance by a wood beam protruding from the building and two delicate-looking chains. It swings in the breeze, creaking slightly.

My palms are sweaty inside my pink mittens as I pull open the heavy door and step inside the building. It's warm but not hot, like Poppy was already thinking ahead and knowingly kept our upcoming sweating in mind when she set the thermostat. My breath stalls in my chest when I spot the four unfamiliar women already waiting.

They all spin in my direction, interest and curiosity sparking in their eyes. Bryce struts to my side, setting a hand on my shoulder. I swallow when she introduces me to everyone, lifting my hand in a nervous wave.

"This is Annalise, and she'll be joining us for today. Hopefully, we can keep her for longer than just today, so please help us convince her to stay!"

"Please be welcoming, or I'll have you hanging on the pole for the entire class," Poppy threatens, coming up to my other side.

Flanked by the two of them, I let some of my nervous flutter away and lift my chin. I really like these two girls, and if they think that I'll enjoy my time here, I'm willing to give it a fair shot. It's not like I have anything else to do today other than sit at home and watch old episodes of *Dateline* again.

"You can call me Anna. I'm excited to be here," I say, attempting to hide my lingering nerves.

"Hi, Anna." The welcoming words are spoken by everyone. Smiles break out around the room, and I return the gesture. Dragging my eyes to the studio, I take my first real look at the space.

The same muted pink colour from the sign outside has been carried inside the studio with matching walls and two velvet chairs settled in front of the infamous firefighter-watching window. The floors are dark wood, the colour similar to the floors in my rental. A hot pink neon sign with the studio name is hung along the back wall, bright enough to blind someone if they stared at it for too long. Six silver poles shine along the room, with one in front of all the others. A wall of only mirrors reflects the poles and the women around them. My stomach swirls at the idea of having to watch myself dance like a fool.

"We usually spend the first few minutes stretching, so just grab the empty pole, and we'll get started," Poppy says a beat later, waving her arm at the other women.

They all drop to the floor, sitting with their legs stretched outward. Bryce grabs one of the two empty poles and nods to the one beside her. We're at the back of the class, and while I won't tell her that I appreciate the placement, I really, *really* do.

Poppy is wearing a cropped T-shirt with the Beautifully Bold logo on the top right corner and a pair of shorts short enough that they cover little more than a pair of underwear. The other women are wearing a variety of similar clothes, with Bryce sporting the same short shorts and a tight tank top. Poppy's glowing, her curves confidently on display in a way that makes me insanely jealous. When she sits on the floor with the other girls and begins to lead stretches, I can't help but stare in awe at the way she moves with such sharp precision, even doing something as tame as stretching.

"I watched her the same way at first. I've been in this class with her since the very start, and I still can't move like her," Bryce says, noticing my stare. She's on the floor now, staring over at me with a soft smile. "She will have you sweating enough that you'll be cursing her name if you don't ditch the coat and boots and sit down to stretch, though."

"Right."

Flushing, I drop my gym bag a few feet behind me and shrug off my jacket, slipping out of my boots and socks next. After discarding them with everyone else's, I sit beside Bryce, waiting for Poppy's stretching instructions.

When I drape my body over my legs and attempt to grip my toes, I nearly cry at the burn that flares in my muscles. I can only reach my ankles, but I don't let that deter me. One glance beside me, and I see Bryce's fingertips brushing the top soles of her feet.

"Doesn't that hurt?" I ask on a rough exhale.

Slowly, she rolls her upper body back up and tucks her left arm behind her head, stretching a new set of muscles. "Not anymore. It used to. The more you do it, the easier it will be and the further you'll be able to reach. For day one, you're off to a good start."

I nod, following the next few sets of movements that Poppy explains to us. Once we're finished with the stretches, she hops onto her feet, and I'm completely unprepared for the sight of her gripping the pole in both hands and hoisting herself up.

Mouth gaping, I watch her swing her body up the length of the pole and extend her legs before spinning. Round and round, she twirls, not even a slight bend in her knees, until she cascades down the pole and her bare feet hit the ground. I wince at the sound of her bare thighs rubbing on the pole, and Bryce laughs at my reaction.

"You get used to that too."

"This is terrifying."

Does Poppy expect me to be able to do that today? *Does the entire class?* I didn't even bring a pair of shorts to change into, just my workout leggings and tee that I wore here and a pair of old running shoes. The only reason I have a gym bag for today is because I got Poppy's text the night after we met encouraging me to bring one for all of my things and panic ordered one online for today. It's embarrassingly empty because I wasn't sure what to put inside. Apparently, a pair of shorts were a good idea.

Another laugh, drawing Poppy's attention from the front of the class. She tosses us a wink, and Bryce says, "She's showing off for you. Nobody is going to expect you to do that today. Half the class can't do that yet."

"I like her," I blurt out. "Both of you. Thank you for inviting me today."

Bryce's sharp blue eyes warm. "You're welcome. We'll see if you still like her once we're finished today."

"She's that harsh of an instructor?"

"Harsh or firm, whatever you want to call it. She loves what she does and wants us all to love it too. Beautifully Bold has been her dream for over a decade, but nobody took her seriously for wanting to open a pole studio here. It was a bunch of total judgmental bullshit, but small towns can be very closed-minded sometimes. Cherry Peak is one of those towns."

Faintly, I hear Poppy telling everyone to chalk their hands, but neither Bryce nor I move from where we sit. Nobody cares much about what Bryce and I are doing right now, including Poppy. Whether she can sense that we're in the middle of an important conversation or just doesn't want to scare me off yet, I don't know.

"I know nothing about small towns, but even so, I hate that she dealt with that. Do the people here still not like it?"

"Most people have warmed to the idea. But we have a very big elderly population, and, well . . . they can't seem to differentiate what we do here and what goes on in a strip club. To them, they're one and the same."

I scrunch my nose. "That's ridiculous."

"I know. We all know that. But Poppy has grown very protective of this space and what we do during class. Sometimes that can come off as mean or harsh to those who don't know better."

"I'm not one to judge. There's nothing wrong with strong, driven women. You don't have to worry about me taking anything the wrong way," I assure her. The smile she gives me in return has my chest warming. Lifting my voice a little, I ask, "Are you ready to watch me make a complete fool out of myself?"

Poppy answers for her friend. "Show me what you got!"

With my head high and a lightness in my soul that hasn't been around in weeks, I let Poppy boss me around.

AN HOUR LATER, I'm sweating in places I didn't know I could sweat and panting like I've just finished running a marathon. My legs and arms are jelly, not a lick of strength left in the muscles that I used today for the first time in years.

But even through the exhaustion and pain, I feel oddly good. Surprisingly strong, even. Not just physical strength, but the mental kind. My mind is clear, my chest light. I'm already counting down the days until the next class.

"Thank you, ladies! See you next week," Poppy chimes, ushering the women out of the class.

Throughout the hour-long class, I've learned all their names, but not much more than that. There wasn't the time for chitchat. It's clear that this class is as freeing for them as it was for me. They were laser focused on what they were doing, and once Poppy brought the class to an end, there was a pep in their step so similar to the one in mine. A new determination in their eyes.

A chorus of goodbyes flood the studio, carried on the wind coming from the open door before it's just the three of us. Bryce squirts water into her mouth and pats at her red cheeks. She's flushed, sweat gleaming on her brow. Poppy looks similar but has a massive grin on her face.

"So? What do you think? Will you come back?" she asks me.

My reply is instant. "Absolutely. I feel really good, even though I'm like a limp noodle right now."

"That means you did a good job." She winks, fanning her chest with her shirt. "We usually go grab something to eat after class as a reward for kicking ass. Wanna come?"

I glance at Bryce for her approval, but she's already nodding. Adjusting the strap of my too-light gym bag on my shoulder, I say, "I'd love to."

Poppy rushes off to change out of her pole clothes, and Bryce jumps right in, asking me questions about myself. I don't balk at the forwardness. Not when I want to get to know them just as well.

Something tells me that becoming their friend will be one of the better decisions I've made in my most recent years.

7

Annalise

"You're telling me that you found your boyfriend of three years cheating on your *birthday*?" Bryce gapes at me, dumb-struck at the information I've just dropped on them.

I might have only winced a handful of times while indulging them on all things Anna and Stewart when we got to the bakery an hour ago. Even that asshole's name makes me feel ill. Like I've swallowed too much cheap tequila on an empty stomach.

"Fiancé, Bryce. Her fiancé!" Poppy corrects her, just as unim-pressed as her best friend.

Bryce's fingers jab into the squishy top of her croissant. "Your fiancé! That makes the betrayal even worse. How is it possible that you only ruined a few of his things? I would have killed him."

"He loved his clothes more than he ever loved me. Clearly. This was better revenge than death," I mutter.

Poppy twists her mouth, sweeping her eyes over the hustle and bustle of people entering and exiting the shop. Our table is tucked in the corner, a bit separate from the rest of the open space. The vibe of the place is incredibly cozy, somewhere you could spend hours working or thinking. It's nice to have some-where like this here. Back in Vancouver, there were a million different coffee shops and cafes, but none of them made me feel this . . . at peace.

I frown. I'm aware enough of my own mind to realize that comparing Cherry Peak to Vancouver has become a crutch of sorts. A way to make my move not feel as scary. But in doing that, am I stalling my progress here? I don't know if I'm going to ever go back, so why can't I let go? The only person who matters to me in Vancouver is my mother. Is she enough to eventually pull me back?

The answer is obvious. If staying with her were enough, I wouldn't have left.

"Have you gone on a date since? You know they say that the best way to move on is to let someone else screw you five ways to Sunday," Poppy says.

"Nobody says it like that," Bryce blurts, fighting off a laugh.

There's no stopping my laugh, though. It tears free and fills the bakery, loud and strong. It's the first time I've laughed like this in months. The realization of that is a sucker punch to the gut. My laugh slowly trickles off.

Bryce halts her croissant tapping and instead places her hand over mine, squeezing. "No. Wherever your head went just now, the answer is no."

"A cheating man is not worth that frown. No man is, cheating or not," Poppy adds.

Bryce nods. "It's one of the reasons I haven't dated one since college."

I blow out a pitiful breath. "I haven't been well and truly single in a long time. Before Stewart, I dated pretty frequently. Maybe that's part of my problem."

"There's nothing wrong with dating a lot despite what society thinks of it as long as you're happy. And I don't just mean happy with dating. I mean with everything. Dating, your life, you in general. You have to love yourself first, obviously, but I don't think the only way to get there is to be alone. Not completely anyway," Poppy says, expression soft.

I'm suddenly struck with the realization that these girls are going to be incredibly hard to let go of if they decide later on that they don't want to be my friends. One pole class and snack date together and I'm ready to make us friendship bracelets.

"That was so incredibly wise of you, Pops," Bryce sighs, her eyes a dimmer shade of blue than usual.

The pole instructor fits with her a sharp look. "Are you being sarcastic?"

"Surprisingly, no. That was solid advice."

"Solid enough for you to take it too?" Poppy counters.

I try not to pay too much attention to that comment and pick at the gingerbread cookie on the brown napkin in front of me instead. It's really damn good, but all this talk of Stewart and loving yourself has my stomach shrivelled up.

Poppy sets her hand over Bryce's and, in turn, mine before asking, "What do you say we do something fun this weekend? The three of us."

"Yes. Absolutely yes," I agree.

Bryce flashes two rows of sparkling white teeth and nods her agreement. Pulling her hand back from where it lay sandwiched between Poppy's and mine, she adds, "In town or out?"

"Doesn't matter to me. I haven't been outside of Cherry Peak since I moved here," I tell them.

"Have you been to Peakside yet?" Poppy asks, eyes on me.

Bryce groans and pushes the rest of her croissant away, as if she's no longer hungry. "We're not taking her to Peakside."

"You just don't want to see Vic. Even you can admit that it's the best place to peruse for a possible rebound. All the fire-fighters go there on Saturday night."

My interest piques at the new name. "Who's Vic?"

Bryce opens her mouth to answer me, but Poppy beats her to it. "Bryce's ex-girlfriend. The owner of Peakside's daughter. We've been avoiding the place for *months* now since they broke up. I'm having withdrawals."

"You're just horny," Bryce grunts.

"And? You're horny too, but you refuse to move on. This is only a prime example of that."

I try and keep up with their back and forth, storing away the information they reveal. For this Vic to be worthy of a woman as beautiful and kind as Bryce, she's bound to be someone that's hard to forget.

"How long ago did you break up?" I ask.

My question drags both sets of eyes in my direction. It's Bryce that answers, her skin paling a bit. "A long fucking time ago."

"Four months and three days, to be exact," Poppy adds.

Bryce grimaces. "Should I be scared that you know that?"

Poppy waves her off. The corner of my mouth lifts the slightest bit. "It might not be my place to say anything, considering I literally moved provinces to get away from my ex, but I think that going out will help. Both of us. There's no time like the present, right? It's not fair to us not to live our lives because of someone else."

Bryce studies me for a moment, features smooth and calculating. Her thick onyx hair is tucked behind her ears, and I find myself counting the number of studs along her right one before moving to the left—ten in total. I don't even have my earlobes pierced. Maybe I'll make an appointment at a jeweller to get that done soon. I've always wanted to wear cute earrings.

How many sets of expensive diamond studs did Stewart get me before he realized I couldn't wear them?

"You're right," Bryce says, some colour coming back to her face. "We've both sulked enough, I think."

"Hell yeah!" Poppy juts a fist into the air. "Word on the street is that Brody Steele is back in town and has been moping around Peakside for a couple weeks now. Maybe we'll have a run-in with him while we're there."

Bryce chokes on a laugh, rolling her eyes. "I should have known you had a secondary reason for wanting to go to that shithole."

I swipe my tongue over my lips and ask, "You know Brody?"

"Everyone here knows Brody. Do you?" Poppy finishes her muffin and crumples the wrapper in her hand.

"No. But I heard he was here. People love to chat when they get their hair done."

It was one of the older women, Marg, who told me he was in town. Or, rather, began complaining to anyone who would listen that the prodigal Brody Steele had returned home at last. Everyone who's listened to country music recently knows who Brody is. He was opening for Killian Granger on his world tour, for Pete's sake. What I didn't know until I moved here was that he was from Cherry Peak.

"People can be assholes. We both knew him in school. He was two grades above us, but he was a nice guy back then and still is now, from what I hear, if not a bit broody. The old folks in this town just give him a hard time because of who his family is. I guarantee they wouldn't give a crap about him if he wasn't a Steele, even with the fame," Poppy grumbles.

"Who's his family?" I can't help but ask.

Bryce sucks on the straw sunken deep in her iced coffee before saying, "Steele Ranch is the biggest cattle ranch in Southern Alberta. He was supposed to stay and help the business but chose music instead. A lot of people in the community hold that against him."

I find it hard to think poorly of those who choose themselves over the expectations of others. A part of me feels for the guy.

"That's unfair."

Poppy dips her chin in agreement. "It is."

When my phone chimes from my coat pocket, I reach behind me to where my coat drapes over the back of my chair and pull it free. My already aching muscles in my abdomen scream at the stretch.

My scowl is immediate when I read the message.

17805559540: Ignoring a man's apology is rude.

A furious growl slips from my lips as I swipe open my phone and shoot daggers at the text. Bryce and Poppy lean toward me, and I glance up just in time to catch the curious looks they give each other.

"You'll laugh if I tell you," I mutter.

Poppy shakes her head furiously. "You have my word that I won't."

"Ditto," Bryce says.

Huffing, I extend the phone to them. Poppy snatches it from my grip right away, and Bryce laughs at her. For the next few moments, they scroll through the messages I've exchanged with the rude stranger. When they get to the one that sparked my distaste, Bryce clucks her tongue.

"He's an ass," she says.

"So, it isn't just me, then? That was an insult, right?"

"I think it was more of a case of a tangled tongue than an insult, but it was still rude," Poppy adds a second later, handing back my phone.

I purposefully made sure he knew that I had read his message last time, and he'll know the same thing now. The question is whether I reply this time or if I do what I should have done at the beginning of this exchange and delete the number.

"You should reply. Tell him off," Bryce suggests.

I tap my thumbs against the side of the phone before typing out a message.

Me: Tell me one good reason why I should accept your apology.

Showing the girls the message, I wait for them to approve of it before sending it off a second later. "I feel like a teenager fighting with the mean girl at school over email."

Poppy sets her chin in her palm. "I've been needing a bit of drama in my life, honestly."

"This place has enough drama for you. You just ignore it all," Bryce points out.

I lock my phone and slide it back into my coat. "You should spend a few hours at the salon. You'll hear enough drama to last a lifetime."

"Do you like working there?" Bryce asks.

"I do. Despite the gossiping, I love doing hair. I would love to have my own salon someday. It's been a dream of mine for like a decade now."

Poppy's eyes light up at that. "A fellow entrepreneur."

"*Someday.*" I put emphasis on the word this time. "I'm broke after moving, and I'm not making nearly enough to be able to afford a place anytime soon. Plus, a town this size doesn't need more than one salon."

It was one of the things I had to accept when I moved here. Braxton was the one who chose this place for me after I spent a week straight trying to pick somewhere to go. She laid out a map on the coffee table of her rental and handed me a die, telling me to drop it anywhere on the map and wherever it landed would be my new home. When it hit the map directly on Cherry Peak with my lucky number facing up, I took it as a sign and got my plans together. It wasn't until I began to research the town that I realized where I had agreed to move.

It's not like I had the money before this to buy a salon. Not in the Vancouver market anyway. It'll happen eventually. I feel it.

One step at a time, Anna. You'll get there.

8

Brody

I FROWN AT THE CONVERSATION ON MY PHONE AND TAKE ANOTHER swig of my beer. Clearly, I'm a bit rusty when it comes to talking to women if I've already put my foot in my mouth after a handful of messages. I don't want to woo her or anything, considering she's a goddamn stranger, but I don't want to leave such a terrible impression. I was raised better than that.

> Me: Cause I've been here staring at my phone like a wounded pup waiting to properly explain myself.

It's been over an hour since I replied to her, and considering she's made an effort to let me know when she's seen each one of my messages before now, it's safe to say that she hasn't yet since there isn't a tiny *Read* showing.

I'd been so busy this past year that texting more than a handful of people just wasn't a priority. If it weren't for the crew members with me every day, I probably wouldn't have spoken to anyone when I wasn't onstage. I didn't care about the isolation back then, but after a couple of weeks at home, my newly formed habit has been a nuisance.

I could hardly make it through one fifteen-minute conversa-

tion earlier with the new farmhands Grandpa snagged after the
harvest season ended.

The shop is hot, the heavy portable heater pumping off thick
waves of warmth to the right of me. My hands are dirty, oil and
grease caked beneath my nails. It'll take hours to get them
completely clean, and I don't have it in me after the day I've had.
The empty plate at my feet that used to be covered with my
grandma's famous gingersnap cookies is a testament to that.

Like some terrible joke, there are three pieces of broken-down
equipment inside the shop, with another one waiting outside in
the snow. I'm the only mechanic on the ranch right now after we
lost the other two only a few days before I got back home. None
of us can blame them for leaving, not after the sudden family
death that struck them.

It's just me now. Me and a million fucking things to do in too
few hours a day.

I finish my beer and set the bottle on the ground beside the
plate. Stretching my legs out in front of me, I ignore the hardness
of the concrete beneath my ass and close my eyes.

Before I fall asleep sitting up, my phone vibrates in my lap,
and I snap my eyes open, blinking to clear the promise of sleep
away.

> 16045557841: Explain then.

Ignoring that Caleb would give me a verbal chastising about
replying too quickly, I type out a reply and send it without a
second thought.

> Me: I'm not the best talker. Texter either. I didn't
> mean to be offensive. You looked just fine.

> 16045557841: Maybe I shouldn't have bought
> that dress then. No woman wants to look just
> fine, stranger.

I swallow my discomfort.

> Me: Shit. Sorry. It was a nice dress. Can we move on now?

Tiny bubbles appear as she types, and I exhale slowly, a pinch growing in my back from sitting this way for so long. Shifting, I lean back against the steel bench and cross my ankles.

> 16045557841: Move onto what? We can go our separate ways now.

I take my hat off and drop it on my knee, raising a hand to my hair. It's warm, damp from the heat and being smothered all day. The hollow feeling in my chest becomes too hard to ignore as I reread her text. The feeling is loneliness, for fuck's sake. I'm lonely, and talking to this stranger, even if I was doing nothing more than sticking my foot in my mouth, helped distract me from that feeling. I hate that I don't want to stop talking to her.

> Me: Let's talk. Just for tonight.

I send the text without giving myself a chance to be embarrassed by my desperation.

> 16045557841: Just for tonight.

My relief is instant, filling that hole inside of me enough to soothe the ache.

> Me: Will you give me your name? Just so I can change your contact.

> 16045557841: What about a nickname instead?

> Me: Sure.

A pause, like she's thinking about which name to give me.

> 16045557841: What about banana?

> Me: Alright. You can call me Bo.

I don't give myself a chance to change the name before sending the message. The history of that nickname isn't anything I'd like to think about right now. I shouldn't have given it to her, but it's not like she's going to tell anybody. She won't have a chance to. This is only for tonight.

I change her contact name and smile slightly at the ridiculousness of it.

> Banana: Hi Bo. You still haven't told me if you're an old creeper.

> Me: Would an old creeper actually tell you if he were an old creeper?

> Banana: No I guess he wouldn't. He probably wouldn't send me a pic of his hot bod though.

I laugh, surprising myself. The rough sound fills the shop before disappearing.

> Me: Are you saying that in order to not be an old creeper, I have to have a quote-unquote hot bod?

> Banana: Well . . . do you?

> Me: Maybe.

> Banana: Prove it then.

With a glance at my clothes, I wince. Dirty jeans, even dirtier boots, and a grey long-sleeve with splashes of oil across the front and what I can't tell is either mud or cow shit on the bottom hem. I haven't been to a gym in years. I was pushed too hard on the road to have time for breaks long enough to work out, and back home . . . I think my grandparents would find it offensive if I deemed the hard labour here boring enough to seek out a gym.

I'm tall, and while I might not have stacks upon stacks of abdominal muscles, I think I'm pretty built. I haven't had a woman tell me that in a long, long time, though. Long enough that I don't know how I'd take it if I heard it now.

> Me: Are you trying to flirt with me?

Banana: You wish. I'm merely trying to stay safe.

> Me: By looking at a rack of abs?

Banana: A girls gotta eat.

Again, I hear myself laugh, and the sound is still as odd the second time. Fuck, that's depressing.

> Me: Who am I to keep you starving then?

As soon as she reads the message and doesn't reply, I know she's waiting for me to send a photo first. I have no clue what to do now. After another sweep of my eyes over my body, I'm saying fuck it and positioning my hat over the dark stain on the hem of my shirt before opening the camera app. Flipping it to front-facing, I extend my arm and try to get as much of my body into the shot as possible, careful not to include my face.

Screw it all to hell, but I snap too many pictures before choosing the one that looks the least awkward and sending it. It takes her a minute to reply, and for those long sixty seconds, I contemplate blocking her and trying to forget the past few minutes.

Banana: Well howdy there farmer.

> Me: Nobody actually says howdy around here.

> Banana: Tough crowd. Did you get in a fight with a jug of oil today? God your clothes are dirty.

> Me: I've been dirtier.

> Banana: Kinky. Where does one go to buy a pair of those boots? I've never had a pair before.

I store that piece of information away, even if I'll never need it.

> Me: Depends where you're from.

> Banana: Nuh-uh. Just because you have a nice looking body doesn't mean you aren't old nor a creeper. Nice try.

> Me: Since a photo didn't prove anything, the demand for it was just to get your rocks off huh?

> Banana: My rocks are still very much on, you filthy cowboy.

> Me: I don't think I've been called a filthy cowboy before. I like it.

Not nearly as much as I like having a stranger tell me I have a nice-looking body. Albeit a stranger with great legs and curves for days, from what I remember from that quick glance at the photo. I haven't looked at it since. It feels like an invasion of her privacy to do that.

> Banana: I aim to please. Now, tell me how many cowboy hats you have. I'm going to guess and say . . .

Banana: Fifteen.

Me: Not even close.

Banana: Twenty?

Me: Three. They're hats not underwear.

Banana: You have twenty pairs of underwear?

Me: Do you always turn everything into a question?

Banana: I do when it involves conversing with a stranger.

Me: Is that something you do often?

Some tiny, annoying part of me hopes that it isn't. Dammit, I need to get out more. Do anything besides hide in this shop and ignore the world outside of it. Cows and tractors are shit conversationalists, and while my throat still kills, I need to talk to someone. Someone who isn't judging me for something they'll never understand or pretending to want to speak in order to get something.

I don't know when my life turned into such a fucking embarrassment, but I need to figure it out. Soon.

Banana: No. My sister would actually kill me if she knew I was doing this.

Me: Older or younger sister?

Banana: Older. Only by a few years. Do you have siblings?

Me: No. I'm an only child.

Banana: What about pets?

Me: Not technically. You?

Banana: No, but I've been contemplating getting a cat. Thoughts on them?

Me: I've never actually had a cat as a pet.

Banana: No offense, filthy cowboy, but your life sounds kind of boring.

Me: Because I don't have siblings or a cat?

My eyelids droop as I stare at the time at the top of the screen. It's late, too late for me to be awake when I have to get up in five hours. Is she in the same time zone as I am?

I struggle to keep my eyes open, waiting for her next message to pop up, but with the steady thrum of the heater and the tick of the clock on the shop wall behind me, I'm dead to the world before I get a chance to see them the two of them come through.

Banana: Call it a gut instinct. It's a shame we only agree to tonight, because I could have helped bring a little sparkle to it.

Banana: Goodbye Bo.

9

Annalise

I'VE NEVER WORN JEANS FOR A GIRLS' NIGHT BEFORE. NOT THAT I'VE been on that many girls' nights that didn't involve my sister and two bags of butter-drenched popcorn.

Going out on the town in Vancouver usually meant dressing up in an outfit you found earlier that day hidden in the back of your closet and a pair of shoes that you know will have you limping home afterward. Maybe I ran in the wrong crowd of people not to spend my Friday nights in small pubs or easygoing bars. I'm sure there were more than a few of those near my condo in the city, but none I ever ventured into. It was always uppity clubs with guest lists and long lines out the door.

Peakside couldn't be further from what I'm used to.

Bryce and Poppy don't hesitate to saunter inside, both dressed like I am in jeans and simple tops but somehow managing to pull it off in an entirely different way. Naturally, almost.

Never in my life have I seen a pair of pink cowboy boots like Poppy's. They're slightly scuffed near the sole, but not a single one of the dozens of glittering studs lining the sides is missing. A pair of deep blue skinny jeans are tucked inside the boots, and a white puffed coat that falls just past the swell of her hips hides the black shirt she's wearing beneath.

Bryce is dressed similarly, but instead of pink boots, she has a pair of black sneakers peeking beneath the legs of her jeans and a coat to match. Neither of them chose to leave their hair down tonight like I did, and I'm beginning to wonder if that was a mistake on my part.

"Don't stand out in the cold, Anna," Poppy says, pausing in the doorway, urging me inside with a wave of her hand.

Bryce is already inside, hopefully securing us a table. My legs still don't move. "Are you sure we can't just go to my place? I'll let you win at Monopoly."

"I blame Bryce for you knowing about my love for Monopoly. But no. We're going inside. You look too good to spend the night at home."

"Do I?" I cringe at my lack of confidence.

"You have the ass for those jeans. Trust me, you look hot." Her wink makes me choke on a laugh.

"Thank you." I mean it. Really, really do. Finally, my legs cooperate, and I move in her direction. "I know I must sound pathetic."

"You absolutely do *not* sound pathetic. You sound like a woman who's just gotten out of a relationship with a man who diminished her confidence. It won't come back instantly just because he's gone. You'll have to grow it back up."

"Well, let's hope that it doesn't take forever because I can't stand this feeling," I admit.

"You've got this. We'll be here to shower you with compliments until you can start giving them to yourself." The words sound like a promise, and I believe her.

When I reach her side, the smell of the bar hits me square in the face. It's not necessarily a gross smell, just a strong one. One I wasn't anticipating. A mix of frying oil and beer.

There's a sticky sort of heat in the bar as we walk further inside, the previous topic dropped. Conversations drawl on around us from the several packed tables. A few of them halt for a breath before continuing when we pass by, as if they're slightly surprised to see us here. Or me, I suppose.

We catch up to Bryce as she lingers near the bar, and then I follow the two women, letting them pick where we sit for the night while secretly hoping for somewhere a bit out of sight. A momentary sense of relief crashes into me when I see them turn for the booths lining the wall behind the bar before noticing that they're heading to an already occupied one, one so full of men that the two on the outside are nearly falling onto the floor.

"Poppy—" I start, but it's too late. The first man catches sight of us and flashes a sparkling grin, his hand rising to wave us over.

"If it isn't Darren's little sister, Poppy," he shouts, drawing dozens of eyes in our direction.

Poppy doesn't balk at the attention. Instead, she waves back and says to the entire table, "Don't forget Bryce and our new friend, Anna."

Bryce slings her arm over my shoulder when the entire table of men looks at me, checking me out from bottom to top. It's with curiosity more than interest, and while that still makes discomfort flare, I'll take it. I use the opportunity to look at them right back.

The man who called us over looks like he could be the youngest, with a smooth baby face and bright green doe eyes. Beside him, the man watching us looks slightly older, as if he could be Poppy's twin. He smiles at me, a dimple popping in his right cheek. He has the same swooped nose and naturally swollen-looking bottom lip as Poppy. Brown hair and brown eyes. Gosh, maybe they're twins.

"Anna, meet Darren, my brother," Poppy says, pointing to the man I suspected could be her brother. I greet him a bit awkwardly before she introduces the other men.

Across the table, three guys sit shoulder to shoulder. The one on the end has red hair and a sly grin, the type that I'd bet more often than not gets him whatever he wishes whenever he wishes it. Sandwiched in the middle, the next guy is maybe the oldest-looking of them all, maybe thirty years old or close to it.

My throat tightens to the point it's a struggle to breathe when I finally slide my eyes to the last man on the bench. A squeak escapes me, and two deep blue eyes slowly slide my way. Annoyance ripples across his features as he takes in my sudden shock, and I bristle beneath that look.

I hardly catch the next three names until finally, my attention snags on the last one. The one who appears completely bothered by my presence. "—and finally, Brody."

I'm not one to get starstruck, but I would love to meet a single person who wouldn't gape at Brody Steele the way I am right now. God, that's *exactly* what I'm doing, but I can't seem to look away. It's the striking, rugged beauty that does me in. The scraping of stubble along the strong lines of his hard jaw and the backward baseball hat with messy hair jutting through the cut-out and curling around his ears. Lips that I've watched purse around pretty lyrics on TV but I bet kiss hard and demanding. Even the bags beneath his eyes can't take away from how beautiful he is. I wonder if he were to smile right now if he would have dimples like Poppy's brother or if it would be harsh instead.

It's dangerous for a man to be so good-looking. A goddamn crime that I plan on keeping myself well away from.

Pulling myself together, I shut my mouth and flash a weak, close-lipped smile. Brody Steele only scowls at me, eyes tracing the length of my body once before he's diverting his attention to the plate of chicken wings in the middle of the table. My stomach turns over when I catch what appears to be disgust in his tight expression.

"Hi," I croak.

"Nice to meet you, Anna. Poppy hasn't stopped blabbing about you since you guys met. I was just telling the guys how crazy it is that you've moved to Cherry Peak from BC," Darren says. His smile is sweet and friendly, and while it doesn't help me relax, at least it doesn't make anything worse.

"Don't talk about my friends when I'm not around, Darren," she warns lightly. "And it's not crazy that she moved here. We might be a bit small, but we're good people."

Bryce, the woman who never seems to miss a goddamn thing around her—including the expression I swore I saw on Brody's face just now—keeps her arm tight around my shoulders and says with a sharp tongue, "Brody is all bark and no bite. Don't worry about all the scowling."

I highly doubt that, but instead of saying exactly that, I look at Brody and smile saccharinely. My next words just explode from my mouth before I can think twice about them.

"My sister's a vet, so I'm not afraid of rabid animals."

The howl of laughter fills our side of the bar, and I don't shrink from it this time. The guy on the edge of the left booth raises his arm and offers me his palm. I step forward awkwardly and slap it.

"Pull up a couple chairs, ladies. I'm all up for watching the new girl spank Brody's ass," the man squished between Brody and the redhead hollers.

"We would, but we don't want to," Bryce says, patting my shoulder. "It's girls' night, Caleb. Anna doesn't have time to entertain you beer fiends tonight."

"What about another night?" the redhead beside him asks, that dangerous smirk attempting to sway me.

"Doubt she'll be in town long enough to entertain you, Trev," Brody grunts, not so much as flicking his eyes in my direction.

"What makes you say that?" I snip, my cheeks flushing red.

Another look at my body, or my outfit, maybe. "You really want me to answer that, sweetheart?"

Steam nearly shoots from my nostrils as they flare. "You've known me for five seconds."

"I only needed three."

My fingers curl as my lips twitch. "To finish? And that's something you're proud of?"

Silence, and then Bryce's body begins shaking, her laugh forcing mine out. I look at Poppy and find her grinning, approval sparkling in her eyes. Neither of us pays any mind to the fuming celebrity who's no doubt planning his comeback.

I don't care about whatever he wants to throw back at me. Brody Steele is just like every other guy I've ever met. An arrogant piece of work with a stick so far up his ass I bet he can taste it. I moved here to get away from my ex, not to wind up a verbal punching bag for someone far too similar to him.

He doesn't know me. His judgment can kiss my juicy ass, even if it disappoints me to know someone with his talent is so careless of his treatment of others.

"Let's go, Viper. No need to draw any more blood tonight," Poppy says, doing a terrible job of hiding her amusement. When she speaks to the men, she does so with such confidence that they can't help but watch her, hanging on to her every word. "See you."

"Nice to meet you all," I mutter with a weak wiggle of my fingers in front of me.

Bryce doesn't bother saying anything to the men before leading the way to what appears to be the only empty table in the joint. Cluing in to my confusion once we slip into the booth, she says, "This is our table."

Poppy shrugs off her jacket. "I'm shocked Vic doesn't have this table full every night regardless."

"Don't say her name. You'll summon her from the pits of hell," Bryce hisses.

I laugh lightly and unzip my jacket, still feeling flushed. My toes cramp in the boots I borrowed from Poppy, an ache already building in the sole of my foot. The boots might be my regular size, but my wide feet aren't meant for them. My entire outfit has me feeling so unlike myself.

"What exactly happened between the two of you?" I ask Bryce.

Bryce blows out a long, harsh breath and taps her nails on the table. "I need at least three drinks before we crack open that can of worms."

"Let me start us off, then," I announce before slipping out of the booth. This is girls' night, after all, and no man will ruin that for me. "What do you two drink?"

Please don't say beer.

"Vodka and cranberry juice for me," Poppy sings.

Bryce thinks for a beat before saying, "Same as her, but add a round of tequila shots."

Poppy's groan matches mine, but neither of us fights our friend on it. If she needs tequila, then we all need tequila.

With that, I spin on my heels and head for the bar. After ordering our drinks, I lean my forearms against the smooth wood bar top and check my phone. I reply to my sister asking what my plans for the night are and then hesitate to open the conversation with Bo for the millionth time since I sent that final text last night, and despite my agreement with only speaking that single time, I've contemplated sending another message.

It's reckless to want to speak to a stranger, but it was easy to speak with him. Fun, even. We got along really well, and it turns out that he even has a sense of humour similar to mine. It's too bad we shouldn't speak again.

I force myself to shove my phone into my back pocket and smile at the older woman behind the bar as she starts setting three glasses full of red liquid on a black tray. The tequila comes next, and I crinkle my nose in anticipation of the taste of it.

"Thirsty?"

I jolt, hair flying as I turn my head and find Brody standing there, arms crossed over his wide chest. Up close, he's really damn tall. Like I have to tip my head back to meet his eyes tall. I've never felt shorter in my entire life than in this moment. *Great.*

The woodsy scent of his cologne drifts in the air between us, and I immediately hate how good it smells. I would prefer him to smell like skunk spray or something equally as disgusting.

"Yep. Parched," I snip.

When I reach for the tray of drinks, he snags it out of my reach. My blood boils as I snap my gaze upward. The scowl I'm starting to believe he was born wearing has somehow deepened, as if I've already done something to offend him again.

"I'll carry it for you," he grunts.

"So you can dump the drinks over my head once I turn my back to you? Not a chance. I can carry them myself."

"I'm tryin' to be nice."

"Well, you're doing a terrible job. Leave me alone."

He closes his eyes, inhaling deeply before opening them again. "You'll be lucky not to trip in those boots."

"I'd rather trip than be pushed by you. Seriously, go away."

I don't have the chance to be shocked at my rudeness before he's sidestepping me and pulling the tray toward him, out of my reach. He doesn't wait for me to fall into step beside him before walking toward my table.

"If this is your attempt at an apology for your utter asshole-ness earlier, you're doing a terrible job!" I raise my voice just enough he'll be able to make it out over the music and chatter.

He freezes, glancing at me over his shoulder. The exaspera-tion in his expression threatens to sever my last nerve.

"It wasn't an apology."

"Your friends ordered you to come help me, then?"

One long leg shifts in my direction, the tight material of his jeans cupping his thigh as it strains with the movement. I tighten my jaw, annoyed with myself for noticing that.

"Let's chuff it up to a moment of weakness," he snaps, not coming any closer than that single step. "Won't happen again, sweetheart."

"Don't call me that!" I demand, but he's already walking away again, this time quicker than before.

I watch as he drops the tray of drinks on my table and mutters something to the two women that has them glancing my way before he's stalking away again. He doesn't go back to his table. No, he blows right past it and leaves the bar entirely.

Bryce offers me a sympathetic smile, but I'm already reaching for one of the three shot glasses and lifting it to my lips. The tequila burns the entire way down.

Hate at first sight.

How romantic.

10

Annalise

MY MOUTH IS DRY. I SWIRL MY TONGUE AND LICK THE INSIDE OF MY cheeks, the lingering taste of alcohol turning my stomach. A pulse beats between my brows, so I keep my eyes closed, too scared to open them. My eyelids are sticky, and my mind is groggy, heavy with exhaustion.

I sift through my memories of last night and try to piece together what happened. From my current state, I must have drunk a lot more than I planned to. The last solid memory I have is sitting at the table with Bryce and Poppy while they tried to calm me down after my one-on-one run-in with Brody fucking Steele.

Even just the slightest remembrance of that conversation intensifies the pain in my head. I don't have a lot of experience meeting celebrities, but now I'm positive that I don't want to ever meet another one. Not if they're going to stomp all over my minuscule expectations of them by being such total assholes! I don't even know why he took such a strong dislike to me so suddenly. Poppy and Bryce assured me that he's a nice guy, but I couldn't disagree more.

With that thought, I finally peel my eyelids open and squint at the beaming sunlight shining directly onto my bed. Groaning, I lift a hand to my face and shield my eyes.

"You're awake!" Poppy's voice ricochets through my skull.

"What gave me away?"

"The groaning. You sounded like an angry bull."

I blow out a laugh and grip the blanket at my chest, turning onto my side. My first look at Poppy takes me aback. "How long have you been awake?"

"A couple of hours. There's coffee and bagels in the kitchen." She's dressed in workout clothes, her hair tied back and cheeks flushed. Blue eyes bright and soft, she stares at me, assessing. "How are you feeling?"

"Like roadkill. How do you look so good? Did you *work out*?"

"Yep. Both you and Bryce were dead to the world when I woke up, and after last night, I figured you both needed the extra sleep. How much do you remember?"

By the slight twist of her mouth as she shifts her weight back and forth on her feet, almost like she's holding herself back from blurting out what happened, I can tell it probably wasn't anything good.

"Nothing. Explain it all to me, please."

Loud, uneven footsteps sound before Bryce appears beside Poppy. She looks about as great as I feel. Bags heavy beneath her eyes, skin pale, and hair stuck up in every which way, she's the picture of hungover. I don't even want to know how I look right now.

"I'm going to guess and say it has to do with why I have pink paint beneath my nails?" she asks, examining her hands.

Alarmed, I bring mine in front of my face and gawk at the pink crusted beneath my short nails. Poppy has the nerve to giggle at our reactions.

"It was Bryce's idea," she tells us.

"What was?" I stammer.

Bryce is grimacing now, her face somehow becoming paler. "Tell me we didn't."

My eyes flick between the two of them, anxiousness swelling in my stomach. "If one of you doesn't tell me what we did right now, I'll kick you out in the snow."

"This is all you, Ice," Poppy urges her best friend. The nickname is new to me, and I make sure to make note of it.

Bryce hides her face behind her hands and sighs. "We went to Vic's, didn't we? Her favourite colour is pink."

"Oh, we went to Vic's alright. After the both of you got ten shots of tequila deep and demanded we leave the bar. The moment we stepped outside, you started ranting about Vic and explained to Anna here about what happened between you. Then, we spent a solid half hour painting pink dicks all over her front fence before the devil herself nearly caught us," Poppy explains, face red with the effort it's taking her not to laugh.

I roll my lips and blink slowly, trying to pry open my memories in search of what happened, but I come up empty. Maybe that's a good thing.

"Fuck my life," Bryce mutters. She drags herself to my bed and throws herself onto her back, the mattress shifting with her weight. "She's going to try to ruin my life now."

I sit up and stare at the top of her head. "I hate to say this, but I don't remember anything about Vic or what we did last night. I'm sorry."

"Long story short, Vic tried to bring a third person into their relationship, and when Bryce said she wasn't comfortable with that, she dumped her on the curb and dated him instead. The first time Bryce saw them together, she kicked the guy hard enough in the crotch that she cracked his dick like a glowstick. She spent the night in a jail cell until I came and got her. Luckily, Vic had the decency to feel guilty enough to convince him not to press charges," Poppy explains.

"I'd say the pink dicks were only fitting, then," I declare.

Bryce tilts her head back and gives me a half-smile, pushing her fingers through her knotted hair. "I'm scared to turn my phone on. If she saw it were us, there's no telling what she'll do now."

"This is karma, babes," Poppy says.

I nod. "This isn't any worse than what I did to Stewart's things after I found him cheating. If anything, this is less evil."

Poppy leans her shoulder against the door frame. "This isn't all that out of character for you either. No offense, but you're not a terribly sweet person."

"That's not exactly true. I can be sweet," Bryce corrects her.

"You can, just not to many people. There's nothing wrong with that, B. I just don't want you to start thinking poorly of yourself because of something you did not only just out of anger and hurt but under the influence of tequila, of all things. What's done is done, and if I'm being honest, that little witch deserved it," Poppy explains.

The adoration heavy in her words, despite the seriousness of the conversation, makes my chest warm. I had this same support from Braxton, but I've never had friends like Bryce and Poppy. Having someone who isn't family that chooses to love you in the same way is an experience I haven't had in my life yet.

I've had friends in the past, but none that clicked the way the three of us have over the past few days. This friendship makes me hopeful that Cherry Peak really could be my new home. A real one and not just a passing blip on a map.

"You're worth more than what she did to you," I tell Bryce.

She nods appreciatively, some of the shadows in her features disappearing. "Thank you."

"Anytime."

"Alright, it's time for you two to eat. Get dressed and come have the bagels I braved the cold this morning to get for you. You need something to soak up all that booze," Poppy says a beat later.

Without another word, she turns on her heel and heads for the kitchen. Bryce laughs, flashing me a final smile before pushing herself off the bed and following our friend.

"Toothbrushes are in the bottom drawer in the guest bath!" I shout, getting a *thank you* in return.

Once I'm alone again, I heave a sigh and reach for my phone on my nightstand.

The stretch along my side as I bend is tight, and I mentally curse Poppy for the soreness in my muscles a couple of days after my first pole class. I could hardly move yesterday, and it's only gotten worse.

My stomach threatens to shoot through my throat when I swipe along the notifications on my phone and spot the newest text message. Terror spikes.

> Bo: Good morning.
>
> Bo: Sorry I didn't answer you last night, my phone was off.

As I open the conversation, my cheeks burn like they've been lit on fire. Fuck. My. Life.

> Me: Hi. I know we said 1 night but I changed mi mind.
>
> Me: Sorry that was weiiiiird to say
>
> Me: Are u sleeping? Do u wear ur boots to bed?
>
> Me: I don't. Anyway idk y I wanted to talk 2 u, but I do
>
> Me: Srry I'm being weird. G2G! xo

There isn't a reply from him until the two from five o'clock this morning, three hours after I sent my final embarrassing text. I don't know why I opted to message him, of all people, but maybe it's because of what happened with Brody. The encounter that's solely responsible for this headache and dry mouth.

I barely know the guy, and he's already enemy number one

in this small town. If he were more like Bo, maybe we would have gotten off on a better foot. *God, what am I talking about?* I don't even know this Bo guy either.

They should both be completely off limits. No more interesting text convos or butting heads at crowded bars. But then again, where would be the fun in that?

I stare at the screen for an embarrassingly long time before typing out a message and forcing myself to send it.

> Me: I'm shocked you didn't block me.

When there's no answer after a couple of minutes of me staring at the screen, I toss the phone onto the bed and slide out from beneath the blankets. The carpet is a shaggy type of material, and while I hate vacuuming it, it does beat setting my feet on a cold wood flooring in the morning.

I have a quick shower—scrubbing at my nails until the pink disappears—and get dressed in a pair of sweatpants and a baggy shirt before grabbing my phone and joining the women in the kitchen. Bryce hasn't showered, but she looks a bit more refreshed as she chomps on a bagel, a to-go cup of coffee on the kitchen table in front of her.

Poppy notices me first and slides the unclaimed cup of coffee across the table to where an empty chair sits. Like all of the furniture in this place, the dining table and chairs came included in the rent. I got lucky when it came to finding this place. It's not like I had any furniture after I left Stewart. I had sold all of my own furniture back when I gave up my apartment to move in with him.

"What are the odds that you could fit me in for a hair colour this week?" Poppy asks, sipping from her own drink.

I slide into the empty chair and wrap my hands around the warm cup before taking a test drink from it. The coffee is warm but not hot and sweet enough without being too much for my sensitive stomach.

"Probably pretty high. I've mostly been doing walk-ins since I started. What are you wanting?"

"Something that she'll hate in a week and demand you change back," Bryce teases. It's nice to see her eyes bright again.

"Don't pick on me," Poppy chastises her and then says to me, "I just want some new highlights."

My phone buzzes in my pocket as I say, "Let me know when you're thinking, and I'll make it work."

Her grin is blinding. "Will do."

The conversation dulls before Bryce switches gears and brings up an idea she has for the pole studio. I let them talk and grab my phone, reading the message on the screen.

> Bo: Maybe I should have, but I didn't want to. How's your head this morning?

> Me: Angry, but I'll live. I'm sorry again. I don't know why I texted you.

When his reply comes back right away, I fight back a smile.

> Bo: I'm not complaining about it.

Flicking my eyes up at the women at my table, I'm grateful to find that they're still talking amongst themselves and not paying me or my totally weird smile any attention.

I might like texting Bo, but I'm not about to explain anything more to them than I've already shared. It's hard to explain something you don't even understand yourself.

For now, he gets to be my little secret.

11

Brody

> Banana: Alright . . . so, what did you do last night?

I don't know why I'm standing out in the cold with my gloves off and my fingers bare to the whipping wind as I tap at my phone screen, but I make no move to stop. My lips are numb as I rub them together, snow plastering to my bare face. A small head shoves against my side as the calf beside me tries to get me to abandon my texting and pay attention to it again.

"You're a needy thing," I tell it, dropping one hand to scratch behind its ear as I use the other to finish typing.

The calf is only a couple of weeks old, having been one of the last births of the season. The mom's close by, but this guy's been on my tail all day.

With frozen fingers, I send off the text and pocket my phone before shoving my hands back into my gloves.

> Me: Nothing as fun as you, apparently. I worked on a truck that's not much more than rusted parts that belong in a dump yard until I went to bed.

From the chaotic, misspelled texts I received from her last night, I knew she was either drunk or suddenly half-blind. I wasn't expecting to see a text come in from her at all, but I was actually relieved when it did. It saved me from having to be the one to reach out, whenever I worked up the nerve to.

Even though I wanted to, I most likely wouldn't have. Maybe that would have been a mistake.

With a final pat to the calf's head, I head back to the shed. Each step has my legs tingling, the cold seeping into my bones the longer I'm outside. The snowstorm is supposed to slow soon, but it hit us hard last night in another unforgiving dump.

The wind howls when I slip inside the barn and blow out a clouded breath. Pulling my hands out of my pockets, I press them to my lips and wait for them to stop burning before pulling my phone back out.

> Banana: Do you like working on trucks?

The question surprises me. I don't remember the last time someone asked me that. Long before I left town, maybe. Now, the only time someone mentions mechanics to me is when they inform me of something having gone wrong on one of the machines.

> Me: I love it. Last night was the first time I've worked on something just because I wanted to in a really long time.

> Banana: That's sad. You should make yourself a priority more often. I hear it's good for the heart.

I bark a laugh, shaking my head.

> Me: Where'd you hear that? A fortune cookie?

> Banana: And what if I did?

> Me: I'd say that I need to buy them in bulk.

The typing bubbles appear for a few beats before her next message comes through.

> Banana: I had a pretty shitty evening yesterday.
> Wound up trying to drink my problems away.

> Me: Did it work?

It didn't for me. Turns out it's a bit difficult to hold a wrench steady when you've nursed a bottle of whiskey for a couple of hours.

> Banana: Maybe. I don't remember much of the night. I paid for my choices this morning.

> Me: Anytime you want to talk, try me before the alcohol. Your head will appreciate it the next morning.

> Banana: That's a bit forward.

My throat clogs. Was it? Jesus Christ, of course it was. I begin typing an apology when she texts again.

> Banana: I like it. Consider yourself my new therapist.

> Me: Do I get a certificate or something?

> Banana: No, but you can offer me the same job in exchange.

I chew on the inside of my cheek, contemplating the offer. Is that something I'm willing to do? Give a stranger access to all of my problems when I don't so much as share them with so much as Caleb, my best friend.

Maybe that's the safer thing to do. She doesn't know who I

am. There's nothing she can do with my secrets besides listen to them and maybe judge me for them in secret.

> Me: Deal.

> Banana: Pleasure doing business with you, Bo.

> Me: Likewise, Banana.

My GRANDMOTHER IS a woman of many words. Oftentimes, far too many.

That's especially true whenever we're on a supply run. If my grandfather knows the entire ranching population, then my grandmother knows double that number. She's kinder, more welcoming to newcomers, and loves to gossip. We can't make it three steps into the grocery store or feed shop before she's catching up with someone she claims she hasn't seen in a month or two.

The woman raised me, though, so after a couple of decades of being forced to suffer through these long conversations, I'd say I'm used to it now.

That's why I'm not surprised when we don't even make it past the cart corral inside the grocery shop before she's taking me by the hand and dragging me over to Mrs. Sullivan and her daughter. I'm already prepared to endure the conversation with a smile by the time Grandma grabs their attention.

"Marty! You're so grown up!"

Marty jolts at the volume of my grandmother's voice but smiles kindly at her a beat later. Her mom does the same and meets my grandmother halfway, kissing both her cheeks.

"It's so great to see you, Eliza. You look happy and healthy," Mrs. Sullivan greets my grandma.

"Same to you both. I feel like the last time I saw Marty, she was graduating high school with my grandson!" Grandma says.

I fight back an eye roll. She knows damn well she's seen them both in the last *ten* years. This is most likely her trying to get me to take her friend's daughter out on a date. Ever since I've gotten back, all she's seemed to want me to do is date someone. I hate disappointing her, but I don't have any plans on dating anytime soon.

Marty seems to sense my train of thought and smiles sympathetically. "I've spoken to Brody a couple of times since he's been home. He's a good friend."

"I told the firefighters about your idea for the library fundraiser, and they're interested, by the way. Darren said to text him the details," I reply.

Marty is a beautiful woman, with strawberry blonde hair and two dimples that flash every time she smiles. But friends is all I'm interested in, and I think it's the same for her. It's hard to date as an adult in a town as small as Cherry Peak. We all grew up together, and more often than not, if someone was going to start dating, they would have done it long before now.

It's the older generation that can't seem to accept that. If they had it their way, we'd all have married a high school sweetheart, had six kids, and already bought matching headstones.

"Thank you! I'll talk to him today and get it set up. The kids are going to love it," Marty says.

"What fundraiser is this for again?" her mom asks, attention whirling to her daughter.

Marty nearly glows at the chance to explain her idea. "I was hoping the fire department could help me with a small carnival inside the library in the new year. There would be a toy drive, and the money from the carnival games would be used to help give the kids section of the library a bit of a makeover. It's extremely outdated."

"You're right. It's far too dark in there! Let me know what the Steeles can help with, and we'll do it," Grandma offers.

Marty nods, opening her mouth to reply, when there's a crash from one of the aisles close by. A muffled female curse is followed by another crash, smaller and quieter this time. What sounds like cans rolling along the floor and metal clanking has my curiosity sparking, my feet carrying me in the direction of the sound.

My decent mood is snuffed out the moment I see the woman currently attempting to sweep a dozen cans of soup off the floor and into her arms.

"Really? This is really going to happen to me right now?" she mutters to herself, scowling at the tin cans.

I cross my arms and watch her lose her grip on the armful of soup for the second time. They hit the floor with a bang, and it's nothing short of a miracle that they don't bust open. She scrambles for them, and then I'm moving toward her.

When she notices me coming, she glances at the ceiling and mutters, "Fuck." When her brown eyes meet mine again, they tighten at the corners. "Are you here to make fun of me?"

"I was going to help you, but I can leave."

"I don't want your help."

"You look like you need it."

Rage makes her nostrils flare. "You're arrogant."

"You seem to bring that quality out of me, sweetheart."

Shooting to her feet, she takes the cans she's managed to secure and slams them onto the shelf. I drag my eyes down the curves of her body, gritting my teeth as I'm reminded how outrageously beautiful she is. Brown eyes aren't usually my thing, but hers aren't simply brown. They're warm and soft, a complete contradiction to Anna from what I've seen thus far.

Her pin-straight hair is a shade of brown so deep it's nearly black, depending on the lighting, and it reaches just past her shoulders. Instead of jeans and boots that very obviously don't fit her properly, she's wearing black leggings that fit a little too well and dirty, worn sneakers. Her dark jacket is the one she wore last night. It looks a bit too thin for the current weather here right now, but I keep my mouth shut about that.

"No boots for you today?" I sound condescending as fuck, but I ignore the guilt that follows. She doesn't look at all like she did yesterday, and that tells me everything that I need to know.

Posers aren't welcome in my life. I've encountered enough of them to last a lifetime.

"Is that what your problem with me is about? My *boots* last night?" she hisses.

I shrug and drop to a crouch, gathering the rest of the cans. "If the boot fits."

"You're hilarious. And a jackass. What a fantastic mix of traits."

"Happy to entertain you . . ." I pause, arching a brow. "What was your name again?"

I almost flinch at her expression. Fuck, she might very well chuck one of those cans at my head.

"If you've forgotten my name, you never deserved to know it in the first place. The fact you have any fans at all is beyond me. You wear a great mask, though. I'll give you that," she grits out.

Diverting her eyes, she keeps her shoulders tight while finishing arranging all the cans. I wait until she's backed away from the shelf before taking the ones in my arms over and doing the same.

I change the subject before I can say anything that will have her truly beating my ass with a can. "How did you even knock all of these off?"

"Changing the topic, are we?" she counters.

"You're impossible."

"That's rich coming from you."

Blowing out a long, exasperated breath, I finish with the cans and back away from her. "You're welcome for the help."

"Considering I never asked for the help, I'm not thanking you."

She's a stubborn woman, that's for sure. Stubborn and

somehow able to get on my very last damn nerve with little to no effort.

"Noted. I'll make sure to stand by and watch you suffer next time you look like you need help," I reply.

"Brody Steele! That is no way to speak to a woman!"

12

Brody

My grandmother's voice has me holding back a groan. The sound of her boots hitting the floor in quick succession would usually be enough to make me cower had Anna not been standing in front of me. I can just picture the smug grin she'd give me if she were to witness that.

Grandma reaches my side far too quickly and swats lightly at the back of my head when I remain silent. A beat later, she stares up at me expectantly. "Well? Aren't you going to introduce us?"

I dare a look at Anna and find her watching me. Holding her stare, I say, "Grandma, this is Anna. Anna, this is my grandma, Eliza."

At my knowledge of her name, Anna blinks in surprise before quickly grinning at my grandma. "It's nice to meet you, Mrs. Steele."

"Mrs. Steele," Grandma echoes, slapping my arm and returning Anna's smile. "You have better manners than Brody."

"That's hurtful," I mutter.

"It wouldn't be if it weren't true," she sings.

Anna's smirk is just as nerve grating as I knew it would be. "I don't want to say I agree with you, but you might be onto something."

"I blame how many hours he spent out in the barn with his grandfather and all those cows as a boy," Grandma says.

"That's right, I heard you were cattle ranchers! I've never actually seen a cow in person before," Anna admits, confidence heavy in every line of her body. I hate the way I admire that about her.

From the way my grandmother is staring at her with hearts in her eyes, she's obviously feeling the same way.

"You should stop by the ranch sometime. Brody can give you a proper tour," Grandma offers, completely oblivious to my dislike of the woman she's *just* met.

Anna looks at me, amusement making her eyes glitter. "That would be really nice of him. Maybe I'll take you up on that offer sometime."

"Great," I say through my teeth.

"You're new to town, right?" Grandma asks. Apparently, she's either naive to my annoyance right now or just doesn't care about it. Knowing her, it's probably the latter. That woman never misses anything.

Anna tucks her hands into her jacket pocket and nods. "I've only been here for a couple weeks."

"How are you liking it? Where are you from?"

"Let's not give her an interrogation in the middle of the grocery store," I interrupt.

Anna waves me off. "I don't mind."

I force a smile. "Great."

"Stop being rude, Brody," Grandma chastises me again.

I don't think I've been given so much shit from her since I was a teenager.

"He'll warm up to me," Anna replies smoothly.

Grandma scowls at me while threatening, "If he doesn't, you let me know."

"Will do." Anna smirks.

I use the break in conversation to lay a hand on my grandmother's arm and say, "Are you done?"

"I suppose so. If we don't hurry, I'm sure I'll have a dozen hangry men to deal with come a couple hours." Offering Anna a soft smile, she tunes me out completely. "It was lovely to meet you. Please take me up on the offer to come around sometime. It's always nice to have another woman around the ranch from time to time."

Her casual words poke at the dormant ache in my chest, and it comes slithering out of hiding. My mood plummets further, memories I've forced into locked boxes pounding fists against my mind, begging to be set free. I push back, shutting them up again.

Anna's looking at me again—I can feel the sear of her eyes on my face—but I stare at the toes of my boots. I can't seem to tangle a sentence together, so I don't bother. Instead, I turn and leave the aisle, my heartbeat pounding in my ears and blocking the sound of the two women telling each other goodbye.

A WEEK LATER, I've had better luck avoiding Anna than I have my grandmother. The ride home from the store was awkward, and despite how hard I tried to pretend what she said hadn't brought back too many dark memories, she knew it did and, in typical style, wanted to dig deep into my feelings. One firm no from me, and she dropped it.

We haven't picked up the topic since, and I doubt we will anytime soon.

There are some things we Steele men don't talk about. Not to each other and not to anyone else. Anything that hints at my mother's death is and always will be one of them.

Clearing my throat, I focus on the doctor in front of me as he begins to pull the endoscope back out of my nose. The numbing spray he used before shoving the fucking thing into my nostril and down my throat did its job, but the discomfort of pressure is still there. I've had my vocal cords checked this way twice since the day following my last show, and both times were like this. I'd love never to experience this again.

"You still don't have any lesions, Brody. I'd say you're healing quite well," he says once he's set the equipment off to the side.

Caleb speaks up from the chair beside me. "What exactly does 'quite well' mean?"

The best throat doctor in the province, who we drove nearly three hours this morning to see, peels his gloves off as he explains, "It means he's on the road to recovery. I don't want to give a concrete timeline, but I'd say he has maybe a couple more weeks of rest before he should be able to at least attempt to sing again. Speech therapy will come after in that case."

"So, until then, he just keeps doing what he's doing?"

Dr. T nods, sitting on his rolling stool, eyes locked on my throat as if he's trying to look inside of it. "Yes. No yelling or shouting. You can still carry on how you normally would, still speak in small amounts. Just don't overdo it."

Caleb shoots me a look. "That means keeping Rita out of Alberta." Turning to the doctor, he adds, "She's the reason the pain came back. Some bullshit about wanting to see where he was at by making him attempt to sing."

Dr. T's eyes bulge with alarm. "You sang? When was this? You absolutely cannot be doing that if you want to heal. Singing at any level right now, before you've fully healed, could ruin all the progress you've made, Brody."

"There are some things I can't say no to," I rasp, pushing past the returning ache in my throat. Like the wedding I promised an old friend that I'd sing at in a little over two weeks from now.

Both men shake their heads at me, disappointment radiating off of them. I should be ashamed, but I'm more pissed than anything. Rita knows I shouldn't have been pushing myself like that. She works for *me*, not Swift Edge Records. The order to test me came from Garrison Beckett, head of the record label that owns my soul, but Rita was the one who forced it on me when she knew she had no place to do so. I shouldn't have entertained the idea, but fuck if guilt didn't play a huge part in my decision.

I screwed over a lot of deals and lost a lot of people money when I left Killian's tour early. Giving Rita and Garrison what they wanted was my way of paying them back, I guess. It was stupid and reckless, but what's done is done.

Garrison will never admit that he's responsible for the unrelenting pressure he put on me before the tour and the after-effects of that pressure. The damage caused to my voice that we're all lucky is reversible.

"Well, if you ever want to perform again, you'll figure out a way to say no."

I stiffen at the doctor's tone but nod and say, "Alright."

Caleb pats me on the back. "I'll keep him on the straight and narrow, Doc. Our boy here will be healed up and ready to go again in no time."

"Good. I'll have the front desk schedule you a follow-up in two weeks. If things are looking good then, we'll talk about next steps," Dr. T says before standing and opening his office door.

Dismissed, I thank him before leaving. The receptionist avoids eye contact with me the entire time it takes her to book me a follow-up, and I somehow manage to hide my discomfort until we get outside.

Tapping my fingers on my thigh, I climb into Caleb's truck and ignore the incessant urge to check my phone for any new messages. I've become glued to the damn thing this past week, every buzz making my stomach jolt.

Continuing to refer to my newest friend as Banana is a bit annoying now, but I haven't gotten the nerve to ask for a real name. It seems too forward, too personal. But she has become my friend, and I guess that makes the personal thing a little more acceptable.

She's become someone who listens to me complain about what went wrong during my day and tells me something ridiculous to make me forget about it. I do the same for her, although I'm not nearly as good at coming up with replies as she is. We haven't asked each other many questions about our real lives, nothing specific that would give me any hint as to who she is outside of our conversations, but that hasn't seemed to matter to either of us.

I've kept my conversations with her hidden from everyone so far, and I want to keep it like that for as long as I can. I'm not ashamed of speaking to her—that couldn't be further from the truth. I just feel almost protective of her and our friendship. That's acceptable . . . right?

I take the time alone in the truck to give in to my urge and check my phone. The awaiting texts settle something restless inside of me.

> Banana: Do you have a hairy chest?

> Banana: You know what, it doesn't matter. I vote no.

> Me: I wouldn't consider it hairy. Why, are you into hairy chests?

> Banana: No. I'm just watching TV and the medical examiner is about to perform an autopsy on a man who has a chest as hairy as a dog. It made me shudder. I like a bit of hair, but not this much.

The truck door opens, and Caleb slides in, so I stifle my laugh. I shoot off a quick reply before tucking my phone under my thigh.

> Me: What show? I need to see this for myself.

I never watch TV. Never have time to. But for some reason, I'm suddenly very interested in whatever she's talking about.

"You happy about the news?" Caleb asks.

I swallow before asking, "What?"

"Are you happy that you're healing?"

"Yeah . . . why wouldn't I be?"

He turns over the engine, and cold air starts to blow from the vents as it warms up. "You're smiling. I assumed it was because you're happy to know you'll most likely sing again soon. Am I wrong?"

"Nope. You're dead right," I answer, my smile slowly fading as the real world starts to set back in. "I can't wait to get back to work."

13

Annalise

WEDNESDAY MORNINGS AT THE SALON ARE TYPICALLY ALWAYS SLOW. Most days are in a town this small, but we can usually make do. It's Wednesdays that have us filling the time between clients with cleaning and rearranging and gossiping.

Wanda's music plays through the speakers like it always does. She typically chooses an upbeat pop-style playlist, but today, country music plays. It's a nice change for once, and not a single one of us complained when we arrived at work this morning.

The owner of the salon is hardly a few years older than me, and while she was born and raised in Cherry Peak, I've learned from the town gossips that she doesn't tend to stick around for too long before she's gone again. She didn't hesitate to give me a job here the day I asked for an application, even though I doubt there was demand at the small salon for another employee.

Rumour has it that Wanda's the daughter of Lee Rose, one of the most successful country stars in history. She's never confirmed or denied the rumour, and whether it was her choice or not, they don't share a last name. Having such a famous father could explain her lack of financial worry when it comes to keeping a full house of employees with hardly any income coming in, but it's not my business. I like her just fine either way.

Speaking of the devil, she shouts at me from the back room, "You can take lunch if you want, Anna!"

The other girls are gone on their lunch breaks already, but I stayed behind, still full from the two breakfast sandwiches and cup of coffee Bryce dropped off at my place this morning. She's been bringing me breakfast every second day for the past two weeks on her way to town hall. I've never had anyone make a point of bringing me food in the morning or stopping by with lunch in the afternoons, but between Bryce and Poppy, I've been . . . taken care of.

The pain in my chest lessens every day, and the memories of Stewart and our relationship fade with each new one I make in Cherry Peak. Moving on from heartbreak is never easy, but surrounding yourself with people who care about you and want to see you happy sure does make it easier.

"Not hungry!" I swipe the cloth in my hand over the front desk and then set the keyboard back in its place. Twisting the cup of lollipops back around so the front of it points at the entrance, I add, "Are you going out?"

"Got a salad in the minifridge. I'm good," she replies.

I blow out a breath and grab the cleaning supplies from the desk, bundling them in my arms before putting them back in their proper cabinet along the far wall. As I walk back to the front, the door flies open, and the bell above it jingles through the salon.

"Hi! Do you have an appoint—oh. What are you doing here?"

I set a hand on the front desk and pop my hip, staring Brody down where he stands with one foot inside the salon. He's wearing a cowboy hat again, his dirty-blond hair curling beneath it. His boots are dirty like the last time I saw him, but his jeans look clean. The T-shirt he has on is plain and black and tight enough that the sleeves hug his biceps when he tucks his hands into his pockets and steps all the way inside, letting the door shut behind him.

Devastatingly handsome. That's what he is. *Dangerously so.*

"Can't say I've ever had such a warm welcome at a salon before," he quips, taking his hat off to shake out his hair. The movement draws my eyes, snaring them before I can grapple for my self-control.

"I'm honoured to be so many of your firsts."

Impatience ticks across his features, making me look away. "Wanda here?"

"She is."

A quirk of his brow. "Can I talk to her?"

"Is she expecting you?"

"No."

I shrug, shifting my weight to one foot. "She's a very busy woman."

"Are you really goin' to make me walk back there and get her myself?"

Without tearing my gaze from him, I shout, "You have a visitor, Wanda!"

"I'm stepping out for lunch!" she shouts back. *Liar.*

Pushing out my bottom lip, I tell Brody, "Seems you're out of luck, big guy."

"Whatever," he grunts, and then he's attempting to move past me.

I slide into his way and plant a hand to his chest. His eyes widen before dropping to where I'm touching him and then crawling back up again. That stupidly good cologne fills the air between us. The hard muscles beneath my fingers thump harder and harder, and I realize with a start that it's his heartbeat. As quickly as I've touched him, I retract my hand, dropping it to my side.

Clearing my throat, I ignore my burning cheeks and say, "You're not dirtying the floors I just cleaned with your muddy boots. Take them off first. I'm assuming you want Wanda to cut your hair?"

"She always does it." His voice is deeper than usual, his annoyance with me blatantly obvious.

"I'll do it today. Take your boots off and sit at the last station." I wave a hand at the far back chair.

He doesn't move. "You want me to trust you with a pair of scissors that close to my throat?"

"It's either that or you continue to grow out the mullet."

"I don't have a mullet."

"Don't you?" He doesn't. His hair may be long, but it's well-kept, the front pushed back out of his face. "I'm assuming you chose now to come because you knew everyone would be out for lunch, so I'd hurry and decide what you want before they come back."

Turning my back to him, I ignore the burn of his stare on my back and begin fiddling with my station. Everything is already out and ready to go from my extra time spent organizing this morning, but I need something to keep me busy until he figures his shit out.

While being around him might light a blaze of agitation in my belly, there's something else there too. A searing attraction that fights to tangle my tongue the moment our eyes meet. No good ever comes from an attraction like that, especially not when it walks hand in hand with such a strong sense of annoyance.

This is the same man who judged me unfairly and harshly and who hasn't even so much as apologized for it. I'm certain he doesn't feel the same attraction to me that I do him—he's made that very clear with the disgusted looks and rude comments.

I'm only offering to cut his hair so he'll leave as quickly as possible. He's not about to taint my workspace with his rude, alpha-male energy, that's for sure.

"Alright," he agrees, albeit reluctantly.

I glance over my shoulder at the boots still on his feet. "Boots first."

Shoulders stiff, he toes off his boots one at a time and then pushes them off to the side. He even wears thick wool socks well, for God's sake.

"How long have you worked here?" he asks once he's seated in the chair.

He's so tall that to reach the top of his head, I have to lower the seat as far as it'll go. Even that isn't perfect, but I'll make it work. I drape the black cape over his shoulders and clip it at the back before meeting his stare in the mirror.

"A few weeks," I answer. "How do you want me to cut it?"

"Just take a couple inches off. My grandfather's been givin' me shit for letting it grow this long."

Before I can convince myself not to, I run my fingers through the curls at the base of his neck. His hair is surprisingly soft and thick, the curls strong. I pretend not to notice the goosebumps that spread over his neck and pull my hand away.

"Alright."

"Do you want me to wash it?"

"Nah, I gotta get back to the ranch as quickly as I can."

I nod and grab my spray bottle before starting to wet his hair. Whether he's aware of the fact he hasn't stopped staring at me in the mirror or not, I can't help but feel the pressure of doing a good job. Do I really want to be the woman who's known as the reason Brody Steele started rocking a buzz cut because she cut his hair so badly?

Focusing on keeping my attention on his hair and not the deep blue eyes watching my every move, I set down the spray bottle and pull my comb from my apron. I take my time combing the knots out and then lift a section of hair trapped between my fingers for him to see.

"This much okay?"

It's only just over an inch, but I'd rather start small. To be honest, longer hair fits him. It gives him a more rugged appearance, although I'm sure someone as good-looking as him could pull off short hair too.

Fuck my life. *That's enough, Anna.*

"Yeah, that's fine," he says.

I nod and focus on my *job* and not how good he smells or how he shivers every time I brush the back of his ear with my finger. The first snip of my scissors severs through those thoughts, and I blurt out a question to distract myself.

"What do you do on the ranch?"

He double blinks, seemingly surprised by my question. "Whatever my grandfather orders me to do."

"That's vague."

"Do you really want to know anythin' about me? Aren't you just askin' questions to avoid awkward silence?" he counters.

"Does it matter?" I continue cutting the hair at the back of his head, slowly working my way to the first side. "Considering how often we run into each other, maybe it would be better if we didn't start a cat fight every damn time we speak."

"And asking about my job will help that?"

I scowl, finally meeting his awaiting stare in the mirror. His eyes are slightly narrowed as he watches me, as if he's trying to see into my head. He'd have a heyday with what he'd find if he succeeded in that.

"Are you always so hard-headed?" I ask.

"Honestly, no."

"So, this is all an act for me, then?"

"If you want to take it that way, then sure. I just don't like posers. I can't say I've ever wanted to tell one all my secrets."

His arrogant tone makes me pause, my scissors poised to cut a chunk of hair far too short.

"You think I'm a *poser*?"

"Aren't you? With the borrowed country clothes and your dramatic gaspin' when you first saw me at Peakside? Bryce and Poppy are too nice to try and set me up, so I have to assume you put on a pretty impressive show in order for them to bring you somewhere I'd be."

Despite what he thinks of me, my flinch is genuine. So is the hurt in my eyes that I can see reflected in the mirror.

I release the hair between my fingers and slide the scissors and comb into my apron. The flash of guilt across his face doesn't register to me as I glance at the clock on the front desk and inhale for three calming seconds before exhaling.

My voice is as hard as steel when I look back at him and speak. "If you don't mind waiting, the other girls will be back any minute. I'm sure one of them would love to finish up here."

"Shit," he mutters, throat bobbing. "I shouldn't have said that."

"But you did."

"Because I'm a jackass. I'm sorry. Please don't stop."

Against my better judgment, I nod and slowly pull my scissors and comb back out. "Alright."

He rubs a hand down his face, his next words exasperated. "I'm not usually like this."

"I moved here a month ago because I needed to start over. Not because I'm a fan or wanted the chance to meet you. I'm not a poser; I'm just trying to fit in. The clothes and the boots were Poppy's idea. So was the bar," I explain.

I know that I don't have to explain anything to him, but this feud? It's not what I had in mind when I decided to start a new life. Especially not a feud fuelled by one man's misplaced opinion of me. I'm a big enough person to overlook those things and start over, even if only to not have to worry about running into him somewhere and starting a fire with our words.

"You moved here to start over, and I moved back to run away. Funny how that works," he says briskly.

I want to sink my fingers into that admission and peel it apart layer by layer, but I have a feeling that would send me running with a half-cut head of hair. Instead, I send him a soft smile in the mirror and start cutting again, a simpler kind of silence now budding between us.

14

Brody

ACCORDING TO MY GRANDFATHER, I DIDN'T CUT MY HAIR SHORT enough. I had a feeling he would feel this way unless I asked Anna to take a pair of shears to it and leave me bald, but hearing his snippy remarks still annoyed me.

I've been holed up in the shop for the past couple of days since. Or hiding, more like. I'm far too old to be avoiding the old man, but I prefer my hide on my back, not hung on the back fence, and I have a feeling that if I go near him right now, I won't be able to keep myself in check.

The weeks of tension and unspoken feelings regarding my past actions have kept the entire ranch on their toes, always prepared for the blowback. The fact it hasn't happened yet is alarming. Everyone has something to say about my leaving besides my grandfather. He's been focusing on nitpicking the million other things I'm doing wrong instead.

> Banana: You're a bit prickly today. Anything you want to talk about?

I think back on the text that I saw before leaving to grab

lunch and frown. My mood was shit when I woke up this morning, and I didn't notice that my attitude had travelled through cyberspace. Talking to her has become the one thing I've been looking forward to every day.

I still don't know who she is or what she looks like outside of that singular photo, and as much as I hate to admit it, that's starting to frustrate me too. I'd have to be delusional to deny that I want to meet her in real life.

Would we get along just as well as we do now? Does she listen to my music, and would she admit that to me in person? Would her knowing who I am change anything between us?

Shaking my head, I turn off my truck and open our long thread of messages before typing a reply.

> Me: Sorry. It's just family drama.

The parking lot of the grocery store is nearly empty, and I'd bet the only other cars here belong to the employees. I linger in the truck, delaying having to step out into the snow. The heat starts to dissipate the longer I sit here, though, the chill from outside starting to seep in by the time my phone buzzes.

> Banana: Oh, I know all about that. How about you tell me something and I'll do the same?

> Me: Alright. My grandparents resent me for choices I made a few years ago. They've never forgiven me.

My lack of hesitation should be alarming but isn't.

> Me: Your turn.

> Banana: My father tried to sabotage my sister's relationship with her now husband because he's a self-serving bastard. None of us speak to him anymore.

I suck in a breath.

> Me: I'm sorry.

Banana: I'm sorry too.

> Me: Do you miss him?

Three dots appear for longer than usual as she types but never sends a message. I'm prepared to take my question back when she replies.

Banana: He's my father. I think a part of me will always miss him, but I won't ever forget what he's done. For that reason, I'm going to continue living my life without him having a place in it.

Banana: Do you miss your grandfather?

> Me: I haven't lost him. How can I miss him?

Banana: You don't have to lose someone to miss them. Not physically.

I reread the message over and over again, trying to understand how she can be so aware of my feelings. My chest tightens as I shift gears and focus on her admission to me.

> Me: Your father doesn't deserve you. Your bravery is admirable.

Banana: Thank you. So is yours. I couldn't spend every day with someone who held resentment toward me.

> Me: I've worked on a lot of trucks because of it. Turns out I didn't forget anything while I was away.

Banana: Will you ever tell me where you went?

I type out a message before quickly deleting it. Will I ever tell her? I want to, but not like this. The way we're speaking now. If I decided to tell her who I am, it wouldn't be when I don't know who she is.

> Me: Will you ever meet me in person?

> Banana: Is that something you want?

> Me: I think so.

> Banana: Let's start with a phone call and go from there.

My stomach bottoms out. The chill from outside suddenly doesn't register as my skin heats on its own.

> Me: Just tell me when.

> Banana: I'll let you know. I have to go, but we'll talk later?

We've spoken every day for the past month. As if I'd change that up now. I doubt it's even possible at this point. I've become attached to her.

> Me: Yeah, we will. Bye, Banana.

Her goodbye comes instantly, and then I'm pocketing my phone and stepping into the cold.

WITH A BAG of jerky in one hand and a bottle of Coke in the other, I stalk through the store toward the front tills. My wet boots squelch on the tile floor, the sound grating along my spine. At least the heat is blasting to fight the cold.

It's almost unheard of to step away from the ranch to pick up lunch, considering my grandma's love language has always been feeding hungry mouths, but I've been skipping most of her meals for a while now.

I love her food, but the company that comes with it, not so much. A half hour spent tensely eating across the table from my grandfather and his withering looks isn't my idea of an ideal break. So I've been driving into town every afternoon to grab something to dull my hunger and taking my dinner straight to the shop every night. It's a miracle I haven't been called out on either yet.

There's only one till open today, and I double blink when I notice the woman setting her items onto the conveyer belt. I ignore the urge to run my fingers through my hair, the ghostly feeling of hers doing the same just the other day slamming into me head-on.

She wasn't supposed to be the one to cut my hair, but fuck if I wasn't going to just accept her help and get on with it. I didn't mean to treat her so poorly, and I've regretted being the one to bring that wounded look to her eyes since the moment it appeared. My judgment was misplaced, and she was undeserving of it.

I just hope my apology for everything sticks.

Anna speaks to the male cashier with an easy smile on her face, and for some reason, I'm almost jealous of the ease with which she speaks to him. There's never been that ease between us. I haven't allowed there to be.

He asks her if she wants a bag for her items, and she nods, taking it from his extended hand before starting to pack up her items. I narrow my eyes on her premade salad and sandwich, piecing together that she must be on her lunch break too.

I reach the till and hesitate to drop my items on the belt. Anna has her back to me, not noticing me yet. Her hair is up today, the slick length of it swinging back and forth across her back. She's wearing that jacket again, the one that's not warm enough. A pair of pink mittens stick out of the left pocket, so at least she's not baring her fingers to the cold. The tips of her ears are red, though, so she didn't wear a toque.

When she finishes bagging her items and turns around, she catches sight of me and jumps, rosy lips parting. I laugh, lifting the jerky in my hand and waving it around in greeting.

"I'm starting to think you're following me," she says. The slight quirk of her mouth gives away her amusement.

Finally, I set my things down and move closer. She's so much shorter than me but seems to hate that fact if the way she fixes her posture to make herself as tall as possible is anything to go off.

"I'm just a man lookin' for something to eat," I reply.

Her eyes fall to my lunch on the belt. "I took you for a Cherry Coke guy."

"I'm not a fan of overly sweet things."

"The more bitter, the better, then?" she challenges, the double meaning in her question hitting home.

I can't stop my laugh as it tears free. The cashier watches our interaction closely, no doubt making note of it to tell his friends later. I don't care what he does with it, and that surprises me.

"Are you goin' to pay anytime soon?" I ask, changing the subject without giving her an answer to her question.

"Right," she mutters. After she steps up to the debit machine, the guy reads how much she owes, and she reaches into the jacket pocket stuffed full of mittens. As she pulls her hand back out, her cheeks flush. "You've got to be kidding."

The anxious pitch of her voice has me on alert. "What's wrong?"

"My wallet's at the salon."

Oh. I shrug a shoulder, looking to the cashier. "Just add my stuff to hers, and I'll pay."

"Alright," he says before reaching for my beef jerky.

Anna jumps toward me. "No! You're not buying me lunch."

"Why not?"

"I don't want you to."

I laugh through a half-smile. "Consider it a real apology."

"You already apologized," she notes, still so damn stubborn.

It's no wonder we butt heads so much. We share one of the most polarizing traits.

I don't reply to her until the guy has finished scanning my items and tells me the new total. The slap of my card over the machine hardly sounds before she's swatting at my hand.

Laughing, I turn my hand and capture hers, pulling it away from the card machine. Her palm is soft and warm in my grip, her fingers so much smaller than mine. They're delicate. I'd bet she's appalled at the state of my hands. The scars and calluses must feel so off-putting.

Remembering myself, I drop my hold and thank the cashier before moving past Anna and dropping my things into her packed bag.

"Are you goin' back to work now?" I ask her as we leave, the bag in my left hand.

The wind howls when the automatic doors slide open, and we step outside. She shivers, the movement causing our arms to brush and the thin material of her jacket to become even more bothersome to me. When I snag the mittens out of her pocket and hand them to her, she doesn't fight me on taking them and slipping them on.

"Yeah. I walked, which probably wasn't the best choice, but I don't like driving on these roads yet."

Are her cheeks pink from the cold or embarrassment?

"What part of BC are you from?"

"Vancouver."

I nod, spying my truck in the parking lot. Something claws at my subconscious, a plea to consider whether I'm really going to let this woman walk back to the salon in this cold fucking weather. Especially in that goddamn jacket.

"This is definitely new for you, then. Have you driven much around here yet?"

She diverts her stare at the question. "Not once, actually. The idea of the car sliding out of control terrifies me."

We stop walking when we reach the start of the parking lot, and I release a long breath. The angel on my shoulder grins proudly. Fuck me, I'm really about to do this.

"I'll drive you," I huff.

She whips her head in my direction, eyes full of curiosity. "To the salon?"

A deep breath. "The salon. Home later. To work tomorrow. Just tell me when."

"You're offering to be my chauffeur?" It sounds even more ridiculous coming from her mouth.

"Don't make me take the offer back."

"Is this you still apologizing?"

"My grandmother would kick my ass if I let you continue to walk in this weather. It's only goin' to get worse. This is nothin' compared to what will come in January."

Playing it off doesn't help make me feel any less of a loser. I don't have the time to be driving her around town. I'm already pushing the limits stepping out for lunch every day. It'll be a miracle if I can sneak off the ranch in the morning when everyone's up and rushing around.

"You're sure about this?" she asks, voice suddenly sounding shy. The tone is out of place enough that I can't help but focus on it. "I work every Monday to Friday from nine to five."

I force myself to nod. "That's fine."

"If you're sure . . . then that would be really nice. Thank you."

The appreciation shining in her eyes as she stares up at me is almost too much. The brown is even softer now than before, warm like melted chocolate. My chest is twisted up, and before I notice what's happening, I'm grinning at her.

Grinning like I haven't just complicated my life with a woman who three days ago made me want to shout into a pillow.

Great.

15

Brody

My truck's heater blasts into the cab as I wait outside the salon that evening.

The sun has already set despite it being just after five. There's not nearly enough light on the street without it, and I make note to mention the addition of some extra outside lights to Wanda. Cherry Peak is safe enough, but knowing Anna— *or any woman* —has been walking home alone in the dark doesn't sit well with me.

The reminder of why I'm here has my eyes darting to the coat on my passenger seat. I searched my closet high and low for one that wouldn't either drown her or cover her in dirt before finding that one. Thick and lined with sherpa material inside and over the folded collar, it's the nicest and cleanest jacket I own. I don't know if she'll even accept it, but I didn't have time to stop at the store to grab one for her, nor do I even know what she would have liked if I had.

Fuck, I don't even know her well enough to pick a winter jacket out. What makes me think I have the right to toss her one of mine and expect her to wear it?

It must be my manners. I was raised to put women first always, regardless of who they are to me. That's what this is. I'm being thoughtful, protective in a very standard way. What kind of man would I be to continue letting Anna freeze half to death whenever she steps outside?

I shut my eyes and lean my forehead against the steering wheel. If my grandmother could see me right now, she'd lose her mind. It wouldn't be long until she was shaking wedding bells and calling every living Steele relative with the news. Which is precisely why I lied to her when I left before dinner.

As far as anyone at the ranch knows, I've started stepping out every afternoon to meet with a member of Swift Edge Records while they're in town to keep tabs on me.

I'm hoping it won't be a lie for long, despite how badly I don't want to be guilted into going back to work. It's only a matter of time until Garrison sends someone else to guilt me into returning early or to remind me that my next album is supposed to be completed by the end of the year.

I startle when the passenger door opens and Anna hops into the truck as if she's done it a million times and not only just once earlier today when I dropped her back off at work. Before sitting completely, she holds herself above the seat and grabs the jacket before her eyes lift to mine.

"Can I move this? I don't want to sit on it."

My throat is tight when I say, "It's yours."

"Mine?" she echoes, a hint of bewilderment in her tone.

I scratch the back of my neck, suddenly too hot. "You can't be walkin' around town in December with the jacket you have. If you don't want that one, I won't be offended. Just please use it until you get another."

Something far too similar to pain flickers across her face. My brows scrunch at the reaction, not expecting it as guilt churns my stomach. Alarms blare in my head when she blinks and whips her head to the side, a hand coming up to rub at her cheek.

"I didn't mean to upset you." The words are stumbled, awkward.

Fuck.

She shakes her head furiously, as if she's angry. "You hardly know me. Can barely stand me, really."

"*We* can hardly stand *each other*," I correct her, attempting to lighten the mood. It doesn't work.

"And you still thought to bring me a jacket so that I didn't freeze? *Your* jacket?"

"I don't use it anymore." As if that's a valid reason.

"That wouldn't matter to most people," she whispers.

I don't have an answer to that. She's right, and we both know it.

After a beat, she turns to me again, and I search her face for tears. The thought of them marking her pink cheeks is an unpleasant one. But there's no sign of them after that first swipe of her hand. Instead, her mouth is quirked.

"Can I put it on now?"

I shake off my shock and nod. "Yeah. Yeah, of course."

The cab of the truck is big enough that she doesn't have to struggle with taking off the too-thin jacket and dropping it to her lap before sliding her arms through mine—*hers*.

It's a good two sizes too big for her, but with the sleeves rolled up once, it's good enough. At least it's warm and will keep her from turning blue with the true winter temperatures approaching. Her approval lights up her face and the whole damn truck.

"It's perfect. Thank you."

"No worries."

She zips up the jacket and rubs her cheek on the lining on the collar. "I'm sorry I was a couple of minutes late today; I had a client run long. I'll try to make sure it doesn't happen again if you choose to continue driving me home."

"It's not a big deal." I adjust myself in the seat and wait for her to do up her seat belt before putting the truck in reverse. It's dead quiet on Main Street tonight, no other cars on the road besides us as we pull away from the salon. "I don't have a lot to do in the evenings anyway. Where am I dropping you off?"

"I'm a couple houses off Second Street. The one with the red roof."

"Got it. There's the crabapple tree in front of the back gate, right?" No amount of time away will fog my memory of every nook and cranny of this place.

"That's the one. And you're telling me you don't go out with your friends all the time after a long day? I figured you'd be spending most nights with them at Peakside."

"Caleb loves to drag me out with him, but I'm supposed to be relaxin', not joinin' him and his friends in drunk karaoke." I glance across the truck and catch her worrying her lip like she's holding something back. "You can ask what you want to."

"You sure?"

"Yeah. If I don't want to answer something, I won't."

There are some things I can't hide from, and Anna's knowledge of who I am is one of them. I can't imagine that it's easy being around someone with as much drama surrounding them as I have and not wonder.

My headlights beam off the snow of the intersection as we stop at a red light. Anna taps her fingers on the centre console before saying, "Fair enough. So, how bad was it? Your voice? They kept it vague in the media, and I didn't really pay much attention to that until, well, I saw you here."

More guilt for judging her the first time we met nips at me. I couldn't have been further off about her.

"Bad enough I got permission to leave the tour and come home. It could have been worse, but it could have also been a hell of a lot better."

"How long are you home for?"

Something sours in my stomach. The thought of leaving again . . . "At least another month."

"And you're upset about that?"

"Nashville is very different than Cherry Peak" is all I say.

"Would you stay here forever if you could?"

When I look at her again, she's already watching me thoughtfully.

"I don't know. But Nashville was never my plan." The sign for Second Street appears, and with it, I put her in the hot seat. "Do you plan on stickin' around long?"

"For as long as I can. I like it here."

"You'll have to learn to drive in this weather if you stay. You realize that, right?" I tease.

Her following laugh is warm, welcoming. I like it. "Why would I do that when I get to have you driving me around instead?"

My laugh joins hers. "You make a strong argument."

"Work smarter, not harder, Brody."

"Maybe I ought to bring you out to the ranch sometime. My grandfather could use a verbal smack talk from you about that."

She hums. "Grandpa Steele working you too hard lately?"

He'd be disturbed if he heard her speak of him that way. The idea of witnessing such an event amuses me far too much.

"Lately? Hard work is what fuels him. There's nothin' like skipping a workaround for a problem simply because it's either too easy or not the way he was taught to do it back in his youth. It's the difficult way or no way." The complaints seem to fall from my lips of their own accord. I don't have time to feel guilty for them before she's speaking again, having already digested everything I've admitted.

"Is that an odd way of thinking for an older-generation rancher?"

I slow the truck when her house comes into view, and I contemplate doing a lap around just to talk to her longer before flinging that idea into space.

"Not at all. But times are changin'. He doesn't take my ideas into consideration often, and I think that's because he doesn't want to deal with the responsibilities of them when I inevitably leave again. I can't make any promises to him."

"What if it wasn't inevitable? What if you stayed?"

I contemplate the questions, wishing I had a better answer. But the one I want to say just isn't possible. Not anytime soon.

"There's no use in hopin' for the impossible."

"I'm sorry, Brody," she says.

I shrug nonchalantly, even as my chest grows tighter and tighter. "Thanks for listenin' to that. I'm sorry to dump it all on you."

"I asked. Despite the rocky start to our relationship, I'd like to be your friend. These are things friends know about one another."

Pulling up in front of her house, I put the truck in park and shift to look at her fully, taking in her timid smile and cautious eyes. She's most likely worried I'll reject her, and I don't blame her for that. Not after everything I've done and said so far.

I've taken the boot out of my mouth, and now I've got to earn the forgiveness she's gifted me. It's a shocking revelation to learn that I want to earn it and get to know her in the process.

"I'd like to be your friend too, Anna."

Those timid eyes grow more confident as she reaches across the console to pat my shoulder and says, "I'll see you tomorrow morning, then, friend."

And then she's slipping into the cold night, bundled up in a jacket that I can rest easy knowing won't leave her teeth chattering and a pair of pink mittens on her hands.

I only head home once she's made it inside and waved me off from the front window. The drive is as quiet as every other I've taken before today, and I find myself missing her chatter the entire time.

16

Annalise

"You've been holding out on us," Bryce mutters, leaning her head on my shoulder.

My friends have been in a state of disbelief since they arrived with takeout in their hands and spied my new coat on the rack. Poppy nearly dropped the bag of burgers and fries all over the carpet while Bryce grabbed my shoulders and shook me twice, asking if I'm truly myself and not a clone.

"You guys better sit down for this one," I told them before spilling all about Brody showing up to save me like a total hero. We've been cuddled on the couch ever since.

Poppy pops a fry into her mouth, her jaw moving against my shoulder as she chews. Our legs are all extended, feet crossed on the soft ottoman. I'm the middle of our sandwich, trapped between the two of them.

"This is the furthest thing from what I expected from the two of you," Poppy says.

"And just what did you expect?" I ask.

She hums. "I was picturing something out of one of my favourite romance novels. An enemies-to-lovers storyline that had you at each other's throats until you couldn't deny your feelings any longer and fucked like crazed animals."

I choke on a laugh, thankful there wasn't a mouthful of pop in my mouth. "Your imagination is fascinating."

"You should have heard her in our teen years. She would have lived in the pages of a book if it weren't for me forcing her out into the real world," Bryce says.

Poppy waves her off. "We're not talking about me right now. We're talking about Brody and Anna."

"There's no Brody and Anna. We're hardly even friends yet."

Bryce tries to hide a laugh behind her fist but fails miserably. I shrug her off my shoulder and glare. "Don't give me that look, Anna. You think Brody Steele would give you his jacket if he didn't like you? Don't tell me Stewart ruined every romantic part of you."

"Brody hardly speaks to the women around town. Other than what the tabloids claim they know, I don't think he's dated since college," Poppy adds.

I stand firm. "Nothing good would come from catching feelings for this guy. Not only have we just barely buried the hatchet, but he's leaving in a month. His stay here is temporary."

"Temporary, my ass," Poppy mumbles, and I scowl at her.

"Don't start."

She swings her hands before dropping them dramatically in her lap with a heavy sigh. "You never know unless you try. And ignoring the obvious isn't trying."

"You could still sleep with him," Bryce says nonchalantly.

Until I met Bryce, I'd never known someone so at ease with sex and their sexuality in general. It's a refreshing mindset to see.

I've never been opposed to casual sex, but I haven't done it often. I'm not equipped to handle that lack of emotional connection with someone. I may not be a woman who's spent her whole life dreaming of a fairy-tale love story, but I still want a real partner. Marriage is off the table for me, but everything else is still something I'm interested in. Who wouldn't want someone to share their life with? Someone to love and to be loved by?

Even with everything Stewart did and broke within me,

those wants remain untouched. I don't want to remain single for my entire life. He didn't break me or my dreams. Just my heart. The one I'm slowly but surely stitching back together.

"Casual sex with Brody Steele wouldn't stay casual. Not for me." Our differences wouldn't matter. Once we reached that level of intimacy, I'd become completely wrapped up in him. Everything would mean that much more. "And let's not get ahead of ourselves. He hasn't given me any hint that he's considered me in that way, and he probably won't."

This talk is only going to make me look for any sign of interest, and I'll end up more disappointed than anything else when I never catch it.

"I don't blame you there," Poppy says on an exhale. "Just keep us in the loop on how things go the next few days. He's picking you up tomorrow morning, right?"

"Yes."

"You should bring him coffee or something," Bryce suggests, and when I catch the slight curve of her lips, I roll my eyes.

"I don't even know how he likes it."

"A guy like that? Black for sure," Poppy states.

I pull my hair behind my shoulders and lean back, staring at the ceiling. Giving him coffee in exchange for the rides to and from work seems like a safe thing to do. It's the first solid suggestion my friends have had today.

"If he's a latte guy, you're both dead," I warn.

Poppy snorts. "If Brody is a latte guy, then I'm a whiskey girl."

"Okay, I get it. I'll try the coffee sometime," I relent.

Bryce reaches for the rest of her burger and then returns her head to my shoulder. "And you'll text us as soon as you get to work tomorrow."

"Whatever you want, Brycie."

The pinch in my side from her sharp nails makes me howl a laugh, the sound of it acting as another stitch in my chest.

Bo: Good morning. What's your favourite colour?

Me: Pink. The hot kind. Yours?

Bo: Blue. The tropical ocean kind.

THE GOOD-MORNING TEXT was waiting for me when I woke up. There have been similar ones every morning for the past week, and I'd be lying if I said I hadn't started to look forward to them.

It's always a random question, something to help us get to know each other. So far, I know that he prefers salty over sweet, morning over night, fall over summer.

The friendship between us has grown so organically that it should probably be a bit scary, considering he's still ultimately a stranger. It's safer for me to keep him in that box until we meet in person. If we ever meet, that is. Everything has started falling into place in Cherry Peak, and I've grown content with my new life. Any new changes and I might lose that feeling.

For now, he'll continue to be a cozy spot in my life, tucked away in the safety of my texts until we take the next step.

A glance at the clock above the stove and I'm grabbing the jacket from its hook by the door and slipping my arms inside. The soft material glides over the bare skin of my arms, and the same way I did last night, I ignore the scent clinging to it. Cinnamon and something woodsy. God, getting such a strong scent of it makes my toes curl. It's ten times stronger than the few times I've smelled Brody.

Just the thought of his name in relation to my new jacket makes my chest ache. The act of generosity and care that came with the gift was almost too much. Almost *is* too much. He didn't have to do that, but he did anyway.

It wasn't until he told me it was mine that I realized how

truly low my standards had become while being with Stewart. Not only did he make me feel terrible about myself, but he also ruined my expectations of others. While an incredibly thoughtful gift, it shouldn't have hit me so hard that a man—a friend—wanted to make sure I was taken care of without expecting anything in return. I mistook Stewart's habits of gifting me things as sweet gestures, when really, it was his way of controlling me.

I can take care of myself, but I also deserve to be taken care of if I wish to be. *Truly taken care of.*

Three knocks hit my front door, and I squeak, snatching the to-go cup of coffee before running to the front window to find a big red truck parked out front. My knees lock as I notice the lack of exhaust puffing out into the cold.

Did he actually come to my door?

By the time I pull open the door, my mind glitches when Brody is indeed standing on my front porch. With his hands in the pockets of a jacket similar in colour to the one he gave me, he looks me over with a slight, tired smile. He takes up most of the doorway with his wide shoulders, but for once, I'm not intimidated by his size. It's almost . . . overwhelming, in a way that I refuse to dig into with him watching me like this.

"You didn't have to come to my door," I tell him, only half meaning it.

It was thoughtful of him to come up.

"That's not the way I was raised, Buttercup." The words roll off his tongue with a natural finesse, and not for the first time, I question if he picked up the slight twang in his voice from his time in Nashville.

I zip up my coat and wait for him to back up before stepping outside and locking up. "No more sweetheart?"

"Do you prefer that name?" We walk down the sidewalk, our strides in sync.

"I've never had so many to pick from before. Let me feel special for a moment," I tease.

His chuckle is gruff. "My apologies. Feel away."

"This is for you, by the way." I extend the cup of coffee to him, eyes tracking his every reaction. He hides whatever he's thinking well.

"Thanks," he says, taking the cup and popping open the lid to smell it. "Coffee?"

I nod. "I wasn't sure how you took it, so it's just black."

"Black's good."

Pride blooms in my chest as we reach the truck. Just like he did the first time I rode in this red beast, Brody opens the door for me, nodding for me to hop in. The snow in front of the door is deep and heavy, and my winter boots sink into it. When I set one boot onto the running board and grip the handle to try and push myself up, the slickness beneath it has my body shooting forward, my legs whooshing out from under me.

"Ah!" I yelp, my arms flailing in an attempt to grab onto something. But the only thing I can grab onto has already failed me, and I brace myself for the incoming impact.

Hands grab onto my waist, their grip tight as I'm pulled backward toward a hard, sturdy body. Strong arms wrap around me, that woodsy cinnamon scent exploding everywhere, making my toes beg to curl in my boots. Breathing is a foreign concept.

"Careful, it's wet," Brody rumbles in my ear, and fuck it all to hell, I give in and let my toes curl.

"No shit," I blurt out between sucking back gulps of air.

His arms flex around my waist, the steel coffee cup still sealed shut and pressed to my side. I swirl my tongue around in my mouth to try and cure the sudden dryness before pushing out of his embrace.

I keep my back to him while I grab the handle again and ask, "Can we forget that ever happened? I'll never recover from the embarrassment."

"You'll never recover from what?"

His presence is a weight at my back as I try again to get in the truck. I know he has his arms spread behind me, most likely holding the body of the truck on either side of my body so if I fall, I'll topple onto him instead of the snow. That thought fills me with too much warmth.

He's protective of people. It must be a deep-rooted instinct for him to fall into the role of protector so naturally.

Never mind that it's an incredibly attractive instinct as well.

"Exactly," I reply.

Thankfully, I make it into the truck this time without another incident, and once I'm seated on the leather, I'm gifted with a flash of his broad smile before the door is shut and he's out of sight.

My toes curl again.

17

Brody

THE GATE SWINGS SHUT BEHIND ME, THE METAL CLANGING OVER THE sound of hooves hitting the snow. My grandfather comes to a stop a few feet back, a bulky midnight-black horse beneath him that I'd recognize anywhere as Kip.

Despite his age, Grandpa is the head of the ranch, and he intends to keep that position until he isn't physically able to any longer. I've never understood his love for this place, his obsession with it. We were both born into the life of cattle ranching, but he feels like it's what he was meant to do. I don't. I never have.

Horses were more my thing when I was young. From sun-up to sundown, I was in the stables with my mother either brushing manes or fixing my saddle to go for a ride. My mother was just like me. It might have been her blood right to take over for Grandpa, but she wanted nothing to do with this life or the expectations that came with it.

When she married and got pregnant with me, there was finally hope that the Steele legacy wouldn't die with my grandfather. My father was taught everything there was to know about cattle ranching, and he got along with my grandfather fine. He loved my mother deeply and took the brunt of everything for her. For us.

The break allowed me to spend more time with my mom in the stables. Days, weeks, years. It was me and her and our horses.

Until it wasn't.

Until I lost both my mother and father within the span of a single year. The trip down memory lane is unwanted, but it's been happening more and more since I got back.

"Renner is broken down along on the far west fence. Need you to go bring him back before we can send a tow out," Grandpa orders stiffly.

I wipe my gloves down my thighs and drop the locking mechanism over the gate. "Alright. I'll grab my truck."

His lips thin. "Be faster if you jumped on a horse. We don't have time to waste around here with a man down."

"I'll get my truck," I repeat.

Tension stiffens my muscles. He's been pressuring me to get onto a horse since I got back. If he's so against wasting time, he should drop the whole thing.

He must realize that now's not the time because he nods sharply and tightens Kip's reins. "Get it done and be at the house for dinner. Your grandmother misses you."

"I'll be late. I have plans before dinner."

"Aren't those studio folk getting bored hanging around this town yet? Either go back with them, or tell them to leave so you can get back to work. Don't hurt your grandmother's feelin's by missin' another one of her meals, Brody." His words soften at the mention of my grandmother, and guilt slashes me.

"Can you ask her to wait for me? I'll be half an hour late. This isn't something I can cancel, but I'll be back as soon as I can," I promise.

If my grandmother knew I've been late to every meal this week because I'm fulfilling a promise to a woman, she'd be the one to shove me out the door. Her husband, on the other hand? I don't know what he would do.

"Get Renner. I'll see you later," he says, and then he's urging Kip into a trot toward the house.

My exhale is heavy with frustration, but I start toward the house regardless. The sooner I get this done, the sooner I can take a break from this place and the reminders of a past that can't seem to let me be.

Banana: Are you busy right now?

I PUT the truck in park and wait for Renner to hop out before replying to her text.

Me: I'm never too busy to talk to you.

The drive back from picking up my grandfather's oldest ranch hand was filled with a lot of awkward conversation. We don't know each other well at all, and while he may work for the Steele family, he's my grandfather's friend before anything else. His opinion is tainted by whatever it is my grandfather is holding against me.

Banana: That phone call I mentioned before . . .
I have a few minutes to talk now.

My eyes bulge as I read the message. The ranch house is in front of me, the lights warm and bright. My grandmother is inside, no doubt already working on dinner. I have to leave to pick Anna up from work, but . . .

I'm calling Banana and connecting her to the Bluetooth in my truck before I've even made it out of the driveway. Nerves buzz beneath my skin, but I don't back out. This is my friend.

"Hello?"

I tighten my grip on the steering wheel at the sound of her voice. Her very female voice. If I was unsure that she might have actually been a man this whole time, I'm not anymore.

I clear my throat and say, "Hey."

She blows out a breath, and I do the same.

"You sound young," she notes.

"Disappointed I'm not old and creepy?"

"You could still be creepy."

"Fair enough."

The road back to town from the ranch is gravel. It's a bit hard to drive on with the amount of snow we've been getting, so I try and keep my mind focused on the road and not the soft voice in my speakers.

It's a difficult task, especially when she says, "I was expecting you to sound more hillbilly, to be honest."

"Hillbilly?" I roll my lips before the tug up into a grin. "Sorry to disappoint ya, darlin'."

Her laugh is too fucking sweet. And almost . . . familiar. The slight increase in pitch at the end tugs at my brain. I want to chastise myself for not remembering where I last heard it.

"Now, that's more like it," she says.

I notice how close I am to turning into town and slow my speed slightly. Checking my rear-view mirror, I confirm there's nobody behind me to complain about it.

"Wanna tell me why you wanted to talk right now?" I ask, unable to help myself.

"It's one of those days. I've been a bit cranky and figured that talking to you might help."

My chest tightens. "That was a bit of a risk. What if I'd been someone you weren't expecting and I made your day worse?"

"It was worth it," she states confidently.

"I agree."

I turn into town and get hit with a mix of feelings. I'm . . . excited to see Anna. To see her smile and listen to whatever she wants to talk about. But at the same time, I want to continue this phone call. Is that messed up? Fuck, I can't even tell anymore.

"I have to go soon, but thank you for calling. Even if it was only for a couple minutes. You always help when I'm feeling down," she admits.

I swallow. "You can call me whenever you want. You're in Canada, right?" Close to me too. "There was no long-distance warnin' when I called."

"I am. So are you, then. I figured with the area codes, but wow. I want to ask where in Canada you are, but I don't want to sound creepy."

"Creepy is supposed to be my thing."

"You should ask, then." It's a dare, and I haven't backed down from a dare since high school.

"Alberta."

Her sharp inhale is all I need to know, but she still replies, "Alberta for me too. Now anyway."

"Now?"

"I'm originally from Vancouver."

The truck jerks when I accidentally press hard on the brake. My tires lock up on the icy road, and I bark a curse while releasing the brake and finally gaining control of the truck again. My pulse thumps in my throat as I carefully pull onto Main Street.

It's just an eery coincidence. Don't think too much into it.

"Are you okay?" she rushes out, panicked.

My reply is weak, confusion distracting me. "I'm fine. I have to go, but I'll text you later."

"I—alright. We'll talk later."

"Bye, Banana," I mutter.

"Bye, Bo," she replies, and then our call drops.

I try to ignore the worry in those final two words as I park in front of the salon and stare at the window, still bright with light. When Anna glides into view, I can't look away.

Instead of having her hair tied back like it was this morning, it's hanging free down her back. I haven't seen much of her body beneath her bulky jackets, but I wasn't expecting the sight of her without one to leave me so breathless. She's wearing a tight grey long-sleeve that emphasizes the curves of her waist and generous chest. Generous is an understatement. I've never looked before, and maybe that's a good thing. It's hard to drop my gaze, but once I do, I feel my cheeks burn.

The twitch of my dick in my jeans makes me feel like a perv. I knew she was gorgeous, but I didn't know she was like that *everywhere*. I won't be able to forget that fact now that I know it.

She steps out of view, and the lights go out. My throat works with a thick swallow as I wait for her to lock up. On instinct, I'm out of the truck and rounding the hood at the same time she starts heading toward me. As if accepting that I'm going to open the door for her every time, she smiles at me and waits for me to do just that.

"Thank you," she says, accepting the gesture.

"'Course."

I step up behind her, lingering as she pushes herself up and into the truck. Once she's settled, I shut the door and try to steady my steps on the way back to my side.

She's skipping through the songs on the screen when I'm back behind the wheel. A swirl of discomfort moves through my stomach when the opening notes of my latest song fill the speakers. A brow quirked, Anna looks at me from the corner of her eye, as if testing my reaction to the song choice.

"I'm going to guess from that look that you don't listen to your own music?"

"Not unless I'm singin' it," I answer honestly.

Interest flares in her eyes as she stares at me head-on. "Would you ever sing for me?"

I sling my arm over the back of her seat and look over my shoulder while reversing the truck out of the parking spot. The sherpa collar of her jacket tickles my fingers. I stroke the pad of my finger over it, feeling the heat radiating from her neck.

"I keep forgetting that you like my music."

"I doubt many people don't like your music, Brody."

"You'd be surprised."

I pull onto the road, the ice still slick beneath my tires. Anna's breath hitches when we fishtail slightly. Before I can think twice about it, I'm shooting my arm out and placing my hand on her thigh, gripping it tight. I meant it to be reassuring, calming, but when she stops breathing altogether, I snatch my hand back, the warmth of her leg burning my palm.

"I'm sorry," I stammer, twisting the leather steering wheel over and over again.

Her exhale is shaky, but at least she's breathing now. "It's fine! I just wasn't expecting that."

Me either. "I don't go around touching women without their permission. It won't happen again."

"I was more concerned about the ice."

"Oh."

Her laugh is smooth before climbing in pitch at the end the way it always does. It's a soothing sound, at least for me.

"I'm a good driver. I won't let anything happen to—"

That laugh.

My promise dies in my throat. I want to look at her. Want to ask her to pull out her phone and show me her messages. But I'm *not* going to do that. Fuck, that's an asshole thing to even consider.

How many women have similar laughs? And moved from British Columbia to Alberta recently? Anna Banana? I'm ashamed that I didn't put that one together.

God, even her body makes it all that clearer. I don't remember details from that single accidental photo, but I remember seeing curves and pale skin. And the memory of Anna in the window earlier is as crystal clear as ever.

It's obvious now.

Anna is my mystery woman.

18

Annalise

BRODY'S WORDS COME TO AN ABRUPT HALT.

Something sour twists and turns in the air. "Did I say something wrong?" I ask softly.

He won't look at me. I tell myself that's because he's concentrating on driving, but that wouldn't explain the grip he just had on my thigh. The way he thought to reach for me when I was anxious as if it were a simple instinct despite the road conditions.

I've never known a man to have that instinct around me before.

The heat from his palm still burns my thigh. I can feel every indent of his fingertips as if he never removed his hand at all. I've never wanted to be manhandled before, but if that was anything like what I could expect from a guy like Brody, maybe I've been missing out.

"No. You've never done anything wrong to me," he says.

"Then what's going on?"

I should tread carefully and not push him to open up, but I can't help but want to know everything about this man. Every ideal and personality trait that he's been hiding. The things that make him smile and laugh freely. I want to crack him open and see if he's as mushy inside as I expect he could be. That starts with something as simple as this.

"I'm just tired, Anna."

I nod, fighting the voice in my head that begs me to keep poking. "You work hard. The long hours must be exhausting."

"You work hard too." It's a briskly spoken statement but sincere nonetheless.

"Thank you. One day, I hope to have something to show for it all. A salon of my own, maybe."

He nods silently, and I finally tear my gaze away from him, staring out the windshield. Tucking my hands between my thighs, I roll my lips and try not to pay too much attention to the glistening of the half-plowed roads. I have to get over this fear sometime. It's not healthy to rely on someone else to take me places. The lack of food in my fridge from not going shopping is a prime example of that. Brody doesn't reply to my statement for the rest of the drive. Something is going through his head that he doesn't want to share, and I don't have any business forcing him to. Letting someone sit in their feelings has always been something that I've struggled with. It's hypocritical, considering I like to do the same thing when I'm upset.

Five minutes later, he pulls the truck into the same tire tracks he left behind this morning and shifts it into park. I fidget in my seat, unsure of how to say goodbye. Am I just supposed to hop out without a word?

When he breaks the silence first, I sigh in relief, uncaring if he notices.

"Monday morning?"

"Yep." I keep my voice steady so he can't pick up on my nerves.

Maybe it'll be warmer tomorrow, so I can walk to my pole class. Or, worst case, I'll somehow buy a damn snowsuit.

Another curt nod. It's all I need to push myself to open the door. A blast of cold slaps my cheeks. I don't look to see if he's staring at me when I jump down into the snow. Don't need to.

I'd have to be numb not to feel the heat of his stare against the back of my head.

"Thank you, Brody. See you Monday," I say before shutting the door and beginning my trek through the heavy snow on the sidewalk up to the house. My first task for tomorrow is to shovel before I wind up face first into the snow.

Maybe a snowsuit is a smart idea after all.

I DIDN'T HEAR from Bo all night, and at half past noon on this Saturday morning, it's still silence. For the first time in days, no good-morning message greeted me when I woke up. It was jarring, to say the least.

The only texts on my phone today came from my sister, reminding me of my flight to Ottawa for the wedding creeping up on me, and Poppy telling me how excited she is to have me back at class today.

It shouldn't be so disappointing not to hear from him after a single day, but after our first phone call, I guess I just expected him to talk to me even more, not less. His rushed goodbye yesterday took me by surprise, but I didn't think too much of it. Now, though? It's all I can think about.

Analyzing every single word he spoke has kept my thoughts in a knot all damn day.

I've been staring at my front door for ten minutes, the winter boots on my feet making them sweat. My car keys are clutched tightly between my fingers. I need a push. Someone to shove me out the door and into my car.

It's minus thirty degrees today, which means no walking to the pole studio without risking frostbite. I didn't tell Brody about my plans today because I didn't want him to have to feel responsible for carving out even more of his time to chauffeur me there and back, especially after his gruff attitude when he dropped me off last night.

Bryce or Poppy would have driven me, but they both go to the studio early, and I stupidly hyped myself up about driving this morning instead of reaching out before they'd left. Now I'm stuck with either bailing on class or toughing it out and climbing behind the wheel.

"Just drive the damn car, Anna," I grit out.

Lifting my chin, I roll my shoulders and step outside. The sun is near blinding, and I have to squint at the porch stairs so I don't trip and fall on the ice there—

There's no ice. *How* is there no ice?

My jaw falls open as I search the stairs and find nothing but blue specks of ice melt. Sharp-looking shards of it lie scattered on top of the new snow piles lining my shovelled sidewalk.

This wasn't me. Was it my neighbours? Unlikely, considering I haven't spoken to a single one of them since I moved in. I passed out early last night and then chickened out this morning, deciding to stay huddled in my warm bed for as long as I could instead. It was a problem for another day, but now . . . gratitude swells in my chest.

The walk to my car is easy without the snow and ice, and I pause when I realize my car has been brushed off as well. I don't even have a snow brush. Haven't needed one.

Maybe it was Poppy or Bryce. Those two women would do just about anything to help me out.

The inside of my car is *freezing*. My teeth chatter as I turn over the engine and gape in horror when it sputters, ticking over and over instead of starting. I try again, and again.

It's dead.

The. Battery. Is. Dead.

My palms hit the steering wheel before my forehead does. Tears of frustration well in my eyes before spilling over. They run down my frozen cheeks, and I'm surprised they don't turn into ice chips.

This is so embarrassing. My neighbours are probably watching me from inside, chattering about how unprepared I was for this winter season. How long did I stand staring at my door before finally gaining the nerve to come out here, only to find my car dead? As if it wouldn't die without being plugged in at all. It's probably been dead since the first cold night.

"Ugh!" I shout, flinging myself back in my seat.

My teeth won't stop clacking together, even when I bite down. The thick jacket can't protect me from this level of cold. I can't sit here and freeze to death. But what the hell am I supposed to do now? I don't know how to boost a car, let alone have cables in the first place or anyone to hook them up to. My father never taught me things like this, and as if Stewart was going to spend his time giving me a lesson on boosting a battery.

I pull my phone from my pocket and focus on keeping my fingers from shaking. Anxiety bares its teeth at me, the distance between my mind and the looming pain of its bite closing in as the seconds tick by. It's a task in itself just to pull up Bryce's contact and press the Call button.

The ringtone continues to drill my eardrums before her voicemail catches the call. I swallow when I look at the time and realize pole has already started.

That leaves me with . . . zero options. Or maybe not. They have to have a tow truck service in this town, right? My fingers have grown stiff and partially numb as I bring up Google and look for one. I laugh sharply when the only one is half an hour out of town.

The next call I make isn't one I understand, but I do it without hesitation. The moment I hear his voice after the third ring, I don't feel so damn alone.

"You okay?"

"Hi to you too."

"Sorry. Hey. You've just never called me out of the blue before."

"My car is dead," I blurt out, unable to keep it in and play coy right now.

A pause. "You're in your car? Were you goin' to drive?"

"I have a pole class. I wanted to drive myself. But it's so cold and I haven't plugged my car in at all since I've been here and I don't have booster cables or even a car to boost it with and it's really cold in here and I just—"

"Take a breath," he instructs, voice dropping into a soothing caress. My next inhale is shaky, but at least I can breathe. "Do you have anyone to call?"

The striking truth of my answer is a hammer to my heart. "Nobody that can come and help me."

There's movement on his side of the call, and I'm instantly feeling guilty for bothering him. Could I hit a lower low? I doubt it.

"Go back inside instead of sitting in the cold. I have to go, but please go inside and think through what to do. Sittin' in your car if it's dead won't help you," he directs calmly.

My stomach drops at the thought of him hanging up on me right now. I have no right feeling hurt by his schedule.

"Okay," I croak.

There's a slam of a door in the background and a loud male voice that doesn't belong to Bo shouting before I hear him tell me to go inside one final time. The familiar beeping of an ended call is my only company now.

I hate the way I stare at my phone, waiting for him to call back when I know he won't.

By the time I slide my hands into the pockets of my jacket and curl them in an attempt to warm them up, I don't know how long I've been sitting in the car or how long I linger, unable to haul myself back outside. Long enough for snot to run from my nose and my legs to have no feeling left in them. The air I suck down is cruel, burning in my lungs.

A scream rises up my throat when my door is pulled open and I'm hauled out of the car as if I weigh nothing. The heat radiating from the hard body behind mine nearly makes me purr, and I think I hate myself a little for that, considering I'm probably being kidnapped.

"You're fucking frozen," my assailant scolds.

It's Brody. Brody, Brody, Brody.

His hot breath fans over my neck, and I moan at the sensation of it against my cold skin, uncaring about the way the sound makes him stiffen against my back. His voice and presence settle my fear, and I begin to go lax in his arms.

"What are you doing here?" I mumble. It's taking everything in me not to spin in his arms and bury my face in his jacket.

His words are quick off the tongue. "I drove by your house on my way back to the ranch and saw you sitting inside of your car. You can't be sitting in a cold car, Anna. Where are your keys?"

"In the ignition."

The sound of protest I make when he releases me and steps toward the car is pitiful. I wish I could feel my blush because I know it's there.

Brody catches my eyes and doesn't look away. It's a soft gaze. Unguarded. "Let me get your keys, and then we'll go inside."

"Both of us?"

"Unless you don't want me to. I can boost your car and then leave," he offers, not a hint of offense in the words.

I shake my head far too quickly. "No. You can come in."

The corner of his mouth tilts into a small smile before he's reaching into the car and pulling my keys free. He's more at ease now than he was the last time I saw him, but there's still something off. I can't put my finger on it yet.

When he shuts my car door and turns to me, I jerk my head toward the house and say, "Come on."

Even with my legs half-numb, I feel my knees shake when he slides his arm around my waist and carefully tucks me into his body before leading us up the sidewalk.

I don't consider pulling away. Not even once.

19

Brody

ALARMED DOESN'T COME CLOSE TO DESCRIBING HOW I FELT WHEN Anna called me—called Bo.

The thought of her driving on roads she isn't comfortable with or knowledgeable of turned my stomach. Even before learning that she was sitting out in the cold, her car dead and hearing those tears in her voice, I was sprinting away from my grandfather mid-lecture and toward my truck.

The pull I feel for her doesn't make sense. It's concerning that my first instinct is to drop my duties and responsibilities for a woman I've known just shy of a month. Her distress is cutting, a shake to the ground beneath my feet.

I'm positive I'll face the consequences of abandoning the ranch when I'm finished here. I won't be able to hide why I left or have been sneaking off once I do. My grandma will smell any potential lies before they've slipped from my tongue.

That's a problem for later, though. When I'm not bundling a frozen woman in my arms who needs to get warm as soon as possible and trying to keep from going completely caveman on her.

Anna shivers in my hold, though not enough to strike another blow of fear inside of me. It's cold out, but we're not teetering on the edge of hypothermia with the amount of time she was outside. If I hadn't come when I did and she continued to sit in a daze for minutes longer, things might have been different. For now, she just needs to warm up and sort her mind.

I unlock her door and hold it open as we step inside. The air is warm, the telltale drone of her furnace pumping through the small house. A sweep of my eyes through the open floor plan exposes some more of her personality.

While the place is small, the way it was furnished makes it appear bigger. If I had to guess, I'd say it was rented out that way, but the small touches tossed around have to be courtesy of Anna.

From the soft, muted green pillowcases on the couch, the teal coffee machine on the kitchen counter, and the picture frames scattered on the built-in bookshelves along the living room wall, I learn more about her.

I wonder if she brought a lot with her when she moved here, and if she did, why there aren't more of her things visible in the space. Why exactly *did* she move here? She said she wanted a fresh start, but I want to know what made her old life so bad that she felt like she needed to move here to start over. Cherry Peak is a long way from Vancouver.

"I'm sorry for the mess," she breathes, teeth still chattering slightly.

When she goes to pull out of my grasp, I stiffen my arm around her, as if my body is against the possibility of letting her go. *She needs heat*, I tell myself. That's why I want her close.

Reluctantly, I release her and curl my fingers to keep from reaching out again. "I've never minded a bit of mess."

"The only company I've had since I've moved in has been Poppy and Bryce, and they're even messier than I am."

I follow her further into the house, past the stacked pizza boxes on the kitchen table and the unfolded clothes in the laundry bin beside them. Honestly, her house is hardly messy at all.

She'll be in for a big surprise the first time she comes to the ranch house. After a busy week, it looks less like a house and more like a dumping ground for every ranch hand we employ.

Not like she'll be at the ranch house anytime soon. Or ever.

"You picked a good couple of friends to make. Those two have always been solid in the community."

"Poppy mentioned that she knew you prior to when we met. Actually, she told me you were a nice guy, and then you were the absolute opposite of nice." Her voice is teasing, but the truth beneath it still grates against the lingering guilt.

"I was an asshole that night," I admit. Anna moves toward the electric kettle on the counter, but I gently brush her aside and snag it from her extended hand. "Do you want some tea?"

She quirks a brow, tipping her head back to meet my eyes. "You know how to use a kettle?"

"First of all, that's insultin'. Who doesn't know how to use a kettle?" I snap open the lid and turn on the tap to fill it up. "And second, please go put on some warm clothes. I like that you're wearin' the jacket, but it's not enough. A hoodie and some thick pants will do."

Once the kettle is full, I turn off the tap and plug it in, waiting for the light to turn red before facing Anna. She's got her hands on her hips in a sassy stance, and I bite back my laugh at the effort to intimidate me.

Not quite there yet, sweetheart.

"I'll take your orders this one time, but don't get used to it. The tea bags are in the farthest cabinet with the coffee pods. Peppermint is my favourite," she says, and then she's walking out of the kitchen before I have a chance to reply.

It's an effort to tear my eyes from her as she moves. The tight black athletic pants make her ass look criminal, and the baggy shirt does little to hide her upper half. A searing burst of want shackles me before I can wish it away.

She's disappeared into what I assume is her bedroom before I regain focus on my task and adjust my dick in my jeans. I find the tea bags easily and then snoop through the remaining cabinets until I find the coffee mugs. There's a lot of them. It seems Anna has a bit of a tendency to collect the damn things. I count at last fifteen in the cabinet alone, and I'd bet there are more in another.

Once the tea bag is in the hot water, I set the mug I chose down on the table and pull a chair out for her before sitting in the opposite one to wait.

My phone begins to buzz in my pocket, and I already know who's calling before I've grabbed it and spied the name lighting the screen. I decline the call.

"Not one for phone calls?" Anna asks. My heart skips at the bite of suspicion that lingers in her tone. She can't know, right?

Anna walks toward the table with a familiar confidence. Her long brown hair now shines in a braid hanging over a hoodie-clad shoulder. The bulky material draping over her torso is black and red with a beavertail in the centre. My brows jump.

"You're a hockey fan?"

She ducks her head to look at her chest. "I kind of have to be."

"Nobody *has* to be an Ottawa fan." My nose scrunches.

"Let me guess, you're a Nashville fan?"

"Fuck no. I'm a Calgary fan 'til the day I die."

Anna sits in the chair I pulled out and wraps her hands around the mug. She lets out a soft sigh at the warmth against her skin and smiles. My chest nearly puffs at the satisfaction of knowing I put that look on her face.

"My brother-in-law plays for Ottawa," she says, pride filling her eyes.

Mine simply widen. "Who?"

"Maddox Hutton."

I whistle, rocking back in my chair. "Wow."

"Are you a bit starstruck, superstar? Who would have thought you were capable of such humility."

The jab is soft, not a pointed edge in sight. I wouldn't have minded even if there was. The similarities between her and my texting buddy are blaringly apparent. So much so that I feel even more idiotic that I didn't piece it together sooner. Neither Anna nor Banana was concerned with holding punches when it came to me. It was one of the reasons I liked them both so much.

I can't help but wonder if she actually has started to piece it together too. That I'm the guy behind the texts. I knew the risk that came with showing up to help her earlier, but like hell I wasn't going to come.

There's a part of me that doesn't want her to know. At least not yet. Maybe that's why I haven't told her the truth.

There's a sense of safety that comes with talking to her via text without her knowing it's me. I know that's ridiculous. It doesn't fully make sense to me, but there's no changing the way I feel about it.

I can tell her things over text that I don't feel comfortable enough to tell her in person. She doesn't know who Bo is, and while it feels terrible to withhold the truth from her . . . I haven't had this bubble of security in a long time. From anyone. I'm selfish enough to want to keep it for just a bit longer.

"You're nearly related to one of the top players in the NHL. Do you blame me?"

"Oh, absolutely not. Be as awestruck as you want, just don't act like this in his presence. He'll never let anyone hear the end of it."

I lean forward again with my hands fisted on the table, my next words coming out far throatier than I mean them to. "Plannin' on bringin' me home to the family, Anna?"

Pink splotches appear across her cheeks before she rolls her eyes and takes a long sip of her tea. It's clear she expects it to be a distraction, but I don't break eye contact with her, my question continuing to hang between us.

Finally, she sets down her mug. "What were you doing in town today? I didn't think ranchers got days off."

"Don't change the subject."

"You're going to smell like peppermint if you don't stop picking on me."

My smirk is sinister. "And why exactly would I smell like peppermint? Plannin' on kissing me?"

"You're unbearable," she says, but there's still no heat in her insult. "I was thinking more along the lines of dumping scalding tea over your head."

I toss her a wink. "My grandparents would agree more often than not."

"Your grandma seems really kind," she says, leading the conversation away from the helpless flirting I suddenly can't seem to put a stop to.

"She is. But don't let that fool you. She can be cutthroat when she needs to be."

"I'd think you'd have to be to put up with such a busy ranch. If the other people there are like you, I don't envy her."

"I'm sure there are few who could do what she does," I agree.

"What about your mom? I'm sure she must be just as strong."

The lingering ache that I've long since grown used to turns sharper, tearing a bit deeper at the question. I drop her gaze, focusing on the veterinarian logo on her coffee cup.

"You don't have to answer that. I like to poke too far into people's personal lives sometimes. I'm sorry," she says, picking up on my every reaction.

I clear the emotion from my throat. "My mom passed when I was young. But yes, she was just as strong as my grandmother. Stronger."

Warmth covers my hands, drawing my eyes from the mug. A small, soft hand covers my much larger, rougher ones. She strokes my knuckles with her thumb, and my breath stutters.

"I'm sorry. I have no doubt that she was an incredible woman."

I can't ignore her stare any longer. The moment I find those brown eyes glistening with grief for me, I turn over my hands and sandwich hers between them. My touch grows brave when she doesn't pull away. Pointer finger exploring, I trace over a small line of raised skin. A scar on the inside of her middle finger.

Something restless settles inside of me. Maybe we're not that different after all.

"Are you up for learnin' how to boost your car?"

Her answering grin strikes me so deeply I'm thankful to be sitting down.

"Yes, please."

20

Annalise

A HALF HOUR LATER AND I'M IN DISBELIEF OF HOW EASY IT IS TO bring a dead car battery back to life. Watching Brody turn his truck to face my car and then haul two cords—one red and one black—from the back had done something to me. That something only seemed to grow stronger and more annoying when he popped both hoods, connected them with the cords, and then ordered me to turn my car on.

It took far too much effort to keep from saying yes, sir, anything you want, sir.

When the engine started on the first crank, I nearly shrieked. That's when the embarrassment had set in. It had been so easy to boost my car, yet I hadn't been able to do it on my own. I didn't know how.

Brody didn't seem to care that I hadn't known how to do it. I think he cared more about making sure I learned for the future than anything else.

That's why he's still here, walking back from his truck a second time with a bag in his hand and a long yellow cord tossed over his shoulder.

The toque he plopped onto my head before we left the house keeps sliding down my forehead as I lean against the car door. I have to push it up to keep from looking away from him when he steps in front of me.

"Is there anything you *don't* carry in your truck?" I ask.

He chuffs a laugh. "You don't even know what I have yet, and you're already bustin' my balls."

"Fair enough. What have you brought me, Oh Mighty One?"

The serious shift in his expression has me sobering. "You can't be driving without an emergency kit, especially in the winter. This has everything from flares to an emergency blanket. Never take it out of your trunk unless you need to use it." He waits for me to nod before continuing, lifting the shoulder with the yellow cord slung over it.

"This is an extension cord for you to use to keep your car plugged in when you're not usin' it. Every time the temperature drops below minus twenty-five, you're goin' to make sure your car is plugged in and that you're startin' it at least once a day. When you start it, have it run for a good ten minutes straight if you're not goin' to be drivin' it."

My face flushes beneath the weight of his instructions and explanations. He's being gentle with his words, cautious as if to not make me feel completely useless. I appreciate the effort, even if it only half lightens the blow.

I lick my wind-dried lips. "You don't need these things in your truck?"

"There are extras at the ranch," he replies with an air of nonchalance that doesn't match the intensity of his stare. I choose not to mention that.

"Thank you. I appreciate this."

Taking a step closer to me, the toe of his boot nudges the side of mine. His hand ghosts over my waist in a steady, comforting touch that lingers before he's moving to the other side of me and opening the back door. My blood heats, and that's enough to have me pushing away from the car and putting some space between us.

Watching him try to squeeze his body into the small space of my back seat is what I imagine clowns look like popping out of a clown car. It would probably take a hearty push against his ass to get him inside.

"Don't worry about it. I'll just plug your car in before I head out," he says.

I didn't notice that I was smiling until I feel it fall. Disappointment falls like a rock in my stomach. What I'm disappointed about exactly, I don't know. It's not like I expected him to stay for dinner or anything.

"Alright," I force myself to say.

When he extracts himself from the back seat and shuts the door, I can't find it in myself to be the first to walk away. He returns to his towering height, and my head tips back further with each step he eliminates between us.

"Where are your exterior plug-ins?"

"I don't know." It's the truth. I've never looked.

His smile starts small before growing. The first look at the dimple in his right cheek has me swallowing a swoon. "Let's have a look, then."

"Why are you smiling like that?" I blurt out.

"Like what?" The fucker somehow grins impossibly bigger.

"Like you know exactly how good-looking you are, especially when you smile like that. Are you trying to seduce me or something?"

His laugh is pure sin. It runs a soft touch down my body before settling between my legs. The involuntary clench that follows makes me breathless and annoyed all in one.

"If I was trying to seduce you, Anna, you wouldn't be thinking so hard," he coos.

I nearly moan. The realization of how easy it's become for this man to turn me into a horndog is enough to relieve me from the effects of his words.

"You said something about finding my exterior outlets?"

Brody

I BARELY MAKE it two steps into the ranch house before my grandfather finds me. My pep talk in the truck on the way home was for nothing. There's not a damn thing that I could have told myself to adequately prepare for the ass whooping my grandpa's prepared.

Leaning against the wall in the foyer, he has his arms crossed and cowboy hat dipped low. The lack of boots on his feet is courtesy of my grandmother, I'm sure. She's stubborn when it comes to her no boots past the back mat rule, even if it weakens Grandpa's rough and tough appearance.

Not only is my stomach empty, but my eyes are heavy, exhaustion a real pain in my ass. Slipping my boots off, I shut the heavy wooden door and wait.

"When are you leavin'?" he asks, the question sharp and demanding.

"Leavin'?"

"Leavin' back to Nashville. I assume you've been plannin' your return over the past couple of weeks with all of your disappearances. Clearly, you don't want to be here."

"Well, with such a cold welcome, I don't see how I'd overly want to be here," I snap.

Grandpa straightens, a hurt look there and gone in the blink of an eye. "It's hard to get too close when we don't know when you'll be takin' off again."

"Don't give me that. I'm still your grandson. You were fine until we went to that auction. What happened there that turned you around?"

It's pissed me off ever since he switched up that day. Sure, he wasn't exactly warm and cozy with my return, but he surely wasn't this cold. Something or, more likely, someone messed with his head.

"I was too hopeful that you'd hang around."

I remove my hat and rest it against my thigh, exasperated by his way of thinking. His fears are on me, I know that. They're the consequences of my leaving, but fuck, that doesn't make it any easier.

"I haven't made plans to leave yet. You need to let what you think I'm goin' to do go. You're only pushin' me away," I tell him.

He guffaws, pushing away from the wall. Tugging off his hat, he smooths a hand over his grey hair. "You pushed yourself away, Brody. I'm sorry if your welcome back wasn't everythin' you'd dreamed of, but it's gonna take some work to earn back the respect and trust you lost when you left."

"What do you think I'm tryin' to do every day? You're the one so desperate to believe that I'm plannin' an escape instead of appreciatin' the time we have together."

"Appreciate the time we have? That's supposed to suffice? I raised you, son—don't give me shit for not taking the scraps you offer us." The old man seethes, a red tint to his cheeks.

I know I'm not going to get anywhere with him tonight. The hurt runs deep, and the Steeles are as stubborn as mules. We don't forget or forgive easily. Especially not when it comes to abandonment. And that's exactly what I did. Whether intentional or not, I abandoned this place. Abandoned him the same way my father did.

"Wade Steele, you go get washed up for dinner," Grandma scolds.

I find her standing in the doorway, a pale yellow apron tied around her waist and a tea towel in her hands. Her scowl is brutal and aimed at her husband. At least he has the sense not to fight her on this, even if the look he gives me promises that we'll continue this conversation at a later time.

He places a kiss on Grandma's cheek as he passes her, leaving us alone in the foyer. My heart grows heavy at the soft gleam in her eyes.

"Give him time," she tells me.

"How much time? I don't have much left here."

She considers that and places a steady hand on my shoulder, looking up at me. "Maybe that is something you have to take into consideration, then. If things haven't turned around by the end of your time here, will you be okay with leaving things unsettled?"

"I've already been here longer than I should have."

"And while I'm grateful for every moment I get to have you back, I'll be honest and say that I want it to be longer. I'll always want more time with you. It makes me sad to see you so at odds with your grandfather, but I'll always urge you to do what will make you happy, my love. If that means you going back to Nashville, then I'll understand. However, I will also want you to stay."

I exhale and wrap my arms around her small frame in a tight hug. She sets her cheek against my chest and sniffles.

"This is dirty work, Grandma," I scold teasingly. "It'll take more than a hug and a sniffle to convince me to stay."

She laughs, and some of my tension drains. "Are you finally going to tell me why you've been sneaking off every day like a naughty teenager?"

Pulling back, I set my hat back on my head and use the brim to avoid looking at her intense stare. Like a beast on the prowl, this one.

"Not yet."

"Fine, don't tell me. But a word of advice: maybe resist carrying the smell of her perfume into the house if you want to keep me from asking," she warns slyly. The moment I look at her with wide eyes, she knows she's trapped me. "Go wash up. You're helping me set the table tonight."

With two pats to my cheek, she spins and goes back to the kitchen. I pinch the collar of my jacket and lift it to my nose, breathing in the mix of lavender and coconut that I've quickly come to recognize as Anna. The scent has begun to linger in my truck and, now, my clothes.

I'm content to let it.

21

Annalise

Bo: Good morning. Pineapple on pizza . . . yes or no?

Me: On. Always on.

Bo: Good. Same here.

Bo: What are three things you would want with you on a deserted island?

Me: Why am I going to a deserted island?

Bo: Your plane went down.

Me: Oh, so this is an in-a-perfect-world scenario?

Bo: Yes. Pretend you had time to pull your suitcase down and grab three things before nearly dying in the crash.

Me: Alright. Since my options would be fairly limited, I'd say mouthwash, a second pair of underwear, and a knife I'd steal from wherever the flight attendants store the knives.

Bo: What planes have you been on before where the attendants carry knives?

Me: You're telling me there aren't steak knives hidden somewhere for the rich people in first class to eat their steak?

Bo: Have you ever flown first class?

Me: Obviously not.

Bo: I've never been served a steak.

OVER THE PAST WEEK, BO AND I HAVE GONE BACK TO NORMAL. IT seems that his couple of days without texting me must have just been a blip because he's been consistent with his silly questions and terrible jokes since then.

The similarities between him and Brody have also become harder to ignore. After the day Brody showed up to help with my car, I've been curious. Possibly too much so, given the slim amount of proof I have that they may be one and the same.

I haven't told him about my weak conclusions, and I don't plan to yet. I'm not even entirely sure if I want to risk it.

If he truly was Bo, wouldn't he have told me the day he swept in to save me like some rough and tough cowboy remixed Prince Charming? If it wasn't pure coincidence that Brody showed up right when I needed him and instead, he knew where I'd be and that I needed help because I had told him—*told Bo*—then clearly, he would have already pieced together that I'm Banana.

I'm interrupted from my thoughts by the loud crunching of snow beneath tires. My head snaps up, and I stare out the glass porch door when Brody pulls his truck up behind my car and waves at me from inside. While I may be used to him getting out of the warm truck to open all of my doors for me, I've started waiting at my front door so I can keep him from wasting his time coming up to get me.

We've fallen into an easy routine this past week. By the time he's stepped onto the snow and rounded the bed of the truck, I'm halfway down the sidewalk. The dimpled grin he flashes me has become a comforting sight each morning, but the blush that beats at my cheeks afterward? Not so much.

Ducking my head, I step around his towering body that radiates far too much heat and hop into the truck. He closes the door behind me, and I take the moment alone to beg my face to cool. The messy farm truck has nearly become a second home for me in Cherry Peak. It's even started to smell like my perfume to the point I tried not wearing it for a couple of days to see if it helped. It didn't, and when I apologized, offering to buy some air fresheners, he waved me off, admitting that he liked the smell. I've returned to using my perfume like normal.

"You should really let me walk to your door. It's a polite thing for a man to do," he says once he's seated beside me.

"You don't need to be more polite, Brody. You've already been my personal driver for the past two weeks."

"There's no such thing as too polite."

I snort loudly, unashamed of how ugly of a sound it is. "I beg to differ."

"Are you tryin' to hint at somethin'?"

I glance at him, batting my eyes. "What could I possibly be hinting at?"

"I didn't take you for the bad-boy type, but maybe you actually are into the whole motorcycle-and-arrogance persona," he teases. "Am I too nice for you, Buttercup?"

"I wouldn't exactly turn down a ride on a motorcycle, but the arrogance thing? I've been there, done that too many times. It's hotter in movies and romance novels than it is in real life."

Something in my voice must give away just how many times

I've been with arrogant men because his next words lack their teasing edge.

"You've never told me why you felt like you needed to start over somewhere."

I stare out the windshield, watching the houses turn into the buildings that mark downtown. The once flaying pain that came with talking about Stewart has dulled exponentially. It still hurts to think about what he did, but it's more like a sore spot now that I've begun to heal. The wound is closed, but the scar remains, so to speak.

"I was engaged to a man who was sleeping with another woman. I didn't know until I caught them sleeping together on my birthday, and I never bothered to learn how long it had truly been going on. Our lives were completely entangled up until then, and the only way I felt I could get free of him was to leave. Maybe it was cowardly, but I'm glad I did. I love my new life here."

I avoid looking at Brody, too scared of seeing disgust twisting his handsome features. The judgment from Stewart's family the one and only time his mother reached out after I left her son standing naked on his yacht was more than enough. I don't want the judgment from Brody. It would hurt me more than I want to admit to myself right now.

"Did you at least try and pawn off the ring?" he asks sternly.

The bluntness of the question surprises me even more than the question itself. My laugh comes right from my chest, and I let it flow, not daring to trap it.

My next words are more of a wheeze than anything. "You sound like my sister. But no, I left it on the bed after I destroyed a few of his favourite things."

He nods approvingly. "He sounds like a fuckin' tool. I'm sorry."

"Thanks. It all happened months ago now."

The clarification comes naturally. Even just the idea of him thinking I might still have feelings for Stewart is bile inducing.

"Have you spoken to him since?"

Does he sound *jealous*? My heart jolts. I'm not the woman who's going to pretend she doesn't like a jealous man. As far as I'm concerned, as long as it's jealousy and not a cover for being controlling, I'm all for it. And jealousy on a man like Brody is all too appealing.

"Not since I moved back. I don't know if I'm hurt that he didn't care enough to try and win me back or if I'm relieved he let me go without much of a fight," I admit.

"Not only did he not deserve you because of what he did, but a real man fights for his woman regardless of whether she's going to hit you in the crotch with a baseball bat while you try to or not," he says, firm and final.

The confidence he exudes has always had a strong effect on me. It's as natural for him as breathing is. I've only been around one other man who carries himself with that sort of confidence before—my sister's husband—and I most definitely did not have the same reaction to him. *Ew.*

There's something so different when it comes to Brody. Whether it has to do with the feelings I'm starting to grow for him or something as clean-cut as pure attraction, he makes my blood sing. Hearing him speak of what a man should and shouldn't do for his woman . . . I squash my thighs together. If I let myself wonder about all of things he'd do for his woman, I'd leave a puddle on the truck seat.

"What's it like to date as a celebrity?" I blurt out, watching him start at the sudden question.

He doesn't answer instantly. Instead, he pulls the truck into his usual spot in front of the salon and puts it in park. When he looks at me again, it's after fully twisting in his seat, facing me as much as he can. I suddenly wish there wasn't a giant console between us.

"I haven't dated anyone in years. Not since I got into music professionally. So, I'm probably not the best person to ask about this, but from the limited experience I have, I can say that it's compli-cated. I think the way I treated you when we first met is a prime example of just how complicated it can be," he explains, another hidden apology in the last sentence. An apology I don't need.

"You're constantly trying to see if someone is being genuine or not."

He nods, trying to hide a wince. "Sometimes it can come back to bite me in the ass."

"It didn't bite you in the ass this time," I muse, the corner of my lips tugging up.

Our gazes lock, holding for longer than normal. The sparkle in his pretty blue eyes makes my stomach flutter. How exactly am I supposed to keep from developing feelings for him when he treats me the way he does? Even as just friends, he's made me feel more important and cared for than I ever have before. God, he's dangerous.

Brody Steele is a land mine hidden in plain sight. I never stood a damn chance in avoiding him or the damage he's sure to do to my heart when he leaves.

Because he will leave. He's told me Cherry Peak was a temporary stop. I knew that and still let myself open up to him and accept him into my life. Only time will tell if that decision was worth it or if I'll end up wishing I never accepted the first ride home.

"No, it didn't. And while I'm sorry that jackass hurt you, I'm glad you wound up here," he says, and the genuine words are enough to snap me out of my thoughts.

My cheeks heat again, but I don't duck my head this time. I let him see my blush and pray he doesn't turn away from it. When his eyes drift over my face, so focused yet soft at the same time, I swallow, and they follow the movement.

My breathing changes beneath the intensity of his stare, turning to sharp, quick inhales and uneven exhales. A new sense of tension yanks at my chest, like a cord has been hooked to the both of us and is shrinking in size, tugging us closer and closer. I want to lean into that tug, but does he?

"Happy I wound up in Cherry Peak or right here?" I whisper.

His eyes turn from soft to sharp so quickly I stop breathing altogether. I wouldn't mind if he cut me with that stare as long as he kissed the wounds afterward.

"Both," he says, voice low and deep.

My eyebrow twitches, begging to lift and for me to say some teasing remark, but I can't. Not when I want to crawl over the stupid centre console between us and plop myself into his lap. And certainly not when we're interrupted by the shrill sound of my phone ringing.

The majority of the tension is gone after the second ring, but some lingers, as if a promise to return.

I find my phone in my jacket pocket and take a steadying breath before answering the call.

"Hello?" God, I sound like I've just run a half marathon.

"Anna! I know you're already out front—please tell Brody good morning for me, by the way—but I've got some surprise family friends stopping into town today and have moved all of our clients around, so I don't need any stylists on shift," Wanda explains.

"Oh! Okay, I'm good for work tomorrow, though?"

"Yes. I'm sorry I didn't let you know sooner, but I didn't know before a half hour ago."

"Don't apologize. I'll never turn down a free day off."

I sense Brody's attention and flash him a small smile. He wasted his time bringing me today, but I won't apologize for the time I got with him.

"You're my favourite. Thank you, and I'll see you tomorrow."

"See you tomorrow. Bye, Wanda."

Tucking my phone away, I say, "Turns out Wanda doesn't need me today. She's got surprise family friends arriving."

Interest flares in his eyes. "Really? Did she say who?"

"Your reaction is making me believe the rumours are true."

A rough laugh. "Maybe they are, maybe they're not. Want me to take you back home, then?"

"Obvious deflection, Brody, but I'll let it go. Under one condition."

The idea springs to life so quick I almost miss it.

"What's what?"

My lips pull into a mischievous grin. "Take me to work with you."

22

Brody

As if I could turn Anna down when she flipped those damn doe eyes on me. I think I'd give her just about anything she wished for if she looked at me like that again.

I'm so fucked.

"I've never been to a ranch before. You'll have to tell me what I should and shouldn't do," she says once we've turned out of town toward the ranch.

I wasn't expecting this kind of excitement from her. Sure, she clearly wanted to go, but there's a genuine excitement to experience what I do every day in her attitude that I'm floored by. I've never taken a girl home to the ranch before, and I'm more comfortable with the idea of Anna there than I thought I'd be. I want her to get to know me more, and this might be the best way to make that happen.

"Alright, for one, you'll want to watch where you step so you don't end up ankle-deep in cow shit."

Come to think of it, the nice winter boots on her feet are an absolute no go. Hopefully, she's close enough to my grandmother's shoe size so we can steal a pair for her today.

Anna makes a sound of agreement in her throat. "What else?"

"If my grandmother offers you lunch, accept it. Feeding others is her love language."

A pause, as if she's thinking that one through. "I haven't had anyone cook for me in years."

Disbelief barrels into me. "What?"

"Family dinners aren't really a thing in my family. They never have been," she answers sheepishly.

"Not even with your sister?"

"My sister moved to Ottawa a few years back, and I've always been the one cooking for her and her family when they visit."

"Your mom still lives in Vancouver, though, right?"

I can't help but keep looking for a valid reason as to why this woman has been lacking such a sense of family in her life. I may have only had my grandparents for most of my life growing up, but they were more than enough. Family time was always a priority for them.

"Yes, she does. But when she remarried, it was like she was born again. Suddenly, she wanted to travel and live her life in a way she couldn't when she was tied to my dad. I refuse to be selfish with her when she dealt with a man like him for decades. So no, we don't do family dinners, and yes, she might be gone on a majority of the holidays, but I'm happy for her," Anna explains. The soft note in her voice makes it hard not to believe her.

"Well, one thing you shouldn't do today is tell that to my grandmother. She'll damn near adopt you, and you'll never be free of us again," I say, trying to lighten the suddenly serious mood. "You'd be wishin' you never had to have another family dinner in your life."

"Somehow, I don't think that would be such a bad thing."

The Steele Ranch gate comes into view, and I flash her a grin, feeling like a damn lucky guy knowing she's about to venture into my world. It's hard to focus on the road when she spots the gate and gasps, awestruck at something as simple as some iron and steel. It's nothing in comparison to the ranch itself, especially not in the summertime. Life dealt us an unfair hand with having her first time here being in the dead of winter.

"Welcome to Steele Ranch, Anna. It's a lot more than meets the eye," I say.

"How big is it?"

"About thirty thousand acres, give or take a few."

Again, her mouth falls open. "That's massive."

"We don't use all of it." Nearly all of it, but still.

"So, you just leave some of it barren?"

I nod, turning the truck through the open gate. The drive up to the house is short, the original Steele generation of ranchers having built it closer to the road to try and help the land not appear so overwhelming to newcomers. Nobody knows if it actually has that effect, but I'd guess not. It doesn't take more than a glance past the house to see the true size of the ranch.

"Most of it is just roaming space for the cattle. I'm not the best person to ask regarding the ins and outs of anything outside of the equipment, stables, and simple chores. I never took an interest in learning much about the cows once they grow from calves."

Much to my grandfather's disappointment. My lack of involvement was the first sign that he was going to need to find someone else to take over for him. For as long as I can remember, as soon as someone started talking about calving season, my attention drifted elsewhere.

"My grandfather would be a better teacher if you chose to learn more. My knowledge is limited to the basics," I add.

Anna's stare is inquisitive enough that I can't help but wonder what she's thinking. "How did your lack of interest go over with your grandfather?"

I blow out a long breath. "About as well as you'd think."

"I'm sorry."

"Don't be. We make it work. I'm still hopin' that my time home will help start to mend our relationship."

"How's it going so far?"

I chuff a laugh. "Not great."

"Will he care that I'm here today?"

"No. He'll probably be too surprised that I've brought anyone here in the first place to worry about who."

Even if he did have a problem with it, it wouldn't change anything. I want her here. That's all that does matter.

I glance across the cab and catch her smile before she looks out the window. Movement on the left has me tearing my eyes away from her. An onyx horse trots alongside the truck, its rider sitting atop him wearing a matching hat and a heavy winter jacket. My grandfather leans forward on his saddle, looking into the truck and quirking a brow at me before I park in front of the house.

"Is that him?" Anna asks.

"Yep," I mutter. "Seems like you'll get a sooner introduction than I planned."

She doesn't appear put off by that. No, her excited grin is anything but put off.

"Let's go," she urges, clapping her hands on her thighs.

I bite back a smile and do as she says. Once I step out of the truck, I face my grandfather, expecting to find annoyance on his worn features but instead find curiosity.

"Your grandma was right" is all he says before taking another look into the truck and adding, "Go on, then. Don't leave her waitin'."

It's only then that I realize Anna's waited for me to come open her door. Pride swims in my chest at that, even if it's more likely that she simply waited for me to open the door to avoid another one of my scoldings. It still fills me with a strong sense of male satisfaction.

It's been weeks since I've heard my grandfather laugh in my presence, and as I round the hood of the truck, the rough sound of it takes me aback.

"What?" I call out.

He shrugs a shoulder and readjusts his grip on Kip's reins. "Nothin'. There's a list of jobs for you on the kitchen counter. It shouldn't take you long with a second set of hands."

"Alright. Grandma inside?"

"Yup. She'll be excited to see your new friend again."

The way he says it has me shaking my head despite the buzz beneath my skin. "Don't get started. I'll have to hear enough of it inside."

"You gonna let me meet her?"

"Will you scare her off?"

His mouth flattens. "Does she need scarin' off?"

"No."

"Then no. I won't."

I tip my chin and finally open the passenger door. Anna's worried expression has my stomach sinking.

"Everything okay?"

"Yeah, he's just surprised to see you. Are you up for meetin' him first? I know it's kind of throwing you in the deep end, but—"

Her hand on my arm has my brain failing to form words. I gulp, ensnared by the warmth in her pretty brown eyes and the comfort a single touch from her can evoke.

Not only can I not form words, but I can't form a single thought other than Anna, Anna, Anna.

"It doesn't matter to me when I meet everyone. I'm just happy to be here with you."

With me.

I don't let myself think twice about my next move. Covering the hand she has placed on my bicep with mine, I give it a squeeze before linking our fingers. I shift our hands to the centre of my chest and hold her stare, grateful for the first time that she opted not to put her mittens on. I like the feeling of her bare skin against mine, the softness far too addicting.

The corners of her lips tug into a delicate smile. "You should probably let go of my hand first, though. You'll be introducing me in an entirely different way if you don't."

"One introduction would probably be better than two," I say, mentally kicking myself in the ass the moment the words are out.

They're unfair. Unfair and premature. Whatever it is that's going on between us is temporary. She's in Cherry Peak to stay, and I'm planning on leaving. Sooner or later, we'll have to say goodbye.

Pulling her into my life by bringing her here was already a big decision that I'll probably grow to regret later. But anything more than this and we'll leave this town in rubble.

So why can't I stop touching her? Why does her goddamn presence make me feel more awake than I have been for the past few years? I don't think I'll have the time to get all of the answers I need.

Especially when I'm keeping the other half of myself hidden from her, withholding the truth about who I'm labelled under in her phone. I have to tell her soon. Preferably today so I can stop carrying this weight around whenever we're together.

I release her hand, forcing a smile that I hope doesn't look as fake as it feels.

"Let's go, then, Cowboy," she teases, tucking her hands into her pockets.

My jacket looks better on her than it ever did on me, and I grit my teeth when one passing glance over her body is enough to turn me rock solid.

I lead her toward my grandfather, subconsciously drifting a hand across her lower back. My spine straightens when he swings off Kip and takes his first real look at her, his eyes slightly narrowed. It's not an abrasive look he gives her, but it's not warm either. I knew it wouldn't be; I can only hope she did too.

"Wade Steele," he introduces himself, extending his hand for her to shake.

She grips his hand in a tight shake. "Annalise Heights, but you can call me Anna."

"Nice to meet you, Anna. Welcome to Steele Ranch. I hope my boy gave you a bit of a run of the land before you got here."

The term of endearment has my chest tightening. "I told her enough."

"Why don't you head inside and say hello to my wife. Last I heard, you made quite the first impression on her. She'll want to get you out of those boots before you ruin 'em out here."

Anna looks down at her boots before meeting Grandpa's waiting stare. "You make a good point." Her eyes flick to me. "Guess we should be getting a move on, then."

I shift closer to her before turning to Grandpa. "Call me if you need anythin'."

He nods curtly before swinging back onto Kip's back and saying, "Was nice to meet you, Anna. Hope to see you around here a bit more."

There's a double meaning there, and I don't miss it.

He hopes to see us both around here a bit more.

23

Annalise

BRODY IS GOING TO GIVE ME WHIPLASH.

At this point, I'm considering buying him a thermometer for Christmas so I'll be able to tell in advance whether he's planning on being hot or cold.

One moment, I'm hoping my breath doesn't stink because I'm sure he's going to kiss me, and the next, he's putting so much distance between us that it's a wonder I can hear him speak over it. It makes it worse that I'm pretty sure I know what's creating these sudden changes in him.

Either he's constantly reminding himself that we're doomed if we wind up falling for one another, or he's just genuinely a misleading tool. I'd say it's option number one, but with my history with men, maybe he'll wind up disappointing me in the worst way.

If I'm right, though, I need to do something about it. I refuse to be the woman I was with Stewart. I'm not going to let opportunities pass me by because I'm scared of getting hurt or hiding behind the glamour of safety.

Because that's what it was with Stewart. Safe. We became something comfortable. A relationship I thought was sturdy enough to carry me forever and not one that made my heart jolt or my stomach fill with butterflies. I don't ever want to go back to that life.

I want banter and new adventures and thoughtful gestures that have my cheeks burning from smiling. Even if it's temporary, Brody gives me those things. I'd like to think that I give him those things too.

There's no timeline for someone to get over a heartbreak, but I'd like to think I've done pretty alright so far, even if it's only been a couple of months. My healing has been slow and steady, and I've learned more about myself than I have in the last decade. I don't think that growth is going to stop here either. My future is too bright for that. Wanting to see where this connection with Brody takes me doesn't seem like such a bad idea.

The heat from the palm pressed to my back as we step into the house has me even more confident that I'm right where I want to be.

The interior of the farmhouse is almost exactly how I pictured it from the outside. Warm wood floors, bookshelves galore with clutter on every shelf, and mismatched rugs spread throughout the spacious entryway. I've never seen so many shoe racks. They're pushed against every wall, and while they're fairly bare now, I can only expect that will change come lunchtime. The warm yellow lighting even makes the space feel cozier instead of outdated like it usually would.

Brody shuts the door behind us, hangs his brown hat on a hook on the wall, and then steps up to linger at my back. His body heat slams into me. I ache to lean into it and dare him to pull away again, but on the off chance he doesn't, I don't trust what I'd do.

Footsteps carry into the entry from further in the house before a familiar face appears around the corner. Mrs. Steele takes one look at me and beams. It's a welcome that I wasn't expecting but greedily accept.

"Annalise!" she sings, arms already open.

I laugh and step into the embrace. Just like the first time we met, I notice her strength first and then her comforting cinnamon scent. It's easy to tell that she's a woman who doesn't turn up her nose at hard work. To be married to a man like Mr. Steele, that seems about right.

"It's nice to see you again. I hope I'm not intruding," I say.

She pulls back but holds me at arm's length, taking me in from head to toe. "Never! I saw you speaking to my husband from the front window and was just twiddling my thumbs impatiently, waiting to greet you properly."

"By saw us, you mean that you were spying," Brody pipes up.

His grandmother releases me just long enough to wave him off. "Let me get you in a proper pair of boots and a new jacket. We can't risk you ruining your perfectly nice things out there. What size are your feet?"

"I was already planning on getting her those things, Grams," Brody says.

"What you should have done was taken her out this morning and bought her her own pair of boots," she sasses.

I swallow a laugh at the ease with which she scolds him. "I don't think I'd get enough use out of a pair of my own."

She gapes at me, offended. "Nonsense." Flitting her eyes to her grandson, she adds, "Tell me she'll be here often. Don't you tease me, boy."

"Don't look at me. It's Anna you should be threatening." Brody's fingers slip beneath the bottom hem of my jacket, tracing the waistband of my leggings. The shiver that racks through me is immediate, and one sneaking glance up at him exposes his smirk.

I try to shove the touch to the back of my mind and focus on Mrs. Steele. Watching the space between Brody and me like a hawk, that woman nearly splits her cheeks with a smile.

"Something tells me I shouldn't worry. You'll be back, my sweet. But let's worry about right now. Boots!" she exclaims before dashing toward the double doors belonging to the entryway closet.

The next few minutes are spent with me sitting on a long bench and Mrs. Steele shoving old cowboy boots into Brody's arms as he kneels in front of me and slips them on one by one. My cheeks grow hotter with each brush of his fingers against the arch of my foot—which I happen to think he's doing intentionally now—until I'm positive they might very well catch on fire.

His stupidly handsome smirk has never been more prominent as of right now. I'm close to giving him a mouthful of old leather.

"How do those feel?" he asks, sounding *far* too arrogant for my liking.

I wiggle my toes inside the boots and nearly moan at the comfort. As opposed to the boots Poppy lent me and the first few pairs Mrs. Steele had me try, these ones don't clinch at the widest part of my foot. They fit snug, yet not too snug.

"They're perfect," I tell them both.

Brody cups my calf just above the top of the boot in his large hand, his eyes transfixed on my feet. My skin begins to itch with nerves, but I stay quiet, hoping that he'll break through whatever he's thinking right now.

Does he hate them? Do I look ridiculous?

He squeezes my calf before finally dragging his eyes up to meet mine. They're dilated, the blue deeper and darker than usual. A shudder works through me at what that could possibly mean.

"Do they look okay?" I ask softly, not hiding the tremor of doubt in my tone.

He huffs a laugh, shaking his head slightly. "I've never seen anyone pull off a pair of boots so well."

I roll my eyes to hide the effect that compliment has on me. "Maybe I'll wear them every day, then."

Slowly, he slides his hand up behind my knee, curling and digging his fingers into the sensitive muscle. A whimper gets stuck in my throat, and I ache to press my thighs together when I begin to throb between them.

"Please." It's a guttural word, hardly more than a groan.

I go to pull his hand from my leg, unable to take any more of this before I jump his goddamn bones, when a horrible screeching sound breaks through the thick tension between us. Flinching, he removes his hand himself and pushes to his feet. After running his fingers through his hair, he plucks his hat from the hook and drops it back on his head.

Mrs. Steele comes rushing back from wherever she slipped off to during the past few moments. "You'd better get out there and see what that was."

I push to my feet at the same time Brody says, "Sounds like someone braked too hard and slid. Shouldn't be anythin' serious. Call me if you need anythin', okay?"

The old woman kisses her grandson's cheek in answer. After tucking a piece of paper into his jacket pocket, she flashes me a soft smile and disappears again, leaving the two of us alone.

Once Brody's handed me a thicker jacket and we've stepped outside, I say, "I expect the best Steele Ranch tour that was ever given while you tell me all of your deepest and darkest secrets."

"You don't hold punches," he replies.

"Nope. The old Anna did, but not this one. I think I've about had it with holding my punches."

"Are you a lot different now than you were before you got here?"

I think about my answer for a minute, wanting to make sure I've collected my thoughts. "In some ways, yes. I'm still me, but depending on who you ask, I might be a better or worse version. I've always tried to speak my mind, but I was engaged to a man who tried to stifle that quirk of mine. It's quite frustrating to think back on all the negatives in my past relationship and the fact I didn't leave sooner."

Brody keeps his expression deceptively blank as he takes my

hand and helps me down the porch steps. I didn't need the help, but I don't think that matters to him.

"I think love makes people do crazy things," he says, that damn steadying hand returning to my back as we start down a flattened snow path. "Careful, it's a bit slick this mornin'."

I heed his warning and watch my step. "Have you ever been in love?"

"In high school."

"Ooh, high school sweethearts, huh?"

"I suppose so, yeah," he hums.

"What happened?"

He exhales heavily. "Young love hardly ever works out. She never understood why I'd want to leave this place, and I didn't understand why she would want to stay forever. I was a stubborn kid who thought he deserved better than to stick it out here forever."

"Does that stubborn kid think differently now?"

"If you're askin' if I'd go back in time and stay instead of leave, the answer would be no. Not for her, not for anyone. I've always loved music, and gettin' the chance to make a career out of it changed my life. For better and for worse."

"It takes courage to stand by your decisions. Especially when you know the repercussions of them," I say.

"Hurtin' those you love with those decisions still hurts like a mother, though."

"Is that woman still in Cherry Peak, then? The high school sweetheart?"

"Last I heard, she moved out East with a husband and a van full'a kids. People change as life goes on, even those so sure they won't."

I nod, reading his expression for any sign of disappointment that she's gone, but find none. My relief is instant.

"I never did learn how your career started," I say, switching gears.

He looks at me, an eyebrow lifted. "Are you telling me that you didn't Google search me the night we met?"

"As a matter of fact, I was far too pissed at you to spend my night researching you."

His laugh is rich and warm. "Fair enough. I actually met Reggie, the head producer at the record label, when I was performin' in a small pub in Edmonton one night. There was sort of a weird talent show thing happenin', and we had no idea that this major producer was going to be there. But he was, and he loved my voice. Told me I had what it takes to succeed in the music industry, and the rest is history. I've really liked workin' with him so far."

"Maybe it's Reggie who I have to blame for your ego, then," I tease, bumping our shoulders. "He was right, though."

"Yeah? I like to think so."

"Clearly enough people think that, or you wouldn't be where you are now."

"You mean back at home livin' with my grandparents while I heal from a workplace injury?"

I frown at the ground. "No. I mean that you're incredibly successful and doing what you love. How many people get to say that?"

His jaw tenses, but not in anger. More like frustration or grief, maybe. "Do you do what you love, Anna?"

The question takes me aback. "I don't know if there's anything that I love doing as much as you love music, but I'm happy."

"Good. I'm glad."

The further we walk down the path, the more of the ranch I can see. The towering stable on our right-hand side is in pristine condition, not a chipped plank of dark wood in sight. The sliding door in front is shut while the one along the side is open, allowing the handfuls of horses to roam freely into the metal pen. My heart leaps to my throat when I spot two babies playing chase while the older horses linger at the other end, watching.

"Oh, my god," I breathe. I swivel off the path and turn to face Brody as I walk backward toward the barn. "Can we start the tour here, please? I haven't seen a horse up close since middle school, and even that was from behind a fence."

A hard-to-read emotion flickers across his face before he takes a tentative step toward me. He glances at the barn and swallows so hard his throat bobs.

"You sure you don't want to see anythin' else first?"

"Are you allergic to horses or something?" I ask, narrowing my eyes.

"No. God help a rancher who's allergic to horses."

"Soooo?"

"Fine," he says on an exhale. Waving toward the barn, he nods for me to go ahead. "The horses inside the stable are either still foals weaning off their mothers or the ones we use on a consistent basis."

"Does that mean your horse is inside? You do have one, right?"

"Yes." It's a stiff word.

My curiosity has me looking at him over my shoulder as I stop at the door. I itch to pull it open, but despite my excitement, I wait for him to do it.

He stands right behind me and reaches beside my head to grip the steel handle. With a white-knuckled hold on it, he pulls it open with little effort, the bicep at my ear flexing in the most delicious way.

I push down the burst of arousal and spin, turning into his chest. My palms meet his chest as I create the slightest bit of distance and tip my head back to stare into his eyes. They're already on me, the weight of them like a soft blanket, warm and reassuring.

"If you don't want me in here, please just say so," I tell him, wetting my dry lips. "I don't want to overstep."

The brim of his hat falls to cover his brows, and I don't think twice before reaching up and pushing it out of the way, admiring the velvet feel of it between my fingertips. His breath catches, and a breath later, he grabs my waist, simply holding me there. I stay still, not wanting to spook him again.

His fingers flex a second before I'm tugged a bit closer, our bodies nearly flush. "Meetin' the horses will make you happy, right?"

"Yes," I whisper, the moment too delicate for anything louder.

"Then that's what we'll do."

Appreciation fills me. It's like this man wants nothing more than to see me smile. How was I ever supposed to keep him at a distance? It almost feels like a trick question.

"Lead the way, Cowboy."

24

Brody

A LONG, NEEDY WHINNY CUTS THROUGH THE AIR, AND I SLOWLY release Anna's waist before stepping back and looking at the second pen on my right. A familiar set of brown eyes dredges up a decade of memories I've long since hidden away.

I haven't been in the stable since the last time I was home months ago, but it's been much, much longer since I've spent any real time in it. Panic claws at my throat as I hold Sky's stare and consider shackling myself to the wall to keep from going over to her like I ache to do. The recognition in her eyes is a sledgehammer to my gut.

She waves her head side to side, whinnying again, louder this time. Her golden mane flies with the movement, and my fingers begin to shake, the only physical sign that I'm struggling to restrain myself. Grief hits me in a wave that dares to sweep my feet out from beneath me.

"Oh, you're so pretty," Anna coos, stepping up to Sky's gate and resting her hands on top of it. "Can I pet her?"

"Yeah." The word is sticky. I clear my throat and bring back up the wall I've let down. "Her name's Sky."

Anna focuses all her attention on my horse but doesn't make

a move toward her. It strikes me then that she's waiting for proper instructions. *This is a first for her, idiot.*

"Extend your arm to her and let her smell the back of your hand," I say.

She does, and it takes Sky less than a breath to decide Anna's a worthy friend. Sky presses her white-striped nose into Anna's palm, and her following laugh is nothing short of giddy. Something tugs at my chest as I witness the automatic ease between the two of them, but I continue to keep my distance.

"Hi, Sky. You're a sweetie, aren't you? Yes, you are," Anna murmurs to the horse, continuing to let Sky rub her muzzle into her hand.

I drift toward to her, unable to ignore the comfort that appears when she's close. "You can scratch her neck."

"Will you show me where?" she asks.

It isn't a completely innocent question. Anna's too observant to have missed the way I haven't gotten as close to Sky as she has or why I haven't made a move to touch her when clearly, she wants me to.

I can't speak past the rock in my throat. Instead, I lean into Anna's body and lift my arm alongside hers, watching as Sky steps as close to the gate as she can and greedily shoves her face toward us. Anna giggles at the touch, and then I'm taking her hand and resting it on Sky's neck, just below her bright blond mane. My hand is so much bigger than hers, and as I press it against the thick muscle, my fingers reach further, brushing soft, short hair.

Dropping my chin to rest on the crown of Anna's head, I inhale deeply, shutting my eyes. I guide Anna's hand down Sky's tan-coloured neck, repeating the motion over and over until it stops feeling so foreign to the both of us. When I feel the thin, silky hairs of her mane tickle the top of my hand, I open my eyes to see that Sky's turned her head to give us more access.

She's always been greedy for affection, but after months without seeing me, I can only imagine that need has multiplied.

"She's yours, isn't she?" Anna asks softly.

A curt nod. "Since I was fourteen."

"I wanted a horse when I was little, but it wasn't exactly possible in the city."

I'm grateful for the small change in topic. "Your parents never put you in lessons or anythin'? I'm sure there were a few places you could have gone around Vancouver."

A pause. "I'm actually allergic to most animals, dogs and cats especially, but my parents didn't want to risk horses either."

"You're allergic to animals, and you insisted I take you here?" I jerk my head back and try to pull her away from Sky, but the stubborn woman shakes her head and plants her feet to the ground.

"Oh, relax. I got more allergy tests done a few years back, and most animals are fine—including horses. Even if they weren't, I only get an itchy rash when I come into contact with them. It's nothing too serious," she explains. "Are you allergic to anything?"

Her confidence allows me to begin to relax. "No. At least not that I know of."

Sky whinnies again before butting her nose against our hands and moving back a few steps. I stifle a laugh at her obvious attitude and take Anna's hand in mine, holding it at her side.

I meet Sky's stare and shake my head. "We're not coming in today."

If horses could roll their eyes, she would have. The breath she blows before stomping her front hoof into the hay is just as bad.

"Has she always been so sassy?" Anna asks, grinning at her.

"From the moment I got her as a foal."

"Huh. I bet that was good for you." She smirks at Sky. "You're probably half-responsible for his good manners."

My mouth curves ever so slightly. "You're probably right."

Realizing she's not going to get what she wants, Sky comes back, hanging her head over the gate for us to pet. Anna takes advantage of the chance, but I put my hands in my pockets.

I'm not ready to touch my horse again yet. Just once was more than enough to unravel every defense I'd spent years putting in place.

"Let me introduce you to the foals. You can spoil Sky with more affection later."

Anna glances over her shoulder, and whatever she sees on my face has her agreeing without pause. With a soft parting pat on the neck, she says goodbye to Sky and follows me toward the open door leading to the outdoor pen.

We pass both empty stalls and ones with horses inside. Most of the stalls inside the stable are for new moms with their foals and the work horses we need kept close. The rest are out in the field behind the stable, able to roam wherever and whenever they please. Kip's stall is the one beside Sky's, his reins and coat missing from the hook on his gate as opposed to the ones hung on Sky's.

Grandpa tried to tell me all about Sky when I got back, but I ignored him, and suddenly, I'm wishing I hadn't. Too many questions linger in my head, from how often she's been ridden since I've been gone to who's been mucking her stall.

I've neglected her over the past decade—long before I took off to Nashville—and I'll never forgive myself for that, even if it still hurts too much to make it right.

She deserves better than me, but she's mine.

"Do I do the same things with these horses that I did with Sky?" she asks.

"Pretty much. Start with the mares and then go to the foals. If they'll even pay you any mind. These two have been serious pains in the asses these past few weeks."

She snorts. "They're foals, not human toddlers."

"They may not be pitchin' fits, but they're just as rambunctious. Steph has been telling anyone who will listen about these two specifically. They were birthed nearly one after the other last spring and have been inseparable since. Their energy is unmatched, hence the chasing earlier," I explain.

Anna's steps falter, her next words sharp despite her effort to appear unbothered. "Who's Steph?"

It's an effort not to appear smug at her jealousy. "The ranch employs two horse trainers. Steph is one, and Randy is the other."

She nods. "That makes sense."

"Would you like a full list of employees, sweetheart? I can name all the women for you," I purr.

She scowls and swats at my arm. "You're an ass."

"Yet you like me enough to get jealous."

"Nobody said anything about jealousy. I certainly didn't."

"You didn't need to. It was all in the tone."

Her brows fly up. "The tone? Well then, read the tone in this, Cowboy—"

Whether it be from seeing her connect with Sky, or wearing those damn boots like she was born to, or even just every moment spent with her over the past few weeks combined, something gives inside of me.

Before she can finish ripping me a new one the way only she seems able to, I'm turning her to face me and taking her cheeks in my hands, placing my mouth on hers.

She stands frozen for a heartbeat, but then she thaws for me. Leaning up on her toes, she parts her lips, and I groan at my first taste of her. Soft and sweet, like cotton candy without the stomach ache.

I drift a hand behind her ear and thread my fingers through her hair, using the hold to tip her head back further and deepen the kiss. She swipes her tongue along my bottom lip, and I let her explore, close to begging her to do whatever she wishes with me.

Our toes touch, both of us having drifted closer as if pulled by an invisible string. We're flush together, and the rapid rise and fall of her chest has me throbbing behind the zipper of my jeans. I'm breathing just as frantically as she is, but fuck if I'm willing to end the kiss so soon because of it.

In this moment, it doesn't matter that this isn't forever. Not when the right now is so damn good.

Her hands find the front of my jacket, taking two fistfuls of it and using it for leverage so she doesn't lose balance. I know I need to pull back, but it takes every ounce of willpower to do it.

Dragging the tip of my nose up the length of hers, I inhale the sweet scent of her perfume. She pants against my lips, and I do the same.

"Better?" I murmur.

"Better?" she echoes.

"Are you still jealous?"

Her eyes snap open, and I chuckle when they roll. "You couldn't help yourself, could you?"

"When it comes to you, that's the one thing I can't seem to do."

25

Annalise

I'VE NEVER UNDERSTOOD WINTER WEDDINGS.

They're cold, there's no colour outdoors for pictures, and travelling can oftentimes be a pain in the ass. But I suppose when you have money overflowing from your wallet like most NHL players do, the season with which you decide to get married doesn't really matter. Money won't fix the temperature, but it can certainly buy greenery and compensate unexpected travel expenses.

In all honesty, over the past few weeks, I'd completely forgotten about the wedding Braxton's forcing me to attend. Between work, pole, and spending as much time as possible with Brody, I feel like my life has been moving on three-times speed. December is halfway through, and with it, I'm facing my first unforgivably cold winter and a trip to Ottawa for a wedding I'm terrified to attend.

I haven't been back to Steele Ranch since that first and only time last week, but that hasn't stopped me from hanging on to Brody every chance I can get. I'm surprised he hasn't gotten annoyed with driving me around yet.

We haven't kissed since we were in the stables either . . . despite how much I've hinted at doing it again. A woman's pride can only take so much gentle rejection before she backs off. To make matters worse, he's made me so damn horny with his lingering touches and sweet gestures lately that I've had to recharge my vibrator three times this *week*.

It's cruel, and I've begun wondering just what exactly I must have done in my past life to deserve this level of teasing in my present one.

Having Brody around on the regular has also all but completely cut off my conversations with Bo. It didn't take me long after spending the day with Brody at his family ranch to confirm my hunch, and I refuse to keep up the ruse. The two men are one and the same, but for some reason, he's known and hasn't made an effort to tell me.

Maybe the guilt from keeping his conclusions to himself has kept him from kissing me again. Something tells me I'm not far off. I could tell him myself, but a stubborn part of me wants him to do it. He realized first, after all.

"You look even better in that dress in person," Braxton muses.

Scrunching her curly hair in her product-coated hands, she continues gawking at me in the mirror. My older sister is gorgeous, so hearing compliments from her never fails to hit harder than any others.

The master bathroom in her and Maddox's new house is magazine-worthy, and I'm still struggling to pick my jaw up off the floor at the overwhelming sight of it. It's a white marble palace with a spa tub triple the size of my regular tub, a stained-glass window above it, and a long vanity with two sinks and a cabinet built between them. The shower looks like it could fit ten people. I've already made Braxton promise to let me use it at least once before I go back home.

When she first told me Maddox was planning on hopefully finishing his career in Ottawa, I knew it was only a matter of time before they upgraded from their first house to their forever one. This place is perfect for them, and I'm so happy for my sister. She deserves everything she has. A beautiful son, successful career, and a husband who would lie on hot coals just to form a bridge for her to walk across them.

"With such a beautiful date, it's only fair I try my best," I reply.

"You'll have to be the one to break that to Maddox. Poor guy thinks I'm going to the wedding with him."

I scoff, dragging my fingernail along the edge of my bottom lip to clean up any lipstick. "As if."

"That's what I'm saying. My sister is in town, so obviously we're going to be attached at the hip."

"I missed you like crazy," I admit, turning to rest my back against the counter. Braxton leans a hip against it, her eyes going soft.

"I missed you more. Have you spoken to Mom recently?"

"Not for a few weeks. Last we talked, she and Cliff were waiting to board their flight to Arizona. Have you talked to her?"

Braxton twists her mouth. "Not since around the time you did. What about Dad? I got a damn email from him last week that said he wanted our new address to send Christmas gifts for Liam."

"I hope you told him to piss off," I grumble.

"Close. I told him to send them to Maddox's parents' house and we'd collect them when we see them over the holidays."

Our dad has never met my nephew, and he never will. His want to send him gifts is just a way to assert his unwanted presence in Braxton's life. He's undeserving of that honour.

"I'm sorry. Don't let him spoil your mood. He's so not worth that."

Braxton straightens her shoulders and pushes away from the counter. The knee-length yellow dress she chose for the wedding fits her curves effortlessly and makes her bright blue eyes pop. I fiddle with the gold bangle on my wrist and bite at the inside of my lip.

"Don't think that all this talking about our parents means I don't want to hear about you. I'm still curious about all of these new friends and the way they keep you too busy to call me as often as I'd like," she says, pushing a sparkling diamond stud into her earlobe.

I smooth the silky material of my dress over my stomach with a laugh. "Are you a little jealous, Brax?"

Her eyes narrow on me. "Me? Jealous? Never."

"Mmhmm. Well, I think you'd really like Bryce and Poppy. Bryce reminds me of Adalyn sometimes."

Maddox's little sister, Adalyn, is as outgoing as they come, and I've enjoyed every moment I've spent with her in the past. There aren't many people in Braxton's life that I don't know, especially those in her husband's family. Considering Maddox and Braxton were childhood best friends, I was around his family quite often.

"And they've actually got you to join a pole class?"

"Is it really that hard to believe?"

"Not because I don't think you'd succeed at it. There are very few things you wouldn't succeed at. You've just never done something like that before. I like it for you, Anna."

I smile softly. "Thank you. It's definitely out of my comfort zone, but I think that's why I like it. It makes me feel powerful."

"You *are* powerful. Maybe I'll have to give a pole class a try sometime."

My brows knit together. "Why? Are you not feeling powerful anymore?"

"We're not talking about me right now. Don't think that if you distract me, I won't keep poking around in your life. There's more than just those two women keeping you occupied," she says pointedly.

I spin, hiding the blush I feel warming my cheeks before leaving the bathroom.

"Annalise! Don't make me chase you."

"I'm just going to put my shoes on." I make a dash into the bedroom and find my black heels waiting on the carpet.

"Uh-huh, and I'm just asking about your secrets, not demanding to hear them all."

"You're terrible."

"Ditto, babes."

The master bedroom is bright and airy, a California king bed beneath a canopy against the wall opposite an electric fireplace. Floor-to-ceiling windows cover the length of one wall, and a set of double glass doors lead out to their private balcony. It almost seems criminal to put the bottoms of my heels on the plush, white carpet, despite them never having been worn outside before.

"Maybe you don't know me as well as you used to," I say, knowing damn well I'm spouting nonsense.

Braxton's harsh laugh tells me she knows it too. "This reaction is just telling me everything I need to know already."

"Perfect! I'll keep my secrets to myself, then."

She pinches the back of my arm and pushes me to sit on the edge of the bed, my heels forgotten. When her hands find her hips, I sigh. "What gives? You never deny me gossip. Especially not boy gossip."

Again, my cheeks flush, and I reach up to cover them with my hands before stopping, remembering the makeup I spent an hour applying. They fall to my lap as I tip my head back and stare at the ceiling.

"I'm a bit out of my depth with this one," I mutter.

When I look forward again, I find Braxton staring at me in disbelief. "What do you mean? You've *never* hidden a guy so hard from me before."

"I'm not hiding him."

"You just left the room in order to keep from talking about him. Is something wrong with him? Did he hurt you?" The protectiveness in her voice rings loud, nearly making me flinch.

I shake my head, exhaling heavily. "It's nothing like that."

"Then explain it to me." She sits beside me and takes my hand in hers. "You can tell me anything. Always."

"You have to promise that you won't be weird."

"I promise."

"Do you know who Brody Steele is?"

A pause. She blinks slowly, lips parting and closing before she manages a nod. "You're kidding."

"I'm dead serious."

"How?"

My heart skips a beat. "He's from Cherry Peak. We met at a bar and got off on a very wrong foot, but now . . . now he's just everything. He's been driving me to and from work every day because I don't feel comfortable enough driving on the winter roads, and on top of that, he's constantly making sure I'm taken care of. We get along so well that it's almost creepy, and he even took me to his family's ranch and introduced me to his grandparents."

I leave out the part about Bo because it would only lead to more questions that I don't have the answers to yet. They're questions I need him to answer face to face.

Her expression gentles alongside her voice. "So, why did you try to hide him?"

"I wasn't hiding him; I just wasn't planning on telling you about him yet," I defend myself. *If ever.*

"That's just as bad. I would have thought you'd want everyone to know about him if he makes you so happy."

My chest tightens as I say, "He's leaving soon. Going back to Nashville. Cherry Peak was only a pit stop for him."

She makes an angry noise in her throat. "I refuse to accept that."

"There's nothing to accept, Brax. It's the truth. And *I've* accepted it."

Braxton drops my hand and shoots to her feet, glaring down at me. A fierce determination lights her eyes. "You know, I waited *three years* to hear that emotion in your voice when talking about Stewart, and I never did. We have one conversation about Brody, and it's already there. That's all I need to know."

"It's not that easy, and you know it. It was never that easy with you and Maddox," I argue.

"Maddox and me were different, and *you* know it."

Fair enough. "Please just let me do this my way."

"Fine."

I arch a brow. "Fine?"

"It'll be easy enough for me to corner him in person and ask him how he feels about you myself."

"What?"

Her smirk is devilish, and my stomach drops. "Didn't you know that he's performing at the wedding tonight?"

26

Brody

"My man!"

The growly shout belongs to an old friend, someone I spent years playing hockey with in Cherry Peak before he was drafted into the NHL. Walker Morales is the starting goalie for the Ottawa Beavertails and, today, a goddamn *husband*.

"All those years apart and you still look like a prepubescent boy," I joke, welcoming him into a tight hug.

He pounds a steady fist against my back, howling a laugh at my weak insult. His thick beard puts any facial hair I can grow to shame. "And you're still a damn country hick. Would it have killed you to leave the hat at home for a day?"

I swipe a finger along the rim of the hat in question, grinning. "Care to be reminded just how much of a country hick you were before the NHL stole you away? And don't talk shit about my hat. Is my suit not enough for you?"

"I get enough of a reminder from my parents. They'll never let me forget my cowboy roots." Walker's smile is loose and wide, a pure, rare breed of happy in his expression. "I'm surprised you didn't show up in jeans and a greasy shirt, honestly. I'll take the suit and the hat. You look good, buddy. Are you sure you can do this today?"

"Wouldn't be here if I wasn't."

It's a little white lie. I shouldn't be here, and my doctor agrees. My first appointment for vocal rehab isn't until next week, and the doc was tied in a million knots when I told him my plans for today. It's a stupid, reckless risk to sing today, but I promised Walker long before my injury that I'd do this for him, and I'm a man of honour. I don't go back on my promises.

It will only be a couple of hours' worth of strain. If I can't do this today, then I might as well stop hoping for a comeback anytime soon. I rehearsed this morning after swallowing a couple of painkillers just in case, and I sounded fine. I *feel* fine. My body is just that. Mine. And I know my limits. I knew them the first time too, but I chose to ignore them. That won't happen again.

"Good to hear it. Have you met the rest of the wedding party?"

"Most of 'em," I say.

The wedding ceremony earlier was an intimate event, and with that, only the bridal party and close family were invited. I used the time they were off tying the knot to prepare for the reception at the hotel ballroom venue. The staff were running around to get everything finished up, and I was grateful for their distraction in case I sounded like a dying animal instead of the Brody Steele everyone is expecting.

Walker's wife is a sweet thing, originally from Ottawa, with a weak French accent I learned she picked up while living in Montreal for a few years growing up. Walker looks at her like she's his lifeline, and I'm happy to note that she watches him in the same way. We may not be as close as we were back in our peewee days, but some friendships you don't lose despite how crazy life gets.

"Good. I hate introductions, and I've had to do enough of them today," Walker says.

"It's all worth it, though, yeah? All of the stress of a wedding?"

"Without a doubt. Was worth it from the moment I saw her walking down the aisle."

I tuck my hands into the pockets of my slacks and lean against the wall of the dressing room the groomsmen used to get ready this morning. There are only a few minutes until the bride and groom have to make their grand entrance into the ballroom and I get called out to sing their first-dance song.

It's always nerve-racking performing in front of people, but I've grown used to the stadiums and festivals. It's rare that I'll have a twisted stomach before a show. Tonight, however, it's in knots.

"I'm surprised you're not off with your new bride already. Aren't you supposed to be joined at the hip now?" I ask teasingly.

"Wanted to check on you first. You're doing us a huge favour tonight."

"It's no skin off my back, man."

"Maybe not, but I still appreciate it."

Sincerity shines in his eyes, and I pat his arm. "Anytime. Now, go find your wife."

"Try not to ruin my first dance, yeah? I won't be able to live it down in the dressing room. I've bragged about you a little too hard leading up to today," he says.

My muscles loosen as I laugh, nodding. "You got it."

"Save me some time tonight to grab a drink, okay? I wanna catch up before you head back to CP."

"You got it."

"I'll see you out there, then, buddy."

Once I'm alone in the room, I pull my phone out and instinctively open my text conversation with Banana. The last text was from over a week ago. It's safe to say that the cat is out of the bag for the both of us.

I've been contemplating how I'm going to bring it up to Anna for too long. This performance was the last thing I was waiting for before doing so.

I didn't piece together that she would be here tonight until a few nights ago when I found myself scrolling through our earlier messages and reread her first text. The mention of the Morales wedding wouldn't have necessarily meant much had it not also been for knowing her sister was married to Maddox Hutton. There is only one Morales wedding starring an Ottawa Beavertail player tonight.

It was hard to keep this knowledge from her, but I needed to be sure about what I was going to do before opening my mouth too soon. Tonight, I'm going to tell her the truth and make her mine. The word *temporary* whispers in the back of my mind like a sick joke, but I ignore it the same way I have been since I decided I wanted her.

You don't meet a woman like Annalise Heights and not make her yours. Especially not when you share the same natural chemistry that we do. The same unadulterated want for one another.

Whether or not she wants to risk it with me is still up in the air. I'm positive that my nerves won't settle until I know her answer. This is my most important performance to date, and the star of my show is completely unaware of her importance.

My ribs constrict as I scroll through our past messages, some old and some recent. Some so fucking funny and laid-back that it makes me completely in awe of my inability to realize it sooner. I met my dream woman *twice* and still took this fucking long to make a move.

What's even harder to believe is that I never knew what I truly looked for in a woman until I met Anna. I didn't know that I wanted a funny city girl with a snarky attitude when annoyed and a fierce passion for helping others. Not only is she fierce, but she's also incredibly easy to talk to. There isn't anything that she wouldn't listen to me talk about, even if I didn't need her to say anything back. But if I did, she would give me the best advice.

One kiss, one taste of her was all it took. Fuck, I'd let her string me along forever if it meant I'd get another one of those.

Someone clears their throat in the doorway, and I lock my phone, slipping it back into my pocket before acknowledging them. Rita keeps her face blank despite the impatience in her eyes. The crow's feet beside them try to tell me that at one time, she smiled often. I haven't gotten the honour of witnessing more than a small handful of those.

"You ready?" she asks, staring down at her cell phone.

For the millionth time since I got back home, I'm contemplating why I keep her as my manager. She's hard-shelled and, more often than not, harsh and cold. Swift Edge Records encouraged the partnership shortly after I signed with the label, and I was too naive to know better.

"I'm ready," I answer her.

"It's good you're doing this, Brody. Videos will hit the internet by tonight, and the world will know that you're ready to come back better than ever."

I scratch at my jaw, noting the thicker facial hair that I've begun to grow. It reminds me of a younger version of myself. I always wanted a beard, but Garrison wasn't a fan, so it disappeared.

"I'm not ready to come back yet. I need a few more weeks."

Finally, her attention lifts from her phone and settles on me. "What do you mean you're not ready?"

"Exactly what it sounds like, Rita. I want more time at home."

"Want or need? Because they are two very different things. Especially in this business," she snarks, her condescending tone scratching along my nerves.

I swipe my tongue along my lips, agitated enough to begin fidgeting. "Both. Reggie told me I had a full three months if I needed it. That time's not up yet."

"Reggie is not your boss."

"He's as much my boss as his son is. I appreciate everything you've done for me, Rita, but you work for me. It would serve you best to remember that."

"That sounds a lot like a threat."

I stiffen further at her attitude. "I didn't mean it as a threat, but don't think that can't or won't change."

Three more weeks isn't enough with Anna, but it's a start. I need that time with her. To really be with her. To show her that maybe, just maybe, this thing between us wouldn't have to come to an end once I leave. It's a hopeful thought but the one I've been contemplating most as of late. There are so many variables in play when it comes to a potential relationship with me outside of Cherry Peak, which is why tonight is so important.

I'm about to welcome her into my world. I just hope to God she doesn't run.

"You have bigger balls than I thought you did," Rita mumbles.

I furrow my brows. "Thanks?"

"I wouldn't take it as a compliment. I'll tell Garrison you need the time, but it'll be him you have to fight this battle with, not me."

"I don't even have doctor sign-off yet. I'm not healthy enough regardless of the fact I want to stay longer."

She digests that, rolling her lips for a moment before saying, "Fine." Her phone pings, and she reads the screen with a nod. "Time to go."

"Any last-minute words of encouragement?" I swallow my panic before it has a chance to surface.

She pins me with a steady gaze that lacks her usual coldness. "You know the songs. Know the pitch. I've never heard you give a bad performance."

I pull my head back slightly, surprised. "Thanks."

"Thank me after you've had a good performance. This is a wedding and not an opening show in New York. Try to remind yourself of that."

If only she knew that having Anna out in the crowd at this wedding feels like a bigger deal than any stadium show I've ever done.

27

Annalise

My leg bounces beneath the table, the lace tablecloth tickling the bare skin of my thigh exposed from the slit in my dress. I can feel the cool breeze of the air conditioning blowing over my shoulders, but the heat beneath my skin doesn't fade like I wish it would.

I haven't been able to tear my eyes from the stage at the head of the ballroom since we arrived at the hotel. The navy and plum colours of the wedding are everywhere, from the gorgeous floral centrepieces and frilly material hung along the length of the head table to the petals on centre stage.

The same centre stage that Brody will be standing on any minute now. My nerves mix with a dull throb of annoyance. He knew I would be here. If he was always meant to be the entertainment for this wedding reception, then he damn well knew once he saw my initial text and pieced together who I was that we would be at the same wedding.

He knew and didn't tell me.

From the moment Braxton told me he would be here, all of my past insecurities flooded back, damn near choking me. Two hours later, I'm still nowhere close to okay.

I hate that I've let myself think negatively, but I'm only so strong. Only so damn brave. I've fought falling into a spiral, and even that took too much energy out of me.

It's obvious to me that I would have wanted to go to this wedding with him had I known that he would be here too. I would have loved being his date, if he'd have wanted that too. Clearly, he didn't want that at all. He didn't want it badly enough that he hid his plans from me.

My first thought was that he was embarrassed of me. That I was only a woman he wanted around when he was at home, away from the spotlight of his normal life. That was the most painful conclusion. It tore me up deep, and the small pulse of pain in my chest as I recall it is proof enough of why I refuse to let myself wander there again.

From what I know of Brody so far, he isn't the type of guy to hide a woman from anyone. I've met both of his grandparents and a handful of Steele Ranch employees. So why the secrecy now?

I swallow the lump in my throat and tap my fingers on the tablecloth, glancing around the table. Our table number has been burned into the wood sign beside the floral centrepiece, and our names have been written out in a gorgeous cursive over thick parchment and laid out on top of our napkins. The decorations are very rustic but with a soft glam vibe that fits really nicely. All in all, it's nice enough that I forgive the bride for her ridiculous wedding dress approval process. It did lead me to Brody, after all.

This is the first wedding I've been to since my sister and Maddox married. I always thought mine would be next. It should have been. But I'm not as devastated by that as I anticipated.

Marriage wasn't for me long before I met Stewart. I was a fool to believe a man had changed my perspective so easily. Accepting his proposal was a moment of weakness after a lifetime of bravery. A desire to be taken care of by someone who I thought wanted to do so for the rest of his life.

Boy, was I wrong.

"You look deep in thought," Braxton says, brushing a strand of my hair behind my ear.

Maddox flexes his arm where it's resting along the back of my sister's chair and strokes her shoulder. "You okay, Little Heights?"

"I'm trying not to run out of here," I tell him honestly.

"Before I get to see you give your man an ass beating? Not allowed," Maddox argues.

I scowl. "He's not my man."

"Does he know that?"

"I'd figure so, considering we're both here dateless."

Braxton tries and fails to hide her giggle in her husband's bicep. "She's going to be beating *your* ass instead if you keep arguing with her."

He smiles sympathetically. "Sorry, Anna, that's Braxton's job."

I scrunch my nose in disgust. "And she can keep it."

"Maybe he just didn't tell you he would be here because he was nervous?" Braxton asks.

I want to tell her that that's most likely not it, but without her knowing the entire story, she wouldn't understand. Plus, we're not alone at this table, and even with our voices quiet, I don't want to risk anyone else overhearing.

"Yeah, maybe," I reply.

Maddox nods toward the stage, anticipation heavy in his features. "I don't think you'll have to wait much longer to find out."

My muscles stiffen as I drag my eyes back to the platform, this time finding it occupied. I stop breathing when Brody grins at the wedding guests and waves at the bride and groom. It's clear there's a relationship there between them with the ease in which they smile back and the groom pats his chest.

I've never been struck stupid by someone's good looks before, but if anyone were to change that, it would be Brody. It's almost hard to look at him for too long without risking getting stuck in his trance. *So handsome it hurts.* It should be a warning given to every person that gets too close.

I've grown so used to seeing him in dirty ranch clothes, but today, he's slipped into a slim-fitting black suit with a plum-coloured tie. The top two buttons of his white dress shirt have been left open in an unsurprising way, but it's the hat on his head that has me trying not to start panting. Instead of his soft brown cowboy hat that I've become accustomed to, he swapped it for one so dark brown it's almost black. It makes his dirty-blond hair stand out, the curls loose and messy beneath it. Even his short beard has grown on me, and I've never been a fan of facial hair.

I trail my eyes down his body and stare at the clean boots on his feet, tugging the corner of my mouth up. I don't know how he managed to convince the bride to allow him to wear those, considering her other crazy outfit rules, but I shouldn't be surprised. He could convince a nun to sin just for the slight glance at his smile.

The guitar slung around his neck by a plum-coloured strap is a new, refreshing sight. I've gotten so used to Brody Steele the rancher/mechanic that sometimes it's hard to remember he's also Brody Steele the country star. One of the quickest-growing musicians on the scene right now, to be exact. There's an entirely new side to him that I have yet to meet, and I guess there's no prolonging that any longer. It's now or never.

I flush from my forehead to my toes once I lift my eyes and find him watching me, a little slip of a smirk transforming his features into something devious. Like he knows something I don't.

Arching a brow in defiance, I mouth, "You are in trouble."

That smirk transforms into a smile that's as close to shy as a guy like Brody is capable of, and then he's mouthing two words back. "I'm sorry."

With a twist of his body, his guitar swings from his back to his front. He holds my stare until the lights begin to dim and a spotlight is shone on the bride and groom. Only then does he turn his attention to them. It's polite in the way someone should be at an event like this, but right now, I don't feel all that polite. All I want to do is stare at him, and even after the MC announces that the newlyweds are having their first dance, I fall into that desire. I tell myself that I don't know the couple personally, as if that's reason enough not to pay them a lick of attention.

The first deep, throaty sound of his voice into the microphone is enough to have me gasping for breath. Plucking lightly at the strings of his guitar, he sings in a tone so soft and warm I want to curl up in it. It's a comfort like I've never known. Or maybe I have, that one time in the stables, so wrapped up in him I couldn't tell up from down. There was only his smell and warmth and touch and this utterly devastating feeling of rightness.

His singing voice is the equivalent of that. Something that feels an awful lot like coming home.

My body sways to the music, a serenade that I wouldn't mind having stuck in my mind on replay every day and night. I don't dare look away from Brody, not for one heartbeat. Finally, when the song trickles to an end, our eyes catch again, and the affection shining so brightly in his is almost too much for my love song–infested brain to comprehend.

One song blends into three, and then the DJ I spotted earlier in the corner of the dance floor takes over—for how long he'll be in charge, I'm not sure—and the guests join the bride and groom. My sister lays a hand on my wrist a moment after a fast-paced throwback song blasts through the room and whispers gentle words of encouragement that have me already up and out of my chair, searching for the man who is no longer onstage.

My heels clack on the dance floor as I slip past the wedding guests watching and laughing while the groomsmen break into a choreographed dance for the bride. I stifle my own laugh at the terrible coordination before slipping out the side door, back into the hotel lobby.

The duo of security guards chatting a few feet to my right pay me little mind as I begin my search. It's pleasantly empty out here, as if the bride and groom reserved the entire hotel for their special night. They probably did. Tonight isn't the night to be interrupted by hockey fans or reporters itching to sell a story to *Sports Weekly*. With Brody here, it probably only made their decision easier. He deserves privacy just as much as they do.

The hotel carpet muffles the sound of my footsteps as I continue down the long stretch of hallway that I hope will lead me to a dressing room of some sort. So far, I've only seen a closed hair salon and what I think must be a bridal boutique.

The sign for the bathrooms appears when I turn the corner, but then I'm being tugged toward one of the two bathrooms, a hand on my waist and another wrapped tight around my front. I'm pulled against a hard body, but before panic can sluice through me, I take a deep pull of woodsy cologne and melt in the arms around me.

"This is the second time you've grabbed me like this. Some would say that's a bit of a creepy habit to have," I say, rolling my lips to hide a smile.

Brody's chest shakes against my back, his laugh vibrating beneath my skin and damn near into my bones. "Only have a habit of grabbin' you like this, sweetheart."

"If you're trying to suck up right now, you've gotta try harder than this."

His chin presses to the back of my head as he nods. "I know. Come with me so we can talk in private."

"Is there a 'please' in there somewhere?" I ask, nipping at the inside of my cheek.

His lips brush the back of my ear, and I shiver, goosebumps decorating my skin. "Please."

"Okay. Alright."

He pushes his shoulder against the door behind him and

leads us inside. It takes more effort than it should to leave the warm hold of his arms, but when I do, I watch him flip the lock on the bathroom door. My stomach lurches with both excitement and nerves, wondering why he felt the need to ensure we weren't interrupted. It must be more than just not wanting a quiet space, right?

He turns back to face me, and I'm not anywhere near prepared to see his blown black eyes taking in the sight of me in this dress. I was hoping he'd like it, but he's already seen it, and I won't lie and say that thought hadn't been messing with my head all day.

"Beautiful, Anna. Fuckin' prettiest thing I've ever seen in my entire twenty-eight years of living. A far cry from just fine," he admits, awe so heavy and clear in his voice that it takes me aback, makes my eyes burn with tears I can't blink away fast enough. The call back to our first messages is too much.

"Don't cry," he says gently, closing the distance I've put between us in a single step, his chest brushing up against mine. Carefully brushing away the wetness beneath my eye without ruining my makeup, he rests his other hand at the curve of my waist, the fit of it perfect.

"You aren't allowed to make me cry from your pretty words when I'm upset with you," I whisper.

His lashes flutter as his eyelids fall to half-mast, the intensity in the blue beneath them fierce and strong. "That's fair. Don't want you to cry anyway. Especially not because of me."

I focus on my breathing as I release a calming exhale. "Why didn't you tell me who you were?"

He doesn't need me to clarify. I would have if he asked, but Brody is a smart man. Without having to read my mind, he knows what I mean.

The warmth of his palm seeps into my cheek as he holds me there, tracing the outline of my lips with his thumb in smooth glides.

"I didn't tell you I was Bo because I was scared. Scared of

what it would mean to open up that final door between us. I thought I needed more time to keep my secrets and hide behind some metaphorical wall of privacy. But you were already knockin' down those walls plank by plank with every one of your sweet smiles and understanding touches. Even that smartass mouth that I want to kiss more often than not had me all twisted up inside. It was only wasted time not takin' that step sooner, on my own. I knew you'd accept me for all I am long before tonight, Anna. You're too good a woman not to."

Emotion balls in my throat, making it impossible to swallow my whimper. It's a soft, quiet sound, but one that emphasizes how much his words mean to me. Pretty words can be just that. Empty and soulless yet beautiful. But sometimes, pretty words can also be those that you reach for in your worst moments, when you need something good to hold on to.

These will be words I hold on to forever.

"And tonight? You could have asked me to come with you. I would have. I'm pretty sure I'd go anywhere with you," I admit, not ashamed of my vulnerability.

Brody leans down and braces his forehead against mine, holding me steadily in place with the hand cupping my cheek. I fight the urge to shut my eyes and soak in this gentle moment, forcing them open and holding his. Blue with grey specks, like clouds cast across a clear summer sky.

"And I'd go anywhere with you. Should have asked you to be my date. I'd have arrived with the prettiest one out there. I'm sorry I didn't. I just knew that if I brought you with me, I would have blurted out the truth without collectin' my thoughts the way I wanted to. It's been torture enough not kissin' you since I watched you handlin' my horse with more care than I've ever seen anyone do other than me. You're a gentle soul, and even Sky knew it. Recognized it on first glance the way I wish I had. I wouldn't have lasted five minutes with you on my arm here without taking your mouth again, and you deserved this moment first. These answers."

Each word is a declaration. A promise without the pinky swear. Maybe tomorrow, I'll wish I had been more stubborn, that I had made him work harder for my forgiveness, but I didn't need some grand gesture. Just honest words and a sincere smile like the one right in front of me.

"I like Sky almost as much as I like you. I'm not sure how I'm supposed to like her more when you go and say such beautiful, honest things like that to me. She's just a horse at the end of the day," I tease, lifting my hand and bringing it to his face, indulging in the feel of the thickness of his beard scraping my palm before sliding it behind his neck, the soft curls there tickling my fingers.

The velvet feel of his hat blocks off the majority of his hair, and when I tuck my fingers beneath it, he seems to get the memo. In a swift movement, he sets the hat down on the counter, giving me free rein to run my fingers through his hair. I succumb to the invitation, threading them through the thick curls without hesitation. My nails scratch at his scalp, pulling a rough sound from his throat.

"And what am I?" he asks, nearly groaning the question.

Digging into the well of my confidence, I answer, "My man."

He answers me by pressing me flat up against his chest, our hearts beating perfectly in time, and kisses me so hard I see stars.

28

Brody

My man.

Her man. Hers, hers, hers. It's the most important title I think I've ever had. Would bet money on nothing ever coming close to it. Hit me like a pair of hooves to the chest that day in the stables, but it had been brewing long before that. My feelings are so prominent they have a heartbeat of their own, thumping in time with the one in my chest.

Her perfume floods my senses, drowning out the room, the white marble tiles and constant drip of one of the sink taps. Even the lingering ache in my throat fades, my voice weak enough that one song took more out of me than recording all damn day used to.

Our mouths move in time, both of us famished for more. More of this connection that can't seem to stop zapping between us. I tangle our tongues before nipping at the soft cushion of her bottom lip, swallowing her surprised moan.

Anna's nails scratch at my scalp, the grip on my hair her anchor as she tugs me closer, allowing me to devour her mouth with a vigour that she returns with equal force. A sharp possessiveness thrums through me, urging me to bring her even closer, to tuck her into my chest and keep her there forever.

Never loved the feeling of a woman in my arms as much as I do this one. That thought drives me as I drop my hold on her and shrug off my suit jacket. Wide brown eyes watch my every move, lust blown as they trace the lines of my arms and shoulders, even lingering on my hands as I fist the jacket before laying it flat on the counter behind her.

"You keep lookin' at me like that and it'll give me a complex," I warn before grabbing her by the waist and perching her on top of my jacket.

"Looking at you like what?"

Her swollen lips part as she stares, the counter levelling our height difference so I don't have to crane my neck when I kiss her again, letting the taste of her fill my mouth. Soft and sweet and mine, a heady combination I want to drink down for the rest of my days.

I drag the length of my nose down over her cheek and along the underside of her jaw, scraping the smooth, pale skin with my beard. Inhaling, I palm her thighs, just above her knees, before spreading them enough to wedge myself between them.

"Like you want to lay claim to me," I groan, curling my fingers in the heavy silk of her dress. It falls open at the movement, and a glance down at her lap has my cock kicking in my slacks.

She sucks in a breath that draws my eyes from the bare expanse of thigh exposed from the high slit of her dress and back up to her deep brown ones. "I do. So, so badly."

A deep, purely animal noise escapes me at her confidence. Her teeth pull at her bottom lip, sinking deep into it before my thumb is there, untucking it. I pinch it between my fingertips and tug, rolling the soft plushness until it reddens the colour of a fresh-picked raspberry.

"Go ahead. I'm aching to do the same fuckin' thing."

I barely get the words out before she's grasping at my button-up and popping it open with a surprising amount of skill. Inch by inch, she exposes my chest, leaving the bottom few buttons closed before grabbing my hair again, forcing our lips back together. I can't stop kissing her. Can't stop the exploration of my hands either, not as they cup her thighs and her waist and then her thighs again, gripping higher this time. She's hot to the touch, burning with the same desire I feel deep in my belly.

"Do it," she gasps, peeling our lips apart to arch her neck, offering it to me.

"Tell me to stop at any time, Anna. I mean it. Refuse to cross any lines with you, but I have to touch you now. Can't wait any longer."

I'm half out of my mind, all the blood in my body running south to the rigid length of me. I'm behaving like a caveman, but she goes soft in my arms, melting like butter in a microwave.

"Yes, Brody. Please."

She spreads her thighs as far as they'll go in the confines of her dress, and I take the offering like the greedy, desperate man I am. Finding the bottom hem of her dress, I grip it tight and glide it up her thighs, trying to steady the excited shake of my fingers as they scrape along the length of smooth, delicate skin. I grind my teeth together, damn near close to blowing at the feel of her alone.

"So soft," I breathe. The higher I climb, the hotter she gets. "So hot and smooth."

She hums low in her throat, forehead falling forward to rest on my chest so she can watch as I explore. "You forgot something."

"What's that, sweetheart?" I still my hand, waiting for the answer. Nothing prepares me for it.

"Soft, hot, smooth, and very, very wet."

"*Christ,*" I hiss, throat growing tighter and tighter.

I'm burying my face in her throat and sucking the skin into my mouth before I can think twice about it. Pushing my hand higher up the inside of her thigh, I bypass the thin barrier of her panties and delve my fingers through the wet skin I find waiting for me. She whimpers, stifling a cry while leaning back on the counter and tipping her head back. Chest arched, she presents her covered breasts and the hard peaks of her nipples to the ceiling. I'm quick to stroke her slippery pussy while freeing her tit from its place in her dress and taking her nipple between my lips.

Twirling my tongue around it, I watch her from beneath my lashes, taking in her every reaction to my touch, searching for what she likes best. The first brush of my thumb over her clit makes her jump, nails digging into my shoulders through my shirt. I do it again, just once, before circling her entrance with a careful finger, exploring softly.

"More," she gasps, hips shifting into my touch.

I hover my teeth over her nipple and apply gentle pressure, a warning. "Don't rush me. Want to explore you and learn what makes you scream. What will have you drippin' down my wrist."

"Brody."

It's the most beautiful my name has ever sounded.

"Been a long time comin', baby. I want to devour you."

"So devour me. I don't need slow. I need to come so bad after all the teasing you've done these past few days."

My patience slips further and further with each pleaded word, but I tighten my hold on it. Laving at her nipple with my tongue, I twist my wrist and cup her pussy, feeling the slick coating my palm. Applying pressure to her clit, I slide one finger inside her hot hole, reeling at the tight grip that meets me.

"Yes, yes," she chants, pushing up on her hands, feeding me more of her nipple. I release it and trail kisses between her breasts and over to the next, paying it the same attention. "So good!"

"Fuck yeah it is."

Her hips swirl, so I add another finger before beginning to fuck her with them. In and out while increasing the pressure of my palm and twirling my wrist. She coats my fingers with her desire, growing louder with each thrust inside.

"I make you come, Anna, you're mine. No more goin' in circles. You'll be my woman."

Her eyes focus on me, bright and clear. I swallow, meeting her stare with equal sincerity. Every move on my fingers inside of her makes her clench, quivering with the tease of an orgasm. The power that gives me is better than any high I've ever felt. More fulfilling than every scream in a crowd of thousands.

"Tell me you understand me. Let me give you that relief," I beg, curling my fingers on every thrust.

"I've wanted to be yours for weeks. Take me," she breathes, exposing so much of herself to me with just a few words.

I break.

My patience snaps.

I'm on her quick, savaging her mouth and throat and chest until I'm sure she'll bear my marks in the morning. Wet pools on my knuckles before the first drip falls from my wrist. I groan, thrusting my fingers faster and harder, filling the bathroom with her pleasure.

Her tiny hands wrap around my neck, holding me in place as the dam breaks and she comes all over my hand, pussy squeezing tight around my fingers, clit pulsing against my palm. Each cry that slips from her swollen, red lips strokes my balls, driving me further out of my mind.

By the time she quiets, I'm blowing harsh breaths from my nose in an attempt to calm down. Every inch of my skin is sensitive, the hand moving down my chest, lingering over my sternum, almost too much. But I don't brush it aside. I cover it with mine instead.

"Hope you know what it means to be mine, Buttercup," I warn lightly, half out of breath.

"I could say the same thing. I'm not an easy woman."

I slip my fingers free and keep my eyes on her, ensuring she's snared in my gaze before lifting them to my mouth and sliding them knuckle-deep. Her taste explodes in my mouth, and the groan that follows is pure and honest, turning her cheeks pink.

After sucking my fingers clean one final time, I release them and tuck some hair behind her ear, stroking her cheekbone. "Never liked easy."

"I get jealous. Often. I hate shaving my legs and avoid it at all costs. There's an entire drawer in my nightstand that's full of candy and chocolate bars because I'm a late-night snacker, and finally, I turn into a massive bitch when I'm on my period," she rambles, hands still clasped around my neck, hanging at the base.

I chuckle, resting our foreheads together again. Our lips are a breath apart, but neither of us closes that final distance. Not yet.

"Before tonight, I wouldn't have considered myself a jealous man, but one look at you out there and I knew I would have fought every single person who thought to come up and ask you to dance. Body hair hasn't ever bothered me. You already know I prefer salty to sweet, so as long as you make a bit'a room for me in that drawer of yours for some chips, we'll be peachy. I grew up around stallions and bulls, so trust that I can weather a few days of attitude while you're hurtin'."

I'm confident I'd have an answer for every argument she threw at me. Anna's mine, no doubt about it. I'm positive I'm making the right choice here.

There's a lot that's going to come next, decisions that have to be made and important speeches to be given, but for right now, right here with this gorgeous woman in my arms, her staring at me like I'm the goddamn king of her heart, body, and soul, nothing else matters. Only this.

"There's not a damn thing you could say that would change my mind," I declare.

She twists her lips deviously. "You know what this means, right?"

"Tell me," I murmur, my eyelids drooping, lips brushing hers.

"I'm going to need my own pair of cowgirl boots now. Since

I'm going to be spending so much time with you at the ranch and all."

Her cheek-splitting smile steals the breath straight out of my lungs.

"You'll send me to an early grave in a pair of your own boots, Anna. But fuck if I'm not going to take you shopping anyway."

29

Annalise

MINUTES LATER, AFTER HELPING READJUST MY CLOTHES, BRODY RUNS his steady, strong hands over my head, smoothing my messy hair. When he presses a kiss to my forehead, I almost purr, so languid and relaxed. *Happy.*

His declarations flow through my mind on repeat, settling a part of my soul that I didn't know had been so uneasy. The silence following the aftermath of hands down the best orgasm I've ever had is soothing in a way that reminds me of snuggling beneath a warm blanket after a long day out in the cold. Add the presence of Brody, and I'm tempted not to leave this bathroom again.

The wedding reception has most likely moved on to dinner while we've been away, hiding in our own special place in time. With no way to tell how long we've been gone, it's hard to know for sure. I almost feel bad for keeping the entertainment hidden away with me, but not enough to rush our exit.

This is our time, our moment, and I'm going to be selfish with it.

I lean my butt against the edge of the counter, shifting my weight on my heels as I button his shirt back up. The short, coarse hairs on his chest brush my fingertips with each button I finish. It's disappointing to tuck it away, to hide it from view once more, but I don't need anyone else gawking at him once we leave. That's my job, and I plan on being employee of the month.

Brody watches me closely, his chin tipped and chest rising and falling steadily. His hat remains on the counter, leaving his messy hair exposed. The ghost of the strands whispers between my fingers, the memory of tugging them hard still fresh in my mind. Reaching up, I sweep away the few loose waves that have fallen over his forehead. His eyes visibly shudder, zeroing in on my mouth.

"If you kiss me again, we'll miss dinner completely," I warn him, dropping my hand to finish fixing his shirt.

"I wouldn't mind eatin' you instead of whatever they've got out there."

Desire blooms in my belly, turning my cheeks fire-engine red. "Tempting, but when that happens, I don't want it to be in a public washroom. I'm surprised nobody has tried to break in here yet."

His gaze remains fixated on my lips for a breath longer before, reluctantly, he lifts it. "I'd rather take my time with you anyway."

"Ditto, Cowboy." I toss him a wink before spinning to grab his suit jacket from the counter and moving to his back. The wide expanse of strong shoulders and thick muscle trips a wire in my brain. "Extend your arm."

"More than capable of puttin' my own jacket on," he says, but when he moves his arm for me, I know he actually doesn't mind the help.

"I know. I just want to do it."

Sliding his arm into the first sleeve, I guide the jacket over his back and move to the other arm. Once both are inside, I release the material and take a step back. He shrugs the jacket on fully, stretching his arms in front of his body before turning to face me.

"Look good?"

I arch a brow. "Searching for compliments now, are we?"

"From you? Absolutely."

My chest flutters. "You're the most handsome man I've ever laid eyes on, let alone had as my own."

"Now you know how I feel every time I look at you. Come here," he orders softly.

I step into his body, sighing at the immediate comfort that comes with having his arms around me. He strokes up and down my back with a firm touch as I press my cheek to his chest and sigh.

"Tell me how this is going to work," I whisper.

"What do you mean?"

"Once we walk out of here. How is it going to work? I've never been with anyone like you before, and I'm not just talking about your outrageous good looks. I'm talking about your fame. Your career. God, I don't even know why I'm setting myself up for heartbreak when you have to leave in just a couple of weeks. Maybe that makes me a fool."

He pulls back, expression tight with anger. "You're not a fool. Don't talk like that about yourself."

I reply with a tense nod. "Alright. I'm sorry."

He blows out a breath and pinches my chin, lifting it until I have no other choice but to hold his gaze. "It's too late to worry about turnin' out as fools. Been thinkin' about you daily for weeks now. Either way, I was fucked. I don't want to focus on the after right now. Not when I have you in my arms like this for the first time. Maybe that's not a fair thing to ask of you. But all I know is that you're my woman now, and I don't give a shit what anyone else thinks about it."

"But how do I act out there, Brody? What do I do, and what do I not do? I don't want to ruin anything for you by doing something wrong in the public eye. We aren't still in Cherry Peak, where nobody cares who you are or what you do. I've never cared much about social media or whether or not people like me, but I've seen what my sister has dealt with from hockey fans, and while Maddox's fans aren't yours, they can't be much different."

I've been surrounded by public figures for years now. Braxton married into a family full of them. From her husband and father-in-law the hockey superstars, to her sister-in-law the social media influencer, and even to her damn brother-in-law, who just so happens to be one of the biggest names in rock music. I'm not new to seeing the fans and constant judgment that comes with a high follower count. But I've never been nose-deep in it.

"This isn't a red carpet, sweetheart. The only thing you need to do out there is let me keep you close and be yourself. Every-thin' else will fall into place," he soothes.

A spark of insecurity slips past my defenses as I blurt out, "And if it doesn't? If we both wake up tomorrow to see a Twitter thread about the girl you were caught slumming it with at an NHL player's wedding?"

He shakes his head, smiling so slightly I almost miss it before he's brushing his lips over my mouth. "I've never cared much for the opinions of others. Not those outside of my family, and in case you haven't noticed, Buttercup, my grandparents would damn near adopt you if given the damn chance. They like you nearly as much as I do, and that's sayin' somethin'."

The confidence in his words is good enough for me. Right now, at least. Whether or not it will still be tomorrow or the day after, I'm not sure. All I am sure of is that I'd rather have Brody for a couple of weeks than not at all. I've fled from important choices in the past, ones that could have held the potential to change my life, and I won't do it again. I've let others help dictate what I should and shouldn't do, but this is the new Annalise, the badass that doesn't cower.

Let the country music fans judge me if it comes to that. Let the potential heartbreak drive me back to the place I was post-

Stewart, because this right here, this skip in my heart and warmth in my bones, is so fucking worth it.

"It makes sense now," I whisper.

His brows tug together slowly, thumb moving back and forth over my chin. "What does?"

"When I heard that you wrote most of your own music. You naturally know just what to say."

"It's easier for me to talk to you than it is to write. It's one of the first things I realized when we first met, both via text and in person. Was easy to talk to you. Easier than it's been to talk to anyone for months."

I nip at the inside of my cheek, fluttering my lashes. Pride blooms in my chest. "Good."

"Good," he repeats, his voice a breathy, surprised sound, as if he's in awe of my simple answer.

"Yeah, good. I'm glad we're on the same page because I could happily talk your ear off every damn day."

With a low laugh, he kisses me just once, even as I chase his lips for more, and releases my chin, tucking me beneath his arm instead. I catch sight of our reflection in the mirror and feel the rightness of the picture in every thump of my pulse and rise of my chest.

He has a few inches on me, even with the additional height from my heels, his chest lean with hard-packed muscle and hips narrow. I fit into his side like a missing puzzle piece, the plump curves of my hips and chest evened out with the strong width of his shoulders. My dress is the colour of his tie, the plum colour the married couple loves so much. There's only one thing missing from the picture, and I quickly snap my hand out to grab it.

Brody's eyes are intense, hot on my skin as I lift his hat between us and push up on my toes to set it atop his head. Once it's back where it belongs, I tap the front, tipping it slightly before dropping back to my heels.

"There we go," I say, unable to hide a great big smile.

He tugs me tighter to his side, the arm draped over my shoulder a pleasant, reassuring weight. "Ready to get back out there?"

Taking in the sight reflected back at us one last time, I nod. "Feel up to meeting my sister and brother-in-law?"

He straightens, determination flaring to life in those pretty blue eyes. "Anytime, sweetheart."

"Then lead the way, Cowboy."

BRAXTON'S JAW nearly hits the table when I walk right up to her with Brody's arm still hanging securely over my shoulders. I'm all too aware of the curious eyes watching our every move, but I focus on not letting the discomfort that comes with that judgment show on my face. This is a good moment. The best of the best. Nobody can ruin this for me.

To my surprise, the reception hasn't moved on to dinner or speeches yet. The bride and groom are speaking to an older couple near the main stage while the guests chat amongst themselves. Our table isn't cluttered by any means, but it's quite full. Eight chairs, five of which are occupied by people I've never met before. The only empty seat is mine, but I make no move toward it.

Maddox boldly looks Brody up and down, donning a mask of indifference. I could cry at the obvious show of protectiveness. His big-brother sense must begin to tingle because he meets my stare and winks. I push every ounce of appreciation into my expression, hoping he understands just how grateful I am for him.

Growing up, my sister and I never had anyone other than Maddox to be protective of us. When it came to my sister, Maddox was protective for his own reasons, most of which stemmed from being in love with her his entire life, but he picked up the responsibilities that came with being my big brother too, warning the boys away and threatening ultimate destruction if they broke my heart.

Dad didn't really care what we did or who we went out with, so long as we didn't embarrass him or the family, and Mom . . . she was too busy not trying to drown in the terrible marriage she was stuck in to worry about our dating lives. Having Maddox around filled a hole inside of me that I didn't realize was so gaping.

My sister couldn't have married a better man.

"You must be Brody," he says in a no-bullshit tone.

I wait for Brody to tense up beside me the way Stewart had when he met my brother-in-law for the first time, but he doesn't. Instead, he extends his free arm toward him, and they shake hands in a rough and tough alpha-male way that usually has me rolling my eyes. The grip with which they shake has me looking at Braxton to find her hiding a smile.

"Pleasure to meet you, Maddox," Brody replies.

I twist my body further into his hold, inhaling his woodsy scent as it swarms my senses. "The gorgeous woman beside Maddox is my sister, Braxton."

Braxton beams. "How's the hand? My husband has quite the grip."

"Fuck me, I think he might have crushed my bones," Maddox groans, shaking his hand out in front of him.

Brody huffs a deep laugh. "I've been shaking hands with men used to gripping bull rope since I was a boy."

"You don't say?" Maddox retorts.

Braxton lays a hand on her husband's back and coos, "Poor baby. Will you be okay?"

"Don't mention this to anyone, and I'll take it easier on you than I usually do Anna's boyfriends," he tells Brody.

My man just nods and slides his hand from my shoulder to the back of my neck, palming it. "Works for me."

"Where are you sitting for dinner?" Braxton asks.

Good question, sis.

"I have a spot at one of the tables around here, I think," he answers.

I worry my lip, selfishly wanting to keep him close. I've never felt so possessive of a guy before, but I can't help but want to keep him glued to my side all night. Having him sitting somewhere else tonight while he's not onstage singing singes my insides.

"We can pull you up a chair at our table," I suggest, feigning innocence, as if I'm not itching to drag his ass down on *my* chair and plop myself on his lap. "You know, so you don't have to go wandering around this busy ballroom and risk missing dinner."

A deliciously smug grin spreads his lips, one brow arched. "I don't think it would take me that long to find my spot."

"Dinner isn't for half an hour anyway, Anna," Maddox adds, goading me.

My glare is vicious as I pin him beneath it. The douchebag howls a laugh in response. Even Braxton—*my own sister*—lifts a hand to hide her mouth and avoids my eyes.

Brody tightens his grip on my nape. The sensation of hot breath in my hair, against my ear, makes me shiver.

"It would be my honour to sit with you tonight, sweetheart. All you had to do was ask," he purrs, his country drawl thicker than I've ever heard it. As if he called upon it just to drive me out of my mind.

Fuck, it works. Suddenly, I ache to rub my thighs together, the throb between them alarming so soon after what happened in the bathroom. I'm used to it taking me a good few hours after an orgasm to be even remotely interested in having another, but apparently, that's not the case anymore. At least not right now.

Planting my palm against his solid stomach, I twist and lean up enough that only he can hear as I whisper, "Find a chair, Brody. Before I use your face as mine."

His following cough has me patting his middle and taking

my seat beside Braxton, a wicked gleam in my eyes. The red flush on his cheeks as he rushes to find a chair is one of the most beautiful things I've ever seen.

30

Brody

MY STOMACH MUSCLES BURN FROM LAUGHTER AS I LEAN BACK IN MY chair with Anna tucked into my side. Empty plates lie scattered around the large round table, wineglasses and beer bottles beside them. The cooler in Anna's hand has to be warm by now, but she still doesn't set it down. She continues to sip on the fruity drink and tap the tin in time with the low music, anything to keep from moving from my arms. Her chair is as close to mine as it can be, but I'd prefer her to abandon it in exchange for my lap.

Luckily, the other group of people at the table couldn't have cared less about us, so we haven't had to worry about getting interrupted thus far. Even though this wasn't my original table, I'm considering giving Walker a giant thank you for the guest placement.

I bury my face in Anna's hair and sweep my thumb over the ridge of her belly button through the silk dress. She leans further into me and rubs her cheek against my forehead, letting me soak her up for as long as I want to.

Fuckin' hell, I could stay here forever.

"So, how do you know Walker, Brody?" Maddox asks, setting down his dewy long neck beside his wife's glass of water.

"Grew up together in Cherry Peak and played for a shit triples team in Calgary. He was always a better player than me, clearly, so I quit while he kept on climbing. I haven't seen him in a couple of years now."

"You played hockey?" Anna asks me.

"Mmhmm. I never took it seriously, but it kept me busy. Gave me an excuse to fight off a lot of my teenage angst."

"Not a damn part of me believes that Walker Morales is from a blink-and-you-miss-it hick town," he muses before grunting in pain when Anna shifts her lower body and then smirks across the table. "No offense, man."

"Saying no offense after saying something rude doesn't mean there's actually no offense, Maddox," my woman lectures.

I kiss the side of her head and meet Maddox's awaiting stare with an easy one. "It's alright. Walker is the furthest thing from a cowboy, so I get it. He's always been like that. Bigger than life with dreams to match."

"I'd say you have big dreams too, considering your career," Braxton says.

"Yeah, I guess I do. I'm one of the lucky people who gets to make a livin' from what I love."

"That's an understatement. You're amazing at what you do. I think we can all agree on that," Anna adds, palming my knee.

I almost haul her onto my thighs then and there. "It's been nice to have a break, though. Been a long time since I was at home to help out."

The couple across from us nods, a shared look of sympathy there and gone in a flash, making way for understanding.

"I get you. Nothing compares to the feeling of being gone for a long stretch and getting to come home," Maddox says, gazing at his wife with a lovesick expression that has me saying fuck it and tugging Anna right into my lap.

She doesn't fight me, just relaxes into the motions and slips onto my thighs, leaning against my chest like there's nowhere else she'd rather be. I rest my chin on her shoulder and appreciate the lack of gawking her family does at our new position. Braxton looks away from her husband and at me, smiling softly, the lightest tip of her chin making my throat swell.

"How long are you home for, Brody?" she asks carefully.

Not long enough. "A few more weeks."

"And then?"

"And then we'll see," Anna cuts in, stiffening enough for me to notice.

I press my lips to her shoulder, over the thin strap of her dress and the delicate skin beneath, before tightening my arm around her stomach and pulling her further up my lap, chest to back.

The sound of a clearing throat from behind me has me shifting, glancing over my shoulder. Rita stands a couple of feet back, arms crossed and one long finger tapping at the watch on her wrist.

"The crowd awaits," Anna breathes, spinning in my arms to face me.

The encouraging glint in her eyes hits me right in the gut. I don't know if I deserve her. Too bad I'm gonna take her anyway.

"Not yet. Not until I've danced with you first."

Her eyes widen, as if she can't believe I'd fight to do this with her, and it's enough to have me ready to drive my fist through her ex's face. That stupid asshole did a real number on her if she truly believes it's surprising that I'd want to spend more time with her.

"Really?" she murmurs.

I bury my anger for the moment and nod, trailing my fingers along the curve of her jaw and chin. "I'll be right back, and then you're gonna do me the honour of joinin' me on the dance floor. I'm not missin' this chance for the world."

Her lashes flutter, hiding those pretty brown eyes from me as she presses into my touch. "Alright. I'll be here."

Reluctantly, I drop my hand in my lap before Anna settles back in her own chair, leaving my body jarringly cold in her absence. Another cough behind us, and I'm out of my chair, flashing an apologetic smile at Maddox and Braxton.

"I'll be back. Excuse me."

They both nod and jump back into conversation with Anna as I turn and head to my manager. Rita stalks away from the tables of guests beginning to get up and move to the dance floor, waiting for me against one of the walls behind the impressive donut tower display. I'm grateful for the volume of the music playing around us when she pins me in place with a hard glare.

"You needed to be ready to go up onstage ten minutes ago. Instead, I find you PDA'ing it up with that woman. Do you have any idea how many photos have already been posted of you here tonight? You're at a wedding for one of the best-playing NHL players in the world! This isn't an empty karaoke bar where you've decided to get your kicks off after a few lonely nights!"

Her anger was expected. The digs were too. But the photos . . . I should have expected those. When Rita nods sharply, as if reading my mind, I realize that maybe my wince wasn't as well hidden as I hoped it was.

"Does she know that she's about to end up in photos with you tonight? That they're going to be spread all over social media by tomorrow?"

Looking back at the table, I fight back a smile at the furious movement of Anna's hands as she speaks animatedly to her sister. Her eyes are alive; it's obvious even from back here. I already miss her. *Fuck me.*

I grit my jaw when I dive back into this conversation. "My personal life isn't your business, Rita. She knows who I am and what comes with that. And as far as needin' to sing, I still have time before I'm up. I'm damn well gonna spend it dancin' with my date."

"Your date? Brody, I'm going to seriously encourage you against that. The photos of you two at the table can be easy enough to brush aside, but dancing with her out there won't be.

This is going to be a PR nightmare." She's already texting on her phone before the final word lands.

"It's a good thing that I don't want to brush her aside, then. I'm dancin' with my woman, Rita. End of conversation."

She inhales sharply, glancing up from her screen. "Your woman?"

I straighten, crossing my arms. "Yeah, my woman. Tell whoever you need to, but I never agreed to sign off on this shit before. Take it or leave it, but I'm not talkin' about this any longer tonight."

"You have . . ." She looks at her screen again. "Seven minutes. Make them damn well count, and then finish what you were invited here to do."

My damn manners keep me from storming off without replying. "Got it. Enjoy the rest of your night. It's an open bar."

"I'll keep that in mind," she snips, but I'm already walking back to the table.

By the time I'm standing at the back of Anna's chair and resting my hands on her shoulders, she's finished off her warm cooler, leaving it by the collection of dirty plates that have yet to be cleared away.

She peeks up at me, happiness twinkling in those gorgeous eyes. Unable to help myself, I'm damn near folding my body in half to get a long, greedy taste of her lips. I taste the fruity drink mixed with the naturally sweet flavour of her and pull back before she ends up hauled over my shoulder.

"Got everything sorted out?" she asks, the words hushed, just for me.

I bury my fingers in the silky-smooth hairs at the back of her head and use the hold to gently tip it back, tempted to kiss her again but holding back. Her stare is innocent to the watchful eye, but it sets my skin on fire.

"Yeah, sweetheart. All sorted." I take a step back and offer her my hand. "Dance with me?"

Picking up on the song playing, she flicks her gaze to the DJ before looking back at me with a brow raised. "I'm a terrible two-stepper."

"He'll change the song by the time we get up there. Don't tell my grandmother that, though. She makes dancin' her sole personality trait at every weddin' we've ever been at."

"I'll have to ask her for some tips, then."

"If you want bonus points, ask about the Cadillac Ranch. It's her favourite."

"Consider it done, Cowboy," she says, setting her hand in mine.

I help her up and tighten my grip on her tiny fingers while leading her to the dance floor. Just like I was expecting, the DJ changes to a slower song a beat later, but the sound of my own voice comes as a shock. Anna's abrupt laugh calls one of my own to the surface.

"Do you think that was on purpose?" she asks, fighting a smile.

When I catch Walker waving at me from the bridal party table, I shake my head, laughing incredulously.

"Oh yeah, it was on purpose."

"At least he chose one of your best songs," she offers, the hint of a tease in her tone.

Stepping onto the dance floor, I twirl Anna into my arms, catching her against my chest with a grin. She relaxes in my hold, sliding her arms up and around my neck, holding me tight. The soft expanse of her lower back feels like a gift beneath my hands as we start to sway.

"Are you hintin' that not all of my songs are good, Annalise?" I tease.

She wiggles her brows. "Oh no, you brought out the full name. Did I brush a nerve, Brody?"

I dig my fingers into the curve of her hip and tug her until we're close enough to hold a piece of paper between us. Her eyes spark with such pure happiness, and I nearly lose my breath at the beauty of it. She's

"Nobody brushes my nerves the way you do. I don't let them get close enough," I admit.

"Yet here I am."

I release a breath heavy with the weight of my thoughts and nod. "Yeah. Here you are."

To stay, if I have anything to do with it.

31

Annalise

POPPY LEANS FORWARD, HER NARROWED EYES LEVELLED ON MY FACE in a deep, speculating stare. It's a bit intimidating, to be honest, but I continue to sit across the couch from her, my legs tucked beneath my butt, unflinching.

"Walk around for me a little bit," she orders.

I blink. "What? Why?"

"She wants to see if you're bow-legged," Bryce answers from her knee-slung-over-knee sitting position on the soft ottoman facing us.

"We didn't have sex!" I shriek, face suddenly on fire.

"I don't believe you, Miss Liar Liar," Poppy sings.

"I didn't lie to you."

Bryce cocks her head at me. "Lying by omission is still lying."

When both women appeared at my house earlier this evening with pizza and wine in hand, I let them inside without a second thought. My exhaustion from flying home on an early flight this morning after a long night at the wedding was quickly forgotten when it came to spending time with them.

I sure as hell wasn't expecting to get hit with the fifth degree the moment the door shut behind us. While I didn't go to the wedding knowing that Brody was going to be there, I didn't exactly tell them once I did. The photos of Brody and me last night that Poppy showed me a breath after setting the two bottles of wine down in the kitchen came as a shock. Only to them, however.

I knew they were coming, and just like when Brody warned me after we finished dancing and he was set to go back onstage, I refused to let them ruin the night.

Guilt lashes through me. They still don't know the truth about Bo either.

"Okay, that's fair enough. But in my defense, I didn't know that he was going to be at the wedding before I got there. My sister told me before we left," I defend myself.

"You could have texted us at some point after learning about it. Clearly, you needed some confidence boosting or peer pressure since you're claiming you didn't sleep with that hunk of a man," Poppy chuffs.

"Just because we didn't have sex doesn't mean we didn't do *anything* else. There wasn't a chance for us to so much as even spend the night together anyway. He was performing for the rest of the night after those pictures were taken, and then I went home with my sister and her husband."

Much to Brody's displeasure. If he had had it his way, he would have cut out early and danced with me all night before taking me back to his hotel room. We wouldn't have had sex even if I had gone with him, but a night just lying in his arms would have been incredible. I couldn't miss out on that extra morning with my sister and nephew, though. Not when I hardly see them as it is. The small breakfast we shared before I left was perfect. Enough to last me until I see them after Christmas.

I felt silly worrying about Brody's reaction to my wanting to stay with my sister, but for the millionth time, he proved just how out of Stewart's league he is. After kissing me breathless, Brody walked me to Maddox's SUV and went as far as to even buckle me in before telling me good night. He stood waving until we got too far to see him.

"Okay, don't tease me, then. Tell me what you *did* do. Let me live vicariously through you. It's been forever since I've been with a real man," Poppy begs.

Bryce's expression is exasperated. "Your collection of sex toys keeps you occupied."

"Well, *excuse me*. Sorry I like to have a man's helpful, steady touch with my orgasms sometimes," Poppy retorts.

I untuck my legs before they fall asleep, stretching them out over Poppy's lap. "I had Brody's helpful, steady touch last night, and it was fucking amazing. So stop arguing with each other and fawn over that with me."

It's Bryce who gasps, gripping her knees. "Where? How? More than one O?"

"Before we get into that, I have to tell you something else. If I don't, the reason for why we wound up in the bathroom won't make as much sense," I start. Poppy scrunches her face at the mention of the bathroom, but I hold up a finger for her to wait. "He was very gentlemanly despite the location, so don't even start."

She raises her hands and shrinks back into the couch as if I brutally scolded her. The CEO of dramatic, this one.

"You remember that guy that I accidentally texted for dress approval?"

"The one that was a douche to you afterward?" Bryce asks.

"Yeah, that one. Well, he actually turned out to be really nice, and we kind of kept talking . . . and before you say anything, Poppy, I already know that it was dangerous. But it was worth it. Really, really worth it," I rush to explain.

Poppy looks about close to bursting from keeping silent, so I pause, gesturing for her to speak.

"You sent a picture of yourself to a guy—a stranger, might I add—and then proceeded to continue texting him . . . Did you want to wind up the victim on one of your weirdo crime podcasts, Anna?"

Bryce laughs, flicking Poppy on the knee. "As if you would have blocked the guy."

"I would have!" she shouts before bending under our disbelieving stares. "Fine, maybe I wouldn't have. Just keep talking."

"In my defense, he had sent me a photo of his body soon after we started talking, and it was nice enough the prospect of him being creepy didn't matter as much," I add.

"You shallow bitch," Bryce teases, earning a laugh from both Poppy and me.

I don't try to deny it. My comment makes me appear incredibly shallow, but I would love to meet someone who hasn't had their judgment swayed by a beautiful human being. "I am what I am."

"At least you admit it," Poppy mutters.

"And I didn't need to be shallow for long. It turns out that the stranger I was talking to over text message was Brody. I started to figure it out after he came to help boost my car, and now . . . now we're just kind of combining all of our text and in-person conversations into one big picture. Joining the two separate halves of our friendship, I guess. But that's how we wound up . . . you know, last night. We both just came out with it. No more running around the bush with the secrets."

A warmth fills my chest at the simple fact of speaking about this now. It's like a weight is off my shoulders, even if I didn't need to carry it for as long as I did.

I want to shout to the world that Brody's mine. The photos and videos of us dancing last night might have taken the initial opportunity to do that away from me, but I'm not going to stop until everyone is *sick* of me.

My two best friends are silent for a few moments, both of them staring at me like they don't know how to respond. It makes me giggle, proud of myself for finally stumping them.

"It's a lot, I know," I add.

"Don't even try me right now with that friendship bullshit. You're not friends with the guy. Not from what I saw on social media this morning. What have I been saying for weeks now, Bryce?" Poppy asks, the first to speak.

Bryce leans forward on the ottoman, twisting her hair behind her shoulder. "That Brody's been into you, Anna. Ever since he gave you his jacket, we both knew. It was only a matter of time before he finally grew the balls to make a move."

"It doesn't matter when. You guys keep swaying from the point of what I'm saying. We're definitely not just friends, but we started that way. Both via text and in person. That's crazy, right? That I met a guy I liked not just once but twice?"

"It is crazy. Crazy enough that if you don't end up marrying him, I'm certain I'll die a crazy spinster," Poppy says.

"You're not going to die a spinster, Poppy." I ignore her mention of marriage, not wanting to open that can of worms right now.

"You're right. Because you're going to lock down your man. You found each other before his career totally exploded too. It's going to be adorable to watch you together on red carpets and for him to write songs about you! Oh, my God! He's going to write albums upon albums about you." Poppy lifts her hands to her mouth, eyes wide. "Alright, I'm swooning."

Bryce buries her face in her hands and laughs, her entire body shaking. "Trust Poppy to go the extra mile in terrifying you."

"I'm not terrified."

And it's the truth. I'm the furthest thing from scared when it comes to Brody. That might be the scariest part of our entire relationship.

It's odd. Unusual. There are a million things you should worry about when it comes to dating someone new. From your official label to the hows and whens and whats. The subject of his career should be an entirely separate fear all on its own. But for some reason, it's simply not.

Maybe it's my age or my past with Stewart, but I'm more excited than I am fearful. Life is too short to pick apart every possible bad outcome. I'm in a really great place right now, and Brody is confident in me and in us. I don't feel insecure or curious as to where we stand. He's put the effort in to ensure that I feel this way.

There's only one thing that could crack the solid foundation we've laid beneath our feet, and I refuse to think about it. Not yet. Not until I have no other choice but to watch him leave Cherry Peak behind. For the first time in his life, with me left standing here.

"No, I don't think you are. If I didn't know any better, I'd think that's because you're falling in love with him," Bryce says, her words taking an axe through the thoughts in my mind.

I meet her waiting stare and smile. "I think you're right."

"Oh shit," Poppy breathes.

"A good oh shit or a bad oh shit?" I ask.

Bryce answers, nudging Poppy with her foot. "An incredible oh shit, right?"

"Yeah. That."

"Is it really that surprising?" I ask softly.

Poppy shakes her head, quick to clarify. "Not in the way you're thinking. I just mean, you haven't mentioned him all that much recently, and I know you've been really busy, so I shouldn't be surprised. I'm being selfish, is all. Greedy for your attention and to spend more time with you. I wish you would have told me the extent of your feelings and that you were talking to that stranger before you knew who he really was. We're here for you, Anna. Boy talk is like the best part about having a best friend."

Suddenly, it's not guilt that floods my belly; it's appreciation. Such a strong, crippling sense of appreciation and love that my eyes start to burn and drip all in a matter of seconds.

The lack of female relationships I've had outside of the one I share with my sister didn't mean much to me until I met Bryce and Poppy, and now that I have, I don't think I'd be able to survive without them. In just a couple of months, they've integrated themselves so fully into my life that I'll fight tooth and nail to keep them here.

"Don't cry, baby," Poppy hushes, sliding my feet from her thighs to crawl toward me on the cushions.

She brings me into her arms, and a beat later, two more wrap around me. My best friends cocoon themselves around my body as I cry. Cry because I'm happy and overwhelmed and healing. Because I'm so grateful for the things that brought me here, good and bad.

"I love you guys," I whisper through a hiccup.

It's Bryce who replies. "We love you more."

32

Brody

> Me: Fancy coming with me to the city tomorrow? I'll be there at 10 if you say yes.

> Banana: What do you have planned, Cowboy? Miss me already?

> Me: Missed you from the moment I watched you leave.

I SENT MY ORIGINAL TEXT AS A LONG SHOT AFTER MY FLIGHT FROM hell back to Calgary last night. Turbulence doesn't usually bother me, but the sky was on a mission to punt us to the ground. With a swirling stomach and a new appreciation for the ground, I strode out of the airport with one thing on my mind.

Annalise Heights.

We didn't get enough time together at the wedding, and I want to make up for that. Sending her off in her brother-in-law's SUV was like having my favourite dessert drifted beneath my nose and being told I couldn't take a bite out of it. Except I did have a taste, and it was delicious. Still taste her two days later.

Even as I pull up in front of her house this morning, I'm desperate to see her. See her and feel her and kiss her. It's like

I've gone back in time and become a teenage boy again with a crush to end all crushes. My grandmother would never let up if she knew the way I'd been thinking recently.

I leave the truck running as I climb out and step over the snowy curb onto her clear sidewalk. I've taken to shovelling for her, not wanting her to have to do it herself. The appreciative grin she gifts me every time she steps outside and sees that her sidewalk is clear is more than worth the effort.

Christmas is fast approaching, and I've been itching to invite her to the ranch to spend it with me. It's not my place, though. Not when she probably wants to spend the holidays with her family. The bond she shares with them isn't one I would ever think to try and get in the middle of.

Anna's already slipping out her front door and onto the porch before I've made it halfway up the sidewalk. Picking up my pace, I take the steps two at a time and take the key from between her fingers, locking up for her.

"I was going to do that myself," she chastises me.

"When's the last time I haven't come up to your door?"

"Fair enough."

I tuck her key back into the pocket of her jacket and dip my head to kiss her warm lips. She hums in the back of her throat before resting her hands on my chest and nipping at my mouth.

"Mornin', Buttercup," I breathe.

"Good morning indeed. Is this going to be my greeting every time you pick me up from now on?"

I take one of the hands lying on my chest and carefully lead her down the wooden stairs. "If I have anything to say about it, yeah."

On solid ground again, she grabs my arm and leans into my side, our legs moving in time. The walk to the truck is too quick.

"Can I know what we're doing today, or is it supposed to be a surprise?" she asks once I've opened the passenger door for her.

"I'll tell you once you get your fine ass into my truck."

Unable to help myself, I emphasize my point with a sharp smack to her left ass cheek. I watch with a twitching dick as it ripples beneath her tight jeans with the force, the sight damn near enough to tempt me to grip her hips and fit her ass right to my groin.

Anna's squeak flies into the cold. My laugh is a throaty sound as she whips around to swat my arm. "We're playing like that, are we?"

"Better get used to it, sweetheart," I tease.

Even though she hasn't tripped getting into the truck since the one and only time, I still linger at her back, waiting until she's plopped safely onto the seat with her belt done up before going round to my side.

The truck is warm when I slide into my seat and turn the heat down a bit. Anna unzips the first inch of her jacket and shifts to face me.

"My fine ass is in the truck now," she smarts, the corner of her mouth quirked.

Pulling the truck from the curb, I say, "So it is. We need to get you a pair'a boots before you can step back onto the ranch. A pair all your own."

"You were serious about that?"

Risking a quick glance at her, I frown when I notice she's frowning. "Why wouldn't I have been? I want you around as much as possible these next few weeks. We've gotta start somewhere."

"I believe you. I thought maybe you were just being nice."

"I don't have it in me to do things just for the purpose of bein' nice, sweetheart. You're here with me 'cause there's nothin' else I'd rather do today than spend time with you," I say firmly, not leaving anything for her to contemplate.

The soft pull of her lips as she relaxes in her seat has me nodding to myself, pleased with the trust she has in me. After turning out of town, I let her fiddle with the radio while I lift the top of the centre console to grab the brown bag of gingersnap cookies my grandma shoved in my hands this morning.

"Hungry?" I ask, offering her the bag.

Anna takes it gingerly, appreciation heavy in her features. The crinkle of the bag fills the cab when she slides her hand into it and grabs a cookie.

"Grandma?" She brings it to her nose and sniffs, hearts filling her eyes.

Taking the bag from her, I set it on top of the console and continue stealing looks across the truck as she bites into the cookie. "'Course it was. She whipped those up the moment I said I was seein' you today. Stayed up way past her bedtime doin' it too."

"She's incredibly sweet. Tell her thank you for me, please."

I nod, my chest cavity suddenly feeling far too small for all the feelings I've got for this woman. "Eat up. There's a spot I want to take you when we get to Calgary, but we got a couple hours still."

"Before or after we find boots?"

"Before. It's a drive-in that I used to go to all the time as a boy. I was thinkin' you could get a banana milkshake." I watch her for a reaction, far too pleased when, just as I expected, her cheeks flush a pretty shade of pink.

"I was waiting for you to start teasing me about that," she mutters.

"Banana? Were you called Anna Banana as a kid?"

"My sister actually calls me that. I don't know why I decided to have you use it as my contact name."

My stomach pinches as I draw a deep breath. "My ma called me Bo. Not sure why I offered it to you either. Especially not before I knew a damn thing about you."

"If you ever want to talk about her, Brody, I'm more than willing to listen."

I tighten my grip on the steering wheel as we hit the highway, swarmed on both sides by snow-dripped pine trees. Frozen mountain streams lie beneath, flanked by wire fencing meant to keep animals from wandering onto the road. It's beautiful, even in the winter when the grass is dead and brown beneath the heavy layers of snow. The air is clear and crisp, so different from the polluted city air I'd grown accustomed to in Nashville. It's home, the root of all my childhood memories.

Clearing my throat, I give myself a gentle push. "She loved horses. Loved them more than I thought possible. We bonded over that shared love and passion. There wasn't a day we didn't spend out in the stables together. Every day after school, she'd be waiting by the fence to ride alongside my bus up the ranch road."

"She sounds incredible."

"Yeah, she was. Sweeter than cotton candy but a rebellious risk taker. She loved horses a little too much. Wanted to heal the broken ones, even when they didn't deserve it." My throat is scratchy; every word I speak sounds garbled.

"Does she have to do with why you were so at odds around Sky?" she asks, always so observant.

"I stopped riding shortly after Ma died and my dad took off. Couldn't bring myself to get close to them afterward."

Anna fidgets in her seat, looking between me and the console separating us over and over again. When her leg starts bouncing, I smile weakly, a soft laugh collecting in my chest.

"Would you like me to rip the thing out and toss it out the window?" I ask.

She keeps her voice steady in a no-bullshit tone. "That would be great, actually. It's a giant pain in my ass right now."

"We can talk about this later, yeah? Today is supposed to be easy."

And ripping open sore wounds isn't exactly what I had in mind. Not even if the idea of having her help sew them shut again is tempting.

"Consider the subject changed," she announces, ripping off a chunk of cookie. When she reaches over the console and holds it in front of my face, I go to take it only to have her pull it back an inch. "Open your mouth."

I double blink but part my lips, letting her push the soft treat past them. Her following grin sends my heart into overdrive as I chew.

"This is one of my official Passenger Princess duties, babe. I'm at your service for the next two hours," she sings, beaming proudly. "We should get a little sign for my seat so everyone knows what's up whenever you're out without me."

I stifle my laugh, enjoying her possessive train of thought. "What would the sign say? Property Of Anna?"

"Something like that. Or Passenger Princess's Only. Which-ever you prefer."

"I'm not sure Caleb would appreciate that sentiment, but if anyone could convince him, it would be you."

"I appreciate that, but he seems like he'd be an alright co-pilot. Maybe we should try and find a double-sided sign. Passenger Princess on one side and Co-Pilot on another."

I scratch at my jaw, glancing at her from the corner of my eye. "I'd leave your sign up for everyone. As far as I'm concerned, that's been your seat since the first time you sat in it."

If I didn't have to pay attention to the road, I would have kept staring at her forever. It's especially hard to look away when her entire face lights up and she busies herself with her cookie, popping a piece in her mouth. She licks along her pillowed bottom lip, collecting the crumbs, and I shift in my seat, growing hard in half a second.

"Open again," she orders, and I jolt, snapping back to the road while hating how potentially bad my staring could have been.

I open my mouth without a second thought, and another piece of cookie hits my tongue.

"Do you think Cherry Peak will ever grow big enough to have need of a second hair salon?" she asks a beat later.

"I think potentially. Why? Are you wantin' to open your own?"

"It was always a dream of mine. I thought I'd do it someday in Vancouver, but I realized after moving here that it's probably not a very viable option. Not for a long while anyway."

"The town has doubled in size since I was a kid. It wouldn't surprise me if in a few years, it's grown enough to need a second salon. Everyone needs their hair done, right?"

She laughs softly. "Yeah, that's true. I'm just still learning all about small-town living, I suppose."

"It's different. I didn't know anything different until movin' to Nashville. After livin' there for a few years, Cherry Peak felt odd. It was hard to readjust. Have some grace with yourself."

It's a far reach, but I drape my arm across the console and turn my hand over. The comforting weight of her palm against mine comes a moment later. I lace our fingers tight.

"Where do you prefer? Here or Nashville?"

There's no hesitation in my reply. "It's always been Cherry Peak. My love for this place has only grown as of late."

I don't explain further, and she doesn't ask me to. There's no need. Not when it's already so obvious. If I never had to leave Cherry Peak again, I wouldn't. And when the time comes that I do, I'll be leaving half of myself here.

With her.

33

Annalise

AFTER A MORNING OF DRIVING AND GRABBING FRIES AND A milkshake at by far the best drive-in I've ever been to, we've spent the past hour in the boot store. The *best* boot store in Alberta, according to him.

"What about these ones?" Brody asks, towering over me where I sit on a short, cushioned bench.

A giggle builds in my throat at the sight of him in front of a tall shelf of boots, a baseball cap tugged low over his brow and a pair of large-rimmed sunglasses hiding his pretty eyes. Paired with his tight-fitting Levi's, a dark brown set of boots, and a heavy Carhartt jacket, the glasses throw off the rough and tough look a bit. It's a testament to his good looks that he can still pull it off. Though, I doubt he isn't capable of pulling off just about anything.

"Anna? Do you like these ones?" he repeats, watching me with a casual smirk.

I clear my throat and ignore his cheekiness. "They're cute."

He's dangling a pair of reddish-brown boots with a square toe and black swirls along the sides. They're not completely my style, but we've gone through at least a dozen different boots already, and none have spoken to me.

"I don't think I like the square toes. Or red," I add, attempting to help narrow down the search before we wind up walking out of here with our hands empty.

Brody sets the boots back and then faces me again, gnawing on the inside of his cheek. Gripping his hips in a wide, powerful stance, he dips his chin. "Be right back."

I fold my hands in my lap and watch him leave, leaning forward to peek past one of the rows of shelving just to catch a glance at his ass. The store is quiet today, but I have no clue if that's out of the ordinary for a place like this. I'd bet it's not. I doubt cowboys are bothering much with gossip when they're shopping for new boots.

Either way, I'm relieved that we haven't had to avoid many shoppers. Brody's disguise isn't exactly state-of-the-art. It wouldn't take much for someone to recognize him despite it, so it means a lot to me that he risked that for me today.

I wiggle my toes in the thick wool socks he brought in with us—another one of his considerate gestures that sent my belly flapping. Road trips have never been my favourite, but with Brody, I think I could get used to them. Driving the same roads I did the day before while coming home from the airport took on an entirely different look sitting beside him today. The two and a half hours weren't boring or exhausting. They were the complete opposite. Lively and full of laughter and thoughtful conversation.

I think it's safe to assume at this point that most things would be different with Brody by my side.

"Okay, give these ones a try."

Twisting to find Brody headed toward me with a dark brown box in his hands, I untwist my fingers and splay them flat on my thighs.

"Where'd you find these ones?" I ask.

He winks, flipping open the lid for me to look inside. "That's a secret. Grab one and take a look."

As I trail my eyes over the boots, my breath catches in my

throat. Slowly, I reach toward them and pull the first from the box. It's soft in my hands, with a curved toe and a small heel. The light brown grooves in the slightly darker leather are in the shape of sunflowers, and I look at Brody, catching his soft, relaxed features and wishing I could see his eyes.

"They're beautiful," I murmur.

"Try 'em on."

I do instantly, sliding the first boot onto my foot before greedily reaching for the next and repeating the motions. The fit is snug with the wool socks but not too tight. Brody kneels down in front of me, running his hands up and down my calf and ankle as if to check the fit, but I think he's just using it as an excuse to touch me. The thought has me feeling incredibly giddy. Horny too. But that's nothing new.

"Stand up and see how they feel," he instructs.

I alternate between leaning on my feet and pushing forward on my toes before walking a small path back and forth on the carpet. "They feel good. I love them."

"Love them enough to wear them often?"

"Enough to never go anywhere without wearing them."

He stares at me for a moment, head lowering before rising again, and I can't help but push on my toes to pull his glasses off. A full-body shiver racks through me when I finally see what he's been hiding behind them—a heat that licks the flames already building between my legs. That taunts it, begging it to come out and play.

I'm too damn weak-willed for this because it takes all of five seconds staring at those sexy blue eyes before I'm poking the bear. "What do you think? Do you like them?"

"I'm thinkin' that I want to toss you over my shoulder and haul you back out to my truck. I'm thinkin'—" His large steps eat the distance between us. "That for some fuckin' reason, I got lucky enough to call you mine."

I try and steady my breathing, but it's a useless effort. "I've never been carried over someone's shoulder before."

A slow lift of his brow. "Don't tempt me, sweetheart."

"Well, if we're done here, then we can leave. Go back to town and have dinner."

"Where would we have dinner? Out?" he asks, skirting around the question we both know he wants to ask.

I shake my head slowly.

"Are you invitin' me over, Anna?" His voice is so low, a ghost of a sound.

"After today, it's only right to thank you with dinner."

Calloused hands cup my cheeks, hot breath fanning my lips as he leans in close and whispers, "I'll come over. But not under the pretense of just dinner. I'll take dessert too."

I flush from head to toe. My panties grow soaked, a near automatic response when it comes to this man. I exhale a shaky breath and lean forward, kissing him softly. He presses back harder, his lips coaxing mine open just enough that he can taste me fully before he's pulling back.

"This is going to be the longest drive home of my life," he confesses.

My laugh is breathy, quiet. "You're telling me."

AN HOUR LATER, I'm damn near choking on the sexual tension rippling in the dark cab of Brody's truck. The inner thighs of my jeans have probably begun to pill from the consistent rubbing I've been doing.

After Brody paid for my incredibly expensive boots—his request—we left the shop and immediately set off for Cherry Peak. I slipped on my new boots as soon as we hit the highway and haven't been able to stop looking at them since.

I've caught Brody's heated stares as well. They've only made my arousal worse. It doesn't matter how many times I change the radio station or check my phone, not a single thing has managed to distract me from how badly I want to shove the centre console up and climb into his lap.

Desire coils low in my belly, making my skin sensitive to every blow of the heater, and my lungs burn from the effort of controlling my rampant breathing.

Leather groans, and I look at the steering wheel to see Brody gripping it so tight his knuckles are white. He rubs the leather back and forth, and fuck me, the veins on the backs of his hands flex and bulge. I drop my head back to the headrest and close my eyes, tapping at the window.

The old Anna never would have considered taking charge here . . . Never would have done what I'm about to.

Brody flings his head to the side when I shove the console up and unbuckle my seat belt. The sun has set, and I let that calm some of my nerves. Nobody but him can see as I scoot into the small middle seat and lay a hand over his lap, right over the bulge beneath his zipper. My eyes go wide at the thick ridge of him, so hot I can feel it through the thick jeans.

It's my first time touching him this way. My blood boils beneath my skin, heady with my want for him. A peek up at him through my lashes, and I see him grinding his jaw, a harsh breath exploding through his parted lips. I pause, wanting to make sure it isn't discomfort that has him so tense.

Dark blue eyes snare mine in a look so intense pleasure spikes between my legs, like an invisible slap to my clit. "Swear to fuck, Anna, you pull me out of my jeans right now and I'll be takin' that pretty mouth. I'm barely holdin' on here."

Relief plows through me before it's replaced by determination. Fingers shaky with need, I unbutton his jeans and tug. He lifts his hips for me, and I curse as his cock comes free. Long and thick and wet, just for me.

"Kiss me," he orders gruffly.

I twist, setting my knees on the seat and reaching to press my lips on his. He's waiting for me. The moment our lips touch, he's grabbing the back of my head and holding me in place, continuing to stare out the windshield as he devours my mouth.

It's reckless. Even under the cover of night, the highway is busy. Headlights shine through the cab one after the other, but I don't sit back down and hide. Not until he gives me permission. He tastes too good. Feels incredible.

I'm anxious to please him, and when I grip his cock in my fist, stroking once, his hiss fills my mouth before I swallow it. He tugs on my roots, separating us by a hairsbreadth.

"Try not to make me crash the truck. Got precious cargo," he breathes. The order in the teasing words doesn't go unnoticed.

I've found myself a dominant man, and the idea of that thrills me.

I slink down his body like water, pooling on the seat at his thighs. His muscles are tight, bulging as he shifts, legs spread as wide as possible in his jeans. My grip tightens around his shaft, and he throbs, his torso vibrating against the seat and fingers straining in my hair.

"I'll try my best," I promise, eyes trained on his groin.

My own arousal is a lingering song in my ears, but I ignore it in exchange for this moment. With slow strokes, I work his cock in my fist, bending at the waist almost subconsciously as I get so close my breath fans over the red, wet head of him.

My ass is in the air, and the button of my jeans digs into my stomach, but I stay in this position, unable to back away. I'm drunk on lust, intoxicated by the feel and taste and smell of him. My tongue slips from my mouth and traces the edges of his tip before dragging a hot line over the slit, collecting the bead of precum pooling there. I moan, loud and wanton, and repeat the action twice.

"*Fuck.* Just like that. Again," he grits out.

I do as he says, but only for a moment. Then, I'm taking him into my mouth, working the rigid length of him as far as I can before pulling back and sucking in a breath. His fingers are locked in my hair but frozen in a tight pull, keeping still. I drop my head again and move it side to side, careful to keep my teeth to myself but hoping he'll get the memo.

He does. I grin wickedly when he starts using his hold to guide me, setting a pace that he likes. I'm a willing servant, my body strung so tight every one of his groans is a plunge of a finger inside of me. I've never gotten this sort of pleasure from giving a blow job before. I'm a live wire, his for the taking. I rub my thighs together, eyes drifting shut from the sparks I create between them.

Brody doesn't miss my movements. He waits until I've taken him deep before shifting his hips, pushing deeper. "Touch yourself, Anna. Show me how wet you are."

I gag, eyes beginning to water as I rip open my jeans and dive my hands into my panties. I'm drenched, the pretty lace soiled, but I already knew that. The first press of my fingertip to my clit has me bucking, Brody's cock brushing the back of my throat before I pull back up.

"Show me," he hisses.

"Okay," I whimper.

I dip my finger inside myself just once before offering him my hand. With my lips spread around the tip of his cock, I watch as he releases my hair and takes hold of my wrist, bringing my finger to his mouth and sucking it clean. I clench around nothing, my mind splintering.

"Perfect," he groans, returning his fingers to my hair. I shut my eyes, pushing back into his touch. "Get yourself off for me, sweetheart. Come with me."

I'm already so close that I know it won't take long. Sliding my hand back past the waistband of my jeans, I whimper at the pleasure my fingers bring. I work my clit with quick, hard circles, not needing much else.

Brody starts working himself into my mouth, helping speed up the pace as I stroke what I can't fit and moan without a care. My cheeks burn with the strain of sucking them in, and my back begins to ache from being bent over, but the pain only drives me.

Combined with the overload of pleasure, it's not even a minute later that I'm coming, crying out around the cock in my mouth. My limbs shake and eyes go dark with pleasure before I hear him curse and pull me off his shaft.

I force myself to keep my eyes open and my grip on him strong as I stroke him hard and fast. He spits a curse before thick ropes of cum fly, painting the suddenly bare, muscled expanse of his lower stomach. My blinks are lazy when I tug my brows together and set my cheek against his thigh, catching my breath.

"Why did you pull me off?" I whisper.

The fingers curled in my hair relax and turn gentle as he strokes my head, his breath just as ragged. "I asked you what you wanted me to do, but you didn't hear me. Didn't want to risk it."

I grin despite myself, pulling my hand from my jeans and wiping it on my thigh. "Yeah, I think my hearing blew for a bit there. For the record, you don't have to pull me off next time."

"Alright," he says softly.

Still wearing my silly grin, I help get his jeans back up and buttoned before sitting on my ass and grabbing a napkin from the glovebox to wipe his stomach. He takes the dirty napkin and shoves it into a plastic bag before reaching into the back seat to dispose of it for now. Reluctantly, I start to shift back to my seat before he stops me with a heavy palm on my knee.

"Stay here. There's a buckle hidden between the seats some-where. Don't want you all the way across the truck."

My heart thumps. "Okay, but I can't promise that I won't fall asleep on your shoulder."

He shakes his shoulder and gives me a crooked smile. "It's all yours, Buttercup."

The words strike harder than intended. I'm more positive now than ever that I'm all his too.

34

Annalise

BRODY STEPS INTO MY HOUSE AND IMMEDIATELY KICKS OFF HIS boots. I follow suit, our socks matching in a stupidly cute way. I grin stupidly at our feet before we shuck off our jackets. Leading him inside, I kick up the temperature on the thermostat on the way past, chilled from the cold walk up.

"Thank you for today, Brody."

Just like I thought I would, I passed out for the rest of the truck ride home. One moment, I was tucking myself into his side, and the next, he was gently shaking me awake, parked in his spot in front of my house. It was instinct to ask him to come inside, even if we already indulged in dessert on the way back. I'll take any time with him that I can get.

"My pleasure."

"Do you want to stay for a while and watch a movie or something?" Heat trickles up my chest at the juvenility of the question.

He doesn't seem to care, though. "Would love to."

"Do you have a movie preference?" I ask, sitting on the couch, eyes eating up the confident sway of his body as he follows.

"Not really. I'm pretty easy."

"What about a Christmas movie?" I turn the TV on and start sorting through the online movies. An idea sparks in my mind, curving my mouth. "A Hallmark one?"

He sits beside me, the cushion dipping beneath his weight. I don't bother pretending I don't want to be close to him. In two scoots, I'm curled around his side, his arm automatically draping along the couch behind my head.

"Only if you pick the worst one there is. I want ultimate cheese, Buttercup."

"Now we're talking," I say, sorting through a few more movies before choosing one.

His laugh is loud, soaring from deep in his belly. "Jesus Christ."

"What?"

The opening credits flash across the screen before the title appears. *A Cowboy's Christmas Wish.* My stomach cramps from holding back a laugh.

"This is going to be brutal," he muses.

"You don't think it's going to be incredibly accurate to your real life?" I ask, feigning shock.

He stretches his legs out, resting his feet on the ottoman. My heart jolts when he grips my thigh and drapes it over his lap, keeping his hand firmly in place after I'm settled. "I'll try not to pick it apart too much for you."

"Go ahead. I love ripping apart movies."

And that's exactly what we do. For the next hour and a half, we make notes on everything in the movie, belting out in unattractive, loud laughter at the cheesy dialogue and terrible acting. I'm half sprawled over his body, cheek pressed to his sternum and knee nestled between both of his by the time the couple rides off on the back of a horse together, hooves kicking up snow behind them.

"So, do all cowboys naturally know how to dance?" I tease, drawing swirls with my fingertip over the thick muscles of his abdomen as I recall the repeated theme of line dancing in the movie.

I've never felt abs like Brody's before. Stewart was fit but not this muscled. Brody's body has been honed by hard labour and whatever it is he does to keep in shape in Nashville. Weightlifting, if the steel cut of his biceps is anything to go off.

He continues playing with my hair, alternating between twirling pieces around his fingers and scratching my scalp. "Fuck no. But my grandma put a lot of time into ensurin' I could hold my own. Was I decent enough of a partner the other night?"

"More than decent, actually." Resting my chin on his chest, I look upward, catching his waiting stare. "You know there are pictures of us online now, right?"

"I know. You okay with that?"

"I don't have much of a social presence, so I'm not too concerned for me."

"But you are for me?" he asks, although it sounds more like a statement than a question.

"Should I be?"

"You can't answer a question with another question."

I laugh softly. "I think you're a grown man, and if you weren't confident enough about us to be photographed together, you wouldn't have put us in a position to be. It's my own self-doubt that's the problem."

Like the reoccurring, pestering thought that I'm not good enough to be seen beside him. Or that he won't remember me once he's gone. That I'll be a memory he won't bother recalling.

Brody guides me up his body, bringing us face to face. I ignore the flutter in my stomach and focus on listening to the words he speaks. "If I ever meet the man who's behind the worry in your eyes, baby, I swear to fuck I'll ruin him."

"I'd like to see that," I admit. Give me caveman and ultra-protectiveness. I'll never turn down the chance to watch this man protect my honour. Fists or words, it wouldn't matter.

He cups my jaw so, so softly, as if he's suddenly afraid I'll crumble to dust in his palm. "Never been prouder to be seen with a woman than I have been with you. That's the truth, Anna. I've just been tryin' not to scare you."

"It's a good thing I don't scare easily, then."

His smile reaches his eyes this time, almost unnaturally beautiful. "Yeah, I'm learnin' that."

The credits continue to roll, doodles decorating the black screen. One in particular of a short, fluffy animal catches my eye, and I can't stop myself before I'm switching gears, blurting out, "Do you have any fluffy cows at the ranch?"

Brody's chest begins to shake with laughter beneath me. "Fluffy cows? No. I don't think we ever have."

"Not even one as a pet?"

"The sky would fall before my grandfather took cattle as pets, sweetheart."

I nod, deflating a bit. "That's fair."

"Why the random train of thought?"

"They're all over the internet right now. I fell down the rabbit hole a few weeks ago, and they're the cutest damn things in the world. I was just curious whether you've ever had one."

"Would you have a fluffy cow as a pet?"

"I'd love one. They're like dogs that can live outside instead of shedding all over the house and making a mess of things."

"True enough. I've never considered getting one."

"Well, now maybe you should."

"Maybe I will."

I kiss his chest, lips lingering to feel the thump of his heartbeat against them. "Good. Want to watch another movie?"

He presses a kiss to my forehead and nods. I duck my head and get back into my previous position. It doesn't make me long to pick another movie, but this time, I hardly make it halfway through before I'm falling asleep.

I don't wake until the room has gone silent and a soft warmth feathers across my cheek. I'm moved from my seat and hauled into the air, held against a hard body. I keep my eyes closed, not wanting to fully wake just yet.

Strong arms hold me close to a chest that moves steadily against my cheek. I rub my face against it, sighing out contently at the security that washes over me, soothing my most damaged parts.

I inhale deeply, picking out the smell of the peppermint candle I burned earlier through Brody's cologne. His breath fans the top of my head before his arms tighten just once. I'm clutching onto his arm when he pushes open a door and goes to set me down.

"Stay," I plea, squeezing my eyes shut.

He pauses. "You sure?"

"Positive."

"I'm stayin' on the couch."

I nod quickly. "Okay. Just stay. There are extra blankets in the linen closet. Take one of my pillows."

I'm not ready to let him go yet. Call it desperation or neediness, I don't care. The thought of him walking out the door right now has my stomach in a fist-sized knot.

"I'll stay, sweetheart. Get into bed for me."

The thick socks on my feet protect them from the cold bite of the wood floors as I steady myself and then crawl beneath the lifted covers. It takes more self-restraint than I thought it would not to tug him right down beside me. I nearly crack and do it when he leans down to brush my hair back and kisses my nose and then, finally, my mouth. It's a sleepy kiss, one full of soft meaning. The most beautiful kind.

"Sweet dreams, Anna. I'll see you in the morning."

I let my eyes flutter closed and nod, humming my agreement. "Good night, Bo."

THE NEXT DAY FLIES BY.

I woke to find Brody already up and pouring two cups of

coffee, yesterday's clothes on and wrinkled. I'm still unsure how long he'd already been up by the time I was ready to head to work, but I wouldn't be surprised if it was before dawn broke.

He drove me to work and headed out to the ranch with the usual promise of being back at the end of my shift. I've been a ball of energy all day, bouncing around from client to client. I feel refreshed, alive. Happiness is a drug. One hit of the good stuff and I'm nose to the ground in search of another.

Wanda has picked up on the attitude as well, picking at me all damn day with a dirty smirk. I finish taking payment from the last client and glare at her from across the salon when I notice she's lingering by my station.

"I want whatever you're on today, Anna. I ain't ever seen someone blow-dry that much hair in such little time in all my life," she says.

I tuck the debit machine away and shift to face her, leaning against the side of the desk. "I'm skilled with a hair dryer. What can I say?"

"Don't act coy. You can't outplay a player."

"I just slept well last night. I'm refreshed."

"Oh, I bet you slept like a million fucking bucks with a man like Brody Steele beside you."

I can't fight the red that blooms on my cheeks. With a quick look around the salon, I confirm we're alone. "We didn't—haven't slept in the same bed. Not that it's any of your business, Snoopy."

"I'm not gonna tell anybody, sugar. Just razzing you a bit."

"I know. I know. Sorry for jumping at you."

She waves her hand, swaying toward me. The nails that tap the desk beside mine are painted with candy cane stripes and mistletoe. "We don't know each other well, so I can't blame you for being guarded. I haven't spent too much time at the salon as of late, but it's nothing personal. I've been in town for too long and am in need of a change of scenery soon."

"You're a bit of a move-arounder, then?"

"'Flighty' is I think the word my father likes to use," she says with a painfully fake smile.

I shrug a shoulder. "So you like to explore. Who cares."

"My mom, for one. Most of the judgmental pricks in this town, for another. My dad took off for most of my childhood, and now that he's retiring soon, everyone assumed I'd stick around to play catch-up and wait for him to *maybe* come back. It's ridiculously sad, but I keep starting these businesses with the hope he'll finally start to pay attention to me. I've never even liked cutting hair, let alone owning a salon. But I think I've had enough of trying. I have to stop putting my life on hold for the off chance he was *finally* ready to give us the time of day, y'know?"

"I do, actually. It's not exactly the same, but I haven't spoken to my dad in three years. Sometimes you have to know when to look out for yourself regardless of the familial obligations you think you have. It's not always worth the stress and hurt."

Wanda nods, eyes sparking to life. "Exactly! God, I'm so tired of hearing the guilt trips. Especially around the holidays. I've been fending off my mom's phone calls for weeks."

"Are you seeing anyone for Christmas?"

"Nah. I'm thinking I might book a trip somewhere hot. Laze the days away on beaches littered with shirtless surfing men."

I tip my head back and laugh, my chest full and warm. "I'd join you if I could. It's looking like I'll be spending Christmas alone. My sister's going to spend the holidays with her husband's family, and I don't feel like being a cling-on while she's there."

Wanda doesn't look at me with pity. No, she's too busy looking behind me. I spin on my heels and immediately grin at who I find in the doorway.

Wanda moves to greet the customer but stops at my side, our shoulders brushing. Dropping her voice, she says, "Looks like the mother-in-law is here."

I pinch her underarm, and then she's breezing past me, her boots clipping the tiles.

"Mrs. Steele, this is a lovely surprise," I call, following Wanda.

"Eliza," the older woman corrects me gently before pulling me into her arms and hugging me tight. "And I figured I better stop in to get this old mop of hair done right up for Christmas."

"You came on the right day. Anna's the best I have." Wanda winks at me, leaning back against the desk.

As soon as I'm out of Eliza's arms, I'm thanking Wanda with a subtle nod. "I try my best."

"But first, what is this I hear about you spending Christmas alone?" Eliza asks, voice firm, like I imagine it would have been back when she had to scold a young Brody.

Wanda sucks in her lips while Brody's grandmother stares fiercely at me, expecting an answer and a damn good one at that.

Gesturing toward my station, I suggest, "Let's get started on your hair first."

"No. Tell me first so I don't have the chance to get sidetracked," she demands. "You are under no circumstances spending Christmas alone."

"Well, I don't want to spend another year hanging around my brother-in-law's family. I've done that before, and they're nice enough to include me, but it's not the same."

"I don't see anything wrong with spending the holidays alone, Eliza," Wanda puts in.

"Well, then you can call me Mrs. Steele, Wanda," Eliza tuts.

The salon owner huffs a laugh and pats Eliza on the back. "Just for that, I'm not going to give you all the mini samples you love so much."

"Okay, you two, break it up."

I make a show of placing myself between the women before Brody's grandmother takes my hands and lifts them between us. I soak in her soft gaze, letting it fill me up inside.

"You'll come to the ranch and spend Christmas with us."

Her words are kind, but they hold a firmness to them that tells me she's more so telling than offering. I nearly melt right then and there. It's truly no wonder Brody is the way he is. Not when he was raised by a woman like this.

"Are you sure I won't be overstepping? I don't want to impose."

"Dear, I don't think you could impose on our family even if you tried. I'm sure you're the only thing on Brody's Christmas list anyway."

There's no stopping my smile. God, it spreads so wide my cheeks burn from the stretch. "Then I'd love to spend Christmas at the ranch. I can't wait."

35

Brody

I WASH MY HANDS IN THE KITCHEN SINK, WATCHING THE WATER TURN pink in the white basin. The scent of paint lingers in my hair and on my clothes. An old, ripped tee and dirty jeans. I speed up my washing, not wanting my grandmother to catch me in here looking like I just crawled out of a barn. Even if that's exactly what I've just done.

"Is that you, Brody?" she calls, voice distant enough I know I have a couple of minutes to get gone.

I twist the taps to cut the water and don't waste time drying my hands before I'm slipping out the back door, sights set on the guest house. It's a bit of a walk, but that makes it all the more private. I need the time to myself the walk will grant me. I'm a mess of nerves, more than I've felt in a long, long time.

Over the past few years, Christmas has become a bit of a tense time around here. Before coming back home those few months ago, I hadn't been back for the holidays since the first year I moved to Nashville. The resentment my grandfather held for me was too strong to endure for days at a time. Snide comments and unnecessary digs at the dinner table. It became too much.

So, I hid. I came up with a million excuses, knowing damn

well each one was hurting my grandmother deeper and deeper. She'll never tell me that I hurt her, but she doesn't have to. I'm aware of my actions and the consequences of them. That's how I know having me home this year means so much to her.

She invited Annalise for two reasons. The first being the most obvious—that nobody should spend the holidays alone. Hearing that Anna was going to be alone for the holidays poked at her strong caretaker instincts, urging her to take her beneath her wing. The second reason is the one she's tried to deny. That she was thinking of me. That this was a matchmaking effort. One I didn't need her to bother with.

I told her as much when she got back from her hair appointment.

Grandma walks into the dining room, bouncing her curls against her open palms and grinning up a storm. "Do you like my new do, Brody?"

Something in her voice makes the hairs on my arms stand as I look up from my seat at the table, a glass of water in my dirty hands. I've just finished fixing up the bucket on Grandpa's broken-down skid steer, a near crick in my neck hurting like a motherfucker.

"Looks great. And let me guess, you asked Anna to fit you into her schedule?"

"As if I'd have anyone else touch my hair now that that sweet girl is available."

"Well, she did a great job," I say, not falling for her oh-so-obvious trap.

"You should get her to give you a trim again. Maybe on Christmas."

Suspicion flares. "Why would she want to cut my hair on Christmas?"

She glances around the room, eyes wide and too innocent. When she makes for the bowl of apples on the table, I tug it out of reach. Her grin only grows in size.

"You want the apples to yourself? Go ahead, I know how much you love them."

I fight a cringe. I've hated apples since I was a boy. Used to sneak all mine out to the stable and hand 'em off the to the horses.

"You're trying to distract me from the fact you stuck your nose somewhere it didn't belong, aren't you?"

Her lips pop open. "How dare you?"

"How dare I? Grandma, you might be old, but you're not that old."

"Brody Christopher Steele, you did not just mention my age!"

I belt out a laugh as she stalks toward me, so short she hardly reaches my shoulders but tough as iron. Her hands come flying at me before fingers dip into my sides and stomach. I slap them away, jerking backward as she scrunches her brows in concentration.

"I'm not a child anymore, Grams. You can't just tickle me whenever you want to in order to get your way."

"If it keeps you from being such a stubborn mule, then so be it!"

"I'm a stubborn mule now?"

She drops her hands to her hips, giving my stomach muscles a break. "Were you really not going to invite your woman to Christmas?"

I blink slowly. "I figured she had plans of her own."

"If you'd have asked her, you'd know she didn't. It seems her family is otherwise occupied this holiday season."

The quick bite of judgment in her tone has me jumping to her family's defense. "They're good people, Grams. They just live far away from one another."

"It doesn't matter either way. I invited her, and she'll be here for Christmas. With us." *She pushes her shoulders back, chin high.* "We'll make her feel like family."

The sentiment warms my belly like a long swig of hot chocolate. I want Anna to feel at home with my family, want her here over the holidays. I'm a fool not to have asked her myself the way I want to.

"If you're doing this just to play matchmaker, I don't need the help. I'm doing pretty well on my own."

She sets a hand on my forearm, staring up at me softly. "I've done my part. The rest is up to you. Don't play it safe and risk missing out *on important moments, Brody. Figure out what it is you want, and do everything in your power to make it happen."*

She left me in the dining room a beat later, claiming she needed to change before getting started on dinner. As if she didn't just want to leave me to sit in my thoughts. The days since have been much the same.

She'll ask me the same few questions about how Anna's doing, if she's excited for Christmas and what she's been up to. I spent a lot of time searching for Anna's Christmas gift, and Grams was extremely giddy about that. It took nearly the two weeks since the idea sparked to not only locate what I needed but to complete my vision. Now that I'm done, I'm left with a bucket load of nerves and the hope that she loves what I've done.

Trees and bush separate the main house from the guest house, wrapping around the front and providing a necessary sense of privacy in such an open space. Long gravel roads connect the two houses, now covered in thick snow. The ranch is a sight to behold in the summertime, and there's an ache in my chest when I think about not being here to witness it again. It's been so long since I've been home in the summer, to feel the sun baking my shoulders and watch the breeze dancing through the fields. Fuck me, I've gone soft.

The guest house is big. Big and spacious and fitted with upgrades that the main house lacks. I had it built a few years ago, spent my first big paycheque from the label on it, knowing I needed a place of my own for when I came back home.

My first apartment in Nashville was the shits. I found a place that was rough and outdated and, most importantly, dirt cheap so I could focus on finishing up my place in Cherry Peak first. I never told anyone back home that little fact. They thought I was living it large in Music City. I was living well but not large.

Grandpa hated that I was the one to get the house built. He's old-fashioned that way, but if me adding a piece of property to the ranch meant I'd be coming back home to them, he kept his mouth shut. I'm surprised he didn't burn it to the ground when I decided to stay away.

I shove those thoughts aside as I walk inside and flip the lights on. My boots come off before I head for my bedroom, triple-checking along the way that I haven't left a mess for Anna to see anywhere.

Today'll be the first time she's been inside this place. Unlike the main house, these walls are mine. Everything inside of them is mine. Memories and keepsakes. Mementos from my career as of late and back when I was a teenager playing no-good covers at the diner on Saturdays. Pieces of me are everywhere. Everything I had in my grandparents' house growing up is here now.

Inviting Anna here feels a lot like slicing open my chest and baring my soul to her. But I don't want to keep her out any longer. She's already pried me halfway open and taken what she can anyway. There's no use in fighting giving her the rest.

Pleased with the lack of mess, I take a quick shower and change before tossing my hat on and making my way back to the front of the house. I've gotta pick her up right about now, and I'm itching to see her.

I've hardly tugged one boot on when I hear tires roll over the packed snow outside. I put on the second boot before opening the door and stepping outside, arms bare in the cold.

The small, clunky red car comes to a stop seconds before the passenger door is flying open and Anna's hopping out. Fit with tight blue jeans, my old jacket, and her new boots, she's a fucking dream. I'm entirely unprepared for when she reaches back into the car and then sets a light brown cowboy hat on her head. With a beaming smile, she takes a gift box from Poppy before shutting the car door and jogging toward me.

"Merry Christmas, Brody," she calls, each step bringing her closer and closer until finally, she's in my arms.

I scoop her up and lift her feet from the ground, spinning us around. "Merry Christmas, sweetheart. I was just about to come get you."

Glancing at the car in front of my house, I wave at Poppy before she returns the gesture and leaves the way she came.

"Poppy stopped by to drop her gifts off, and I couldn't wait any longer to come. It feels like I haven't seen you in forever."

"Three days without kissin' you and I'm damn near outta my mind," I mutter before I'm remedying the problem.

Our kiss isn't soft; it's hard and fierce and desperate, chock full of a longing that I don't think I'll ever fucking understand. It's been a long two weeks of trying to take my time with her. Of trying to learn her body with my hands and tongue while giving her the opportunity to learn mine in the same way. We haven't had sex yet, been holding off as long as possible to take that last step, but I've about run out of time.

Vocal therapy was a pain in my ass. It kept me away from her more often than I'd like, but for as good a reason as any. My vocal cords are nearly back to where they were before I came home. I'm relieved not to be hurting anymore but dreading what comes next. Going back to Nashville. Leaving this place, this woman, behind.

Anna's the one to pull back, running a soothing hand up and down my back as I try and pull myself together. She presses up on her toes and butts my nose with her own.

"Don't think about it. I'm trying not to," she says, reading my mind.

"We gotta lot to talk about the next two days. Don't plan on lettin' you leave here without us figurin' somethin' out."

"Alright. How about we step inside before you end up spending the holidays with a cold?"

I step into her body and take a deep inhale of her perfume before cupping her cheek and bringing her in for another kiss. This time, I take my time with her, tasting her lips and tongue, drawing it out as long as I can. She feels like heaven, soft against my hard. Warm to my cold. It takes everything in me to keep from taking her to bed right now.

"I'll grab my coat, but then I wanna give you your present," I murmur against her swollen mouth.

"Already?"

"I have more than one, but this first one is special. You'll love it."

Her eyes twinkle when she backs up and holds my gaze. "I've never been one to turn down a gift. Get your jacket!"

When her hand comes down on my ass, I choke on a laugh and hightail it into the house.

36

Annalise

LAST CHRISTMAS, I LET BRAXTON CONVINCE ME INTO GOING TO HER in-laws' house. The Hutton family is big and loud but so loving it's almost hard to believe. If I hadn't witnessed the relationship that family has with my own eyes, I would have called bullshit.

I've never seen another family so tight-knit. So full of love and life. Not until meeting the Steeles.

Brody and his grandfather may not get along right now, but their love runs deep. Their disagreements come from that place of fierce devotion, which is what makes them so strong and all consuming. That's how love is supposed to be. It's supposed to turn us into fools so driven by the want to keep each other close that sometimes we say the wrong things and act poorly.

I'm comfortable here. There's an aura of rightness that sinks deep in my subconscious whenever I step onto the Steele Ranch. This family, small in size but not heart, means something to me. It means a lot.

Spending Christmas here feels like a blessing.

Brody's gloved hand is solid around mine as he leads us down a snowy path that leads to the cattle pastures. My excitement spikes. Despite the chill, I've never been happier to be outside. The fresh air and open sky tickle something deep in my brain, a spot left untouched all my life.

"Did you buy me a horse for Christmas? You know I don't even know how to ride one, right?" My steps are damn near bounced, our pace far too slow for my liking.

His laugh is a deep sound. "I didn't get you a horse, Anna."

"Okay, good."

"Your gift is a bit past the stables, though. You won't be able to miss it once we get there."

We pass the stable, and a few moments later, I find the small structure just inside the first cattle pasture. A . . . pink one?

Picking up my pace, I tug him behind me. He starts to laugh, louder this time, and I ignore him, focusing on the little pink structure as it comes more into focus.

"Brody."

I hear the smirk in his voice. "Anna."

"What is that for?"

"What's what for?"

"Don't even try me right now."

I spin to face him and forget how to think. Forget how to breathe. The adoration glimmering in his eyes is intense, heart stutteringly intense.

"Go ahead, sweetheart. Take a look," he encourages, tipping that hat-covered head toward the miniature shed.

It hurts to look away, but excitement helps soothe the wound as I jog toward the pink structure, my hand slipping from free from his hold.

The closer I get, the easier it is to tell exactly what colour pink the smooth, tall planks of wood have been painted—a pastel shade that appears almost peachy in the bright sun. There are words and a couple of doodles spread above the back side of the shed. The bright yellow banana catches my eyes first before I stop dead a foot from the structure and read the name beside it.

"There's no way Wade signed off on this thing," I choke, emotion clogging my throat.

Brody moves behind me. There's no need to look to confirm. I feel the prickle of awareness on my neck and the heat at my back. My knees wobble as I wait for him to touch me.

When he does, wrapping a strong, supportive arm around my middle, tears spill from my eyes, dripping down my cheeks.

"You haven't even seen the good part yet and you're already cryin'," he points out, his hand sliding beneath my jacket as his fingers splay across my stomach, stroking them everywhere they can reach.

"I don't have to look inside to know. You listened to me."

"I always listen to you."

"The sky hasn't fallen," I say on an exhale.

"It definitely hasn't."

"You said you don't keep cattle as pets."

"I said my grandfather doesn't keep cattle as pets. Didn't say nothin' 'bout me. Or you," he corrects me.

"You or me," I echo, hands itching to reach for the door. "I wasn't expecting this."

"That's the whole point of a surprise, Buttercup. Not knowing what to expect."

"I don't think most people expect surprises like this either, Brody."

"Stop puttin' up a stink and follow me."

I'd been waiting for his permission. The moment I get it, I'm following through the gate and into the pasture. I see the open length of the shed that faces the busy pasture first. Then, the knee-height fluffy animal taking small hops toward us from beneath it. My jaw drops as I watch the cow shake out of his apparent nerves and bounce to Brody, butting its head against his knee.

"Been lonely these past couple hours, have you?" he asks the cow, dropping a hand to scratch between its ears.

God, they're fluffy ears too.

The adorable little thing has thick, off-white fur with a long patch of hair between its ears that hangs down and tickles the top of its pink nose. Calm brown eyes watch me curiously, and I smile at it, as if it can tell that I'm a nice person solely from a smile. A bit ridiculous, but oh well.

"How long have you had it here for?" I ask softly.

"Three days. It took a while to find her, but I think she was worth the hunt. Grandma's taken a likin' to her as well. She's even let her into the house a couple of times when Grandpa's been workin' late. Any other time, she's out here with the other cows. Quite the Ms. Popular, this one."

My brows reach my hairline. "Inside? She can go inside?"

"Apparently so. Like I said—spoiled."

"I don't even know what to do or say or just . . . anything," I admit.

"Let her smell your hand and introduce yourself. She's almost as sweet as you are."

"I'm not always sweet," I say pointedly.

"Pretty damn close to it."

I nip at my lip, hiding a smile as I extend my hand to the cow. Banana, according to the writing on the shed.

"You named her," I whisper.

Banana presses her wet nose to my palm, and I suck back a laugh, not wanting to come off too strong.

"If you don't like it, we'll change it. It's not like she'll be able to tell."

"You got me a miniature fluffy cow," I say, almost to myself.

He snorts. "I did."

I lift my eyes, staring up at him with my heart open, exposed. "Nobody's ever done something like this for me."

"I'm happy to be the first, then."

And the last, I beg him to say. *Tell me you'll be the only one to do these things for me. For a long time to come.* But he doesn't say that, and I hate the way that hurts me. A small fleck of doubt doubles in size.

"Hey." Fingers thread through my hair, turning my head

until I'm forced to stare into his deep blue eyes. "Where'd you go?"

Banana twists her face into my open palm, trying to steal my attention back to her. I would have laughed at that had I not felt twisted up inside. The instant adoration I feel for her helps stabilize me.

"I think that if I'm not careful, it would be so easy to love you."

It's out before I can stop it.

The air around us stills. It grows so, so quiet.

Then, he's moving. Cow forgotten, he holds both my hips in his hands and tugs me close, groin to groin, chest to chest. I shiver at the contact and realize I've just lied to him.

Turns out that I wasn't careful after all. Considering I'm already in love with him.

The words he speaks next have me grateful he's gripping me so tight as my knees wobble.

"It'd be easier to fall in love with you, Annalise Heights. And I've never been a fan of careful."

I DON'T KEEP track of how long we spend out in the pasture with Banana. I'm tucked between Brody's legs, his back to the inner wall of the shed, as our cow bites down on a pink rope, alternating between trying to eat it and trying to tug it front my hands.

I've already fallen in love with the sweet girl. It didn't take much time at all for me to want to move out here with her. Of course, that's not exactly possible. But if I could, I would.

I was pleased to learn that Brody's thought ahead when it comes to her and her new life.

He built this shed himself, with help from a few willing ranch hands who didn't mind staying late after already long days. It's not for much more than just a shelter if she or any of the other cows ever needed or wanted it. There's another shed much like this one but bigger and further out in the pasture. She'd fed with the other cows but, of course, gets far more treats than they do. And in the summer, she'll have an unlimited supply of grass to mow down on all day.

She's spoiled. Utterly spoiled. Almost as much so as I am.

I lean back further in Brody's embrace, exhaling happily when his arms flex around my middle. He sets his chin on my shoulder, and his bearded jaw scrapes my cheek in a dangerously sexy way.

As much as I love my new hat—a gift from Poppy—I'm grateful he took it off when we sat down. Nothing's in the way of his ability to touch me so freely now.

"Are you going to keep your beard when you go back?" I ask, unable to help myself.

He drags said beard harder against my skin. "Yeah. I figure I'll keep it for a while."

"Good. It suits you."

"Makes me look a bit more rugged than the first time you saw me."

"More rugged but just as handsome."

Lips soothe the burn from his beard. "Sure as shit didn't expect to wind up here with you after that first meetin'."

"No? You didn't have a vision of buying the woman who verbally spanked your ass in front of a crowd of people a fluffy cow on your family's ranch?"

"Nah, but I wish I had. Would have saved a bit of time runnin' around the bush that way."

"I think I like the way we started. It was unique," I admit, releasing the rope toy and letting Banana have a win.

She jumps back and then forward adorably before discarding the toy in search of another.

"You're goin' to have to be here often to see Banana," he says, as if I don't already know that. Or plan on it.

"Even when you're gone?"

A pause. "Especially when I'm gone."

"Do you know when you leave?"

I don't want to know, but at the same time, I need to. He can only delay his return to Nashville for so long.

"Next week. Rita sent me the plane ticket last night."

My stomach churns, and I squeeze my eyes shut, wishing the sudden nausea away.

"How long will you be gone?"

"Just a few days. I'm meeting with the label, but it shouldn't take long."

"And then?"

He tightens his grip on me, and I let him. "Then I'm comin' back until I know what comes next. Until *we've* decided what to do next."

"As in us? You and me?"

"Yeah, us, sweetheart. You and me. I don't want to say goodbye once I go back. Plan on keepin' you as long as I can."

I spin in his arms, tucking my legs into my chest as his bracket my body. He slings his arms over his knees, eyes watching intensely as I rest my arms on his shoulders and lock my fingers behind his neck.

"Do you think long distance will work?" I ask calmly. Maybe too calmly.

His expression is tense, so damn concentrated. But those blue eyes are sincere, settling some of my nerves.

"I know it will. For you, I'll make it work. We have a lot to figure out, but we still have time. Today isn't for that conversation, though. I want to just be here with you. Spend the holidays with my woman. I'm confident enough in us to ask you to let me do that."

I soften at the plea in his tone. Words won't suffice in answer. Untucking my legs, I lean forward on my knees and meet his stare, loving the way his eyes track the length of my tongue when it wets my lips. My arms feel like they weigh a thousand pounds hanging on his shoulders as I close the distance between us, tasting his mouth.

The kiss starts soft and sweet before turning hard, frantic. Weeks of sexual tension have all led up to today. I feel the rightness of it in every rise of my chest. We've both been teasing ourselves, but that ends today. Tonight. Now. I don't care, as long as it's soon.

He groans into my mouth, and I suck it down, greedy to hear another one. I sink my fingers into his hair, my nipples hard and aching. Heat pools between my legs, a desire so potent driving me that I tune the rest of the world out. It's just us here. Brody and me.

His large hands possessively cup my ass, kneading it through my jeans. I want them on my bare flesh, want my pants gone.

But, God, I know we can't do this right now. Not here.

It takes everything in me to tear my lips from his and whisper, "Tonight. We can't do this here."

His eyes are still shut when he leans his forehead to mine. "Fucking Banana."

My laugh is loud. Cleansing. It draws his eyes open, the blue in them so sharp and clear it makes me shiver.

Yeah, I think it's safe to say that I'd do just about anything to be with him. Long distance included.

37

Brody

"THERE THEY ARE!" GRANDMA CHEERS, CLAPPING WHEN ANNA AND I enter the kitchen.

I keep Anna close to me, unable to let her go for any amount of time. It took several minutes to will my erection away after nearly taking her in the shed, and I'm still not fully recovered. I feel hot and frazzled. The mess of hair on my head is a perfect example of just how out of my mind I am. I ran my fingers through it too much on the way back.

"It smells amazing in here, Eliza," she says, grinning so damn brightly. "Need any help?"

Grandma returns her smile. "I'd love some. Brody and his grandfather could eat me out of house and home on a regular day, let alone Christmas dinner."

Anna moves to step out from beneath my arm, but I scowl, barely reining in a grunt of denial. My grandmother goes from smiling to glaring at me in a heartbeat. Reluctantly, I drop my arm, and Anna stares up at me with wicked amusement before rushing to my grandmother's side.

Traitor.

Soon, she'll be all mine, I remind myself. And once I have her alone, I won't be letting her out of my sight so easily.

"Don't be so grumpy, Brody. Go keep yourself busy and set the table for me, please," Grandma says, but she's already steering Anna to the sink, instructing her on the easiest and most efficient way to peel a potato.

I linger in the doorway, watching the two women interact, so bubbly and bright. They get along so easily, like old friends. That knowledge does something to me. Twists me up inside in a way that I know comes from a place of love. Because that's what it is. Love.

I love Anna. Deeply and all consumingly. In a way that should terrify me but doesn't. It settles me. Completes me.

I'm whole around her, my missing pieces clicking back in place.

I accept those feelings with open arms, completely unafraid of them. Carrying that completeness with me, I stroll out of the kitchen and grab the good china from the cabinet in the dining room before beginning to set the table.

Laughter and hushed conversation keep me company as I finish my task. Even the stomp of heavy footsteps coming in from the back door doesn't interrupt the two women.

Grandpa's low, deep rumble of a voice cuts in, interrupting them. "Hell of a storm comin' in. They're callin' out for a whiteout on the radio."

"It'll be a true white Christmas, then," Grandma replies, unbothered.

Anna doesn't seem to share the same sentiment if the nerves in her voice are anything to judge. "Will it be bad?"

I step into the kitchen before anyone can answer her. Her eyes find me instantly. They're drawn to me the same way mine are her. I arch a brow at my grandfather when I notice his obvious curiosity as he takes us in.

I'm not sure why he's so surprised at my protectiveness, considering I learned this particular trait from him.

"It'll be fine. We might lose power for a bit, but we have generators galore here," I tell Anna, hoping to comfort her.

She worries her lip. "What about Banana?"

"She'll be fine. There's a shed out there for her if it gets too much, but she can come inside with us if you want, my love," Grandma offers her.

Grandpa's scoff is harsh before he stilts his reaction, coughing to cover it up. "There's no place for a cow in the house on Christmas, Eliza."

"Is that so?" his wife asks, nice and slow.

"Yes. Don't think I haven't noticed the hoof marks on the floors this past week either. I've kept my mouth shut about that, but not this. Not today."

"That's okay! I'm sure she'll be okay. Obviously, I don't know anything about animals, but—" Anna begins, eyes wide and nervous like a deer in headlights.

I settle at her side and set my arm over her shoulders, tucking her into my body, where she belongs. "She'll be good, I promise. We can check on her again before it gets too rough out there, make sure she's settled."

She tries to play it off, but I feel the tension leave her body at my promise. Pride swells in my chest. I want to settle her like this often. A million more times.

"Thank you," she says on a long, relieved exhale.

"We still have a while yet, and I plan on having a nice family dinner, so Wade, if you wouldn't mind, go wash up. You smell like cow shit." Grandma scrunches her nose and lightly shoves her husband out of the room. He tips his head back and barks a laugh, nodding in silent agreement.

I spin Anna to my chest and tip her chin back to make her look at me. My heart tries to bash through my rib cage at the glimmer in her brown eyes.

"Welcome to the Steele family, Buttercup. Buckle up and enjoy the ride."

THE STORM HITS two hours later, rocking through the ranch with a vengeance. We had just finished cleaning up dinner when the lights flickered twice and then gave out completely, banking us in darkness.

The generators took a few minutes to get started, but once they were up and running, I was bundling Anna up in her jacket and sitting her in my truck. She didn't argue as I drove us back over to the guest house or when I helped her inside, insisting she stay the night. It was for her safety. Mainly. And my own selfish wants. The desire to sleep beside her in my bed.

I make quick work of starting my generator and then a fire in the fireplace, all too aware of the way Anna's shivering from her place on my couch. The generator might be on, but the time with no heat kicking through the house has left it fucking freezing.

The small flames come to life before growing into a blaze, warm and bright. I'm moving toward her in an instant, gathering her in my arms and squeezing, soaking in her touch. I spin us around and sit on the couch, pulling her onto my lap, her legs wrapped around my middle.

It's overwhelming, the strength of my feelings for her. The intensity of my affection and desire to have her by my side. She's everything I never knew I needed. The laughter that fills my quietest moments and the finishing notes in a melody I've always thought would be left incomplete.

Fuck. She's just . . . everything.

I press my face into her neck, my lips curving against her pulse. Happiness rattles through me. This right here is what I was missing these past few years. What I was chasing in Nashville but could never quite find.

I'm not letting it slip away. I'll do everything in my power to revel in this happiness for the rest of my life.

"You're smiling," she whispers, palming the back of my head before stroking it softly.

"I'm happy you're here."

"Me too."

Leaning back just enough to bare my face to her waiting stare, I thread our fingers together and rest them on my thighs. She watches me intently, like she's trying to get inside my mind. If only she knew that the only thing I've thought about recently is her.

A soft humour glows in her eyes as she asks, "Why are you staring at me like that?"

"'Cause I feel lucky. I've got my Christmas present in my lap. The best one I've ever had. And if you let me, I'm goin' to spend a damn long time unwrappin' you."

Annalise

My PULSE THUNDERS in my ears, throat drying like a sponge in the hot sun. I shift my hips, an almost subconscious movement to soothe the ache between my legs. Jean on jean, I grind on the bulge beneath me, my lungs on fire.

I palm the soft material of his old hockey tee, the team logo too worn to recognize, before pressing harder, firmer, wanting to feel the ridges hidden beneath. The heat from his skin burns into my fingers, but it's still not enough.

"You can unwrap me under one condition," I murmur, tucking my fingers beneath his shirt, thumbing the trail of hair leading into his jeans.

"And what's that?" he grunts, his body so rigid beneath me.

It thrills me to know I can make him this way. As overloaded with desire as I am.

I drag his shirt up his chest and stare transfixed at the exposed muscle. Abs thick and prominent enough to be counted, one after the other. And that's exactly what I do, sweeping my nails over the ridges just like the first time in the hotel bathroom. He's breathing hard through his nose, grip brutal on my waist.

"You let me unwrap my gift first," I whisper, shoving his shirt as far as it will go before he's leaning forward and tugging it off for me. "Holy abs."

His laugh is choppy. "Go ahead, sweetheart. Please."

I'm too focused on touching him, greedy for this look and touch without anything in the way, to register his plea. The black ink on his chest takes me by surprise, a beautiful mix of designs that he's kept hidden.

On his right pec, two dates rest beneath a horseshoe drawn with such vivid details it almost jumps off his skin. The initials L.S. lie inside the horseshoe, and my heart pangs, knowing who they must be for.

Cautiously, I trace the design before moving to the next, a thickly sketched *Steele* beneath his left pec. It's a proud declaration. A visible representation of the love he has for his family.

"They're beautiful," I breathe, continuing to trace his tattoos. "You're beautiful."

His stare is heady, so goddamn intimate it's like a stroke along my wet pussy, teasing me with the pleasure that's coming.

"Unbutton my jeans, Anna."

He leans back into the couch and watches me get to work. With shaky fingers, I do as he says before taking it one step further. I slide off his lap and drop to my knees between his spread legs. His fingers curl on nothing but air.

It takes little time to rid him of the rest of his clothes. When I've finished, I stare up at him in awe. In utter disbelief. He looks like a god, a king in his own right, as he sits above me, powerful thighs spread and roped biceps flexing. I take hold of his knees before sliding my hands up his thighs, over the raised skin of thick scars hidden beneath the dark hair. Leaning forward, I take his hard cock in my hand, squeezing as I stroke up to the tip.

"Christ, Anna," he groans, throat working with a swallow so thick it's audible.

I've never loved being on my knees for a man before. Never got pleasure from giving a blow job or feeling the throb of a dick in my hand. Not until now. I rub my thighs together, accepting that I'm drenched between them, another pair of panties soiled because of Brody.

My mouth hovers over the shiny tip of his cock for less than a beat before I'm swiping my tongue along it, moaning from the familiar taste of him. I pulse between my legs, no amount of rubbing doing anything to help my ache any longer.

I squeak when he leaps from the couch and takes me in his arms. He carries me to the space before the fireplace and slowly lowers me to the ground, setting me on the soft carpet. His body moves atop mine, and then his mouth is on my throat, my jaw, and lips.

"It's my turn to taste you," he says, his tongue sliding along my neck.

I'm nodding, speechless. I spread my legs, welcoming him between them as he makes quick work of peeling my clothes off, piling them somewhere out of sight.

"My gorgeous woman," he praises, cupping my breasts in hands marked with thick calluses. They scrape my sensitive flesh, my nipples hard to the point of pain. "So soft and warm and mine."

"Yours," I gasp when he softly twists my nipple. My cry is loud when his mouth takes over, sucking hard.

Grappling for anything to hold on to, I wrap my thighs around his middle and whimper, "More."

He trails his hands down my sides, over the bare skin peppered with goosebumps. When he pulls my legs from around him and drops them to the ground, I shove aside the need to hide my nakedness. My wet inner thighs, thick stretch marks, and exposed pussy, there for his perusal. His eyes flare as he stares at me, *all of me*. A deep, rough noise builds in the back of his throat, and then he's pushing himself down my body, dropping his head between my spread thighs and cursing.

"Fuckin' prettiest pussy I've ever seen. Is all this for me, sweetheart?"

He drags a finger through my slit, his eyes so focused on his task that the fire burning beside us could swallow the house and I doubt he'd notice. My teeth tear into my bottom lip as he dips his head and nips at my inner thigh before taking me in his mouth. He sucks just once on my swollen skin and then brings his finger back to explore.

Another sweep through me, and then finally, a slow, torturous circle around my clit. I jolt, my back arching off the floor, thighs spasming as they press tight to his ears.

"Taste like heaven too," he moans before he's darting his tongue out again, this time lapping at me.

I believe his words, believe that he truly likes what he's doing, and that drives me insane. Out of my mind. My blood burns. I'm hot, hot, hot.

"I've never—" I start before my confession dies in my throat.

He slides a finger inside me, twisting his wrist when he pulls it out in a way that gives him room to bring his mouth to my clit. I can't think, let alone speak, as he flicks his tongue over it, his pace quick and confident. My stomach soars when he teases me with his teeth, the feel of them cool on my overheated skin.

"Never what, Anna?" The question rumbles across my clit.

My eyes drift shut, my hips lifting as I chase his mouth, wanting more and more and more. "Never come like this. Please let me come, Brody. Please," I whine.

"You'll come like this. I won't fuckin' stop until you do," he growls.

He becomes a man on a mission. Possessive hands flatten on my thighs, pushing them further apart, spreading me even wider as he plunges a second finger into my heat and sucks so hard on my clit that his cheeks hollow.

"Yes!" I cry, nails tearing at his shoulders.

I'm half-feral, coiled so damn tight. The pressure between my legs grows, the promise of pleasure so close I can almost taste it. His fingers piston inside of me, brushing an untouched spot every time he curls them just right.

"Right there. Keep touching me there. Oh, my God," I ramble, half out of my mind.

"That's it. That's a good girl. Let go for me," he groans, flicking my clit again in a perfect rhythm.

I jerk on the carpet, my eyes shooting open as I finally get there. My climax hits me like a truck, sending me flying across time and space. I fill the house with my cries, and he urges me on, his praise intensifying my release.

He licks me until I'm back on solid ground, so sensitive but still craving more. Craving him. The curve of my lips as I watch him kiss up my stomach tells him just that.

"I need you inside of me," I tell him.

I'm riding a high unlike any I've ever known. I feel like I'm floating, happiness mixing with desire in a combination so potent it's all I can taste.

The warmth from the fire has his skin glistening. He moves up my body, dragging his mouth and tongue along my curves, his cock hard against my thigh. I sigh, relaxing beneath him.

"You'll get me, baby. Just let me get my fill first," he rasps.

I curl my fingers in his hair. "You haven't gotten enough already?"

Deep, dark blue eyes lift, snaring my stare. "Don't think I ever will."

I hum low in my throat when he buries his face in my hair, breathing deep before sucking at my pulse again. He's leaving marks on me, and I love it.

"Do you want me to get a condom? I haven't had sex for a long time, but it's up to you, sweetheart."

The first brush of his cock over my pussy makes me moan, jerking against the pressure. My reply is instant. "No. I want you bare. Please."

"You don't have to beg."

I nod, biting down on my tongue when he parts me with two fingers and gives my clit a final pinch before notching his cock at my entrance. My exhale is heavy, vibrating with nerves.

"It's been a long time," I blurt out, holding his shoulders. "Stewart and I didn't have sex long befo—"

He shuts me up with his mouth on mine, swallowing the words poised on my tongue. I taste myself for the first time on a man's lips, and maybe I'm messed up inside because I don't hate. Not knowing how it got there.

Stewart hated going down on me. He only did it when I asked him to, and even then, it was a quick, lazy effort that always ended with an exaggerated, fake orgasm. I stopped asking after so many complaints, and the sex came to an end soon after it.

Brody pulls back, punishing me with a tug of my lip between his teeth before he says, "Don't need to hear his name ever. Especially not when I'm about to make love to you. You're with me now, and I'll always make sure you're satisfied and ready. I won't hurt you, sweetheart. You'll take me just right, won't you?"

I'm nodding without realizing it. "I will. You're not him."

His expression shudders. "He's the past. The reason I found you and nothin' more."

"You're my future, Brody," I whisper, reaching between our bodies to hold his cock and lead him into my body.

The stretch is intense, each inch spreading me open, but he's so gentle, so patient. I breathe out, nails pricking his shoulders as our eyes hold, never straying from one another.

"A little more," he says through his teeth.

I rub the tip of my nose along the bridge of his and start to relax when he bottoms out, feeling so incredibly full. He holds himself above me on his hands as he pulls out and moves back in, a little faster this time. Discomfort turns to an intense pleasure as I grow used to the stretch of him.

My eyes threaten to roll when he takes my clit between his fingers and picks up speed, thrusting harder now. He reaches a place so, so deep inside of me. I choke on the promise of another orgasm so soon after the first. It's an experience I'll only ever share with Brody.

My lips part as my next words tumble out so clearly and confidently that I have to look away from him before I ruin this moment with tears.

"I love you, Brody. I love you in the most unexplainable way."

My heart thuds against my rib cage, screaming out for the man above me. I want it to have him.

He pinches my chin, and I force my eyes open. His thrusts are so hard now that my entire chest shakes with each one, bouncing obscenely.

His fingers grasp the side of my throat, holding firmly as he kisses me fiercely, turning my lips swollen. "You don't need to explain it to me. I know. I fuckin' know how you're feelin' because I love you the same way. You're it. Fuckin' everythin'."

"Brody," I whisper, touching every inch of his face as euphoria shakes my bones.

The next roll of his hips pushes him against the spot he found earlier, and I'm soaring again, the world flashing white and then the most beautiful show of colours. I pull him tight to my chest, and he drops to his elbow, pistoning his hips. He buries his face in my throat and slams a hand to the floor as he grinds down on me.

"Fuck. *Fuck*, Anna," he groans as he comes deep inside of me.

I'm sore and swollen when he pulls out, not daring to move off me. I stroke his head, sighing happily as the minutes tick by. My eyes droop, the heat from the fire making me so blissfully warm beneath my man.

His breath tickles my ear, and I grin, letting it lull me to sleep.

38

Brody

I wake feeling eyes on me and nails tickling my stomach.

I'm really fucking hot too. Hot and sore. Light hits my eyelids, and I scrunch my brows. How long did I sleep for? I don't remember the last time I didn't wake to darkness. Or with weight on my arm and chest.

I lick my dry mouth and attempt to stretch my arm before realizing it's trapped beneath a warm body. Hair tickles my bicep and chest as a soft sigh scatters across my nipple. I splay my hand over the soft curve of a hip and squeeze.

"It's been a long time since I've woken up like this," I rasp in a sleep-drunk tone.

Anna rolls half on my chest and rests her chin on her hand. Her brown eyes are heavy with sleep but also alive with happiness. I hope to fuck she can read me just as well as I can her.

"It's been a long time since I woke this happy," she replies.

I don't give a shit about morning breath as I bring her in for a long kiss. "Merry Christmas, Banana."

She giggles, and it's a glorious sound. "Merry Christmas, Bo."

"You hungry?"

A devious grin. "Hungry for what exactly?"

I shiver as she drags her nails down my stomach. She scrapes them along the dip of the V leading beneath the thin blanket at my waist before her hand disappears, wrapping around my cock. I tip my head back, sucking in a sharp breath. I'm hard as steel, throbbing desperately.

"Are you sore?" I ask on a tight exhale.

"Not sore enough."

I nearly come right then and there when she suddenly pulls herself onto my lap, her naked pussy spread over the hard length of me. She's already wet as she starts to move, grinding on my shaft, slicking me up.

"You gonna ride me, gorgeous?"

Her lips part on a moan, head bobbing. Our eyes lock and hold, so many emotions floating between us. Love, passion, need. Fuck, my head is foggy with how badly I need her.

"Do it, then. Take this dick like a good fuckin' girl," I order gruffly.

Her pupils blow, black flooding the brown as she reaches between us and takes me deep, sinking slowly until I'm buried all the way.

Euphoria. Nirvana. Fucking whatever term is equal to the feeling of connecting with the woman I love in this way. So completely. Our bodies moving in sync, our breaths staggered and strong. I never knew it could be this way. I'll never go back. Not ever.

Anna rides me hard, chasing her pleasure with each grind of her hips. I settle my hands on her waist, memorizing the feel of them in my palms before swatting at her ass and thrusting up inside her tight heat. She folds herself over my chest, and I fuck her hard, the sound of skin on skin screaming through the house. Her whimpers build to screams in my ear, and her nails sink deep into my pecs. I grow harder inside of her because of it.

"Touch yourself. Need you to come with me inside you," I groan, taking two handfuls of her ass and spreading her cheeks wide.

"You touch me. Make me come, Brody."

The demand has me fighting back my orgasm, slowing my thrusts until I have myself under control. "You're so fuckin' sexy, Anna. I've got you."

Her clit is swollen and hot beneath my fingers as I work it, circling it with enough pressure to make her thighs quiver at my sides. She holds herself up on my chest, nipples so close to my mouth I can't help but lean up and suck one deep. I swirl my tongue around it before swapping to the other one, pinching the one I've left behind, wet and so damn swollen.

She tips her head back, chest arched toward me as she comes. Her pussy clenches tight, fluttering around my cock as I go over the edge with her, coming inside of her for the second time.

I release her nipple just as she starts to fall forward again, inner walls pulsing in the aftershock of her orgasm. Pushing her damp hair out of her face, I pepper her forehead with kisses, breathing in deep. The scent of me clings to her skin, mixing with the sex in the air.

Cheek to my chest, she says, "The girls are going to die when they hear about this."

I belt out a loud laugh, kissing the tip of her nose. The entire world has started to learn about her relationship with me, but I'm positive Bryce and Poppy are the only two opinions she cares about. I love her for that. It's too easy to fall into the trap of caring what people think of you. To focus on it and let it change the way you think of yourself and those around you. It took me years to accept that.

Now, I don't bother with social media at all, and somehow, I found a woman who doesn't either. It's impossible to shut the world out when you're in my position, but it does make it a bit easier to handle.

Still, I do worry that my career might become too much for her. It's not an easy thing to live with most of the time, and it won't be for us. My trip back to Nashville is looming, and I have a plan, but fuck knows it could fail. I have a house there, a life separate from the one in Cherry Peak. Friends, expected appearances, long days and nights in the studio recording my next album. It was nice hiding from those responsibilities while I was home, but I always knew it wouldn't last forever.

I never expected to meet Annalise. She threw a wrench into everything, but I wouldn't change a damn thing.

Wrapping my arms around her, I hold her tight, wishing we could stay here forever. "What do you say we have a shower, and I'll make breakfast before we head out and check on Banana?"

"I say yes. I'll trim your hair while we're at it."

And that was that. The start of the best Christmas I've ever had.

A WEEK LATER, I'm shaking off the rain from my jacket as I step into the Swift Edge Records building. Still riding the high from my Christmas with Anna, I smile at the receptionist when she waves me through.

The Nashville location is one of five offices the label has in the United States, with another two locations in Canada. Their main office is in Toronto, and the other is under construction in Calgary. The Nashville building is only the second I've ever been to. The LA office is bigger and far ritzier. I've only been once and wouldn't mind never having to go back. The outrageously large crystal chandeliers and black marble flooring made my skin itch.

I prefer it here. It's still large in space but much calmer. Soft wood floors, brown walls with accents of black spread throughout. Security waves as I step into the elevator and press the button for the twentieth floor, where the boardroom is located. There's only one floor higher than where I'm headed, and it belongs to Garrison Beckett, the CEO and reclusive douchebag.

If I could, I'd skip the meeting and go right to the studio to meet with his father, Reggie Beckett, in private, without the judgmental eyes of every label exec on the payroll.

The elevator doors shut, and I'm quick to pull out my phone. The text waiting there has my nerves slipping away, replaced by an ache I've felt from the moment I boarded my plane to come here. Anna changed her contact name Christmas morning, saying there was another Banana now, so she needed something just for her.

> Buttercup: Good luck today! We miss you already.

The picture attached makes me grin like a fool. I'm so gone for this woman that I've started considering a damn cow a pet. Anna has the phone stretched out far, focusing the camera on her and Banana as they play in the snowy field. She's put the fluffy thing's hair into two tiny pigtails at the top of her head, yellow bows wrapped at the bottom of them that match the one in her owner's hair.

I immediately save the picture, choosing it as my new lock screen before replying to the text.

> Me: Never thought I'd be the father of a cow, but I'm damn proud. You're both adorable. Miss you.

The elevator doors open, and I pocket my phone before striding down the long, carpeted hallway to the boardroom. I'm exactly on time, but everyone is already inside waiting when I get there, staring at me in a way that makes me think I should have been here an hour ago.

"Hey," I say, sitting in the only empty seat. I swallow my annoyance at the placement of it. The side-eye from Garrison is almost enough to make me snap.

Reggie is the only one I truly acknowledge, and his smile is a welcome sight in this room of bloodthirsty piranhas.

"Glad to have you back, Brody," he says, voice genuine and honest.

I nod, unsure what to say back that isn't a blatant lie. I'm not glad to be back. Rather the opposite, actually. But Reggie doesn't deserve to hear that from me.

"How are you feeling?" Garrison asks, drawing my attention.

I look him over, from the perfectly styled and gelled hair on his head to the hairless jaw to the expensive suit fit to his lean body. The watch on his wrist glitters beneath the boardroom lights. He drips with wealth, and it's as revolting as it is impressive.

He's nothing like his father. Reggie wears bright colours and scruffy silver hair on his face. He's artistic where his son is bland, free-spirited where his son has a stick so far up his ass he's gotta taste wood whenever he swallows.

Last I heard, they still don't get along either. Not that that's surprising in the least.

"I'm better. Feelin' good," I answer.

He nods, staring at the laptop screen in front of him. The screen is bright enough I can make out everything written on it. My stomach sours.

"Obviously, we have a lot to catch up on. First order of business is the all clear we received from your doctor last week. We've already gone ahead and scheduled recording time here in Nashville. You can talk more with Reggie later to grab the schedule," Garrison says, making his way down the list on the laptop.

A mousy-looking woman with deep red hair and a face heavy with freckles sits across the table, nodding along in time with him, eyes wide in an "I'm terrified to mess up" kind of way. It's clear by the heavy stack of disorganized paperwork in front of her that she's new. If she's working directly for Garrison, I feel incredibly sorry for her. The apologetic smile I shoot her says exactly that. She offers one back before dropping her stare.

"I'd appreciate a meeting with you as well, Brody. We need to go over a few things regarding the most recent headlines and how we wish to proceed with our response." This from the head of PR, a middle-aged woman named Janice, with a staggering lack of compassion for anyone.

I bristle, and Garrison shoots me a sharp look before speaking. "Yes, Annalise Heights. I'm sure you've seen the media interest. Janice has been dodging calls from a dozen outlets wanting an exclusive. I assume you're wanting to have a say on what we run with?"

"Yeah, I am. I'd appreciate if we just left it alone," I say, my tone just as cutting as his.

"That's not possible, Brody," Janice cuts in, tapping long nails on the glass table. "They're dogs with a bone. Especially after the last round of gossip."

I tighten my jaw. "Give them a piece of kibble, then. Somethin' just enough to keep them quiet. I don't want Anna in a spotlight."

"She's already in the spotlight," Garrison smugly points out.

Rita joins the conversation from her place beside the redhead across the table. "We need to send through an NDA at the very least."

"She doesn't need to sign an NDA," I say.

Garrison sighs dramatically. "She does, and she will. Don't be sensitive about this, Brody. I will only be pushed so far. Have her sign an NDA, and Janice will work on a public statement that will be shared on your social media pages."

"A statement that says what? I don't want any sensitive information shared about her. She's my girlfriend, and that's that. Nothin' personal." I stand firm, Anna's well-being my top priority.

Silence as Garrison turns over my words before finally saying, "Fine. A carefully worded statement confirming a relationship, then. And an NDA signed and faxed back to Janice by the end of the week." He scrolls down his screen. "Let's move on to your tour. We've already begun planning a few dates and stops—"

I interrupt him when rocks fill my stomach. "What tour?"

"Once the album is done, you need to tour it. While you left early, you still played a decent chunk of shows for Killian, and the numbers from your last song are incredible."

"A large number of questions in your messages online are regarding an upcoming tour. Your fans are engaged and incredibly excited for a chance to see you perform live," Janice says.

I bounce my leg beneath the table. "When? Soon?"

"If you can get the album finished in a month, we'll have tickets go on sale in three with the tour starting up in the summer," Garrison says.

Reggie's watching me, concern heavy in his features. Not concern for my voice—a month is a slower pace than I was expecting, considering how I wound up with vocal damage in the first place—but because I feel trapped, and I must look it too.

These meetings are always a lot. A lot of voices talking for you instead of with you and expectations set without a thought of if you can actually meet them or if you'll burn yourself out trying to.

They were bad enough before I met Anna, and now that I've fallen in love with her, the pressure has doubled. How will she take the news of me leaving for months on end to go on tour? A month is a long time to be here recording an album while she's in Cherry Peak. Is she up to visit? Maybe join me on the road?

Do I even want to do any of those things anymore? Fuck, I don't know if I want to go on tour. I've been so happy at home. Will I be happy here now? Music is one of my greatest loves, a passion that I've had since I was a little boy listening to old country in the stables with my ma, but is it worth what I have to risk losing to keep it?

I'll kick myself in the ass later for continuing to push this conversation with Anna from one day to the next until there was no time left before I hopped on a flight here. We need to talk about this soon. I won't be able to concentrate on anything else until I know if she's ready for all of this.

I clear my throat, waiting until I have the attention of everyone at the table before speaking. "I need some time to think about this. I haven't even been back for twenty-four hours. This is a lot to take in at once."

"We're already short on time, Brody. There isn't a moment open to hesitate," Garrison argues.

"I just need a few days."

"A few days more than we have. You don't have kids or a wife. This should be an easy yes for you. Are you not serious about this anymore?" Garrison demands answers I don't have, and I feel like an ass for it.

"We can spare a few days. Take them, Brody," Reggie speaks up, pinning his son with a look only a father can give his son.

Garrison curls his fingers on the table but doesn't put up further argument.

The nod I give Reggie is heavy, weighted with an appreciation that I wouldn't dare verbally give in this room. He gives me one back, and the meeting comes to a standstill.

"We will pick this meeting up in three days. Everyone is dismissed," Garrison grits out before I'm out of my seat and tearing out of the room.

My phone is in my hand before I even hit the elevator, desperate to hear my woman's voice.

39

Annalise

MY INNER THIGHS AND BICEPS SCREAM AS I HOIST MYSELF OFF THE ground. Spreading my legs, bending them at the knee while I spin around the pole, I grit my teeth to keep from exploding into a cursing fit. I'm stronger than I was when I attended my first pole class, more confident too, but it's not gotten any easier. I'm still miles behind all the other women in the class.

I drop from my hold after another second, too exhausted to keep going any longer. The rub marks on my inner thighs chafe as I grab my water bottle from the back wall and take a generous drink.

I've been sleeping like shit these past couple of days, and there's no trying to pretend I don't know why. It's a stage four clinger mindset, but I miss Brody enough to be kept up at night by my mind running circles around when and if he'll actually come back home. Common sense tells me there's no reason why he won't be back, but my fear has a mind of its own.

Today's class was much needed, even if I'm not as present as I usually am. Poppy and Bryce are anxiously awaiting an update from Christmas, and I think I've pushed indulging them as long as I can. Plus, I want to scream about it to someone. About his family and Banana and shit, *the sex*. That deserves an entire moment of its own.

My cheeks flush as I set my bottle down and attempt to zone in to Poppy's instructions for the rest of the class. It's a task, one I fail miserably at, but at least I try. By the time everyone is leaving and Bryce is slipping a sweatshirt over her frame, I'm twiddling my thumbs with anticipation.

"My ass burns," she groans.

Poppy starts wiping down the poles with a spray bottle of sanitizer and a cloth. "It looks good, though."

"I know. Pain is beauty, I suppose," Bryce tosses back.

My smile is instant, a strong sense of comfort filling me. These two are everything I could have asked for from two best friends.

"You're getting good too, Anna," Poppy praises.

"Good? More like I just don't fall to my ass whenever I attempt a lift anymore."

She waves the cloth at me. "Progress is progress. Don't tell me you haven't noticed the changes in your body, because I have."

"It's more than just a change in muscle tone, Pop," Bryce teases.

I roll my lips. "Not sure what you're talking about."

"No? You don't have anything to say about the glow on your cheeks or, I don't know, the walk?" Poppy shrieks, dropping the cleaning supplies before rushing to me. She grabs my shoulders, shaking me lightly. "I've been waiting so long for this. I'm even too excited to give you hell about not immediately calling me the moment you finished riding that cowboy! Honestly, Anna, you made us wait an entire week, and that is just cruel."

I can't help but laugh, my grin fifty shades of bold. "I wanted to tell you both in person, and in my defense, Bryce just *had* to go to visit her devilish extended family for Christmas."

"Trust me, I'd have rather been here than in Montreal. But we're both here now, so spill," Bryce demands.

And I do. I tell them all about Christmas dinner with Brody's grandparents and how at home they made me feel. About Banana and her new home and everything Brody did to make me feel so damn special. I grow hot and sweaty when I get to Christmas Eve and gush about the best sex I've ever had. Our I love you's and frantic round two on Christmas morning. They're both close to bursting by the time I finish. It's Bryce who speaks first.

"I'm fucking jealous, Anna. I wasn't expecting all of that."

"I expected the sex. That man walks like he knows he's hiding a third leg and knows exactly how to use it. But everything else? He got you a damn cow," Poppy breathes, hand to her heart.

"He got me a mini fluffy cow just like I wanted." My smile is dreamy, a visible representation of the feeling swimming through me.

I'm floating on my love for Brody. I'm a total cliché, and it might just be my new favourite personality trait.

"And more than that, he obviously wants you to have an excuse to go to the ranch often, even while he's gone. It's as good an invitation as any," Bryce points out.

Something about my friends has me able to open up completely, and I let my deepest thoughts spill from my lips, knowing they won't judge me for them.

"I've thought about that, too, but worried maybe I was reading too much into it."

Poppy shakes her head instantly. "You're absolutely not. If he didn't want you to be around his family all the time, he wouldn't have gotten you a pet that you had to go to their property to spend time with."

I know she's right. Eliza made that clear to me multiple times over the two days I spent there as well. But hearing it from an outside perspective settles that last wiggle of doubt.

"Thank you," I say, flicking my eyes between the two of them.

Bryce shoulders Poppy away from me and bundles me in a warm hug. "You can thank us by introducing us to the fluffy baby sooner rather than later."

"What about tomorrow?" I offer.

Poppy weasels her way back to me and tosses her arms over both Bryce and me. I exhale, soaking in this moment. Six months ago, I could have only dreamed of this, and now . . . now it's my life.

"After work? I'm picking you up still, right?" Poppy asks as we break apart.

"Yes, please. I really need to get over this stupid fear and start driving myself. I'm too old to be so codependent."

"It's no different than having a fear of planes and refusing to fly. It just makes life a bit more complicated," Bryce says.

"Complicated and annoying," I mutter.

Poppy grabs her abandoned cleaning supplies and finishes wiping the remaining two poles while I slip my sweatpants on over my spandex shorts. "Brody doesn't seem to mind driving you around. I think he rather likes it, actually."

"It doesn't matter if he likes it because he isn't here," I point out, my tone snippier than I meant it to be. "Sorry, that was . . ."

Poppy brushes over my tone. "It was honest. Don't worry about it. I know you're missing him."

Not wanting to continue talking about how damn bad I miss Brody, I try and steer the conversation elsewhere. "Need any more help before we leave?"

"Nah, not today. I'll come back tomorrow and finish up. I'm still recovering my energy from Christmas, and today's class was too much, even for me," Poppy groans. She puts the cleaning supplies back in their cupboard and starts making her way through the studio, shutting off lights and pulling blinds.

Bryce grabs our stuff from the floor while I shrug my jacket on. It smells like me now, Brody's cologne long since worn off. The air has a sharp bite to it when we step outside, boots crunching in the snow speckled over the sidewalk. It's been shovelled recently, but it's been snowing for days now, ever since the storm hit. Luckily, it only took a couple of days for the town to plow the roads despite the continuous sprinkling of snow.

"Let me know about tomorrow. I'll catch a ride with Poppy on the way to your place," Bryce says, the three of us lingering outside Beautifully Bold. She starts her car with the remote in her hand, and Poppy does the same.

I nod. "I will. Drive home safe."

Poppy and I turn around and head in the opposite direction toward her small red car. The headlights beam at the studio windows, lighting up the dark street, and thank God for that. If they weren't, I wouldn't be able to have seen the tall man rushing toward us, a black cowboy hat on his head and one gloved hand held slightly in front of his body.

I startle, eyes flaring wide as I glance at Poppy. She notices the man, too, and immediately swivels on her heels to stare him down. My brows tug together when he gets closer, nothing about him appearing familiar.

"Annalise Heights?" he asks in a rush, reaching the sidewalk and stopping only a few feet from us.

Poppy sets her hands on her hips and, despite the inches he has on her, attempts to look down her nose at him. "Who's asking?"

"Spencer Sharp from *Country Capital*. Would you mind taking a minute to give me an exclusive?"

I stand frozen, anxiety buzzing beneath my skin. "An exclusive on what?"

He lifts his hand, and I notice the rectangular device in his hand. A recorder. My chest tightens.

"If you could just tell me a little about your relationship with Brody Steele, or a confirmation that you are indeed together, that would be fantastic. We've been tryin' to reach his team for weeks but haven't received an answer," he explains. "Is he cleared medically to come back? Will he finish Killian's tour with 'im now?"

The interest in his eyes makes my stomach turn. He's a nosey reporter too far from home if the heavy twang in his voice is anything to go off. His smile isn't a pleasant one. It's greedy.

"You can get lost, Spencer Sharp from *Country Capital*," Poppy hisses, shifting in front of me. "Go back home before you get run out of town."

He doesn't heed her warning; instead, he keeps pushing. "I just need'a tiny statement. A yes or a no."

"You'll get my foot up your ass if you don't get lost. Anna has nothing to say to you."

I set a hand on her shoulder and move to her side. "She's right. Please go. You're not getting anything from me."

His eyes narrow ever so slightly, and I take a step back, tugging at Poppy's shoulder for her to do the same.

"It ain't possible to hide from the public, Annalise. Brody and that team of his know that too damn well to be playin' these games with the media. You tell 'im that, yeah?"

I stiffen, my back straight as a steel rod. "You can tell him that yourself, I'm sure. Now, if you'll excuse us, we'll be leaving."

Poppy bares her teeth at him like a rabid dog before we move to her car, hopping in quick and locking the doors. Spencer Sharp continues to stare at us through the windshield, and I have to shove Poppy's hand down out of view when she tries to flip him off.

"Reporters have been to Cherry Peak before, but not for a few years now. It was crazy for a while after Brody's first few singles dropped and the world wanted a closer look at his life back home. The hype of the small town wore off, though. The people here won't be happy to have that guy in town. He'll be run out quick, don't worry," she rambles as we pull away from the studio and down the main street.

Tucking my hands between my thighs, I attempt to fight off the shock panging through me long enough to come up with a response. Poppy speaks for me.

"You need to call Brody. Tell him what happened."

"He's busy," I mumble, but even I can admit that's a cop-out. It's a reason to keep this to myself so he doesn't freak out. The moment he hears what happened, he'll come home, and it's too soon for that.

If he was ready to come home, he'd already be here. There are still things he needs to work out in Nashville.

She stares at the rear-view mirror before saying, "Call him, or I will."

"Neither of us are calling him. I'm a big girl, Poppy."

"I'm not saying you aren't. But that douchebag is following us in his fancy rental car right now, and there's no way I'm leading him right to your house. So call your man and ask him what he wants me to do here."

I spin in my seat, mouth gaping at the headlights beaming in the back seat. My fingers are shaking when I pull my phone out and dial his number. He answers on the third ring, sounding so happy to talk to me that I almost pretend to lose service before having to tell him what's happening.

"Hey, sweetheart. How was class?"

I swallow. "Good. I'm sore, though."

"Need a massage?" The smirk is obvious in his voice.

A laugh rises in my throat before evaporating into nothing. "Can you talk right now? Are you busy?"

"What's wrong?" he asks stiffly, suddenly on alert.

The headlights behind us continue to flash in the side mirror, making me wince. "There's a guy in town. Says he's from *Country Capital*. He asked me about you."

"When? Where?"

"A couple of minutes ago outside of BB."

"That's not all!" Poppy shouts. I glare at her.

"What's going on?"

I hate this. Really, really hate this. "It seems he didn't appreciate being turned down for a statement. He's following us."

Something slams in the background of the call, so loud I can hear it over the sharp curse Brody spits. "Don't go to your place. Poppy's either."

I relay the information to Poppy, and she asks, "Where do I go, then?"

"The ranch. I'll let my grandparents know you're comin'. Spencer won't get on the property. Poppy can stay with you too. We don't need him knowin' where you both live."

"I'm not bringing him to the ranch and making him your family's problem, Brody. Give me an alternative route."

"You *are* family. And that fucker won't dare step a foot on our land without permission. I'll be home tomorrow."

My next exhale is heavy, tired. "Don't come home because of this. You're not done there yet."

"I'm comin' home. I'm not okay with you gettin' accosted by the media because of me. I can't just sit back and let your life get mucked up by this. Don't fight me on it. I'm comin'," he declares, and I know I've lost the battle.

I'm not stubborn enough to keep fighting him on it, especially not when the annoying part of me wants to beat my chest with pride, knowing he wants to come home early.

"Please give them a heads-up, then, Brody. I want to make sure they're okay with me being there before I just show up."

"I'll call them right now and then call you back." He pauses then, a shaky inhale loud in my ear. "I'm so fuckin' sorry, baby. I didn't think they'd show up there. Should have known better."

"Don't. This isn't your fault, and I don't blame you for it. Get all that out of your head."

Poppy drives another lap around the same block, stalling leading the reporter anywhere close to where either of us lives.

"Yeah, alright. I'm going to call them now. Tell Poppy to head to the ranch, and I'll call back in a minute."

"I love you, Brody," I say sternly, making sure he hears it before dropping the call.

"I love you. I'll be right back."

When he ends the call, I swipe a hand over my hair and mutter, "He wants me at the ranch. You're welcome to stay too."

Poppy nods and changes direction, heading out of town. Spencer's headlights follow.

"Let him come home, babe. I know you're sitting there stirring about it, but trust me when I say that that man won't know peace until he knows you're taken care of. He's not going to want to hear it from anyone else either. I doubt you'll ever be able to convince him otherwise," she says.

"What if he resents me for dragging him back so soon?"

Poppy laughs, but it isn't a warm sound. It's sad. "Something tells me that if he never had to leave, he wouldn't. He's probably relieved to have an excuse to come back."

"His career is important," I whisper.

"That ex of yours really skewered the way you see relationships, Anna. Sometimes being with the person you love outweighs everything else. Even important careers. I'd do anything to have what you two have. To know that I had someone who would drop absolutely anything they were doing to come take care of me when I needed them to."

I reach across the car to touch her hand, my mouth lifting at the corners. "You're very wise, Poppy. Wise and sweet and smart and drop-dead gorgeous. You'll find someone who appreciates you the way you deserve."

She offers me a weak smile. "Thank you. But don't worry about me. I just want you to start accepting more from people. More support and care and love. You deserve it, okay?"

"I'll work on it."

"Good girl," she says, shooting me a wink across the dark cab. My laugh isn't as strained as I anticipated.

The familiar Steele Ranch gate appears up ahead, and I let some of the tension drain from my muscles. It pisses me off that this reporter is going to be anywhere close to this place, but knowing there's no chance in hell he gets on the property is enough for now.

Poppy slows the car as we turn onto the small section of road leading up to the gate and blows out a breath. "Uh-oh. Grandpa Steele is ready to kick some reporter ass."

It takes me a beat to make him out in the dark, but when I do, it's to find him standing in front of the gate, his arms crossed and scowl cold. His usual hat is tipped low over his forehead, and if I didn't know the man the way I do, I'd turn and run for the hills the moment he takes a step toward Poppy's car and waves us through the gate.

Brody hasn't called back yet, and if I had to guess, I'd say he's still speaking to his grandma.

"Do you think Spencer will turn and leave?" I ask her.

"No. If he's stupid enough to try and back Brody's girlfriend into a corner while knowing damn well he's in another country, there's not much help for him."

"I want to hear what happens," I admit.

Poppy stops the car right then and there. Pulling out the keys, she pushes open her door, and I follow suit, the wind harsher in the openness of the ranch.

Deep male voices ripple through the night.

"You're lucky to be dealing with me and not my grandson after cornerin' his woman like that and followin' her back here," Wade barks, voice like a whip.

"I just need a single statement. It doesn't have to be from Anna. If either you or your wife—"

"Get the fuck off my land, boy, before I remove you myself."

An exasperated sigh. "Please. One statement."

I close the space between Wade and me, coming to a standstill beside him while Poppy lingers back a few paces. The older man looks far scarier than I do in my pair of baggy sweatpants and Brody's jacket, but I do my best. Spencer's eyes focus on me, and he takes a step forward.

Wade is moving in the blink of an eye. His arm snaps out, and he grips Spencer's wrist, tugging it hard enough to send him stumbling.

"I'll tell you one more time. Get. Off. My. Land," he spits, releasing Spencer suddenly. The reporter trips over his feet and tumbles into the snowbank, sinking deep. "Come any closer and I'll call the cops."

I watch the entire confrontation with wide eyes and a soaring heart. It isn't Brody here standing up for me but his family, and that hits me so deep I'm fighting back tears as the reporter stumbles upright and, with a shake of his head, gets back in his vehicle. It takes Wade lightly grabbing my arm and leading me back through the gate for my legs to move.

"Thank you," I croak.

Wade drops his arm over my shoulder as he says, "Anything for family."

40

Annalise

After a long, restless night, Eliza sits me down at the table and places a full plate of breakfast in front of me. Pancakes, hash browns, and over-easy eggs just the way I like them. A steaming cup of coffee comes next, mixed to a perfect light brown colour.

"Eat up, my girl. I know you're starving after last night," she says pointedly, continuing to rush around the kitchen.

Stacks of plates, tin containers full to the brim with the same food on my plate, and pitchers of orange juice line the end of the counter. Styrofoam cups come next, and then utensils are shoved in the food.

"I could have helped with all of this, Mrs. Steele. You've cooked for an army."

"You needed the sleep. And this is nothing compared to the meals I cook up during calving season. We're running a thinner crew right now, but these men can still eat like no other any day of the year," she explains.

"When will they come eat? I don't want to be in the way."

Her smile is warm when she faces me, shaking her head. "They might as well get used to the sight of you in this house. Around the ranch too. You just sit and eat your breakfast."

Knowing there's no room for negotiation, I offer her a smile in return and dig my fork into the yolk of my egg, cracking it open. "Thank you."

"You're welcome, honey."

I've nearly finished my plate by the time heavy footsteps trample through the house. I stiffen at the brash laughs and hard voices before looking at Eliza and relaxing. She's excited to see these guys, and that seems to be enough for me.

Never in my life have I met anyone whose love language has so obviously been acts of service. Brody's grandmother truly loves cooking for others and seeing the appreciation on their faces as they dig into her food. Brody's cut from the same cloth, but instead of cooking, he's all about making sure I have shovelled sidewalks and warm clothes and a custom barn for my pet cow.

I jump in my chair when a firm hand grabs my shoulder. Whipping my head to look behind me, I see it's Wade and blow out a breath.

"Didn't mean to scare ya," he says. His dark circles and tired grimace tell me he's slept as well as I did last night. "How was your night?"

"I slept well." When I finally fell asleep, that is.

"Yeah, me too."

"Did you have a chance to speak to Brody before he boarded this morning?"

"No."

My heart tugs uncomfortably. If he didn't speak with him this morning, then he hasn't at all since before he left for Nashville. It wasn't his grandfather that Brody called last night. It was his grandma.

Is Wade offended by that? Does he care enough to be offended?

An idea pops into my head, a no-good, nosey idea, but I let it run free before I can stop myself.

"Would you mind helping me out with Banana this morning? I know you're probably really busy, but there are still so many things I don't know about when it comes to her. It would be really—"

He cuts me off with a squeeze to my shoulder. "You done eatin'? I got some time now."

"Are you not going to eat?"

The kitchen is packed now with so many unfamiliar faces that I try to stack in my memory. Most of them don't bother to sit and eat, instead just holding their plates in their hands and scarfing it back like it's the last meal they'll ever have. A couple of them plunk down at the table in the chairs across from me. They're both young guys, probably a few years younger than me.

One has shoulder-length black hair that explodes in a wild mess when he drops his hat to the table beside his plate, and the other has his blond hair shaved close to his scalp, a ratty baseball cap in his lap.

Their manners are nice to see, especially when it comes to thanking Eliza for the meal. I smile at them in approval.

"I eat before these lazy fucks have even woken up," Wade chuffs behind me.

The guy with the long hair flashes me an easy grin. "Easy, Wade. Don't ruin my chance with the pretty lady before I've even introduced myself."

"Brody'll lock you in the pen with Zeus and feed him the key if you try it with his woman, Johnny," Wade warns, and I laugh at the humour beneath his threat.

"His woman? I'm not seeing him here to compete with me," Johnny replies.

"Cool your jets, Casanova," his friend mutters over a mouthful of pancake. "I'm Thomas, by the way."

"Nice to meet you. Who's Zeus?" I ask.

"The meanest bull on Steele Ranch. A nasty fucker with a love for kicking ribs in," Thomas says with a wince.

Wade releases my shoulder and grabs my plate. He looks down at me, gaze serious. "You'll stay clear of him."

"I've got no desire to meet an angry bull."

"Good. Why don't you go grab a pair of overalls from Brody's old room so you don't ruin your clothes, and then I'll meet you out back."

I eye the plate in his hand. "Between you and Eliza, I haven't had to do a damn thing around here. Please put me to work out there."

"You got my word, darlin'. I'll see you in a bit." And then he's bringing my plate to the sink and kissing his wife on the cheek before starting on the dishes waiting in the bubbly water.

I nod to the two guys at the table and set off to change my clothes. After throwing my hair up, I step into the small closet in the room I crashed in last night and root through the clothes hanging on the rod. I thought this may have been Brody's old room when I first slipped inside last night, but I was too tired to snoop. There's not much to root through anyway, but the clothes left hanging confirm my suspicions. None of the sweatshirts or overalls would fit Brody the man, but they would Brody the teenager.

And hopefully they'll fit me too.

I snatch a pair of denim overalls and wiggle into them, relieved when they fit just a bit too big. I'll have to shove the legs into my boots to keep from tripping over them. Teenage Brody was tall too.

There's a pep in my step as I make my way through the house and put my coat and boots on before stepping on the back porch. Wade is already waiting, his hat and boots on, arms leaning on the deck rail.

"Have you ever mucked a shed before?" he asks, staring at me over his shoulder with a slight tilt of his lips.

"Never. But I'd love to learn."

So for the next half hour, I do just that.

"I HAVEN'T HAD to muck nothin' in years," Wade admits once we've finished cleaning up Banana's shed.

Sweat slicks my forehead and makes the hairs that have fallen out of my ponytail stick to my skin. For the first time since moving here, I'm grateful for the freezing temperature.

"You really didn't have to today either. It wasn't the most complicated thing in the world," I tease. Albeit incredibly gross.

He shrugs and leans his rake/fork-looking tool against the side of the shelter. I set mine beside it, and Banana trails behind me, trotting into the snow. She butts her head against his thigh, demanding some attention. I roll my lips to hide a smile when the rough old man drops his hand to scratch the top of her head.

"Eliza would say the grunt work will keep me young."

"And what would you say?"

"I'd say that it gave me some time with my boy's woman, so I won't complain."

My smile is soft. "He really loves you."

"Love him like a son."

"Have you told him that recently?"

It's out of my mind too fast to rein it in. I should apologize for overstepping, but I won't. After all, this was my plan when I asked him to help me today. I wanted to get him alone and talk to him about his relationship with Brody. It matters to Brody far more than he'll admit.

"No. I haven't," Wade mutters, continuing to scratch Banana.

"He thinks you resent him for leaving. That you hold his career against him and wish he'd done something else. Stayed here, maybe. Is that really how you feel?"

He flinches. "Jesus. Never knew it would kill to hear that."

"I'm sorry."

"Don't apologize for speakin' the truth. Not ever."

I nod slowly, swapping my weight from one boot to the other. "Look, I may not know any of you that well yet, but I do know Brody. And you do too. Enough to realize he's not going to tell you these things on his own. It's my job now to take care of him, and I want to start by trying to help the relationship between you two. Brody is headstrong and *so* damn caring. He won't ever do or say something that he knows will hurt someone he loves. That's where I come in, I guess.

"At the risk of getting thrown off your ranch forever, I think you're going to regret pushing him away all these years, and especially if you continue to do it. I grew up with a father who didn't give a flying crap about me, and I would have loved to experience the type of love you and him share, even shoved down beneath years of pain."

I run my fingers through my hair, feeling like a downright rambling mess, but Wade listens contently, letting me finish.

"What I'm trying to say is that you shouldn't waste any more of your time together. Put the past behind you both and move forward. Life is too fucking short to do anything else."

He doesn't say anything for a long moment. The silence hangs heavily between us, and I contemplate tucking tail and running off when he finally speaks.

"I've never been one to believe in any sort of afterlife. No God and pearly gates. But hell if I'm not considerin' it now." He swallows, staring straight at me. "'Cause there's no fuckin' way my daughter didn't send you here to be with her boy."

41

Brody

EXHAUSTION TUGS AT MY MIND, TRYING TO PULL ME UNDER AS I GRIT my jaw and focus on the road. Another call comes through, interrupting the music on my stereo for the twenty-fifth time since I got off the plane. The past three hours have been tense and angry. A flurry of resentment has built inside of me, aimed directly at the company of people I left behind in Nashville.

Maybe that's unfair. It makes little difference to me right now.

I'm burning up from the inside out, and I won't cool until I've sorted this shit out. Anna's my priority. She always will be, even if Garrison and Rita don't understand it. Which is putting our parting words really fucking lightly. Garrison's growl as he threatened to take everything away from me if I got on that plane still scratches the walls of my mind like nails on a chalkboard.

But clearly, he didn't deter me. Not only does he not mean it, but I can't say I'd care right about now even if he did. I don't put too much more thought into that, though. Not right now.

The ranch gate is open, with my grandfather waiting by the wood fence when I pull up. His posture is stiff, his face unreadable. Preparing myself for a verbal kick in the ass for letting

Anna get dragged into the mess of my life, I unlock the truck door for him.

He hops up and in, setting his hat on the centre seat beside mine. I wait for it. For the lashing and disappointment, but nothing comes. Silence ripples around us, along something heavy I can't pinpoint.

"Let's hear it," I say, breaking the silence. "Tell me I should have done a better job of shieldin' her from this part of my life or whatever it is you're thinkin'. I've already beat myself up enough for the both of us."

"I wasn't thinking none of that."

"No?"

He sets his hands on his lap and cracks his knuckles. The wear and tear on his skin is obvious, a lifetime of marks and scars that I don't know the origin of. Those exterior marks have nothing on the damage inside, though. They never have. We're similar in that way.

I've been bucked off horses and broken bones, swam in shallow lakes and cut my arms on sharp sticks. There are more scars on my palms from rope burn than a schoolteacher has paper cuts. No physical mark has carried more weight than the damage my father's leaving caused.

I had years with the guy. Years of happy moments and bonding experiences that I'll never get back. I've long since stopped thinking about the pathetic excuse of a man that bailed on his family when they needed him most. When I needed him most.

A boy loses his mother and expects his father to pick up the pieces she left behind. But that's not what happened here. I haven't spoken to the man since the day he left, and I hope I never do again.

Unlike me, my grandfather wears the pain of my father's abandonment right beneath his skin. Not only did he take my father in and treat him like his own flesh and blood, but he spent years training him to take over the Steele legacy. It was all for nothing. My packing up and leaving town tore deep. It left our relationship in tatters and brought him back to the place he was in when my father left, despite how thoroughly he tried to hide it. I've never forgiven myself for that, and he certainly hasn't forgiven me either.

There's so much ground to cover and nowhere near enough time.

"I was going to say that I'm proud of you for comin' home. I'd have done the same thing for your grandmother," he says.

My throat tightens. It's been a long time since he's said that to me. I didn't know how much I needed to hear it until now.

"You raised me to take care of the people I love. I'm just doin' that."

"I taught you a great deal of things, Brody. But you taught me just as many."

"I don't think so. Where is this coming from?"

"I was just reminded of who you are instead of who I told myself you were. You taught me a full life of lessons, Brody. I didn't have a clue how to raise a son. Your grandmother did most of the raisin' with your mother, and I always regretted the lack of time I spent with her growin' up. She was snatched too soon." His voice cracks, and my chest splinters. "She left us her boy, and I have regretted a lot of things in my life, but takin' my resentment for your father out on you is my worst mistake."

I stare out at the outline of the stable up the road. The echo of my mother's laugh fills every goddamn inch of that place, haunting me the moment I step inside. It's too much. There are too many memories there that I don't know how to move past.

It's unfair to Sky. If I were a better person, I would have given her to another handler years ago. At least she'd have had the attention she deserved all these years. More than the brief moments every few weeks or months that I've given her when the pain of being without her got too strong. It's been twenty years since Mom died. I know Sky's been taken care of and

311 OF MING ALONG

happy enough to continue loving so damn easily. But she's mine, and I don't have a lot of years left with her.

"I wasn't easy on you and Grams either," I say, tearing my eyes from the stable and dropping them in my lap. "You raised me pretty damn well. I think Anna would agree with me on that."

"That girl is somethin' else, Brody. Real special. Your momma would have liked her. I never thought I'd see a city girl so excited to try ranch life, but I gotta say, it fits her just right."

Fuck. The burn in my eyes is a pain in my ass. "I'm too tired to listen to this shit."

He keeps going, ignoring me. "Should'a told most of it to you a lot sooner. You've made me a proud man. Got a boy that wants the world to know his name and isn't afraid to make it happen. I was just a stubborn old fuck who was blamin' you for things you never did."

"I'm not a boy anymore, you know?"

His laugh is watery, and a tear slips from my eye before I can stop it. I swipe it away quickly.

"That's all you got from that speech?"

I snort. "We don't do soft and gushy. We never have. But I'm grateful to have had you raise me. You've been more of a dad than a grandparent to me for the majority of my life."

A slap of a hand on my shoulder and then a squeeze. "Drive us up to the house. You've got a girl inside chompin' at the bit for a look at you."

I put the truck in gear and go heavy on the gas, desperate to see my woman again. "Did she stay with you guys at the main house last night?"

We never had much of a chance to talk last night before she fell asleep. By the time I had my tickets purchased and my shit packed up to go, it was already late. One quick call to check in was all I got before boarding and heading home.

"Yeah. Your grandmother put her up in your old room."

"Good."

A pause. "That reporter won't come back here. He's probably long gone back to wherever the hell he came from with his tail tucked tight between his legs."

"He's from Nashville. Must have been sent up here after I told the label to decline the rest of the requests for statements."

His voice is hard, stern. "This ain't your fault, Brody."

"How is it not? I led them here."

And if that isn't the cold hard truth. I brought the media the first time, and I've done it again. I'll do it another dozen times by the time my career comes to an end. It's unfair, and I'll feel guilty about it for the rest of my life.

"They lead themselves here on a damn witch hunt. This isn't on you, and we all know it. Anna knows it too."

"What am I supposed to say to her? I can't promise this won't happen again."

"So don't. She doesn't expect that from you. There's no doubt in that woman's mind about you. Not your career and not what might come from it. She knows who you are. Has for a while now."

I'm as convinced as I'll ever be without speaking to her myself.

"Thanks, Grandpa," I say, and I mean it.

He nods, and we reach the house a beat later. My limbs are weighed down as I step out of the truck, but the moment the screen door flies open and Anna appears in the doorway, I'm more awake than I've ever been.

She stands there staring at me for a long, strained moment, and then her boots are clunking down the stairs. We don't run to one another; we don't rush. I wait for her like it's the most natural thing in the world, taking her in my arms when she gets close enough for me to smell her perfume.

"You're actually back," she breathes, face buried in the crook of my neck.

I wrap my arms fully around her body and kiss her head over and over again. The fur collar of her jacket tickles my jaw, and I lean into that feeling, not giving a rat's ass at the discomfort of it.

"Only place I want to be is right here," I reply softly.

"I told myself I'd pretend to be upset with you for coming back, but I'm too happy to do that right now."

"You can give me shit later, sweetheart."

I lower her to her feet and release my hold enough she can slip from my arms. Her grin is blinding, cheeks pink from a mix of the cold and her signature flush. She's wearing my jacket unzipped, exposing the ratty jean overalls beneath, tucked into the tops of her boots. I blink repeatedly, checking her out in the new clothes.

"Been playin' in the mud?" I ask, both dumbfounded and surprisingly hard.

"More like hay and cow shit. Wade was helping me muck out Banana's shed this morning."

I glance at my grandfather. He looks right back, an unmistakable pride sparkling in his eyes that hits me right in the gut.

"She's better at it than you ever were," he says.

Anna beams. "Thank you, Wade."

"Don't let him slack off on the muckin', darlin'. Put his ass to work with that damn cow of yours," Grandpa tells her.

I laugh, holding Anna close. "That damn cow of ours is growin' on you, old man. I'd bet it's only a matter of time until she's parked up in the house with you and Grams on the daily."

"When pigs fly, boy."

"Brody told me weeks ago that the sky would fall before you accepted cattle as pets, but don't think I didn't notice the extra chunks of apple you slipped her earlier," Anna teases.

"Is that where all my apples went?" Grandma asks, slipping onto the porch from inside. She pins her husband with a glare, but it's harmless. "Come to think of it, they've been going missing for quite a few days now."

Anna giggles, turning into my body. She tips her head back, and her eyes shine so bright as they meet mine. "I missed you."

Her lips are parted in waiting when I kiss her. She feels at ease enough here to let me kiss her in front of my grandparents. I take her cheek in my hand and stroke her jaw just once, needing to feel her soft skin, before pulling back.

"Are you up to grabbing some stuff from your place?" I ask her.

She bunches her brows. "Am I staying here longer than just last night?"

"It would probably be smart to make sure that man is gone before sending you off on your own," Grandma says. Grandpa grunts his agreement.

"I doubt he's going to do anything other than be a creep and stand outside for a few hours," Anna argues.

I press my finger to her mouth. "Stay here with me. Just for a couple'a days. Please?"

Thankfully, that's all it takes to convince her.

"Fine. Fine! But only until you go back to Nashville."

"Sure."

My grandparents snicker, but Anna ignores them and the realization that if I have it my way, she'll be out of that rental of hers in no time. Even if that's a downright crazy sentiment to most people.

We make quick work of saying goodbye to my grandparents before she's back in my truck, and ten minutes later, we're pulling up in front of her place.

The black sedan parked in *my* spot along the curb has my hackles rising. Anna sucks in a sharp breath before frantically flinging up the lock on the door and diving into the cold. I'm quick to follow her, my heart stuttering in my chest when the driver's door opens and a man steps out.

"Stewart?" Anna shrieks, stumbling over her feet on the sidewalk. "What are you doing here?"

The man turns to her, a wide grin spreading his lips. There's a giant bouquet of roses in his suit jacket–covered arms. I quicken my steps and reach Anna's side before she gets too close to him. She reaches for my hand, taking it in an almost painful grip, and while I love that she's looking at me for comfort, it pisses me off that she feels the need for it.

"I missed you. It's time to come home," he says.

My nostrils flare, blood starting to grow hot beneath my skin. This guy looks just like I imagined he would. Conceited and stuck-up. Too proud to fight for her the way she deserves. He's not here to do that. It's months too late for that. There's another reason for his appearance, and I'll sniff it out. He's not getting within spitting distance of her. Not again.

I drape my arm around her back and press our sides together, rubbing the top of her arm over and over in a calming gesture. It's not likely to do anything, but I'm willing to try anything.

"I am home. I'm not going back to Vancouver, and certainly not back to you," Anna snaps.

He skips right over her words, dragging his judgmental eyes all over her body instead. The slight curl of his lips is enough to have me stepping toward him before Anna tugs me back, shaking her head.

"What are you wearing? You look ridiculous. I've let you play country hick long enough, I'd say," he says, his tone so damn condescending.

The grip I had on my temper slips. "You have a lot of fuckin' nerve, you know that? Get back in your car before you find yourself with a mouth full of pavement."

He glowers at me, his left eye twitching. I'd have laughed at how pathetic I find his attempt at intimidation if I wasn't so desperate to remove him from Anna's general vicinity. I'm confident enough to believe that there's no way she'll leave with him, but that doesn't mean his presence won't affect her.

"You've played house with my fiancée for long enough, Brody Steele. It's time she comes back home to her real life." He looks at her now, dismissing me. "Let's go. From the looks of your attire, there isn't much for you to grab, so let's just skip that step. Your closet at home is still full of your nice things."

"Leave, Stewart. I'm not going with you. And I'm not your fiancée. You made certain of that when you stuck your dick in someone else."

Stewart rolls his jaw, scratching at the hairless length of it. "Annalise. Get in the car. I've tired of these games. While I forgave you for the mess you made in our bedroom, my patience is still very thin."

"Leave. I'm not going with you. And it's not our bedroom anymore. Last time I checked, you hadn't even bothered to try and convince me to come home before right this moment. I'm not sure why you're here now, but that's your problem, not mine," she says, standing firm, chin held high.

I'm so fucking proud of her.

"I was giving you time to get over your hurt feelings. Instead, I learn that you've been living it up in this no-good town with this wannabe cowboy on social media. You've made quite the mess back home. I've had to convince all of our friends that you were simply acting out and not actually involved with *him*," he sneers.

Anna laughs a loud, bitter laugh. "*I've* made a mess? You're insane. The only reason you're here is because you're upset I've moved on and you've seen it in the media. I can assure you that there's nothing wannabe about my cowboy. Not a damn fucking thing."

My heart thumps wildly. Her public claiming makes my cock throb, the time and place not seeming to matter.

Stewart leans a hand against the door of the SUV and lets the roses in the other fall to rest against his thigh. "Your cowboy? Give me a break, Annalise. I brought your ring. It's in the car. Come put it back on. I don't appreciate you walking around without it."

"You'd have to force it on me," she states.

His face grows blank, his mind seeming to buffer for a few moments before rage flares in his eyes. I tuck Anna behind me just enough I don't worry he'll grab her.

"Come here and I'll do just that, then. You'll never get the fucking thing off again."

I don't let Anna hold me back this time. My strides are huge, eating the distance between us and that fucking no-good sack of shit until I'm right in his face. He smells like money. Money and arrogance. The worst combination but the most common with guys like this. He'd get along with Garrison, I'm sure.

Air shoot from my nostrils as I attempt to rein in my anger, but the grin he flashes is a big red flag waving in my face. I'm not a fighter. I've thrown one punch in my life, and it sucked. But I'm teetering on the ledge, my hands in fists at my sides.

"Touch her and you'll lose the ability to use your hands again," I threaten, my tone cold as death.

"Try it. I've never needed to use my hands much with that one. She's more than willing to put in the work in the bedroom. I've never met a woman who loves to ride dick the way she does." He laughs cruelly, dropping his voice to just above a whisper. I pray she can't hear his next words. "Maybe it makes sense after all. You found a cowboy to ride. Even if she had to scrape the bottom of the barrel to find you."

Footsteps pound on the pavement behind me as I throw my second-ever punch. This time, it doesn't suck. It hits its mark just right. Blood spurts from Stewart's nose as I step back and shake out my hand, sharp pain zipping up my arm.

He's immediately grabbing his face, eyes full of bewilderment. "You're so screwed."

"Maybe. But at least I don't have a broken nose." I shove him out of my way and open the driver's door of the SUV before shoving him inside. His head hits the frame on the way, but it does nothing to settle me. "Get the fuck out of here. Now."

"You'll be hearing from my lawyers, Brody Steele." He glances past me, and I know without turning that he's looking at Anna. The flowers fall to the road. "Last chance. I won't be wasting my time with coming here again for you. Not even you're worth this effort."

"Leave and don't come back," she demands.

He doesn't spare either of us another second of his precious time before he's speeding off down the road and, hopefully, out of Cherry Peak for good. Anna softly takes my hand and sighs.

"You didn't have to do that, Brody. He genuinely wasn't worth it. He was just jealous that I haven't been sitting here pining after him this entire time we've been apart."

"Oh, it was worth it, alright. I've wanted to do that for weeks now."

The corner of her mouth twitches. "He might not get any lawyers involved in this, but he won't roll over and do nothing."

I pull her in close and kiss the soft skin of her forehead. "He's welcome to take a shot at me, sweetheart. Nothin' will make me regret punchin' him."

Not even the call I get from Garrison the next morning, informing me that a representative from Swift Edge is on their way to Cherry Peak for an emergency meeting.

I'd do it all over again if I could.

42

Annalise

REGGIE BECKETT IS NOT WHAT I WAS EXPECTING. HE'S AN OLDER man with a blinding aura of sophistication and thoughtfulness. Dressed in a pink-and-red checked shirt and light-washed jeans with worn fabric down the thighs, he takes a seat across from Brody and me at the dining table. A matching red fedora rests beside Brody's hat and the steamy mug of coffee I prepared for him.

I play with my fingers beneath the table, nerves rattling me right to the bone. Brody didn't expect Reggie to be the one who flew down to speak to him, but it was a pleasant surprise. According to him, the alternatives were far, far worse.

"You have a lovely home, Brody. This place is definitely a marvel," Reggie says, attempting to break the ice.

Brody nods tightly, leaning his elbows on the table, hands clasped tight in front of them. "A home this beautiful makes it hard to leave."

I wince at the brutal honesty in the words. The air's been tense, charged with unspoken worry and nerves, from the moment I opened the door and welcomed Reggie into the second home on Steele Ranch. It's so unusual for Brody to be this frazzled, and I'm struggling to figure out how to calm him.

He isn't worried because he regrets what he did yesterday. I believed him when he said he would easily do it again. It's something else, and if I had to guess, I'd say he's expecting the worst from this surprise meeting. For the label to wipe their hands of him, maybe.

He's been home for too long. Lost them far too much money when he left the tour, and now . . . now he's already back. I don't know the details that were discussed in Nashville, and not because he's hidden them from me but because we haven't had the time to talk about much. It's been one thing after the other since he left.

Most of which come back to me.

It was my getting followed by a reporter that brought him back home so soon after leaving, and it was my ex-fiancé that had Swift Edge management rushing here not long after. Guilt is eating me up inside, one savage chunk after the other.

If he were to lose everything he's worked his entire life for, I don't know what I'd do. What we'd do.

Reggie doesn't reveal a single thing in his expression. He's calm and gentle, far too much so considering the heavy topics that have to be coming.

"I can't say I'd want to leave much either with a home like this. I can't blame you for that. Life is unfair this way, though. It would be much easier if we could have everything we want where we want it, no?" he asks.

I'd have expected the sentiment to be spoken in a snarky way, like a parent scolding a child for being stubborn, but there's nothing like that in his tone. I believe that Reggie truly feels that way. It's unjudgmental and honest.

"It sure as shit would, Reggie," Brody replies.

I press my knee to his, and he reaches beneath the table to hold my thigh. His palm is hot, burning through my jeans and acting as a sharp reminder that he wants me here with him. We're in this together. Emotion builds in my throat, threatening to choke me.

"I'm sorry there wasn't much notice of my arrival. I wanted to give you a couple of days to sort through the most recent events, but you know my son. It was a useless effort. I do hope my call this morning was alright, however."

"It was better than nothing," Brody says. "Thank you."

Reggie shifts his attention to me, smiling kindly. "And of course, I'm grateful to have a chance to meet you, sweet Annalise. You're far more beautiful than Brody explained to me."

"Is that right, Brody?" I sneak a look at him, and my stomach jumps at the blatant affection in that waiting blue stare.

He drifts his thumb along my outer thigh, and I have to fight back a shiver. "It's not my fault your beauty isn't possible to explain."

I could sit here and flirt with this man for all hours of the day. But we can't. And the reminder of why we're all sitting here is enough to sober me up.

"Thank you both for the compliments. But we should focus on the real reason for this meeting."

"You're right. I always tend to drift off topic in my old age," Reggie scolds himself. "I'll be blunt with this. You're talented, Brody. Incredibly so. Swift Edge only takes the best of the best, and I'm honoured to have worked with you. I want to *keep* working with you. But I think the question I need to ask you right now is if you want to keep working with *me*. With the label as a whole."

The question smacks down on the table, alarm bells blaring. I tense, and Brody feels it. He splays his fingers out on my thigh and rubs it in small circles. But this isn't about me, and I attempt to put on a brave face.

"Of course I do, Reg. I want to make music for the rest of my life. That's not the problem," Brody answers.

Reggie purses his lips, considering that. "Then please, explain to me what is so we can move past this. Garrison is growing antsy. We need a plan, something we can bring him if you want to continue to work with us."

"The tour. I don't know if I can commit to that. Not right now. I've got a lot goin' for me up here in Cherry Peak."

"What tour?" I blurt out.

Reggie glances between me and Brody. It feels like there's a lot to unpack right here. I shove away my panic and attempt to keep a level head.

"It wouldn't be a world tour right away, Brody. This isn't our first rodeo, so to speak. We know you may need baby steps. Most artists do. You remember how it was with Killian," Reggie says, each word chosen carefully. For Brody's benefit or mine, I'm unsure.

"Yeah, I do. And that's why I'm sayin' no. It was easier to hop on a tour bus and not care when I'd be home a few months ago. Before—" He stalls, and I flinch. An obvious physical reaction to hearing that he's turning down this step in his career because of me.

My chest cracks, guilt slithering through.

"Before I had someone here waitin for me," he finishes.

"You aren't the only artist out there with a family at home. Plenty of people make it work. Killian, for example," Reggie says.

"I'm not talkin' about other artists. I'm talkin' about me, and I'm tellin' you that I don't know if I can commit to it."

I start to gnaw on the inside of my lip, nervous as all hell. There's no way I can let him give this up for me. I'd never forgive myself. Who knows if he'd ever forgive me either. What happens in ten years when he tires of working on the ranch and realizes he could still be living his dream if he hadn't given it up just to stay close to me?

Not only that, but he hasn't stopped for one minute since apparently making up his mind to even ask me how I'd feel about all of this. Because if he had, I would have told him that the distance wouldn't matter. That we'd make it work because I think what we have is worth the effort. But he didn't. He made these choices on behalf of both of us, and I refuse to take that sitting down.

My guilt begins to twist into frustration. A dangerous mixture that's bound to cause trouble. I shift my leg, and Brody's hand falls from it. The lack of his touch helps clear my mind, even if I'm already struggling not to put it right back where it was.

Reggie seems to read me better than I anticipated. He pushes the conversation along instead of feeding into Brody's declaration.

"Don't make that decision yet. There's more we need to talk about today. The man you punched yesterday, for one. PR is already on top of it, but we got lucky this time. Next time, it may not be so easy. While I understand why it happened, I can't say my son does."

"Yesterday was my fault. Stewart was only there because of me and some sick sense of jealousy. He's gone now and won't be back," I say.

Reggie waves me off with a warm smile. "Don't apologize. As I said, his complaint was easily dismissed. When it comes to Spencer Sharp, however, I'd like to apologize to you, Annalise, on behalf of Swift Edge. We didn't think the tabloids would have sent someone out so quickly. That was a mistake on our part, and you can rest assured that it won't happen again," he says, attention fixed solely on me.

I attempt a weak smile in return. "Thank you. It was just a bit of a surprise. Nothing I couldn't handle. Don't worry about it."

"Yes, they should worry about it," Brody grits out, avoiding looking my way. "I won't have this shit happenin' here again. Not to my family. Public figure or not, I don't care. You have any idea how terrifyin' it was to have a man tailin' my woman in the dark?"

I swallow the lump in my throat and reach for his hand on the table. Fuck my frustration—it doesn't matter when I hear the desperation in his tone. For the first time since sitting down with Reggie, I'm wondering if maybe I've overlooked the true reason behind Brody's denial to go on tour. Brody is the most protective man I've ever met, and the thought of leaving me here for long stretches of time without him after the other day must terrify him.

"Brody," I murmur.

His throat works with a tight swallow as he stares at Reggie. I'd have thought he didn't hear me had he not flipped his hand and linked our fingers.

"What do you want me to do? Do you want security here watching Anna? We've already threatened legal action with *Country Capital* and Spencer. News will spread that Cherry Peak isn't the place to be hunting for secrets. But tell me what else you need, and we'll do it," Reggie offers, and I truly do believe he'll do anything to keep Brody as a Swift Edge artist.

Maybe that's what has fear zipping up my spine and words exploding from my mouth. "No security. I don't want it."

Brody whips his head in my direction, lips parted, clearly surprised by my outburst. "What? Why not? It would help settle me a bit to know you're always bein' looked after."

"I'm not a child in need of taking care of. I've never needed that," I argue.

The terrified look in his eyes devastates me. "One day. I was gone for one day, and not only were you accosted by a reporter lookin' for a scoop on me, but your good-for-nothin' ex shows up wantin' you back. How am I supposed to leave you knowin' shit like that can happen at any given moment? What if I'm too far away next time to get back quick?"

"I'm not having my freedom stripped away, Brody. I've found a life here. Started something really, really good. With you, but also with the girls and my job. I don't want to lose those good things."

I'm only half-aware that Reggie is still here, watching silently.

It would be better to wait until he's gone, but I can't seem to tell myself to stop talking.

"I won't live my life out of fear. Not of snoopy reporters or a guy from my past who's long gone by now. More stuff is going to pop up, but shouldn't it be my choice how we handle it? You're forgetting that I have a say in this relationship too."

"I'm staying in a motel a town over. Call me tomorrow. We'll talk more," Reggie says softly, taking his leave without waiting for a response from either of us. I offer him a parting, wince-like smile regardless. It's all I can manage as he leaves us in the kitchen.

The front door clicks shut.

Brody tightens his grip on my fingers, as if reassuring himself that I'm still here. That I wasn't the one to leave. "You do have a say, Anna. You do. But I can't—I just—fuck. I don't know what I'm doin'. I've spent a huge chunk of life runnin' from Cherry Peak. Of pretendin it wasn't home. Now, I'm finally back and so damn happy here, and I'm supposed to give it all up again? I can't do it. I can't lose you."

I shake my head furiously. "The only way you'll lose me is if you try and lock me up in a padded box. I love so many things about you, Brody Steele, especially your protectiveness. Please don't make me resent you for the same trait that played a part in me falling in love with you. All you have to do is ask me what I'm willing to do for you and us. What I'm willing to give to make this work. It doesn't have to be all on you." I'm both begging and telling him, my voice thick with a million emotions.

He pulls our linked hands to his chest, rubbing them over his heart. I exhale, hating the way the simple action makes my eyes burn.

"What are you willin' to do for us, sweetheart? Because there isn't anythin' I'm not prepared to sacrifice to spend the rest of my life with you."

"It's rude to continuously steal someone's thunder, you know?" I ask.

"What?"

"That's the exact same thing I was going to tell you. There isn't anything I'm not willing to do. You need me to join you every few shows on the road? I'll be there. You need me to fly out for days at a time while you record? I'll make the time. Late-night video chats? You've got it." I press our hands to my lips and kiss each of his knuckles. "I love you. I love you enough to beg you not to give up your dream. Not for me or your family and not for this place, even as beautiful as it may be."

His brows knit together, eyelids closing. I can feel the heat from his breath on my face, both of us leaning in until our fore-heads meet. I bump his nose and cup his bearded jaw with my free hand. Love swells in my chest like a balloon so close to bursting.

"I need you to go to Nashville, Brody. I need you to go and figure everything out and give it a chance," I add, my voice little more than a whisper.

He peels his eyes open, those pretty blues dulled with worry. "I'll go. So long as you're here when I get back."

"Always. I'll always be here waiting for you."

I've never meant anything more.

43

Brody

It pains me to leave Anna just as much the second time. I'm itching to call her to check in and make sure there hasn't been any more reporters following her or another appearance from Stewart, but I hold off. We already spoke this morning, and the last thing I want to do is suffocate her.

I can figure my shit out here with the tour and recording schedule and my upcoming living situation. I have to. If I don't, I risk losing her, and that isn't something I'm prepared to do.

There's a knock on my front door before I shout, "Come in!"

My Nashville home is far larger than the one in Cherry Peak. It's newly built, with five bedrooms, four bathrooms, a home gym, and a pool out back. It's hardly lived in. Even now, walking down the hallway with expensive tile flooring and the same sad beige paint on the walls as the rest of the house, I feel no pull to the place. No sentimental feeling that ties me to it.

I wasn't on tour with Killian for very long, so that isn't an excuse for not . . . caring about this house. For not adding any pieces of myself to it or trying to make it feel more like a home instead of a rental property.

Maybe Anna could help with that. She'd turn this house into a home the moment she stepped inside. No more empty walls and bare counters. I want photos hung and clutter everywhere. Ugly wallpaper and colourful paint. I've never wanted those things before, but now they feel necessary.

"The lack of Christmas decorations in this house is a total eyesore, Brody," Killian says from the foyer.

The three-time CMA winner and, somehow, close friend of mine kicks off his black boots and shakes out of his leather jacket before slapping me between the shoulders. His grin is electric, happy in a way I've always envied, but today, I envy it a little less. I'm not the same guy I was the last time I saw him. Not in the slightest.

"Haven't been here to set anythin' up," I tell him, giving his shoulder a quick squeeze before leading us to the kitchen.

Killian's been to the house enough times over the years to know his way around. We met through Swift Edge shortly after I signed, and the guy took me under his wing. Helped me transition from Cherry Peak to Nashville, and when the time came after the release of my first album for me to dip my toe into bigger and grander live shows, he requested me as his opener. It was going great. Everything was, until it wasn't.

I never expected Anna. And I know Killian wasn't expecting me to find someone to tether me back home either.

We step into the kitchen, and he takes a seat at the long marble island while I grab us both a beer from the fridge. After twisting the caps, I hand him his, and he takes it eagerly.

"How was your Christmas back home?" he asks.

"You tellin' me you haven't been keepin' up with me online?"

He takes a gulp of beer and sets the bottle down with a laugh. "You mean the rag mags were tellin' the truth the entire time?"

"That depends on what they were sayin'."

"Only that ya snagged yourself a beauty. Apparently, you've moved back home and settled down. Considerin' that you're here and not back in Cherry Peak yet, I take it they weren't all right."

I shrug. "Half-right. Do have a woman I love and want to settle down with. I'm here tryin' to make that happen. But I haven't moved back there. Not full-time."

"About goddamn time you found a woman. I worried you'd be turnin' thirty alone with nobody to tuck your old ass into bed."

"You're older than me, asshole."

He winks, tipping back the dewy bottle for another drink. Smacking his lips, he says, "Older in age, not spirit."

My exhale is heavy. "I wish it was as easy as just movin' back, but it's not. You know that just as well as I do."

"Suppose I do. But I don't buy that you haven't been figurin' out a way to make it work, though."

"I am. Fuck, I'm tryin'. I don't suppose you have any advice for me? I feel like I'm completely out of my damn league with this. How do you do it?"

Killian swirls the bottle between his palms and leans over the counter, staring at me hard. "Are you askin' how I got my woman to stay for keeps or how I've made it work with a family in this business?"

"Both. Whatever you're willin' to share."

He nods, eyes burning bright as he speaks. "There's no simple answer. No magic formula. You just do it. You fight for it. Lila was mine from the moment I saw her, and I knew I'd never be happy again without her with me. Things got hard like they always do with stress and questions, and for guys like you and me, it ain't easy to put those we love in the spotlight. But there comes a point when you have to ask yourself if you're alright with fear stealin' your happiness from you. Still scared shitless of somethin' happening to my family—that doesn't ever go away. But seein' my woman at home with my babies? That's worth everythin'."

"You make it sound so simple," I mutter, an ache growing behind my ribs.

Killian taps the bottom of his bottle to the counter and laughs straight from his gut. "Not a damn thing simple about it. Lila didn't ask for the expectations that came with being my wife. She never planned to have her privacy invaded and be exposed to nasty comments on her social media every day. I just stepped back and let her choose what she was willin' to sacrifice in order to be with me and made sure I made up for it elsewhere. That's what love is, Brody. I'm riskin' soundin' like a pussy here, but love's all about sacrifices. She gives, and I give right back. A balance, y'know?

"You got to trust that your woman knows what she wants and what she's willin' to do for it. If she's tellin' you she's in, then fuckin' hell, man, take her at her word and bring her in. Believe her when she says she's good and thinks you're worth it. You don't turn away a woman like that. Especially when you love the shit outta her the way you do."

I drop my elbows to the counter and let his words filter through my mind. "I'm lucky to have you in my life, Kill. You're a hell of a lot wiser than I've ever given you credit for."

"Ah, don't go soft on me just yet. Wait until you've actually got your woman for keeps."

My beer is completely unappealing to me now. Anticipation zips through my veins. I want to hop on a plane right now and head back to Anna with this newfound conviction pumping through me, but I know it's not time. Not yet.

"I want to make this as easy on her as possible. I've got so much shit comin' at me right now that I don't have a clue how to navigate yet," I say on a heavy exhale.

"You talkin' about the album?"

"That and the tour. Garrison wants me out in a couple months. The album done in half that time."

His expression is thoughtful, concentrated. "How about you tell me a bit about Anna before I dip back into my well of knowledge? I want to hear all about the woman who's got you this worked up."

I don't hesitate to do just that. From how we first met to our time at the wedding and how fast and hard I fell for her. I tell him that she loves the ranch and that it loves her right back. He nods along with every word, howling a laugh when I tell him that I searched high and low for a Highland cow for her because she mentioned wanting one a single time and that I went as far as to build it its own shed in the pasture.

I tell him all of her favourite things and about her fear of driving on icy roads. His lips tug into a smirk when I mention her dream of owning her own hair salon, and I grow far too curious about that reaction to let it go.

"What?"

He pushes his bottle to the side and scratches the underside of his jaw. "Lee Rose's daughter lives in Cherry Peak, yeah? I heard about her a few months back at one of Lila's little summer shindigs, and my wife hasn't let it go since. Damn, what's her name again? Starts with a W."

"Wanda? Yeah, she's in Cherry Peak. Owns the salon my woman works at."

The topic change is confusing, but I let it run its course. Wanda grew up in Cherry Peak with her mother, not with her father. I've never been close enough to her to ask about her father other than what the town knows, and even if I was, I don't think I would have put my nose in it regardless. There's a reason Lee Rose isn't a Cherry Peak native, and I don't think it has as much to do with his career as it does his daughter.

All I know is that Wanda's been in and out of our hometown since shortly after high school graduation. I've lost count of the number of businesses she's started up just to abandon a few months or sometimes years later. The hair salon is only a temporary interest for her. That knowledge shakes something up inside of me.

"Shit, yeah, that's right," Killian says.

"Why the sudden interest in Wanda?"

"Well, from what I've heard, she's been takin' an interest in dear old dad after all these years. It was pretty common knowledge that Lee was a shit dad who ran off pretendin' he didn't know of a place called Cherry Peak, so Wanda's drawn a bit of attention with her sudden questions," he explains.

I furrow my brows, still confused. "Alright, so he was a shitty dad. That doesn't answer my question."

"That's because you're not lettin' me finish. My wife's a bit of a gossip, which in turn makes *me* a gossip. From what I've learned from her, Wanda's plannin' on takin' off again to confront the old man. I'm not sure for what, but that salon of hers is as good as gone if she disappears."

"She's not goin' to find a new owner? Just leave all her employees high and dry?" I snap, worry and anger swirling in my belly.

Killian leans back in his seat, arms crossing over his chest and a smirk splitting his cheeks. "Not if there's already someone who has a dream of ownin' a hair salon, I'd reckon. Maybe a woman whose name rhymes with banana."

I double blink. "You think Anna should buy it from her?"

"I think *you* should buy it *for* her. Help her with her dream while she helps you with yours. She gives, you give. Knowin' Lila's at home with our babies while also doin' what she loves with her clothin' line makes it easier for me to leave to do what I love. It can be easy to let our careers suck the life out of those in our lives, Brody. I know my woman is strong enough to fight for herself—God knows she's kept my head on straight all these years—but when I got the opportunity to help her with her dream, I didn't hesitate. Anna might tell you to go to hell and that you overstepped, but it's worth a try."

I won't deny that the thought of being able to help her with this would make me feel more accomplished than pretty much anything I've ever done in my life. Knowing she's home and happy and busy doing what she loves while I'm gone doing what I have to would bring me a sense of peace.

Anna wants to be in Cherry Peak. She's found a home there and friends that she deserves more than anything. Owning a salon of her own . . . that would be the cherry on top. The final piece to the puzzle of her new life.

"Does it ever get easier? Even if I do help with the salon, the thought of leavin' her still grates. Tours aren't a few easy days on the road. You know that better than I do," I ramble.

"You'll always miss her. Always wish she was right beside you on the bus or waitin' for you backstage. All you can do is focus on gettin' back to her once you're done. Well, that and bringin' her with you whenever you can. Don't torture yourself with holdin' back from askin' her to join you. I guarantee she'll miss you just as much as you'll miss her. Don't make it harder than it has to be. And before you ask, I know you're worried about recordin' the damn album, but that's nothin'. It's quick time apart compared to the entire future you two have. Don't make it a big deal."

He's right. Too right. I feel like a fool for worrying so much about things with easy solutions. I blame that lowlife reporter for these fucking doubts and fears. I've been an idiot. Anna's in love with me the way I'm in love with her. The move mountains for her just to catch a glimpse of her pretty smile type of love. The burn anyone who so much as thinks to take her happiness from her type of love. No amount of distance could sever that.

My next words come out quickly, hard with determination.

"I guess it's time we get to work, then."

44

Annalise

FOR THE FIRST TIME SINCE I MOVED TO CHERRY PEAK, I DON'T HEAD into work on Tuesday morning.

I woke to a text from Wanda this morning, urging me to take the next couple of days off, and immediately knew better than to argue, even if I could use the money. A free day means I'll have the chance to go to the ranch and visit Banana. My first call after hanging up was to Eliza.

I've been to Steele Ranch nearly every evening for dinner since Brody left last week, but this will be the first time that I'll get to play with Banana in the daylight. Eliza has done an amazing job of keeping me fed and busy the past few days— Brody's orders, I'm sure. I think I've gained at least ten pounds from her amazing food and homemade cookies and muffins. My fridge is so full of Tupperware containers piled to the top with leftovers that I haven't had to grocery shop at all.

The ranch hands rushing from stable to barn and everywhere in between don't give me a second look as Bryce pulls up the drive to let me out. Everyone is rather used to seeing me lingering around, and that makes me incredibly happy. Even Wade has taken a liking to me, flashing me sneaky half-smiles and teaching me facts about the history of the ranch and dos and don'ts with cattle. The knowledge has helped when it comes to Banana. I want to make sure I know how to properly care for her, and Wade seems to want to genuinely help me do that.

One thing I really still want to learn is how to properly ride a horse, but I don't want anyone but Brody to teach me. *Maybe one day.*

"Text me when you need me to pick you up later. And please don't forget to sneak me a couple of Mrs. Steele's cookies. I swear they melt in my mouth," Bryce moans, unlocking the car doors.

"I can get Wade to drop me off after dinner."

"The fact you're on a genuine first-name basis with that man will never stop being shocking to me. He's intimidating as fuck."

"He's actually quite sweet when you get to know him."

She shakes her head in disbelief. "I'll take your word for it. But if he can't bring you, just let me know."

"I will. Thank you for dropping me off," I say with a quick kiss to her cheek.

"Always. Have fun with the sweet girl."

With a promise to send her pictures, I duck out of the car and head up the porch steps. It still feels rude not to knock on the door, so I hit it three times and wait until Eliza's smiling face is right in front of me.

"How many times do I have to tell you to just come right in?" she asks, ushering me inside.

"Probably a few more," I tell her honestly.

The smell of roast fills the house, making my mouth water. I reach for the heavy puffed jacket from the coat hook on instinct and hand it to Eliza. She slips her arms inside just like she has every night after dinner.

"We'll get there, my dear. Now, I've been just itching to check on that sweet girl of yours all morning. I'm so glad you're here early," she says, her boots already on as we step back outside.

The sun is bright but not warm. According to Wade, it won't be for a long while yet. I wonder what the weather's like in

Nashville today and whether Brody's bundled up the way I am with his thick jacket and gloves. We spoke just before Bryce picked me up, but it wasn't for long enough. At this point, I'm positive no phone call will be long enough. Not with how badly I miss him.

There's an ache deep in my soul that won't seem to ease no matter how badly I will it to. There was never a time in the three years I was with Stewart where I felt like this while we were apart. Not. Once. It's scary, but in the best way possible.

I feel alive.

"You're thinking about him," Eliza says softly, walking in time with me down the path to the pasture.

"I always seem to be thinking about him."

"It's hard having him be away; I won't lie and tell you it isn't. However, there's no better feeling than giving him a big squeeze the moment he gets back."

I smile to myself at that. "Can I ask you something?"

The sweet woman who I've grown to care for so, so much doesn't hesitate. "You don't even have to ask."

"When did you marry Wade? You two still look so in love, and I guess that's hard for me to wrap my head around. My parents weren't like you guys when I was growing up and even less like it when I got older."

It feels incredibly unnerving to peel back my protective shell and expose my inner thoughts like this, but with Eliza, I know she won't judge me for it. There won't be anything but a warm understanding that I latch onto tight.

"We married when I was eighteen and he was twenty. Things were much different back then when it came to marriage, but even if they hadn't been, I still would have married him that young. I met Wade and just knew. It was a beautiful moment that I pray every night I won't forget, even when my mind starts to fade.

"True love doesn't require a marriage certificate, but I've so enjoyed being able to call him my husband. It's simply another way I can consider him mine. I'm sorry you never had an opportunity to witness that type of relationship growing up."

"My father has always had one true love—his job. I've accepted that, but I still hold a grudge against him for stealing my chance for me to witness a proper marriage in my most developmental years." I pause, staring at the toes of my boots. "You know that I was engaged before I moved here, but even when I wore Stewart's ring on my finger, I didn't feel the excitement for my big day that I know I was supposed to feel. I understand if that maybe makes you think poorly of me." I hate how small my voice sounds, how insecure.

"That could never make me think poorly of you. There is no rule written that says we all have to want the same things in life. It's all about finding the person whose dreams align with yours, whatever they might be," Eliza declares, her tone fierce.

I blink past a wave of emotion and ask, "Brody's your only grandchild. Don't you want him to get married someday?"

"I want plenty of things for him, my sweet. Marriage pales in comparison to simply seeing him happy."

Her confident words settle me a part of me that I didn't know had been fretting at the idea of stumbling upon this potential roadblock.

A beat later, she unhooks the metal gate and ushers me into the pasture, conversation already forgotten, no awkward thank you needed. Banana comes skipping over instantly, as if she were watching for us all morning. The other cows watch her with interest, a few lingering close by. My heart swells at their protectiveness. Banana has found a herd here the way I have, and that makes me feel both relieved and at peace.

Eliza is the first to reach down and scratch the fluffy girl on the top of her head. "Good morning, sweetie. You've been keeping these heifers in line, yeah?"

"If anyone could, it would be this sassy girl." Banana jumps forward, and I drop to a crouch to give her some pets. "Yeah, I missed you too."

"She's spoiled rotten, this one," Eliza says.

"Yeah, she is. We can blame Brody for that, though."

"I hope you believe me when I say I've never seen him do anything like this for anyone before. You've turned him all inside out with your love, Anna. It's been surreal to watch the change in him these past couple of months."

"He's done the same to me. I've never been this happy. Not once," I admit.

Eliza grins so brightly. "You're in for a blessed life, my girl. You better buckle in tight."

I don't bother telling her that I have been from the moment I met Brody at Peakside.

Brody

MY BODY SCREAMS at me to get back in my truck and drive to Anna's house. God, I miss her enough to nearly give in. If it wasn't for my fear of not being able to get myself back to this place of determination after sinking back into the feel of her at my side, I would have.

I've been running on the same thrill since that conversation with Killian in Nashville. The same desire to get to work and figure my shit out before returning to my woman. It took a few days to get it all together with Wanda, but there's one more thing I have to do now that I'm back on the ranch.

I wish it hadn't taken me so long to get here. To walk this path to the stables with my heart galloping in my throat and my fingers shaking. But now that I'm here, there's no backing out. This is my next step. The move I need to make to press forward in my life. No more hiding from the pain in my chest. I can't focus on the future while holding a chunk of myself in the past.

It's dark when I reach the stable, the motion-sensor lights above the door beaming when I grip the handle and slide it open. Silence fills the stable before hooves on hay cuts through. I flick on the lights above the right side of the stable. Sky's already watching me when I head down the walkway between the stalls, her head hanging over her gate once again.

"Sorry for wakin' you," I whisper, pausing a few feet from her.

Emotion builds in my throat, a pound of rocks dropping in my stomach. The love in those brown eyes of hers nearly rocks me back on my heels. It's too much. More than I deserve.

"I figured you and me could go for a ride tonight."

It's as if she can understand me. She shuffles behind the gate, a low whinny escaping her. My fingers twitch, wanting to touch her again, but I hold myself back. Not yet.

"I take it that's good with you, then. You'll have to be patient with me here. I'm goin' to be a bit rusty," I tell her.

Her saddle is hung off to the side, and I grab it in surprisingly steady hands, the weight of it just right. She waits patiently for me to open her gate and step inside her stall. It takes me longer than I'd like to admit to get her saddled up, but I'm pleased to know I haven't forgotten how to do it. Maybe it was stupid to consider that I could have.

I smooth my palm down her neck, exhaling shakily at the familiar tickle of her soft hair against my skin. The world fades around us, and I fall into the utter rightness that comes with being beside my horse—my best friend through some of the biggest moments in my life. It was wrong of me to stay away from her, but today marks the start of a new beginning for the both of us.

"One step done. Gonna let me hop on now, girl?"

She blows out a long breath and sidesteps closer to me. I chuckle, patting her neck.

"Alright, now, no sudden movements, please."

Her reins are a welcome weight in my sweaty fist as I step into the stirrup and hoist myself onto her back in one smooth motion. She doesn't move a muscle as I sit in the saddle, my thighs tight against her sides. Too tight.

My eyes are squeezed shut, a swell of emotion rocking through me. I'm tense, my head pulsing with memories and a heavy grief that I haven't allowed myself to feel in a decade. A wet trickle moves down my cheek, and I laugh, opening my eyes to find them blurry.

Like being hit in the gut with two bull hooves, I'm out of breath, gulping in breaths of cold air in the confines of a stable my ma helped build when I was a boy. For the first time since I bottled my emotions up and forced myself to be strong for my family, I cry.

I don't register that we've begun to move until the first snowflake hits my face. Sky trots nice and slow away out of the barn and down the same path toward the trees behind the guest house that we would follow every day after school. Readjusting my hold on the reins, I fix my posture and soak in the shift of the saddle between my legs, a feeling I haven't experienced in too long. Sky's movements become my own. The cold doesn't register as we head further and further from the house and into the small lining of trees that separates the front of the ranch from the massive expanse behind it.

We move through the pasture and around the shop. Past the pink structure I built myself and the tiny cow resting beneath it playing with a calf. The ranch takes on a new look tonight as I stitch pieces of myself back together that I've long since accepted as broken.

And once Sky and I close in on the stable again, I lead her right back out, this time with a gentle squeeze of my legs that sends us flying through the night, my laugh healing the both of us.

45

Annalise

THE SIGHT OF BRODY PERCHED ON SKY'S BACK THE NEXT MORNING has me stumbling, nearly getting a mouthful of dirty snow. His posture is perfect and confident. The twinkle in his eyes is nothing short of magical. I wasn't prepared for this visual, but I'm so not going to complain.

I fix my balance and jog toward him, not caring that the path is slick with fresh ice or that Poppy is no doubt watching us in her rear-view mirror as she drives off. It would be worth the skinned knees and the teasing just to get to him as quickly as possible. My heart soars as the distance between us shrinks, Sky's ears pushing forward while she watches me.

Brody gifts me an unabashed smile, one so damn bright my knees threaten to lock at the beauty of it. His hat is low on his head, jacket zipped high and boots tucked easily in the stirrups. I've never seen someone look so regal on a saddle before. Like they were meant to be there, born for it, even. And that's exactly it.

Brody was born to ride Sky, two best friends bound together by nature itself.

I'm an emotional wreck beneath my warm grin and flushed skin when I finally reach the pair. My man doesn't hesitate to slip from the saddle and take me in his arms, palms cupping my face the way they always seem to. Our first kiss after a week apart is staggering. It's a swell of love and want and greed strong enough to steal my breath and intensify the thrum of my heartbeat. The world around us burns brighter, feels warmer, becomes *complete*. Contentment blooms in my belly, a valley of vibrant flowers springing to life in my most hidden places. They smell of him, of us.

I hold him back just as tight as he holds me, putting everything I feel into the way I kiss him back. Sky whinnies from behind him, and then he lurches forward, both of us staggering. Inching back a breath, I peek over his shoulder and find a wide brown eye staring at us expectantly. I shoot her a wink.

"I missed you, sweetheart," Brody rasps, ignoring Sky for a beat longer as he focuses so completely on me.

"Really? After that greeting, I couldn't tell."

I glide my hands beneath his jacket and up his back. He shivers, pressing his lips to the tip of my nose.

"Alright, smartass."

"I missed you too, Brody," I murmur before stealing another kiss and hugging him tight.

"Seems Sky missed you too. The needy thing."

The tan horse, seemingly deciding she's had enough of waiting, butts past Brody and moves toward me. I laugh when she rubs against my shoulder, demanding attention.

"Did he not give you enough pets, beautiful girl?" I ask her, patting her neck and shoulder.

"She's had damn near more attention in the last twenty-four hours than she has in a long time. Now she's just being greedy."

"Were you here last night, then?"

I figured he was when he stopped answering my texts shortly after he got back in town. My first instinct was to run to the ranch the moment he arrived, but some gut instinct told me to wait. I don't know what happened here last night, but I'm just relieved to see him this happy in Sky's presence. He looks like he's shed a heavy weight from his heart, like he's refreshed and simply at peace.

He moves to Sky's other side and gives her soft strokes on the back. "Yeah. We rode until the sun was comin' up. Once I got back in the saddle, I couldn't seem to get off. Even rode into town. Went past your house and up Main Street."

My throat tightens. "That would have been a sight to see."

"Considered wakin' you up and askin' you to join us, but I figured I'd wait until today."

I gasp, my hand stopping midway across Sky's shoulder. "We're going for a ride?"

He chuckles deeply, nodding. "If you're up for it. There's somethin' I want to show you in town."

"Are we actually allowed to do this?"

"I've been ridin' into town since I was a boy. Haven't done it for a long time before last night, but I gotta admit that I don't really care if anyone's got a problem with it now. Not today."

I roll my lips, a smile begging to break through. My pulse races with excitement. "Then, yes! Yes, yes, yes. But don't think this means you're getting out of telling me all about what happened in Nashville this past week. I've been waiting very impatiently," I warn him.

He doesn't fight me on it, just drifts close and grabs me by my hips, pulling me flush to his front. The feel of him against me is addictive and enthralling, threatening to turn me into mush. Especially when he winds a hand through the hair at my nape and buries his face in my neck, inhaling with a deep, desperate groan. I swallow, and his lips find my pulse before they part and he licks a hot trail up the underside of my jaw.

"Never loved being bossed around, Anna, but when you do it, my cock turns to steel. I'd let you order me around any fuckin' day if it meant I got to hold you like this after." He digs his teeth into the sensitive skin below my ear and whispers, "I've jerked off to the memories of you ridin' me for a week now. Have you touched yourself thinkin' of me?"

"Oh, my God." A shiver so violent it becomes nothing short of a full-body shake moves through me. My body grows tight with arousal, my clit throbbing. "You can't say those things to me out here. Not when anyone could walk by and hear."

"Anyone with half a mind wouldn't consider comin' out here for a damn second when I've finally got my hands back on you after bein' gone a week. It's a fuckin' miracle I haven't taken you against the side of the stable already with how out of my mind I feel right now."

I drop my forehead to his chest and curse the rough scrape of my hard nipples against my bra when any slight movement has pleasure rippling down my spine.

"Take me on a ride to town first. If I let you fuck me right now, we won't make it out until tomorrow, and you've got me too excited to wait. We have plenty of time together still, right?"

His eyes snare mine, so focused and intense, the flare of arousal forgotten for the time being. "We got time, baby. I'll devour you later, all damn night long if I get my way."

"Sounds perfect."

"Let's get you in the saddle, then. Slide your left foot in the stirrup, and then grab the reins in your left hand."

I follow his instructions, too excited to think of anything besides riding Sky. A squeak escapes me when Brody uses his grip on my hips to give me a boost when I push off my right leg to throw myself up and into the saddle. I settle onto it with a rough exhale before loosening my hold on the reins, feeling a hell of a lot higher up than I actually am. I'm grateful when Sky doesn't move as I try and find a natural position on the saddle.

"Good?" he asks, hovering at my side, touching Sky's neck. "It's normal not to feel steady yet, but she won't move until we're ready for her to. Keep your back straight and hold her reins, but not too tight."

He mounts Sky with much more grace than I had. In the blink of an eye, he's perched behind me, his back to my chest.

We hold her reins together, and then we're moving at a calm, slow pace.

"Try and move with her. Relax your legs and let yourself sway," Brody says gently, his mouth so close to my ear.

"It's a lot easier in theory," I admit.

He hums in agreement. "Riding a horse takes practice."

"It's a good thing I have a great teacher, then."

"We'll have you ridin' on your own in no time," he says, leading Sky through the open Steele Ranch gate and onto the road to town. "Up for goin' a bit faster?"

Despite my nerves, I blurt out, "Yes."

Brody slides an arm around my waist, fingers curling in my belt loop before Sky picks up speed. She doesn't take off, but the uptake in pace shifts how I sit in the saddle, the bouncing motion taking me by surprise.

"I won't let you fall. Relax your legs and let yourself move with her," he instructs, his tone gentle.

It's hard to think of much other than the steady feel of him behind me, holding me protectively, but I try. Slowly, I begin to relax, fighting off the discomfort of being jolted around. The rhythmic sound of her hooves in the snow travels through me, and I try and lean into it.

"How did you manage to stay away from her for so long? This is amazing. I feel so free," I say, bewildered by the sudden love I have for this new experience. Something clicks into place, a sense of rightness, maybe.

Brody tightens his hold on me, hot breath fanning the back of my head. "I was a stubborn ass too terrified to acknowledge a lifetime of pent-up grief. My mother loved to fix broken horses. Her entire career revolved around how many wild ones she could tame and heal from past tortures. That passion took her from me."

"What happened?" I ask, going off my instincts when they tell me he's not going to tuck tail and run. He's ready to talk about this now; I know it deep in my gut.

"It was a freak accident. She always wanted to push boundaries and do what nobody else thought was possible. That night, that same drive led her and one of the battered mares too far out on the east side of the ranch where she knew nobody would come lookin' for them. Nobody found her for hours after she was bucked off one of the wild ones she'd been workin' with. Wrong place, wrong time, wrong horse. The entire thing was wrong. There were too many rocks, and when she flew off . . ."

I release the reins in my right hand and grab his from its place on my middle, clutching it tight, hoping he can feel the strength I'm offering him. "You don't have to continue. I'm sorry, Brody. I'm so, so sorry."

"Thank you." He slides his fingers between mine. "I couldn't touch another horse for years afterward. Only Sky, but even that hurt too bad after a while. I hated all of them for what happened, and it wasn't fair. It was just easier to put the blame on them instead of the universe for takin' my mom from me."

"What changed?"

Brody leans forward and presses our cheeks together, his beard tickling my jaw the way I've grown to love. "You. Wantin' a future with you and realizin' that I've been hidin' from far too much in my life. I want to talk about her again—with you—and be able to do all the things I love with the woman I love. It was just time."

My vision blurs as I lean in his embrace and turn my face into the collar of his jacket. His warmth is a welcome break from the wind, but it only makes me that more aware of the tears spilling down my cheeks and every shuddered exhale as I fight back a wave of sobs.

Brody doesn't say anything else, not for a long moment, as Sky slows. I'm grateful for his silence. I'd be too overwhelmed if he tried to tell me much else. This is all so hard to understand. The man behind me is incredible. One I didn't see coming until he was standing right in front of me with his cowboy hat, dirty boots, grease-stained fingernails, and gorgeous blue eyes.

Brody Steele was my biggest surprise but greatest blessing. The last piece to the puzzle that makes up my new life. And fuck, it's a great life.

"Take a look around, sweetheart," Brody whispers a few minutes later.

With a pitiful sniffle, I quickly dry my cheeks and face forward, taking in my surroundings. "Why are we at the salon?"

He leads Sky to the curb, and she stops just outside the front doors. The street is empty, nearly abandoned the way it usually is on a regular weekday. I'm sure the few people who decide to head out today will get quite a kick out of seeing Sky in Brody's usual parking spot instead of his truck.

"I did a lot of thinkin' in Nashville, Anna. About you and us and my career. And a fuck ton about the future." He slides off Sky and drops to his feet. I stare down at him as he extends a hand. Taking it, I let him help me down. Once we're face to face and on solid ground, he closes in on me, pressing me back against Sky's solid weight. "Cherry Peak is your home. It was waitin' for you all these years just like I was, and I want you to have everythin' you've ever dreamed of here. With or without me, I want you to be the happiest you can be."

"That sounds perfect to me, Brody. That's all I want. I want you," I declare on a thin exhale.

"You told me about your dreams once, and I haven't forgotten about them. It's only fair that if I get to live mine with you by my side, you get the same in return."

"What are you talking about?" The question is weak, breathless as I grip his jacket in my fists to keep my fingers from shaking.

"I listed my house in Nashville for sale, and unless I'm tourin' there, I don't plan on goin' back. Cherry Peak is my home, and it's where I plan on stayin' when I'm not in Calgary at the new Swift Edge office or on the road. I've already requested that you have the option to join me on tour whenever you want to, and I sure as fuck hope you do that often. There's only one thing left now," he says, his expression relaxed but eyes wild with excitement.

I watch as he glances behind me, at the salon, the place that took me in when I had nothing my first week in this town. With my heart in my throat, I twist, really looking at the building this time. The lack of the sign above the door has my mind moving in overdrive.

"It's yours. All of it," he tells me, sensing my confusion.

My jaw slacks as I spin back around and shake my head at him. "What do you mean it's mine? Where's Wanda?"

Brody peels my curled fingers from his jacket and takes them into his grip instead. I know I look like a shocked fool when he laughs loudly, the deep sound of it making my toes curl, even now.

"She's headin' to Toronto next month, sweetheart. I'll leave the details as to why up to her to share, but this place was goin' up for sale in her absence," he explains. His eyes bounce between each of mine, searching them for something. "A friend warned me you might very well tell me to shove it and that I shouldn't have done this but that it was worth the risk. I'm havin' a hard time tellin' if you're about to tell me just that."

This time, despite my overwhelming feeling of disbelief, it's my laugh that fills the street. I tip my head back and push up on my toes, kissing him softly just once before falling back on my heels. "I'm never going to be the woman who turns down a grand gesture, Brody. This is just the most unbelievably incredible thing anyone has ever done for me."

He beams with pride. "Really? You mean that?"

"I do. I really, really do," I promise. There's no doubt in my mind that Brody is my forever. "I've never been more excited for anything than I am my future with you."

One blink and I'm in his arms, safe and warm and loved. He breathes me in, and then we're kissing, his taste exploding through me. We stand in each other's embrace for minutes, hours, maybe. Time is nothing more than a figment of our imagination as our lips move and tongues intertwine.

I wouldn't have believed it if someone told me three months ago that I'd be here right now. That this would be my life. But somehow, it is, and I wouldn't change it for the world.

EPILOGUE
ONE MONTH LATER

Brody

THISTLE AND THORN IS PACKED FULL OF CHERRY PEAK RESIDENTS. Young and old, loud and quiet, everyone mingles, indulging in the mutual excitement from a new business opening. Anna's salon has been completely renovated inside, the walls painted a soft pink and the old furniture swapped for new colourful pieces. Wanda's personality was so heavy in the space before Anna began making it hers, but now, a month later, you'd never know this place belonged to anyone but her.

My heart is triple its regular size as I take everyone in, witnessing their genuine awe and pride. It's not every day we have a big party like this here, and everyone came out for it. To support Anna.

I'm instantly searching for her in the crowd, finding her tucked between Bryce, Poppy, and a woman who, while older, could be a spitting image of Anna. I start pushing through the crowd, smiling at those who turn to look at me on my way.

Poppy spots me first, wiggling her fingers and winking. I huff a laugh beneath my breath and step to Anna's side, my arm sliding around her waist on instinct. She twists in my hold to stare up at me, a perfectly elated grin tugging her lips.

"Hey, sweetheart," I greet her for the second time tonight, kissing the top of her head.

She has her hair in a fancy twist and a deep blue dress hugging her body beneath a light-washed denim jacket. I don't have to look at her feet to know she has her comfortable sneakers on, opting not to risk wearing a pair of heels after blistering up her heels in a new pair of cowboy boots yesterday. The memory of her with nothing but those boots on last night while I fucked her over the kitchen counter has me twitching in my jeans.

"Hi, Brody," Bryce all but sings, a smirk prominent on her face.

Anna ignores her friends, speaking just to me. "Where did your grandparents go?"

"Grandma's minglin' and draggin' Grandpa behind her while she does it."

While I may have driven them both to the party, Grandma didn't make it five seconds inside before she was accosted by one of her bingo friends. I would feel bad for my grandpa if he weren't so used to it.

"No surprise there," Anna says with an adorable, light laugh. "Now that you're here, I want you to meet my mother, Larissa. Mom, this is Brody."

Anna's mother is already beaming when she takes my extended hand and shakes it. Her eyes crinkle at the corner, their warm shade of brown the same as her daughter's.

"I've heard so, so much about you, Brody. It's a pleasure to put a face to the name," she says.

"Likewise. It's great to meet you, ma'am." I turn to Anna and ask, "Been talkin' about me, have you?"

"Only every chance I get," she deadpans.

Tugging her close, I let her warmth seep into my very bones. "Makes us even, then."

"Mom is a serious fan of your music, by the way. Don't buy her little coy act."

Larissa gapes at her daughter, glancing at her two best friends as if they'll give her some backup. They don't—instead, they're too busy trying not to laugh to offer any saving.

"I'm flattered, truly," I tell her.

"Betrayed by my own flesh and blood. You're lucky I love you so much, Annalise."

Anna jabs a finger at her mother. "You'd do the same thing, don't even try and pretend otherwise."

"I'd like to see that, actually," Poppy puts in.

Bryce hums in agreement. "Me too."

"You guys!" Anna shrieks.

I rub my hand over the dip of her waist and chuckle. "Sorry, baby, but I'd also like to see it."

"I'm safe nowhere. You can get out of my safe space any minute now," Anna grumbles, but there's no heat behind the words.

Larissa hides a smile and pats Anna's shoulder. "Aw, sweetie. We're sorry."

"Don't lie. No you're not," Anna says.

Her mom says something in return, but a pat on my shoulder distracts me from what it was. As I shift to look behind me, Anna slips from my side, and I find Caleb waiting, a microphone in his hand.

His stare is kind as he waits for me to excuse myself from the conversation and steal a kiss from Anna's lip-glossed lips. He leads me through the throngs of people and toward the small stage we had put up in the corner of the salon.

We stop a couple of feet away, and Caleb hands me the mic. "Sound system should be good to go now. Just flip on the mic whenever you're ready. How are you feeling, man?"

"Real fuckin' happy. Proud too. Prouder than I've ever been of anyone before." It's a heavy understatement, but I can't wrap together more than that right now.

I'm too busy playing back my speech in my head in preparation for the next few minutes. I've never had as much trouble stringing words together as I did for this. It's not surprising, though. What I feel for Anna has always been too big for words.

"It's good to see you like this. That stupid grin of yours is a sight for sore eyes."

"I smiled before I met Anna."

"Not like that. Not like you have something really good in life. Like you're truly happy."

I clasp a hand on his shoulder and meet his stare head-on, pushing forward every bit of appreciation I have inside of me for him. "Don't laugh at my speech, you asshole."

His laugh is brash. "Fuck off and get cheesy for your woman."

"Take notes, yeah? Watch a master at work."

"Only notes I'll be taking are what not to do."

I flip him off and leave him standing alone as I step up onstage. With a quick flip of the mic, I take a breath and call for everyone's attention.

"Welcome, everyone, to the new Thistle and Thorn salon. Thank you all for bravin' the cold to come out and celebrate the openin' with us." The entire crowd is watching me now, but I only look at Anna. "At the risk of makin' a lovesick fool out of myself up here, I just wanted to say a couple'a things before handing over the mic to the phenomenal owner of this beautiful business."

Anna's expression grows curious as she watches me, tapping the corner of her smile with a pink-painted nail. I swallow, my heart thumping like a feral beat in my chest.

"For those who don't know Anna yet, I really hope you take the time to do so. I had no idea that she was goin' to swoop in and change my world the way she did, but I've never been more grateful for anything. I'm so immensely proud of you, Anna, and I can't wait to see what the future holds. Gettin' to love you has been the greatest honour of my life." She places a hand over her heart and whispers my three favourite words. I do the same before forcing myself to glance out at the crowd. "Can we give a

big round of applause for her, please? Thank you all for bein'
here."

The clapping is instant, but I don't pay it much attention. Not
when Anna's moving through the crowd toward me. I catch her
in my arms in a blink, spinning her around on the small stage
and burying my face in her neck as her laugh rings in my ears
like my favourite melody.

"Thank you, Brody. For everything," she breathes in my ear.

I meet her stare before pressing my mouth to hers, knowing
damn well she doesn't need more of my words. Not when we
have forever for that.

THREE HOURS LATER, I'm leading Sky past the guest house and the
trees outlining it with Anna against my chest. There's a calm,
comfortable silence before she finally caves, asking, "So . . .
where are we going?"

"Only a couple more minutes."

"You're lucky I don't mind surprises."

My lips quirk upward. "How was your night? Feelin' good?
Everyone loved you."

"Changing the subject, I see. You're not as coy as you think
you are, Brody Steele. But, to answer your question, I feel amazing. Still nervous, but I'm really excited to open for real."

All of the previous clients and employees from when Wanda
ran the salon decided to stay under Anna's new ownership, so
she's going to be real busy for her first shift as boss next week.

I'll be home to help—I made sure of that when planning my
next steps with Swift Edge. Reggie was more than happy with
what I brought to the table, but Garrison was harder to convince.
Tough shit for him, though, since I didn't budge on a damn
thing.

They agreed to let me record at the new Swift Edge Records

office in Calgary when it finally opens this month, and once that's finished, I'll announce my first North American tour. It took several hours of back-and-forth video chats to work out the dates and cities, but with Anna's approval, we finalized everything.

The discomfort that fills me every time I remind myself of leaving for tour threatens to appear again, but Anna squeezes my thigh, pressing back further against my chest, distracting me.

"I can hear you thinking," she says.

"Sorry, sweetheart," I murmur into her hair.

She moves so much easier on Sky now, more fluid with every jolt and bounce. I tighten my arm around her middle and relax against her.

"Want to talk about it?" she asks softly.

Sky recognizes the trail to the plot of Steele Ranch land I've ridden her to a dozen times in the past few weeks, and I let her lead the way, loosening my hold on the reins.

"I've been thinkin' about a lot of things, Buttercup. All of them revolvin' around you."

"Wanna give me something more than that?"

I press my fingers into the sensitive area beneath her ribs and grin as she starts to laugh, shoving me away. "Not yet."

Sucking in a long inhale to catch her breath, she says, "You've never taken me out here before."

"I haven't. This piece of land hasn't been used once in all the time the Steele family has owned it."

"That's a shame. It's beautiful."

The mountains are easy to see here, so daunting yet beautiful. Trees, so thick and green in the summertime, line the outer portion of the land, hiding the fence and gravel road behind it. It's peaceful here, even more so than the rest of the ranch. There's no noise from the cattle or machines during the busy workdays. It's the perfect place to start a life with the woman I love.

Hopefully, she feels the same way.

"I'm glad you think so. 'Cause I took you out here for a reason."

"Why?"

I swing off Sky's back and offer Anna my hand. She takes it, and I help her to the ground. We sidestep Sky, and I settle behind her, staring out at the bare plot of land.

"I've been thinkin' of movin' farther from the main house. The guest house was good before, maybe could still be had I not wanted somethin' more private. Somethin' that's ours. Yours and mine. What do you think about that?" I ask slowly, ignoring my nerves.

It's only been a few months, and maybe this is crazy, but I don't want her back in town at her own place. I want her in a place for both of us.

"You've been here almost every day for the past month, longer than that, even. We've slept in the same bed for weeks. Banana is here, and I know how much you love to spend time with her," I add.

"Brody," she breathes, awe thick in the single word. "The guest house is beautiful. You don't need another place just because of me."

"Another place for us, Anna."

She grabs both of my arms, grip soft yet firm, but doesn't make a move to turn around to face me. "Are you asking me to move in with you?"

"Only if that's what you want. I know you're independent and content with that. I don't want to strip you of that. Fuck, that's the last thing I want."

"You wouldn't be stripping me of anything. I'd never rush into anything I wasn't ready for."

I struggle to find a reply. It's not until she finally spins to look up at me, the love in her eyes threatening to take my feet out from under me, that I have the words. "One last move. One more new beginning. But this time, you won't be alone. We'll do it together."

Tears well in those love-bright eyes. I'm swiping them away before they have a chance to drip down her pink cheeks.

"I love you, Brody Steele, and I'd love to move in with you," she declares, fingers drifting over my jaw before cupping my cheeks.

"Yeah?"

"Absolutely yes. But we really don't have to build a new house. I would be more than happy in the guest house."

I shake my head, filling my palms with her hips. "No more guest houses or rentals. We'll get somethin' permanent. Right here."

"Right here sounds perfect," she murmurs, and then her lips are on mine, so warm and soft.

I kiss her right back, the taste of forever on my tongue.

EXTENDED EPILOGUE
ONE YEAR LATER

Annalise

Brody keeps a steady arm around me as we finish posing together on the red carpet and head away from the first cluster of photographers. The bright white flashes are intense, staggering at first sight. It took me a few minutes to relax after we first stepped out of the limo, but I'm a bit more settled now.

It feels odd to be wearing such a fancy dress and heels tonight instead of muddy coveralls and boots to match. But this is our first award show together as a couple and Brody's first since his album released, so ranch clothes most definitely wouldn't have sufficed.

There was no way Brody wasn't wearing his hat tonight, though, and I'm glad for that. My man looks incredible beneath the rim of a cowboy hat. Maybe too incredible, based on the thousands of ogling eyes that haven't let him out of their sight since we got here. As if sensing my jealousy when I narrow my eyes on a woman wiggling her fingers in his direction, he swirls his thumb over my hip, and I glance up to find him smirking.

"You're sexy when you're territorial," he says, the words far too husky for me right now.

I cover the hand he has holding my side with mine and

thread our fingers. "Don't think I haven't noticed your side-eyed glares at the security guard while we were being photographed."

"Wasn't tryin' to hide them from you, sweetheart. You're the most stunnin' woman here tonight, and I don't have a problem markin' you as mine."

"You do look incredible, by the way. I know I've told you that a million times already tonight, but you do."

I jumped his bones the moment he stepped out of the bedroom dressed in dress slacks and a button-up I've never seen him wear before. It's criminal for a man to have such a nice ass, and one look at it in those tight-fitted pants had me panting.

His beard is trimmed, and his hair is gelled back beneath the brown hat. I've cut my hair a bit, too, over the past few months and dyed it a soft brown with some highlights. It's not much of a change, but it's something to me. I feel refreshed, and every day, I wake up feeling like it'll be even better than the day before.

"You look phenomenal, Anna. I've been plannin' all the ways I can take this dress off since the moment you put it on," Brody murmurs.

I pinch the silky material below my bust, rolling it between my fingers. "Oh, this old thing?"

"Yeah, that old thing. It's gorgeous on you."

My cheeks flame as I chew on the inside of my cheek, focusing on the next set of photographers up ahead and the woman with a microphone in her hand.

"Thank you. How are you feeling?"

I've been checking on him often today, knowing he's nervous about his first-ever nomination for album of the year. It's been a whirlwind of a year with the success of his album and North American tour.

We spent long, late nights on the phone while he was touring, and I came with him as often as I could while running Thistle and Thorn. The business is flourishing, even after I struggled so badly at first. It was a learning curve, a steep one, but I eventually figured it out.

Construction on our new home finished recently, and we've been moved in for only a couple of weeks. It took far longer than expected to build our dream house, but it was so, so worth it. Getting to wake up every day to a view of the mountains through the floor-to-ceiling windows in the bedroom I share with the love of my life . . . there's nothing greater than that.

"Terrified," he answers bluntly.

I curl myself as close as I can around his side and squeeze his fingers. "You've got this, Bo. Win or lose, you've got this. How many artists can say they not only got nominated for an award after only their second album while also performing? I'm in awe of you. Every day."

His throat bobs with a swallow. "Luckiest man in the world to have you beside me, Annalise. Thank you."

"I'm here for you always. Through everything."

Whether subconsciously or otherwise, he rubs the bare skin on my fourth finger, where I once wore another man's ring. A harsh swell of emotion ripples through me. Longing, I've realized recently. Longing to wear Brody's ring on my finger.

He hasn't once pressured me into marriage, even though I know he would take me as his wife any day, anywhere. A man as respectful as him would never pressure me into that. And at one time, I was positive that I never wanted to get married. Was sure of it, especially after Stewart. But over the past year and a half, that's been changing. Those feelings have evolved so drastically that I haven't even told him about it.

I should have known I would want to marry Brody someday. He's everything I've ever wanted and more. Perfect in an imperfect way. Every day I spend with him only emphasizes how foolish I was.

That conversation has to come soon. I need it to.

The second round of photographs moves faster than the first, and then we're being ushered toward the interviewer waiting to the side. Massive cameras focus on us as Brody tugs me along with him, not caring that the woman most likely only wanted to speak to him. We've both gotten more comfortable in the spot-light because of situations like these, our inability to separate from one another longer than necessary.

We greet the woman together, and she quickly moves into the questions for Brody. She focuses on his feelings regarding his nomination and who he's most excited to see tonight before sliding into a line of questioning that we've grown to expect when we're together in these situations.

"You've been together for over a year, correct?" she asks, voice incredibly chipper.

Brody looks to me to answer, and I don't hesitate to do so. "Almost a year and a half, yes."

"I think I speak for almost all of us when I say that you two look gorgeous together here tonight. As you always do," she says.

Brody kisses the side of my head. "Thank you, Jess."

"You look incredible too," I add, and it's the truth. The woman in front of us is glowing, whether with genuine excite-ment for what she does or if she's just happy to meet celebrities, who knows. It doesn't matter to me either way.

She grins at my compliment, and I relax further in her pres-ence. "I hope you forgive me if I'm overstepping here, but we took a few fan questions earlier for you, Brody, and there's one that overshadowed the rest. Would you mind answering?"

He hides his panic behind an easy-going smile, but I know him too well to fall for it the way she does. I shift toward him, sliding my hand across his middle before tucking my fingers in his belt loop.

"Ask away," he tells her.

"Well, the fans want to know when you're going to pop the question. Do you have an answer for them? Will it be soon?"

I almost laugh at the timing of the question. It's like the universe was listening to my pleas just minutes prior.

Brody doesn't have a chance to reach for the same prepared answer to the question before I'm tilting my head back to meet his eyes and saying, "Hopefully soon. I can't wait until I get to be Brody's wife."

Jess squeals into her microphone, but once my man takes my face in his hands and lays a deep, possessive kiss on my lips, I forget all about her presence.

I think it's safe to say that he's just as excited to be my husband as I am to be his wife.

We've only just made it back into the limo when Brody's cell phone starts blaring in his pocket. All of the important people in his life know that tonight is a big one for him and that he probably won't be around to answer calls, so I'm instantly on alert.

Sharing my worry, Brody takes a look at the caller and picks it up, growing tense.

"Reggie?"

The buzz of watching him win his first-ever award threatens to dissipate, but I refuse to allow it to. It doesn't matter what's happening on the other side of the call. Not after a night like tonight.

"Fuck. Yeah, I can talk to my grandpa, but I can't promise anythin'. He doesn't like strangers on his land . . . You're right, he's worse than a stranger. He's made himself an enemy . . . Yeah. Yeah, I will. The guest house is empty. He could stay there, but again, I can't promise you anythin' yet. I'll do what I can."

My stomach tumbles when Brody meets my stare and I see the discomfort sparking in his eyes.

"Yeah, thanks. We made an amazin' album, Reg. This award is just as much yours as it is mine . . . I'll call you tomorrow and do everythin' I can for you here. Garrison doesn't deserve this sorta support from you, but I get it. He's family. I'll do what I can . . . Yeah, good night."

The second he ends the call, the question is tumbling from my lips. "What did Garrison do?"

Brody strokes a hand over his jaw and pulls me onto his lap, my legs falling over his, the material of my dress being pulled as taut as possible. I steady myself with my hands on his strong, muscled chest.

"Somethin' bad enough that his father called and begged for him to stay at the ranch for a while."

"That's what you have to ask Wade about," I note, nodding slightly as I recall his words to Reggie.

"I knew it was only a matter of time before karma caught up to him."

"Wade won't like it."

Brody leans forward, resting his forehead on my collarbone. His heavy exhale says enough without the words that follow.

"No. No he's not. None of us are. But I don't think we have much of a choice. Garrison Beckett isn't fit for Cherry Peak, but it might be the only place that can straighten him out."

THE END.

Thank you for reading Strung Along! If you enjoyed it, please leave a review on Amazon and Goodreads.

Catching Sparks, the second book in the Cherry Peak series is coming May 2024. Garrison Beckett is about to meet his match, and Poppy is prepared to tear up his world.

While you're waiting for more of these characters, jump into my backlist! Curious about Braxton and Maddox or want to learn a bit more about Garrison and Reggie? Start with my Greatest Love series.

The Greatest Love series:

His Greatest Mistake – Maddox and Braxton (Hockey romance)
Her Greatest Adventure – Adalyn and Cooper (Brothers bff, age gap romance)
His Greatest Muse – Noah and Tinsley (Rockstar romance)

To be kept up to date on all my releases, check out my website!
www.hannahcowanauthor.com

If you have not read all of the original love stories in my crazy fictional world, now is the time to do so!

Lucky Hit — Oakley and Ava (Hockey romance)
Between Periods (Novella and BH prequel)
Blissful Hook — Tyler and Gracie (Hockey romance)
Craving The Player — Braden and Sierra #1 (Boxing romance)
Taming The Player — Braden and Sierra #2 (Boxing romance)
Overtime – Matt and Morgan
Vital Blindside — Adam and Scarlett (Single dad, hockey-esc romance)

Acknowledgements

Sometimes there are characters that write their own story. The words flow, and the relationships build all on their own, and Strung Along is one of those stories. I don't have words to describe just how much I love not only Brody and Anna but the girl gang, the Steele family as a whole, and, of course, Maddox and Braxton. Cherry Peak has become my favourite fictional place, and as a small-town girl who grew up only six hours north of this fictional town, I had the time of my life writing this one.

As always, I have to thank my incredible group of women who helped me along the way while I was writing this one. Taylor, Hayley, Rose, Phoebe, Sierra, Cathleen, Nicole, and Becci. My cheerleaders and friends.

To my team of masterminds that work tirelessly behind the scenes, thank you for turning this book into a masterpiece, inside and out.

And to my readers, I'll never stop thanking you. This is my tenth book, and I can't wait to bring you a hundred more.

About The Author

Hannah is a twenty-something-year-old indie author from Canada. Obsessed with swoon-worthy romance, she decided to take a leap and try her hand at creating stories that will have you fanning your face and giggling in the most embarrassing way possible. Hopefully, that's exactly what her stories have done!

Hannah loves to hear from her readers, and can be reached on any of her social media accounts.

Instagram : Hannahcowanauthor
Twitter, Facebook : Hannahdcowan
Facebook Group : Hannah's Hotties
Website : www.hannahcowanauthor.com

Printed in the USA
CPSIA information can be obtained
at www.ICGtesting.com
CBHW051003191124
17640CB00024B/197